ONE OBLIQUE ONE

A Novel from the Inspector Stark Series

KEITH WRIGHT

Reviews of One Oblique One by Keith Wright

'A most promising debut.' Marcel Berlins, *The Times*

'It's a good yarn with a very well-crafted plot.' Jay Iliff, *Sunday Express.*

'An interesting cast of well-observed characters, many of them pleasingly quirky, and depicts them with unsentimental compassion. I look forward to reading his next book.' James Melville, *Hampstead and Highgate Express.*

One Oblique One - **Shortlisted for the Crime Writers Association 1991 John Creasey Award**
Best debut crime novel – globally.

First published in 1991 by Constable & co (now Little Brown)
This revised edition published in 2019
The right of Keith Wright to be identified as the author of this work has been asserted
by him in accordance with the Copyright, Designs and Patents Act, 1988
ISBN 9781070476988

All characters included in this book are fictitious
and are not intended to bear any resemblance to any
Individuals, alive or dead.

Contains realistic and graphic descriptions of death
and includes issues which some readers
may find upsetting or offensive
It is intended for adults only

For the author's blog and news on upcoming books, as well as free short stories, visit his web-site: **Keithwrightauthor.co.uk**

Follow the author on Twitter: @KeithWWright

1

'One murder makes a villain, millions a hero...'
Beilby Porteus (1731 -1808)

It is the summer of 1987.
It is three years away from the world-wide web being in-augurated. It is ten years before the first accessible mobile phone, and a whole twenty one years before the first iPhone is launched. 'It's A Sin' by the Pet Shop Boys is number one in the charts, available on cassette and vinyl. AIDs is rife. Hugging is for hippies and the author of this book has recently been appointed a Detective in the CID. Of course, some things are the same as today; for example, people still get bludgeoned to death in their own homes. Same as it ever was. You just can't tweet about it yet.

Death can be something of a surprise when you are scratching your sweaty balls at the driver's wheel of a police car on a hot summer's day. News of its arrival messes up your plans; forces its priority upon you and darkens your day. Death is both rude and terribly inconvenient.

The police radio crackled out its final instruction to the young uniformed officer, breaking the monotony, delivering the news as he sat watching the crowds of people hurrying to and fro. The fledgling cop repeated the radio message to himself under his breath as if in disbelief. 'One oblique one at 43 Maple Close.' The police code word had only one meaning – 'sudden death'.

The policeman's heartbeat quickened as he acknowledged the message; telling Control he would attend – estimated time of arrival; ten minutes. He shifted in his seat as the full significance of the message dawned on him. With no lights and sirens to turn on, his immediate response was stymied in the heavy morning traffic. Someone thought it a good idea for Panda cars to merely have a single blue beacon on the roof, operable only when stationary. Still, he could make progress by driving like an idiot, flashing his lights and holding the heel of his hand on the horn. This created some sort of a pathway at least, with drivers angrily sticking two fingers up at him, until they realised the maniac blaring his horn was a police officer. They then hastily retracted the sign or tried to style it into something else, such as the pushing up of glasses on to nose or scratching at a mystery mark on their window.

On the way to Maple Close the young cop wound down the window a few inches, allowing the breeze to blow through his blond hair, cooling his now flushed face. He had one focus; to get to the scene. The policeman was only twenty years old, new to the job, still a kid really, and although he knew that one day soon, he would get this type of call, he certainly hadn't expected it to be today. He attempted to concentrate on his driving, despite his mind racing with possible scenarios that might be awaiting him. Hanging? Old age? Accident? Murder? Whatever it was, everyone would be looking to him to take control within a second of his arrival at the scene. This both thrilled and terrified him all at once. His newly given responsibility was hanging around his shoulders like a lead weight, which he couldn't shake off. He wracked his brains to remember the shortest route to Maple Close.

His mirror showed the shops and office buildings give way to urban housing and within minutes he turned into the tree-lined Maple Close, the subdued quiet of a middle-class suburban estate. He turned left, slowly manoeuvring the Ford Escort panda car, on to the gravel drive, which led to the large four-bedroomed detached house. The house was a 1950's design with a garage and a beautifully mown lawn sheltered by conifers and shrubs. As promised by his colleague in the control room, he could see a window-cleaner, arms limp by his side, mop still in hand, standing outside the wooden front door. He had a strange look on his face. As the officer drew up, the window-cleaner came forward to greet him. He looked relieved. The window-cleaner, one Norman Price, was a short, stocky man of about thirty, with curly hair that nestled on the collar of his leather tabard. The probationary PC wrestled with his emotions, in a vain attempt to give off a more confidant air. The strange look on Norman's face remained; it was a mixture of bewilderment and surprise, although the officer was unclear whether this was his normal expression, or as a result of the death he had apparently witnessed. It didn't seem to be going away. Maybe he always had that look about him?

The diminutive Norman had to arch his neck as he addressed the six-foot tall policeman. He pointed, with dripping rag, toward the house; 'It's in there, mate. The door was open a bit, so I just put my head around and there it was. Pretty gruesome, I'm afraid.'

'OK. Wait here, will you? Leave it with me.'

'So, shall I wait here, or leave it with you?'

'Um. Both.'

Norman shook his head and watched the PC set off toward the house, swallowing hard, his shiny boots landing heavily on the gravel drive, which led to the oak front door. 'Was it safe?' he wondered. 'Did he need back-up?'

His heart rate quickened, his mouth uncomfortably dry, as he tentatively approached the darkened space evident by the open door. Norman did as he was told and did not follow. He had seen enough in any case, settling instead to lean on the police car, arms folded, watching the officer from afar with a big incongruous grin on his face. All he needed was a tub of popcorn.

The PC peeked hesitantly through the open door as outlines of images started to draw into his focus. The bright summer sun, whilst illuminating the outside, made the interior darker and troubled the eyes to adjust. He could just about see into the hallway, his feet rooted to the spot. He was aware of his own breathing and could see nothing in the blackness. The PC loitered at the doorway, reticent to take another step. He reached towards his radio. Should he shout up for assistance? Shout up about what? He needed to know what the score was first.

Norman shouted over to him, 'It's inside, mate.'

The PC turned and replied. 'I know, it's, erm, it's just police procedure, I'm going in now.'

He took a deep breath before stepping in. He initially felt the sticky wetness claw at the soles of his boots and then he trod on something. 'What the hell is that?'

It was soft tissue; he looked down: a human hand. 'Jesus H Christ!'

*

Detective Inspector David Stark was the CID boss covering the area of Maple Close. The CID covered all serious and major crime, including murder, armed robbery and rape, and all that good stuff. There were no specialist homicide squads or robbery squads outside of London, the CID dealt with it all. He appeared troubled. DI Stark, in his early forties, normally cut quite a dash, but right now as he sat in the side office, he was as white as a sheet. His hair was wet through with sweat, his chest was tight, and his breathing shallow. Stark always grabbed a side room when these episodes came on. He didn't want it advertised that he suffered from this 'thing'. Whatever the hell it was. It always came on when he had to talk to a crowd of people. It didn't affect his day-to-day work, thank God, this wasn't too regular an aspect of his work, but enough to annoy him, that he should be burdened like this. He would much sooner put some toe-rag with a knife on his backside than face a crowded room. Stark had just spoken to a large group of new detectives and whilst he had somehow maintained his composure to mask the attack, he couldn't sustain it once he had left the room. He breathed slowly and tried to focus on reducing the number of breaths he took per minute. He was fairly accomplished at this by now, but it took him about ten or fifteen minutes to calm down. Stark eventually got back to his normal self and was able to head towards the CID offices on the other side of the campus as if nothing had happened.

'Dishy Dave' as some of the policewomen called him, headed back to familiar surroundings. His large, muscular frame moved easily in his well-pressed grey suit as he strode boldly down the dimly lit corridor. He was back to his normal confidant self; just a little drained. He passed the main CID office to his left, pausing only to shout to his Detective Sergeant: 'Nobby, my office. Now, please!'

'Coming, boss,' came the gruff reply.

Stark was generally an approachable man, despite the scars of twenty years as a police officer. 'You catch more flies with honey than vinegar,' was one of his sayings. He was nobody's prat, however, and he was getting fed-up with Nobby Clarke seemingly taking advantage. It was time to stamp it out. He puffed sneakily on his cigar; which spewed out a cloud of disdain, heralding his visibly angry countenance.

Detective Sergeant John 'Nobby' Clarke rose tentatively from his plastic chair in the main office. How the hell did Stark know? He was supposed to be giving a welcome talk to sprog detectives first thing. Had somebody grassed him up? His well-worn, rugged face contorted as he anticipated the worst. Nobby started his excuse immediately upon entering Stark's bright, roomy, modern office.

'Hey, boss, nice suit, I know I'm out of order being late, but I can explain...'

Stark cut him short. 'Nobby, I am not going to argue with you. It's not up for debate. It's not today's chosen topic on *Question Time.* You are a grown man. I've got a department to run, and this is the second time this week. Now if you, my best DS, can't get here for eight o'clock, how the hell can I expect my DC's to?'

'Fair comment, boss, it won't happen again...'

'You're fucking right, it won't. You're taking the piss, Nobby, you're undermining me, and worse, you are undermining your bloody self. Next time, you're going to get formal notices, because if there is one thing I cannot allow, it is a lack of discipline and a lack of trust.'

The Detective Sergeant sighed. 'I get it, boss, I assure you it won't happen...'

The apology was cut short by the ringing of Stark's desk phone. Stark dropped his cigar into the ashtray as he answered it. He looked at Nobby as he spoke, who was trying to decipher the ones-sided conversation.

'Stark...You're joking?...and we're sure the PC has checked all three are dead?...Yes...I know. Marriott. Yes, of course... We're coming down. Maple Close, yes? Tell the copper who is at the scene to double check that there isn't an offender on the premises, and then seal it off, touching nothing until we get there. OK? Cheers, Pat.'

Stark tapped the handset, before replacing it slowly onto the cradle of the phone, the coiled wire now hanging loosely.

'What is it boss? A murder?'

Stark looked grim. His mind already whirling with a thousand questions requiring answers. 'It's murder all right, Nobby – three of them, in their own bloody home!'

'Three bodies! That's a first. Shit!'

'It's a Mr and Mrs Marriott, apparently, and their daughter, Faye. You'd better get your coat.'

*

Stark and Nobby were in Stark's black Cavalier car. Stark still enjoyed driving it, even with the grimmest of destinations awaiting him.

'Number 43 Maple Close, Dave.' Nobby felt that he could call him 'Dave' now that the tenseness of Starks' reprimand had apparently dissipated.

'It's there, look.' Stark pointed at the house. He parked on the drive behind the police car and the two detectives got out.

The young red-faced policeman stood outside the door. Three of his colleagues had also arrived and were busying themselves putting tape up as a perimeter and generally tramping about the gardens. This was why Stark did not like taking a whole posse up to a scene before it had been forensically examined. 'I hope all this lot haven't been inside.' Stark said to the young cop as a greeting.

'No, only me, sir. I didn't let them in.'

'OK, that's good. Well done. What's the story, then?'

The PC's reply was excited, but nervy, a little falsetto. 'There's three of them, sir, the whole family by the looks of it.'

'How did we get to know about it?' Stark asked.

'The window-cleaner knocked on the door for his money. He didn't get a reply, so he looked through the gap in the door and saw the man, croaked in the hallway.'

'Have you got the window-cleaner's details?' Stark asked.

'Yes, but he's buggered off now, he said he'd be late finishing his round. I asked him to stay...'

'It's fine. Has he been inside the house?'

'No, sir, only just stepped in the hallway, nowhere else. Or so he says.'

Stark was glancing around the front of the building. 'Did he see anyone, or anything of note? Did he say?'

'No, just what I've told you, sir.' The PC looked at the ground racking his brain to make sure he had not missed anything. 'Oh, I've been inside, of course, sir.'

Stark nodded, 'Of course. Scenes of Crime will need your boots when you've done.'

'No problem sir.' That was his next problem, he didn't have another pair.

'Was the door ajar when you arrived?' Stark asked.

'Yes, sir.'

'How long have you been here, son?' Nobby chirped up from

behind Stark's shoulder.

'About thirty or forty minutes I would think, Sarge. Nobody has been in apart from me, and I've only touched the doors. I had my gloves on.'

'Scenes of Crime will want those too.' Nobby grinned.

'OK. There is something else, which I think I should probably mention, sir.'

'What's that?' Stark asked.

'When I went inside I couldn't see that well and so I trod in the blood, the whole carpet was soaked through.'

'That's to be expected, it can't be helped.' Nobby said benevolently on Stark's behalf.

'Yes, but I couldn't see his outstretched arm and I think I trod on his hand, so. . . '

'There will be blood on the deceased's hand that perhaps wasn't there before you trod on it?' Stark finished.

'Yes, sir, sorry sir.'

'As the Sergeant says, these things happen. Don't worry about it. Good job you mentioned it. Anything else?' Stark asked.

'No, apart from the rear window's been forced.'

'Which one?' Stark asked.

'The dining room, transom window, at the far side of the house, at the back.' He indicated generally toward the house behind him, with his thumb, as if that might somehow help.
'Good lad. Did you see anyone hanging around in the area on the way in? Anyone taking an interest?' Nobby asked.

The young cop, diverted his stare to the gnarled detective. 'No, nobody at all, Sarge. It was like...' the boy hesitated but said it anyway... 'a morgue.'

Stark gave his instructions. 'I want you to start a log of every person who enters this house and the time they arrive and leave, understand?'

'Yes, sir. Does that include you and DS Clarke?'

'Yes, it does.' Stark glanced at his watch. 'Right it's 8.52 a.m. and we're going in.'

First responding detectives did not wrap themselves in

white coveralls, some had plastic slip-on covers for their shoes, but Nobby didn't have any in the car. 'Sorry, boss.' As for gloves; instead they would use a pen or a curled knuckle, to open doors or move items, and so avoid ruining evidence or leaving their own fingerprints.

The front door of the premises would not fully open. The legs of the dead man lying in the hallway were the cause of the obstruction. Stark stepped rather gingerly into the hall, carefully avoiding the considerable area of carpet that was soaked in blood. He could never decide whether it was a smell or an atmosphere or a mixture of both, but almost every 'death house' had that air about – an indiscernible, unnatural feeling as if one were a trespasser, an uninvited guest to something intimate and private. A quiet. A stillness; as if all the clocks had stopped and everything had powered down. His face formed into a tight-lipped grimace as he uncomfortably took in the disturbing scene, leaning closer in towards the body to examine every intricate detail of the terror frozen in time.

The dead man in the hall was not young, probably in his mid-forties, and slightly greying around the sideburns. Stark was unsure about the colour of the hair as the blood had matted it into a dark claret. There was a large hole in the back of his head with some bone chips situated around the crater edge with some misshapen clumps of brain matter stuck on his hair and a blob on his cheek. It looked like a blunt instrument injury at first glance, Stark mused. The man was face down, with his head to one side and the face silhouetted against the beige carpet. A globule of blood wobbled from the nostril and threatened to drop to the floor. His expression was one of apparent surprise which had dissipated with the relaxation of expulsion of life. The dead man was dressed for the occasion, wearing a suit and tie, and next to him lay a Yale door key on a metal ring; the open door seemed to indicate he had not had time to close it.

'Keep an eye out for a weapon, Nobby.'

'I already am, boss.'

Stark gently pushed at the white painted internal door off the hallway with his knuckles and entered the living-room. He looked straight into the unseeing eyes of a young girl in her late teens. She lay on the floor, on her back. Her head was tilted and resting against the black television stand. Stark noticed she had a peculiar lop-sided grin on her face, but he failed to see the joke. He could not fail, however, to see the large hole in the crown of her head, not dissimilar to that of the man in the hallway. Her face was clean though, with notably no blood visible seeping from the orifices of the ear, nostrils or mouth. The girl's breasts were exposed, her dress pulled down to the waist and folded up to her stomach, her white knickers twisted around her left ankle. No bra was evident. Her legs were wide apart, displaying a thinly shaved triangle of pubic hair to the two detectives who leaned in to scrutinise her vagina, which appeared excessively reddened. It looked as if the girl had had sexual intercourse before she died. Necrophilia, however, could not be ruled out. Stark felt that her being in this position naturally implied that she had been killed immediately after, or during the act itself. Unless she had been positioned in this manner after her death. That would be a bit strange, but knocking ten bells out of a young girl is somewhat out of the norm also. 'More likely to be rape.' He muttered.

'Sorry, boss?' Nobby queried.

'Oh nothing. I'm just talking to myself.'

'It's the first sign of madness.'

'Is it? Well if I'm only at the first sign after twenty years in this job, I'm doing well.'

Stark's mind was whirling. Male offender. Hurried or inexperienced attacker perhaps? Was that the motive here? Sex? Stark peered at her polished fingernails but could see nothing of note. No fibres, skin or blood. They could still be there, just not visible. It was a much cleaner scene than the blood-stained cadaver in the hall. She had a hole in her head, but not as deep, and there was scarcely any blood.

'Not so much blood in here, boss,' Nobby observed, his voice seeming like a shout in the hushed atmosphere.

'No, I was just thinking that. It's interesting that she's lying on her back, and there appears to be no sign of a struggle at all. I suppose she could have been asleep or drunk when the attacker struck.' Stark observed.

'True. At least it would have been over quickly for her,' said Nobby.

Stark shook his head. 'I'm not so sure.'

'Why not?' asked Nobby. 'You've seen the wound on her head- the first blow would have killed her, well, rendered her unconscious at least.'

'What about her eyes?' asked Stark, slowly removing his little tin of cigars from his suit jacket- pocket.

'What about them?' asked Nobby, as he leaned closer towards her face, which would have been freaky had she still been alive.

'Petechial haemorrhaging, caused by lack of oxygen,' Stark commented.

Nobby stepped back. 'Yes, but, unless I am very much mistaken, we all die of lack of oxygen!'

'Very funny, Nobby. I'm talking about asphyxiation. When a body has been asphyxiated, there are often tiny red spots in the whites of the eyes, where the miniscule blood vessels have burst because of... lack of oxygen.'

'Of course, I can see it now,' Nobby uttered somewhat unconvincingly.

The two men surveyed the antique-filled living room. Stark felt as if they had walked into a freeze-frame of a reel of film, were that possible, with inanimate objects surrounding them, the only movement emanating from themselves. It was as if real life had been suspended and they were ghosts, privy to a scene that required hushed tones.

Nobby's powerful voice again seared through the silence, making Stark wince. 'I see the hi-fi is still on.'

'I noticed that. It's on tape rather than radio. Does that mean it's more likely to have been turned on last night rather than this morning, I wonder? Would you put a tape on, rather than the radio in the morning, or is that stretching it?'

Nobby shrugged. 'We're just guessing, aren't we?'

'Possibly. Anything else jump out at you?' Stark enquired.

Nobby's eyes lit up. 'Ah, the video machine.'

Stark nodded. 'There's a square of "clean" surrounded by dust under the telly stand. Something has been removed.' Stark rubbed at his chin. 'That doesn't ring right, now does it? A poxy video machine?'

'People are killed for a fiver, boss.' Nobby observed.

'Yes, but not when you can have the pick of a place like this, surely?' Stark wasn't going with it. 'Well, whoever did this must have taken the video machine, after the murder. The blood splatters from the girl's head are on the carpet and telly and around the clean bit, but there's none where the video would have been. The video machine will have blood splattered on it.'

The two men ventured into the open-plan dining room, which was decorated in pastel shades. There were no signs of violence in this room. The focus of attention lay at the wooden transom window which was swinging loosely on its hinges, letting in the morning birdsong and the faraway sound of a lawnmower. Closer examination of the window by Stark revealed that it had been forced with a blunt instrument, approximately half an inch wide, near the handle. It appeared that the window had been the point of entry for the sinister visitor.

With nothing else of note, Stark and his associate returned to the living room. 'Oh, Fuck me, Nobby, quick. Shut that bloody door! A fucking great meat fly's come in – oh shit, it's feeding on her head wound, look. Now it's gone on her...just shut the bloody door!'

Nobby hurriedly shut the front door, and they went upstairs, leaving the fly seemingly rubbing its front legs with glee at the welcome sight of the slowly festering flesh.

Out of the corner of his eye, as shoe touched fourth stair,

and his eye line drew level with the landing floor, Stark caught sight of the third body. 'Here's the third.'

Even Stark had never had three bodies in one house. It was a woman in her forties, in a blue dress and cream cardigan. The two men stood, looking down at the pathetic sight. Her skin was grey and sallow; her lips stretched and blue. A closer look showed her glazed and vacant eyes were bulging, and her tongue was grotesquely distended. Filling the mouth cavity and overflowing out, in a silent raspberry that made Stark's skin crawl. A foul smell invaded the insides of Stark's nostrils – the smell of human excrement, some of which was visible on the carpet in a sticky liquid mess. Stark put his hand quickly to his nose. It looked as though the woman had been on her knees and knocked over to one side. Yet again there was a gaping hole in her head but also the item they had been looking for – the weapon.

'She's still got her shoes on.' Stark observed.

'That looks like the murder weapon at the side of her.' Nobby said, his voice muffled through his cotton handkerchief.'

'It sure does,' said Stark. 'She must have been last? Otherwise why leave the bloody thing up here? Christ. That stench of shit is foul!'

The two men stared at the brass ornamental clown, lying on the plain light-blue carpet. It was about fourteen inches long and smeared in blood and tissue. Stark noticed that the upper half of the clown was very clean with a definite line, a cut-off point where the blood started.

'It looks as though the killer has wiped it,' he said. He noticed a small patch of blood smeared at the woman's dress, alien to the rest. 'Yes, the bottom of her dress - look, Nobby, that's where he's wiped it, by the look of things.'

The men checked the other rooms, which appeared undisturbed. Stark made a mental note of a blue diary in a room lined with posters of, he presumed, the latest rock stars, then they trooped downstairs. Stark pressed the button at the side of his hand held radio.

'DI Stark to Control.'

A lilting Scottish accent was quick to reply. 'Go ahead, sir.'

'Yes, start a log please, please.' He paused and let out an audible sigh, 'It's a triple murder, repeat triple murder, three deceased. I'd like the Detective Superintendent here, please, and two DC's, Crime Scene Investigators with full kit, the police surgeon and the undertakers. Nobody else, for now – it'll be enough of a circus as it is.'

'Ten-Four, sir. Superintendent Wagstaff is already on his way.'

Stark and Nobby went back outside to the front driveway for a smoke and to gather their thoughts before the others arrived. Stark asked his friend, 'What do you make of it then, Nobby?'

'I don't like it. It stinks doesn't it?'

'Yep. Literally.' Stark smiled.

Stark loved this. Not the fact of the horrendous deaths, of course, but the challenge that lay ahead of them. The puzzle. Minute one and no-one had a clue who the hell, or even what the hell, had happened at 43 Maple Close last night. But they would. He hoped.

The two detectives had meandered around to the back garden, looking around for other items of interest. None were seen. A neat, mown lawn with a flowery boarder was all there was. No footprints, nothing. They returned to the front of the house just in time to see the portly figure of Detective Superintendent Wagstaff struggle out of his Rover Vitesse car at the second attempt.

Stark had always considered that Wagstaff looked like an outraged, retired Wing Commander, and Wagstaff did little to change the image as he marched rigidly up the drive in his dark blue three-piece suit, twitching his well-groomed white moustache. Stark nudged Nobby, who was leaning against the wall. Nobby straightened himself up and held his cigarette behind his back. The Detective Inspector greeted his senior officer. 'Morning, sir.'

'Is it, David? Is it a good morning, really?' Tell me what the position is, then.'

Stark related the grisly details and then the enquiry began in earnest. The two DC's arrived next, young Paul Fisher, and his older and uglier colleague, Jim McIntyre, later followed by Scenes of Crime. The two detectives presented themselves to Stark. Paul was fresh-faced with blond curly hair. He regretted being paired up with Jim McIntyre, whose pock-marked face did nothing but moan and complain from dawn till dusk. Everything was an effort for Jim. Paul was keen to start. This was only his second murder and he wanted to throw himself into action. Jim, on the other hand, wanted to finish his cup of tea before leaving the station. Paul had stood impatiently at the door, waiting for Jim to drag his shiny-seated backside off the chair. 'Let them wait,' he had said. 'They're dead, aren't they? What's the rush?' Jim's logic had been lost on Paul.

Stark issued his instructions. 'Start house-house-to-house, gents, please, just in the immediate vicinity for now, to make sure that there is nothing staring us in the face that we've missed.'

'OK, sir.' Paul said.

Jim, who had paid little attention to Stark's orders, was true to form. 'Are we going to be wasting our time with this all day or what?' he asked.

Stark replied 'Well, that depends. Are you a bloody detective, or aren't you?'

'All right, keep your hair on, boss. I was only asking.' Jim's voice croaked. He cleared his gullet and spat out a ball of phlegm on to the drive, where it glistened in the morning sun.

'We'll have a bit of a briefing at half-past three, back at the nick.'

'Right, see you later sir,' said Paul. He and Jim turned and made their way down the drive. Neither spoke to the other.

'Come on, Nobby, let's have another look around the back,' said Stark.

43 Maple Close backed on to Yew tree Gardens, the main road

for the estate. A small gate led into the road.

'Careful where you tread, Nobby.' The men's eyes scoured the ground.

'I still can't see any footprints, can you, Dave?' Nobby asked.

'No, nothing; just small fragments of wood where the window's been forced.'

Stark looked through the glass pane into the house. He could see Wagstaff and the police surgeon deep in conversation. 'Come on, let's go and join Tweedledee and Tweedledum.'

The police surgeon, was not a surgeon at all, he was a GP who was paid extra to respond to police call-outs, usually for deaths, sexual offences and taking blood from drink driving suspects.

As Stark and Nobby entered the living room, the police surgeon left, with a nod, having performed the perfunctory task of pronouncing life extinct in the three bodies and completing the all-important task of getting Wagstaff to sign his attendance sheet for his expenses. He seemed quite jolly. Wagstaff addressed Stark. 'Right then, David, once Scenes of Crime have finished, we'll get the bodies shipped off for the post-mortems. Sergeant Clarke can be Exhibits Officer.'

'But, sir, that's usually a DC's job.' exclaimed Nobby.

'Well, now it's your job. It's going to be a complex one, so I want it doing right from the word go.'

Wagstaff turned to Stark. 'David, keep me posted as to how things develop. I'll be in my office for the rest of the day. I'll sort the Coroner out and send the tele-printer message. He'll be all over this one, as will the press, when they get wind.'

'Very good, sir,' said Stark, nodding his head in a semi-bow, as if Wagstaff was the bloody Queen Mother and not a Detective Superintendent counting the days to retirement. Stark peered through the bay window to watch Wagstaff puff and pant into his car before driving away.

The space his car left was quickly filled by the arrival of a plain white Scenes of Crime van.

'It looks like you have drawn the short straw, Nobby, so make sure you do a good job with these exhibits at the P.M. Remember, every teeny-weeny fibre, every solitary loose hair, every miniscule item has to be packaged and labelled correctly.' Stark was smiling as he spoke.

'Don't I bloody know it.' He said.

'I'll take young Paul Fisher to the post-mortem with me.' Stark said, 'It'll be good experience for him. He'll help out with the exhibits for you. Just give him the right guidance.'

Nobby raised his eyeballs to the ceiling and shook his head. Stark tried to reassure him. 'Don't worry there'll only be a couple of hundred items.' he laughed. Nobby didn't. 'Cheers boss.'

Stark watched as the Scenes of Crime officer put on his white boiler-suit and began to walk towards Inspector Stark. The SOCO was holding a silver coloured metal case. As he got close, Stark spoke to him. 'Hello there, I am DI Stark. Do you mind doing me a favour?'

'I know who you are, sir. What's the favour?'

'Well, I've seen a diary upstairs that I'd like possession of, as soon as I can. Will you dust and examine around there first so that I can take it?'

The officer looked thoughtful, and slightly put out. Already someone wanted to disrupt his routine before he'd even started.

'Oh, OK, if you're running the show, and you think it's that important, fine. Show me the way.'

Stark patted him on the back and smiled. 'Good man.' He led the balding officer up the stairs into the second bedroom and indicated the dark-blue diary resting on a white dresser.

'We'll have to wait for the SOCO Sergeant to come up with the video camera before we touch anything. He's on his way up and should be here in a minute. I'll start with my magnifying glass,' He opened his case and went straight for the large glass, which he used to examine the area where the diary lay. This part of the scene examination would have been the same a hundred years ago. He could see only undisturbed dust, and a tiny spider which struggled over the obstacle course of cosmetics that adorned the dresser. It looked as if the diary hadn't been moved for at least a couple of days.

Stark noticed another white boiler-suited figure progressing up the stairs with a video camera, recording the grim scene for posterity, evidence, and spotty-faced trainees, who in years to come would have nightmares about its contents.

Once the bedroom scene had been video-recorded, the magic SOCO box was again opened. It held an array of brushes and plastic tubs containing white, silver and black powder, and various solutions and vials. An apothecary of mystery. There were small plastic squares, cellophane, sticky tape, scissors, a small knife, a magnifying glass, several well-worn brushes and a plastic pot of aluminium powder which he painted over the diary. Its shiny surface was a good one. 'Smooth surface good, grainy surface bad.' The SOCO said. There were three clear fingerprints. The men were confident that these would be those of the dead girl. After lifting the prints, the Scenes of Crime officer threw the diary at Stark. 'It's all yours.'

*

You would think that house-to-house enquiries consisted of well organised questions being answered succinctly by the occupants of the house; to rule in or out, any unusual or significant incidents or behaviours which may be of use to the enquiry. The reality is that each household is different. The whole of humanity is represented; a demographic game of Bingo, the next one out the pot unveiled only by the opening of the door. Things can get weird.

Paul Fisher could not take his eyes off the unfettered breasts of the woman standing on the doorstep of 41 Maple Close. She was in her thirties; Paul was in his twenties and her breasts were in the forties. She wore tight fitting pyjamas, bizarrely patterned with small unicorns.

Jim McIntyre was perfectly aware of the elephant in the room as he jotted down notes on his clipboard, but his mojo had long since departed.

Things did not start well when Paul produced his warrant card with his photo on and said 'CID.'

'Oh hello. No, I've never seen him around here.'

'No, that's not why we're here, that photo is of me, it's my warrant card.' Paul laughed.

'What are you showing me a picture of you for?'

'It's my ID...my identification, to show you that we are really the police.'

'You didn't say that. I thought that was the bloke you were looking for.'

Paul chuckled and Jim looked skywards. 'Shall we start again?'

Mrs Lewis had a shapely figure but was on the turn, where hygiene was losing the ongoing battle with laziness, and there was a slight whiff of fustiness emanating from her. Paul suspected that the pyjamas had not been removed for at least three or four days, morning, noon and night. Her hair was squashed flat at the back of her head, revealing her scalp and the white roots to her dyed brown hair. She wore slippers that had spots of tea stains evident, indicating a recklessness bordering on the 'given-up trying.' She had been waiting for a man to knock on her door and sweep her away for the last six years. It wasn't going to happen. It certainly wasn't going to happen today. But hope springs eternal.

Paul continued with the questions, albeit a little clumsily...

'There was an incident next door, last night, Mrs...?'

'Mrs Lewis – divorced.'

'Mrs Lewis, and we wanted to ask the locals if they saw or heard anything unusual.'

'Oh I see, what's happened then?'

'I'm afraid we aren't at liberty to say just now. Can I ask, what time did you go to bed last night?'

'Not late. I'm on my own you know. I like to get all snug

under the covers.' She smiled.

'I'll bet you do.' Muttered Jim.

'Sorry?' She asked.

'Sorry, nothing, love, carry on, please. I'm just making some notes.' Jim said.

She continued. 'If I'm not in bed for ten o'clock something's wrong, so it would be around then.'

'Did you see anything unusual?' Paul asked.

'No, not at all. I don't look outside I just lock up. I have a routine. It can be frightening on your own.' She smiled at Paul and began to scratch herself under her left bosom causing a certain amount of displacement. Paul was transfixed, then the smell hit him again.

'Did you hear anything? Any strange noises?'

'Nah, just the normal.'

'What do you class as normal?' Paul asked.

'I don't get off straight away...' Jim coughed. 'I lie there for a while, and you hear the odd car and cats and foxes, it's classed as semi-rural round here, you know.'

'Really? Do you get many foxes on Maple Close?'

'Yes, they kind of screech. Same with cats.' She scratched her breast yet again. Paul was again drawn to the place of pleasure and subsequent complications and acrimony, and then the smell again.

'Are you saying you heard a scratch, I mean a screech?' He asked.

'Kind of a screech. Why, what is it that's happened? You say its next door? They're a lovely family. He's a bit off, but she's lovely. She made me ever so welcome when I first came...'
Jim interrupted. 'Could it have been a human being making the noise?'

'No, it was a screech not a scream.'

'Humans can screech, can't they?' Paul asked.

'I suppose so. What's the difference between a screech and a scream?' She asked.

'You tell me, you heard it.' Paul said, a little more tersely than he intended.

She looked over the two men's heads as if to gain inspiration. 'I think a screech is like 'eeeeeeee' but a scream is like 'Heeeeelp!'

Paul shook his head. 'No, that is just the word "help" dragged out a bit. A scream is a noise not a word.'

'I know, but I was trying to show you the difference.'

'The difference. . .' Paul began. Jim interrupted again, as the conversation was starting to descend into farce. 'We get the point; we know what you are saying.'

She shrugged. 'I thought it was a fox, though.'

Paul asked. 'What time was this?'

'Like I say, some-time after ten o'clock. Maybe half past, but don't quote me on it. I'm pretty sure it was a fox.' She wouldn't let it go; she glanced at Jim.

'Was anyone else at the house last night?' Paul smiled.

Scratch time again. 'No, didn't I tell you? I live here on my own?' She smiled at the young detective.

Jim shook his head slightly. 'Yes, I think you have mentioned that. Okay, thanks for your help, Mrs Lewis. Someone will be back to take a statement from you, no doubt.'

'Statement, why what's happened? It must be serious if you want a statement. Will I have to go to Court?'

The two men turned away. 'As I said, someone will be in touch.' Jim scowled.

'Thanks for your help.' Paul shouted over his shoulder. 'Jesus!' He muttered under his breath.

'Keep walking, son, and don't bloody look back.'

*

Stark clutched on to the diary as he left the girl's bedroom. He had blown away most of the aluminium dust residue. Three clean squares were evident on the grey dusty cover, where the Scenes of Crime Officer had fingerprinted it. The aluminium fine powder had been dusted on to the diary and then dusted off with only so much sticking, illuminating the fingerprint mark itself. The clear plastic square is then placed over the aluminium fingerprint mark and smoothed flat. When peeled off the fingerprint sticks to the plastic square and can be preserved for further examination by the fingerprint bureau. It was a messy business and usually it left a silver sheen to everything that was dusted, print or no print, which of course stuck to any fingers subsequently handling the item. Fingers such as David Stark's.

Stark was itching to open the diary but resisted the temptation. As he negotiated his way past the dead woman on the landing, he paused to have another look. She lay grotesque in death, her eyes and skin already starting to gain a marbled hue. In Stark's mind, this was a case that was likely to be solved through forensics. Many murders are. This was a good scene, numerous 'mini-scenes' within a scene. Lots of sticky stuff and contact, and hairs and fibres and bone and blood and even excrement. Plenty to go at. 'Locard's principle' was often the key. The Victorian scientist; Edmund Locard and his ground-breaking ingenuity, had helped Stark and his ilk detect so many crimes over the years, albeit vicariously. The Frenchman was the father of forensic science around the turn of the 20th Century, not only developing fingerprint analysis, but all elements of forensic science until his death aged 89 in 1966. Stark had learned Locard's principle in full as a trainee detective, but couldn't rattle it off now, just the basic element which had given the police the edge for the last hundred years – 'Every human being leaves a trace. He leaves a trace at the scene. He takes something from the scene away.' Simple but true, and no matter how hard anyone tried, it was damned near impossible to beat the principle at a microscopic level.

He stared into the eyes of Mother Marriott. Death was never the problem for Stark, it was always apparent that the soul had long since departed and so it was just a cadaver, no problem. It was when the mind started to consider the person before death, and the immediate circumstances leading up to it, and the fear and the pain, but mainly the fear. That was the most disturbing element, but Stark had got beyond that at his level of experience. This was not his first rodeo. There were so many times he had to put himself in the mind of the dead person to try to establish various hypotheses, that nowadays he was pretty much able to operate in a scientific manner with regard to the whole grisly business.

Still grasping Faye's diary he carried on down the stairs. 'See you later, Nobby. Sort a lift out, I'm heading back.' He shouted, as he passed the kitchen.

'OK. See you later, boss.' Came the croaky reply from the back garden, where Nobby was chuffing on a cigarette. Stark paused to peer one last time into the crater on the dead man's head and noticed that the droplet of blood on the deceased's nose had finally succumbed to gravity and had now dropped onto the carpet.

Stark walked out to his car and opened the diary, his curiosity getting the better of him. He leaned against the side window of the car and leafed through the pages. It wasn't a 'dear diary' type but more an address book, albeit with some scribbling of random notations scattered through the pages. The writing was neat and large looped, a female's writing, he surmised. It was in Faye's' bedroom, it had to be hers. He scanned the list of names and telephone numbers. He estimated twenty or so male names, but there was only one female name, written in capital letters in red ink and underlined – **'CHANTELLE NAYLOR'**.

2

*'I'd rather have a free bottle in front of me
than a pre-frontal lobotomy.'*

Unknown

Stark negotiated a left hand bend in the busy afternoon traffic
a little too quickly on his journey to the mortuary. He glanced
at young DC Paul Fisher who was biting his fingernails. Only
the ticking of the indicator broke the uncomfortable silence,
until Stark said, 'You are very quiet, Paul, what's the matter?'

'Nothing, sir. Well, to tell the truth, I've never been to a post-
mortem before.' Paul tapped nervously on the dashboard as he
spoke.

Stark reassured him. 'You'll be fine. I'll give you a tip, if you
feel you must look but daren't, focus on something beyond
the body and break the image in gradually. That'll help you get
used to it first.'

Paul sought a justification for the visit. 'What's the point in
us going, sir? Why don't we just wait for the report?'

'Because,' said Stark, 'we get instant answers to questions
and if we have anything in particular we want to ask we can do
so there and then with the pathologist at our mercy.'

'I suppose.'

'Plus, we have to produce the exhibits in good order to the
court, so we have to make sure they are preserved and the
chain of evidence is sound and all that sort of stuff. It'll be
good experience for you anyway; these things can be quite
interesting.' Stark nodded at the pedestrian who waved his
thanks at him as he walked across the pelican-crossing.

'Is it like an operation or what?' asked DC Fisher.

Stark gave a wry smile. 'It kind of is, but it can be a lot more brutal, as they know they can't damage the .... erm, "Patient", for want of a better word.' The silence between the two men returned momentarily.

Stark laughed out loud as the memory struck him. 'It's not so bad nowadays, though Paul. You want to think yourself lucky.'

'How do you mean, sir?'

'When I first joined the job the old-timers would play all sorts of tricks on us youngsters. They weren't sympathetic in the slightest. I remember, they locked my mate in the mortuary all night, on one occasion.'

Paul winced. 'Christ.'

'The poor bloke could be heard across the hospital campus, banging and screaming. He was quiet at first, but then when his eyes became accustomed to the darkness he could make out the silhouettes of the bodies.'

'Bloody hell.'

'He was still all right, but, as you know, dead bodies let their gases out gradually, and when the first one farted that's when the screaming started.'

'The bastards. Fancy doing that to him'

'He went sick for a week after that.'

'I'm not surprised,' Paul said.

'This is it here on the left.' Stark's black Cavalier pulled into the parking bay marked 'Morticians'. 'This'll do here – we are the Queens men, after all...are you all right, Paul?'

Paul's face was as white as a sheet as he stared vacantly at the plastic fascia. He answered honestly, 'I don't fancy doing this, boss.'

'You're not going to let this beat you, are you? Come on, mate, you're a bloody policeman. Once it's over you'll wonder what all the fuss was about.'

Paul's stomach churned; he decided. 'Oh, bollocks to it – in for a penny, in for a pound!'

Paul and Stark strolled over to the drab brick building. The cold chilled Stark's bones as he walked into the white interior. The thick strips of hanging plastic, designed as a barrier of sorts, ruffled his hair as he entered.

'It's colder in here than it is outside,' said Paul, his senses now alive to every little thing. 'Why is there that constant trickling of water, sir?'

'They're the post-mortem tables. It keeps the blood washed away.' Stark grew even more concerned about Paul's nervousness. The two detectives allowed themselves a cursory glance around the room. The main area was quite large, with whitewashed walls and concrete floor. There were three slabs; only one of them was vacant. The first was occupied by the naked body of a man of around seventy, the purple staining of his skin; lividity hypostasis, where blood had collected, showing along the length of the base of the body, as it lay on its back. The middle slab was vacant. On the third slab was a girl of about nine, whose mangled legs gave reason for the look of abject terror etched on her little face. Paul didn't dwell on the sight; he took a deep breath. He felt a bit giddy.

Off the main room were what appeared to be an office and two smaller annexed rooms; in them stood white ceramic tables with a curved rim around the edges and a slight tilt towards a hole at the top end. A loud booming voice made Paul jump. 'Hello, the audience has arrived early, tickets please. Stalls or balcony?' His raucous laughter was enough to wake the dead – well, almost.

Stark couldn't help rolling his eyes. 'Paul, this is Tony the mortician.'

Stark wondered what Paul would make of the thirty-year-old mortician? His off-white coat and black, matted, unkempt hair advertised his obvious lack of hygiene, and Stark noticed Paul's reticence to shake hands with him. Why were morticians so damned weird? A coping mechanism maybe?

'You look a bit pale, my friend. It's not your first time is it?' A gleam appeared in Tony's eye.

Stark interrupted hastily. 'No, he's been here a few times, actually. He was out on the town last night; you know how it is.'

Tony smacked Paul on the back. 'Good man! The butcher won't be here for about ten minutes, Mr Stark. Do you fancy a cuppa?'

After what seemed like an age, the pathologist, Mr Hargreaves, and his assistant arrived. When the formal introductions were over Hargreaves ordered the first 'contestant' to be brought forward. Hargreaves was a man of around fifty, with gold-rimmed spectacles. He was ex-public school and spoke with a plum in his mouth. His assistant, a young registrar, hung on his every word.

Tony walked towards one of the metal doors, there were twenty in total, which covered the whole wall, a giant bunk-bed community of dead strangers. 'We'll get the young bird out first,' declared Tony in his best bedside manner. 'It's drawer eight.'

Stark looked at his watch. Right on cue, Nobby came running in, puffing and panting. 'Sorry, boss, I got caught in traffic.' He was weighed down with paper and plastic bags and tape and labels and tubs, everything needed for the exhibits.

'Late again, Nob.' Stark seemed unimpressed.

'Sorry, boss.' He threw the exhibit bags onto the floor at the side of the porcelain table.

'You're just in time as it happens. We are going to start with Faye. Drawer eight, apparently.' Stark told him.

They watched as Tony pulled the drawer open and the cold air streamed out, clearing to reveal the naked body of nineteen year old Faye. Paul was shocked to see there were see-through plastic bags on her head, feet and hands, secured to make sure that evidence falling off would not be lost.

'Shame about the hole in the head: she's quite tasty,' said Tony, crassly.

Stark shook his head at the disdainful comment. 'You're sick, you know that, don't you?' Tony grinned broadly at him. 'Just appreciating the female form.'

He and the assistant slid the body that had once been the beautiful, and innocent, Faye Marriott, off the gurney and on to the white ceramic slab in the annexe room. The men assembled around the body.

The pathologist's assistant took up a large pad and pencil and Hargreaves began the well-rehearsed spiel. 'I am commencing the post-mortem of Faye Marriott, nineteen years, of 43 Maple Close, Nottingham. The time is now 10.32am on Thursday, 16th July 1987.'

'Here we go. Keep taking the deep breaths, Paul,' thought Stark, whilst reminding himself at the same time. The annexe was not particularly large and there was no hiding place for the young DC; however, he stood furthest away, close to the doorway. The pathologist's assistant took off the head bag and handed it to Nobby, who in-turn put the bag in a bag and began scribbling on an exhibit label and then a log-sheet. Paul was overly attentive of Nobby's, activities as it distracted him from having to view the unnatural events taking place.

Hargreaves voice was cold and calculated. 'External examination reveals a large wound at the crown of the deceased's skull, revealing part of the brain.' He placed a ruler at the side of the head wound, while photographs were taken of the wound showing its dimensions.

'The wound is 4.2 centimetres in diameter and does not appear to have clotted too well...I will take the scrapings off each hand and from underneath the finger-nails once we have removed the bags.' Hargreaves turned to the assistant on his left, who hurriedly removed the left-hand bag and passed it to Nobby to preserve and log. The pathologist then took the relevant scrapings and gave the implement and cotton wool directly to the Detective Sergeant to package. Nobby was already feeling a bead of sweat forming on his forehead. He needed an extra pair of hands. 'Paul, you're going have to get involved, mate. Give us a hand, will you?'

Paul began to busy himself, helping to package the exhibits, as Nobby jotted down the time and date and what the item was and who handed it to him. The labels would have to all be signed at the end.

'I also note that there appears to be blood and fluid deep inside the left ear, petechial haemorrhaging to both choroid and pupils of the eyes. There is a bruise to the left forearm.' Each item of interest on the cadaver was photographed when identified by Dr Hargreaves. 'Now, turning the body over, there is a 2.3-centimetre graze at the base of the spine in the coccyx region.'

'Looks like she's been screwed.' Nobby grunted to Paul as they continued to work feverishly on the exhibits.

'Quite right, Sergeant Clarke,' commented Hargreaves, 'and so beautifully put ...which leads me to the vaginal area.'

The pathologist took a smear from the entrance of the vaginal walls and then inserted a large swab, which was sealed and packaged up. He then proceeded to do this with each body orifice. Stark's mind wrestled with the sudden mental image of Hargreaves telephoning his wife: 'I'm sorry I'll be late at the orifice.'

All the hair, including pubic, was combed for lose hair samples; then single hairs were plucked with tweezers, and each comb and hair was packaged separately. It was time for the blood and gore. Stark focussed on the scalpel as it sliced easily through the skin. The pathologist cut in the shape of a large Y, starting at one side of the neck and moving down the front of the young woman's chest. He then cut down the other side of the neck and joined it into the cut on the chest, in a Y shape. Stark couldn't help flinching even though the girl was beyond pain.

Hargreaves peeled back the layers of skin and about half an inch of yellow sub-cutaneous fat insulating it. The girl's breasts lay sagging down by the side of her body, her sternum and rib cage exposed. With great physical exertion the top flap of skin was ripped up over the girl's neck and chin, revealing the bone and muscle in its red-and-white glory. Paul's eyes screwed up as he watched the assistant do the labouring job of sawing through the rib cage with a hand saw, available at all good hardware stores. The noise of the sawing was a new one to the young officer's ears. Small chippings of bone flew on to the slab and floor, and the Detective Inspector noticed Paul take a step back so that none would land on him. It was like some perverted horror story, only this was real, this was necessary, and this could help catch the monster that had caused this young girl to lose her life prematurely. Paul didn't know what he had expected, but it certainly was not this.

'If you can suggest any other way of getting to the cardio-vascular organs, I'll gladly try it,' said Hargreaves, who must have seen the look on Paul's face.

Paul stumbled over his reply: 'No, sir, of course not.'

Once the small hack-saw had finished, a chisel and mallet were used to prise open the rib cage, which was then fully opened manually by the assistant using brute force. A vast dormant pool of blood was revealed, which was ladled away, as if serving up dinner from a massive pot of stew, some of it was sucked up by a tube similar to one a dentist might use to remove saliva. There followed a thorough dissection of every individual organ. Each organ was removed from the body on to a trestle table, then sliced into linear pieces, and the pathologist commented on its condition. Each organ was then thrown into a dustbin liner placed where the stomach had once been. Part of the spleen was dissected and stored in a container; it would have to be frozen so that it could be used for any later DNA profiling. Other samples of blood would be sent away to be given a grouping; these needed only to be refrigerated.

Although the proceedings were gruesome beyond compare, Stark could see that Paul had become more interested. He had begun to crane his neck to observe each organ: the miracle of life was suddenly brought home to him, paradoxically in the examination of its demise. Once the disgusting smell had subsided slightly, he found it interesting to see that some of the food the girl had eaten was visible in identifiable form, once the gut was opened. The contents of the stomach were emptied into a plastic bucket for the toxicology lab to examine later.

The last part of the butchery was the worst, as Paul was introduced to another new implement – the trepan. Similar to an electric drill but with a circular 'bit' four centimetres in diameter. Once the skin had been pulled over and down to the nose area to expose the bare skull, the shrill sound of sharpened steel cutting into bone screeched into the ears of those watching. Hargreaves progressed the trepan around the forehead to the back of the head, completing a circular cut. Mercifully, the drilling stopped, to be replaced by a dull thud as the chisel and mallet prised off the top part of the skull to reveal the brain. This was quickly snipped out at the brain stem, sliced and dissected with a large knife and thrown unceremoniously into the mix of gore and other organs in the bin bag in her stomach area. The empty shell of a skull was filled with a large piece of cotton-wool wadding and the top of the head crudely sewn back on, Frankenstein style.

'One down, two to go.' Stark observed.

*

Hargreaves and Stark strolled through the carpark in the summer sun, discussing the results of the post-mortems. Stark had his hands in his pockets; the pathologist carried his large briefcase.

'Well, sir, now that you've finished all three PM's, can you offer me a view, please?'

The cultured voice was unhurried in its reply. 'Obviously, the official results aren't ready yet, and they won't be until I file the actual report for the Coroner.'

'Of course.'

'The toxicology will take some time to come back, so take it in mind, this is a provisional view. I'm happy to give you a steer though, David, and tell you whatever I can.' The two men stopped and faced each other, 'Faye Marriott was asphyxiated to death -'

'How?'

'She wasn't strangled. Probably a hand or some article held over her mouth and nose for a long enough period of time. She'd had sexual intercourse prior to her death, although I didn't find any apparent semen traces. She hadn't been forcibly raped, in my view, although that doesn't discount that she may have been threatened. I wouldn't speculate.'

'What about the gaping holes in her head?'

'The blow that caused such a wound would undoubtedly have killed her outright. That wound was inflicted *after* her death, however, there is no question about it. It was made with a heavy blunt instrument.'

'Why hit her after she had died? It doesn't make sense.'

'Are you asking me, or yourself, David?' The Pathologist smiled.

'Myself, I guess. Maybe to cover up the asphyxiation. Who knows?'

Hargreaves laughed. 'That's for you to find out, fortunately. It is possible that the killer went into a frenzy and didn't realise that she was already dead. I'm just surmising, I shouldn't, I know.'

'What about her Mother?' Stark asked.

'She, like her daughter, died from asphyxiation, but this was due to actual manual strangulation.'

'Can you be certain?'

'Absolutely, David. The bruising and striation marks showed quite clearly around the neck, also the hyoid bone is fractured and the larynx is damaged. I would say your killer is right-handed if that helps you.'

'Well, that narrows it down...thanks.'

Hargreaves laughed. 'The head wound was also curiously caused *after* death had taken place.'

'What? It seems to imply a cover-up, but what is the point? Hammer or hand, they're dead, it's still murder. Why? What is the point?'

'The mother would have had it the worst, being strangled so viciously. Not a good way to die.'

'Awful.'

'I suppose the only consolation is that she was *not* the subject of a sexual assault before she died.'

'Anything else?'

'Not really. I would say the killer is pretty strong.'

'Why?'

'He almost put his thumb through her trachea. There's substantial damage in that area.'

'What about, father?' Stark asked. He had produced a piece of paper and was scribbling some notes on it.

'He is slightly more straightforward. He was killed by a single blow to the top of the head, apparently with the same blunt instrument.'

'Lucky him. Anything else?'

'A few scratches on his back – you probably saw them in the mortuary. I don't think they were caused by the killer, however.'

Stark shrugged out a laugh. 'Yes, I get what you mean. Mrs Marriott didn't look like the passionate type.'

'I didn't say it was Mrs Marriott, now did I?' He offered sagely.

'True.'

'I'll get the full report to you and Waggers as soon as I can. It depends how long forensic and the toxicology department are. I'll try to hurry them up for you.'

'Thank you, you've been most helpful, sir.' The two men shook hands and parted company. Stark returned to his car, met half-way by Paul Fisher. 'Nobby said to come back with you, sir, if it's okay?'

'Of course it is, let's get back to the nick and see what's what.'

Paul seemed in high-spirits, pleased at having survived the ordeal. 'What did the doc say?' he asked.

'It's a long story, Paul. I'll tell you on the way back, in the car.'

Stark explained the complicated details as he drove

through the city centre traffic. His account ended as the Cavalier's tyres struggled to grip the loose gravel on the police station carpark, kicking up dust in the summer heat.

'Did the pathologist give a time of death?' asked Paul, somewhat naively as they got out of the car and walked towards the station.

'Oh, come on, Paul, that's for Hercule Poirot. Pathologists can't give an exact time of death; all they can give is a rough estimate, based on a table, drawn up after a series of thermometers have been rammed up the deceased's backside on an hourly basis. All we know is that it was some time last night.'

'Can I ask just one more question?'

'Sure, what's that?'

'Who's Hercule Poirot?' Fortunately, Paul's nimbler legs evaded the swift kick aimed loosely towards him by Stark.

The two men used their master keys to gain entry to the large sub-divisional headquarters. They passed along the corridor into the spacious canteen. The serving staff, two girls, busied themselves chopping vegetables and a pall of smoke rose from the area of the deep fat fryer. They had a radio playing a song from a few years back, 'Are Friends Electric' by Gary Numan. Paul and Stark walked up to the serving hatch and studied the small menu stuck to the wall with a drawing pin.

'Ah, liver and onions.' said Stark.

Paul winced. 'You're joking aren't you sir? I've seen enough liver for today. What else have you got cooking, Margaret?' Paul directed his question to the brunette in the light-blue apron.

'You can have anything you want, me duck, so long as it's liver and onions or steak-and-kidney pie.'

Paul winced a second time. 'I think I've just been sick in my mouth.'

'Spare us the detail, Paul.' Stark grinned.

'Can I have egg and chips, please, Margaret?' She tutted at the special request. 'Seeing as it's you, duck, but I wouldn't do it for everyone, that's why we have a menu.'

'I'm grateful, Margaret, I'll remember you in my will.'

Paul looked drained as he shuffled to the nearest vacant table. There was a smell of food and smoke permeating the canteen, but curiously the smell was neither that of liver, nor steak and kidney pie.

Margaret spoke to Stark, still at the counter: 'What's up with him today? He seems a bit down.'

'He's just been to a post mortem.'

'A post what?'

'It doesn't matter, Margaret, blood and gore and all that sort of stuff.'

'Oh.'

Stark handed Paul his egg and chips before sitting down next to him and devouring his liver with relish. The feast was interrupted.

'Scenes of Crime, sir, can I join you.'

Stark turned round, some potato still on his fork. 'Yes, of course you can. Stuart Bradshaw, isn't it?'

'Yes, sir,' answered the gangly, freckle-faced officer, drawing up a chair.

'This is Paul Fisher, one of my DC's.'

'Hello, Stuart.' He nodded an acknowledgement.

Stark continued with his lunch as he asked, 'So what's happening down at the scene?' before swallowing a particularly tricky and sinewy piece of liver.

'I'll give you the full report later, but I can tell you what I know so far. It looks as though the house, as you no doubt saw, was entered via the rear kitchen window. We've taken a plaster cast of the marks left by the tool, so if you find any burglary tools about half an inch wide during the course of the investigation, they can be compared forensically to the striation marks and indentations left on the windowsill. The instrument used to gain access doesn't appear to be in the house.'

Stark addressed Paul, 'Is Nobby coming in for lunch?' Paul shrugged. 'I'll get Special Ops to do a fingertip search anyway, so let's see what they turn up.' Stark said.

Stuart nodded. 'Did you notice that the video machine was taken *after* the killings were committed?'

'Yes, we noticed that.' Stark concentrated on spearing more potatoes on his fork.

'The girl was actually struck as she lay on her back – you can tell by the direction of the blood spattering. It looks as if she did not move at all to defend herself. I think she must have been dead or unconscious when the blow was struck.'

'That's what the pathologist said, interesting about the blood spattering. If I'm right, it's all low level and same direction of tails on the spattering, yes?'

'That's right, sir. Did you notice the petechial haemorrhaging, on the girl?'

Stark placed his knife and fork together on the plate and wiped his mouth with the paper serviette. 'Yes, I did, Stuart, for Christ sake, I'm not a fucking imbecile, I was there you know!'

'Sorry, sir, I...'

'No, woah, hang on, *I'm* sorry, Stuart, it's been a long day, I've got a lot on my plate, but it's no excuse, of course I want you to tell me everything. I shouldn't be so bloody tetchy. Ignore me.'

'No problem, sir.'

'Wrong time of the month.' Paul said.

'Oi!'

Stuart continued. 'It looks as though the offender was standing on the bottom of the stairs when he attacked the man. The Yale key which was at the side of the dead man fits the front door, and a Yale lock has a catch on the inside and the key is only needed when entering the house, not exiting.' Stark glanced at Stuart and nodded. 'This tends to confirm, sir, that he was returning home, and possibly disturbed the offender. I have a theory about the older woman.'

'Okay, go for it.' Stark lit his cigar up.

'I think *she* walked in first, and then realising her husband had been attacked from behind, ran into the kitchen.

She then must have doubled back, when she found the back door locked, and tried to get out through the front door, but couldn't. So, she quickly ran upstairs, and was caught by the killer on the landing. It looks like she went down on her hands and knees to beg for mercy, shit herself, and then was attacked by the killer. How does that sound to you, sir?'

Stark blew out a puff of smoke. 'It sounds about right to me. She still had her shoes on.'

Paul asked, 'What about the girl; Faye?'

Stark answered. 'Dead by then. That's what they disturbed when the mother and father returned. The killer and Faye. It's early days yet. It's a hypothesis, that's all.'

'What about the screams, though? Surely, both mother and daughter screamed?' Paul asked.

Stark shrugged. 'Let's see what house-to-house, throws up.'

Paul looked like he had eaten something rotten. 'Mrs Lewis.'

'Who?' Stark looked puzzled.

Paul explained. 'I started house-to-house with Jim earlier on and we spoke to a Mrs Lewis at the house next door. She heard a noise but thought it was a fox screeching. It may have been a scream.'

'What's the difference between a screech and a scream?' Stuart asked.

Paul put his head in his hands. 'Jesus Christ! Don't you start.'

'What?'

'Never mind, she thought it was a fox screeching about quarter to eleven last night.'

'It's something to work to in the absence of anything else, for now.' Stark observed.

Paul ate his last chip. 'We got no reply at all the other houses; probably at work.'

The SOCO leaned forward. 'Now, the only other thing we've got so far, is that we've found some red fibres on the carpet next to the dead girl and on the older woman upstairs, her cardigan.'

'Nothing else?' Stark asked.

'Not yet. It is early days, as you say.'

'I guess so.'

Stark rose from the table. 'Right, I'm going to ring the missus and explain I'm not going to see her for the next. . . God knows how many days.' He walked back down the length of the canteen. 'See you later, Margaret,' he shouted to the canteen lady, the swinging double doors carrying the farewell further into the room as they rebounded into place.

*

Stark leaned into the black swivel chair and gazed out through the venetian blinds that hung over the window, partially masking the sunlight. He held the telephone to his ear and fiddled with the curly cord which connected it to the dial phone on his desk. Still it rang.

'Come on, Carol...' he muttered to himself. He did not want the unspoken requirement to have to ring his wife, hanging over him, not with all this to concentrate on. He wanted it out of the way.

'Hello?' Her voice had a cheeriness, a vulnerability to it that Dave still loved after all this time.

'It's me.'

'Hello, love. I've just put the dinner on. It's your favourite, lamb.'

'It sounds great, but I'm afraid there's a slight problem with that...'

'You're not going to be late again are you? You know your Mother's coming tonight, Dave. You haven't seen her for weeks.'

'I'm sorry, Carol, but there's been a murder – three in fact – so I'm going to be late for the next few days at least.'

'So, I won't be seeing you in daylight for the next two or three weeks.' Her cheeriness had dissipated somewhat.

'What can I do? It's a triple murder for Christ sake!'

'Are you saying catching a multiple murderer is more important than my lamb dinner?' She giggled. That was more like Carol, resilient and understanding.

'I'm afraid so, Carol, but not in my eyes, darling. Lamb dinner trumps catching a killer every single time, and you know that.'

'It sounds horrific. It's not going to be dangerous is it? Where was it?'

'No danger, Carol. Don't worry about me.'
She sighed. 'It's a shame about you not seeing your Mother, Dave, she's coming up to see you, not me.'

'Don't be silly. You know she thinks a lot of you.'

Carol laughed. 'Great. We'll sit looking at each other all night then.'

'Ring her up, then and tell her to cancel.' Stark could do without the family politics.

'Oh, I'm sorry, Dave. I was just so looking forward to seeing you. I hate being on my own all day and then all night as well.'

'Don't forget the kids, darling,' he offered.

Carol was feeling a little sorry for herself. 'It's not the same, you know that.'

Stark glanced at his watch. He tried to cheer her up a little, adopting a lively tone in his voice, belying his crowded and tired mind. 'Hey, listen I'll make it up to you when I get home, honestly,'

'Now, come on, David, you know damn well that when you get home you will be too knackered to do anything.'

Stark laughed. 'We don't know that for certain.'

'I do.'

'I can definitely promise a cuddle. Will that do for tonight?'

'Looks like it will have to. I'm joking, I will look forward to it.'

Stark leaned forward on his desk and began doodling with his pen on the white blotter that covered most of its surface. 'Don't wait up, Carol, I'll probably be very late back. I've got a funny feeling about this one.'

'And out early as well, no doubt. I'm not surprised you've got a funny feeling; you don't get three murders every day.'

'Seven years since the last one. It's one of those where all is not what it seems, but it's too early to say quite what is wrong.'

'You'll find out. I've got every faith in you.'

'Enough about me,' Stark glanced at his watch again, 'how are the kids? How has your day been?'

'OK. Nothing fantastic has happened. Laura and Christopher are sitting glued to the goggle-box. It's 'Saved by the Bell' – they've taped it. Then Christopher want's Teenage Mutant Ninja Turtles on. Who invented school holidays?'

'It sounds really exciting.' Stark mocked.

'All right, I know it's not as exciting as you Super-cops, but I'm stuck with it here.'

'I'm only kidding, you know I would much sooner be there with you guys,' Carol didn't respond, 'listen, I'm going to have to hang up now, my love.'

'Try not to be too late, Dave. You know I don't like going to bed on my own.'

'I know, if I can't make it, I will send someone round.' He laughed.

'Very funny. Who have you got in mind?'

'Eh, just you be careful, Mrs Stark.'

'Or else what? Mr Stark.'

'You'll see.'

'Ooh, I'm going to be put in my place am I?'

'You wish, look, I've got to go.'

A concern tone came into her voice. 'Please be careful, Dave.'

'I will, it's probably some spotty faced teenager got out of his depth and panicked.'

'Love you.' She smiled.

'Love you too, don't worry, bye.'

'Bye.'

*

The man lay sprawled out on the cheap settee. The brown leather was worn where various sweaty heads had rested against
it over the years it had been there. A large ashtray, almost
the size of a dinner plate, overladen with nub ends, mostly
smeared in lip-stick, balanced precariously on the arm of the
settee. He couldn't smell the funk in the room, he was im-
mune. He had been there too many times to be affected: it
was a combination of a public bar the morning after a stag
party, and the B.O. type haze that hung almost visibly in the
air. It was the same funk that seemed to emanate from many
criminal-class houses, due to neglect. The small television in
the corner of the room was on, but with the sound off: '*Block-
busters*' being the programme of choice. Music was playing
from an overly ambitious hi-fi with twin decks: 'No Woman
No Cry' by Bob Marley.

The room was a pig-sty, and his mind was just as disor-
ganised, with a melt of cannabis numbing his synapses and
dulling the reality of the shit-storm that was his life, and the
knowledge that everything he touched caused heartache to
others, or indeed himself. He was a criminal, and a low life.
This was not how it was supposed to be. How had this happened? It wasn't his fault. He had killed and would kill again,
and he couldn't give a monkeys toss. Why should he? It was
his end game playing out now; the yellow brick road he had
skipped down was leading to the emerald city of prison, or
better still death. The twelve minutes of pleasure he had just
experienced was a sliver of relief in the quagmire of misery,
he endured through the long days and longer nights. His trousers were open and the naked prostitute kneeling in front of
him had finished her unseemly task. He knew her well. He
had known her for over 5 years. She had self-written tattoos
crudely emblazoned on her forearms, stick men and some
fucking triangle or something, adjacent to these were the
myriad scars from her incessant, and in his view, ridiculous
self-harming. Next to these were bruises and pin pricks from

the needles she injected into any vein she could find, every day of her hellish life. Many veins had collapsed, and she had to inject straight into the groin mostly nowadays, or between her toes. Heroin addicts bruise easily, and they will do absolutely anything if there is a chance of some smack at the end of it. He knew her all right. Only four years ago, she wasn't bad looking. She had just left the children's home when he came across her. She was drug free, had not attended school, had no skills, other than her looks, and a willingness to please, coupled with the need to seek some sort of affection from anyone willing to give it her. Prostitution beckoned when her 'boyfriend' of the time persuaded her to give it a try, 'if she really loved him.' Initially she kept most of the money she made; she was a good earner, but her boyfriend became her pimp, got her addicted and henceforth enslaved her into his dystopian world; obeying his orders and believing she could not survive without him. Then the beatings started, and the addiction grew, and here she was fellating a man she both despised and feared. He had helped her back then, but he too had descended from the man he once was to the killer of today.

She smiled briefly through the peroxide blonde hair that was matted to her cheek. Thankfully he had already paid her the twenty pounds which would enable her to get another fix of heroin before the night was out. The primary aim of her existence was fulfilled. When she awoke her first thought was to get a fix, and when she fell into a fitful sleep in the early hours, her final thought was how she was going to get a fix the next day. Nothing else mattered, and if she had to suck the cock of this particularly unpleasant individual splayed out on the settee, then, that is what she would do. She had done much, much worse, and selling herself in this way was nowhere near as bad as the agony she would endure if she could not make her daily fix. It was a no brainer and she was well qualified.

The man leaned forward and grabbed her by the back of her straw-like hair and made her yelp. He was strong and he leaned his face into hers. She tried a nervous smile. He growled at her, spittle from his dry mouth landing on her face. 'Now, get your skinny white body out of my fucking sight!' He pushed her head away and she fell sideways to the floor. She hastily gathered up her clothing and ran into her bedroom situated down the dingy hall, shouting 'Thanks,' as she closed the door.

3

'She has two complexions-a.m. and p.m....'
Ring Lardner (1885-1993)

Stark had spent ten minutes in his office, trying to get ahead of the curve, by doing his breathing exercises ahead of talking to the troops. It felt like it would help to keep a lid on his attack which was rising each time he was about to go and do the briefing. 'This is ridiculous!' he said to himself angrily, glancing at the closed door as he heard footsteps approach, but they walked past. He was in a cleft stick as each time he got angry at getting agitated, he became agitated. With some effort, he managed to partly block out the intrusions in his brain and his breathing began to even out. Now was the time.

He entered the CID general office and spoke loudly above the chatter of his fellow policemen. 'All right, quieten down, please, folks!' The noise subsided. He focused on each of the ten or so detectives, scattered around the room, between the wooden desks and chairs. A pall of stale smoke hung in layers throughout the room, emphasised by the rays of sunlight which shone in strips through the broken blinds, strobing those assembled.

'Bloody hell, it's a warm one today.' Stark said to himself, such that others would hear the reference and mask his churning inner turmoil, betrayed by his sweaty complexion. A fly buzzed around and was periodically flapped at by whomever it irritated. It was always to no avail, and the fly continued to taunt them, pushing its luck.

Most detectives were sitting on chairs, others sought any

available flat surface. Some were smartly attired, with silk ties and handkerchiefs in top pocket, and would not look out of place at a wedding. Others, such as Nobby Clarke, were less glamorous, with cuffs rolled back, top-button open and tie loosened. The desks were covered with lever-arch files, papers, phones, ashtrays, cigarette packets, lighters, jackets, pens, betting slips and newspapers; there was no space for any-thing else to be accommodated, apart from random buttocks seeking a place to rest. Some uniformed officers were stood at the back, pocketbooks and pens poised for the briefing. The uniformed officers felt a little self-conscious at being in the CID office, they were out of their comfort zone.

Stark knew he was in line for promotion and wondered if that was the reason Superintendent Wagstaff had given charge of the enquiry to him. Wagstaff had twiddled his moustache as usual as he broke the news. 'David, this enquiry is down to you, now. If you can sort this mess out, you can sort anything out. I'll be available as officer-in-the-case on paper, and to brief the Chief, and yes, to give you a guiding hand where ne-cessary. I've told those in the Ivory Towers that you are up to it, so don't let me down.'

Stark hadn't really expected to be officially given charge, he just expected Wagstaff to hang around at the back like he usu-ally did. So, he was running the show, at least for now, and it was for that reason that he addressed the disparate group of officers in the room. Steph was the only female present. Women were still few on CID, which Stark found curious, as he had never met a bad Detective Police Woman. They were always cute, not in the Biblical sense, but they seemed to have a wisdom to them, seeing things some men didn't no-tice. He would use them strategically to interview particu-lar suspects, often the hard men who were expecting a clash in the interview room. It disarmed them, and the women often knew instinctively which buttons to press. In this sense, Stark, was ahead of his time although, perhaps letting himself down when he justified this by saying, 'If there is one thing women can do, it's talk!'

He paused and studied some of the detectives who he was to become reliant on, all of them different, but with one common goal: to find the killer before he struck again. Steve Aston, the young aide to CID, fresh from the uniform branch, an unlikely candidate: ginger hair, suede sports jacket. He was quite introverted, a vegetarian, who cycled to work most days. In contrast was Ashley Stevens, a man of twenty-nine whose expensive suits and jewellery put Steve in the shade. His hair was beautifully styled and he drove a Porsche. It was well-known that he received a private income from his wealthy father, and this riled some of the others. He was branded a poseur, and to some extent he was.

DI Stark spoke. 'Go and get Special Operations Unit in here, will you, Steve? They're in the canteen.' He scurried out.

'And put the bloody kettle on!' shouted rotund Charlie Carter, a man in his forties with greying hair, a twinkle in his eye and a paunch. Stark smiled to himself; he had been a DC with Charlie in 1975. Charlie had lived and worked on the patch for twenty-four years – everybody knew Charlie. He looked like a village squire as he sat back in his chair with tweed jacket on and puffing on a tiny cigar.

Stark's attention was diverted by the sound of swearing from behind a wall of large, brown paper bags. He knew that voice well. 'Haven't you finished that bit of a job, yet, Nobby?' he asked, laughing, whilst dabbing at the sweat on his forehead.

The voice sounded desperate. 'I'll tell you what, boss, I reckon I'll still be here this time next week, at this bloody rate.'

'Don't worry,' Stark replied, 'a DC from headquarters is coming to relieve you shortly.'

Nobby's hard features emerged from behind the packages. 'Brilliant. Praise the Lord. Someone to relieve me. Couldn't you let Stephanie relieve me instead, boss?'

The inevitable whoops resounded. Detective Policewoman Stephanie Dawson sat smirking on a side-table, her slim body leaning forward, causing her long blond hair to cascade downwards, and shielding her firm breasts which she loved to show-off and she didn't care who knew it. She was the queen of the CID scene. A lot of these self-appointed studs wouldn't last five minutes in the sack with her, but she knew that it was a huge benefit to her in the office politic that they would very much like to. She used the situation to her advantage. 'It will have to be somebody better equipped than you, Nobby!'

Nobby hadn't finished. 'Come on, give us a kiss!' He walked towards her, arms outstretched, ready for the embrace. The whoops rose in volume as Steph bent over and pointed to her ample backside. 'Kiss this!'

A voice in the doorway halted proceedings. 'So, this is what the CID gets up to, is it?' In walked the SOU, led by the inimitable Sergeant Tuckworth, every man in a blue boiler-suit and carrying, or wearing a navy-blue beret. Some of them had kit-bags, containing various paraphernalia. The Sergeant was of obvious military bearing, a barrel-chested hard case.

'Standing room only at the back, I'm afraid, lads,' Stark said. 'Right, listen up please.' All eyes were on him, and he felt a bead of sweat trickle its way down his spine. 'This isn't going to be a lengthy briefing. I've prepared a rough copy of the parts of the enquiry which will be of use to you. We'll have a more detailed briefing tomorrow, when we have a fuller picture. I just want to highlight the crux of the investigation as it stands at the moment. The Marriott family have been murdered. Walter, the father, Audrey, the mother, and their teenage daughter – Faye. The killer has forced a rear transom window with a half-inch blunt instrument to gain access to the house. Faye Marriott has been asphyxiated, but, prior to this, she had sexual intercourse in the living room of the house. This means either the killer knew her, or that she was raped, or that there is a third party who is unconnected and who has yet to be traced. It looks as though Mum and Dad interrupted proceedings and paid dearly for it. It also appears as though the sex act was interrupted as there are no traces of semen at the scene.

Necrophilia cannot be ruled out. Walter Marriott was killed by a single blow to the back of the head by a brass clown ornament which is about fourteen inches long. It appears that Audrey Marriott, in an obvious panic, ran to the back door to get out, but it was locked and then doubled-back and eventually ended up, on the landing upstairs. The killer pursued her and then strangled her to death with his bare hands. For some reason the killer then took great trouble to hit both mother and daughter over the head with the same brass clown. Presumably this was done to disguise the mode of killing. Who knows? Our killer then unplugs the video recorder and makes good his escape through the front door, taking the video and the implement he used to gain access with him. We've found the operating manual for the video: it's a Matsui and we have the serial number should you require it. The hi-fi was still switched on when we arrived at the scene this morning. Anything you want to tell us about the initial house-to-house, Paul?'

All eyes turned to Paul Fisher, who gulped. Stark took the distraction as an opportunity to wipe at the accumulating sweat on his forehead. Paul answered. 'No, sir, not too much, most addresses will need re-visiting by Special Ops, as the occupants were out when we tried earlier. One woman thought she heard a noise about 10.45pm the night before but has put it down to be a fox screeching, but I would keep an open mind about it.'

'Right, SOU can finish off the house-to-house – three streets in every direction for now - and a fingertip search of the gardens please, Sergeant Tuckworth.' Tuckworth nodded, Stark continued. 'Some red fibres have been found at the scene, which we believe could well belong to the killer, so please bear that in mind, while you are on your travels. Nobby and I, when his replacement arrives, will team up, and Stephanie and Ashley Stevens, if you pair up also. We'll look into the background of Faye. Ashley and Steph, can start on the actions that are coughed up from the HOLMES team, please?'

HOLMES stood for the clumsy pneumonic: Home Office Large Major Enquiry System. Until 1970 most provincial police forces had little experience in dealing with major enquiries and it would be a team of officers sent from Scotland Yard who would be called into help. This would usually be a Superintendent and a bag man, a Detective Sergeant or Detective Inspector. The Superintendent would read all the documents and he directed the enquiry using something called a Book 40, which listed all the actions and outcomes. Contrary to popular myth about Scotland Yard detectives, this was not always fool-proof, and it was not unheard of for the Superintendent to announce on day one who he thought the offender was, and the enquiry would essentially be focussed around proving this hypothesis. Not the best way to approach an investigation. A couple of high profile cases eventually highlighted the limitations that this process had, notably the Black Panther case, and the Yorkshire Ripper serial killer, a case which ran from 1974 to 1981, and which cost the lives of 13 women. A commission was set up and a pre-cursor to HOLMES was born. It enabled the vast amount of information collated during such enquiries, to be captured, and any comparisons or similarities surfacing later in the enquiry to be matched by computer and, in theory at least, not missed. All major investigations were pretty much the same and had been for a hundred years; information received, an action relating to it is raised; an outcome of that action; an action arising from that outcome; and the cycle would be repeated. HOLMES automated this process.

Stark continued giving his directions. 'Charlie and Steve, you can look into Walter and Audrey Marriott. Paul, can you contact Force Intelligence Bureau regarding the modus operandi, and any other comparisons with other features of other murders? I'll arrange a liaison man at the other end. Jim, I want you as office manager for today until the HOLMES computer starts tomorrow, and all the menial thousand-to-one shot enquiries start. We have a diary belonging to Faye Marriott, and everyone in it will have to eventually be seen and interviewed. The officers in this room, will involve themselves with any enquiries of importance: the peripheral stuff can be done by a squad set up at headquarters. That's it for now, any questions?'

The heads shook in unison.

'Right, crack on. Back here at 10 p.m. for a de-briefing. Overtime's been organised, so don't worry Jim, you'll get what's due to you. Let's go and see who would want to kill a nice girl like Faye Marriott.'

Stark walked out the room and straight to the toilet. He used the paper towels to try to quickly dampen his wet hair. He breathed heavily, trying to control it, trying to master it. He was told this would pass. Just give it time.

*

Stark and Nobby stood on the pavement and stared up at the sign: 'Squires Turf Accountants'. Its large front window hadn't been cleaned for weeks, but the black cardboard silhouette of horse and rider was still just about visible behind the glass façade. As Stark opened the door a cloud of smoke billowed out, and the two detectives stepped from the comparative brightness of the bustling street into a seedy world. The tinny voice of an announcer heralded their entrance: 'The two thirty at Chepstow, three-to-one favourite; Misty Morning, and seven-to-two; L. A. Girl, ten to one bar six.'

Smoke stung Stark's eyes as he tried to focus on the images within the dingy den of iniquity. A man of about sixty stood, hands in pockets, staring at the extracts from various racing papers which festooned the walls. He had a stubble chin and a dirty cloth cap resting well back on his head. A cigarette was smouldering its life away in a nearby aluminium ashtray. To the left of the detectives were six television screens screwed to the wall, with lists of horses' names displayed on them. A fat middle-aged woman with a beehive hairstyle and a beauty spot stared disdainfully at the list of runners and riders. Her short, tight-fitting black skirt revealed a glimpse of her varicose veins, and thankfully little else.

At the far side of the betting office was the main counter, with a Perspex shield. Two notices gave the simple instructions where to queue; 'Bets' and 'Pay Out', and an electrical cash-till was positioned under each sign. The carpet beneath the 'Bets' counter was considerably more worn that that beneath the 'Pay Out' counter. Stark focussed beyond the cash-tills to the woman sitting beyond them. Her name, Stark would discover, was Sally Lawrenson; she was around twenty-five years old and stunningly beautiful, with long flowing, jet-black hair and full lips which pursed to form the question: 'Police?'

'Yes, love, Detective Inspector Stark, Nottingham CID. I'd like to see Faye Marriott's boss, please.'

Sally answered in a soft, slow voice, which Stark strained to hear. 'You mean, Bernie, well Bernard Squires? He is unavailable at the moment, I'm afraid. Can he call you on his return?'

Stark allowed himself a glance at Nobby. The phone at the side of Sally rang. Stark was too quick and beat her to the draw. He held the scoop to his ear. 'Sally, tell them cunts, I'm out, get rid.'

Stark smiled and held the phone loosely, removing it from his ear. He raised his voice above the clamour and excitement and overall din in the shop. 'Bernard Squires, eh? Well, will you tell Mr Squires that unless he gets his backside out here sharpish, I'll lay some odds: Ten to one that he won't keep his bookmaker's permit beyond the next twenty-four bloody hours.'

Stark heard the click of the phone hang up on the other end and he replaced the receiver. Sally rolled her eyes. The door to the rear office had been slightly ajar; now it was opened wider by the forty-something year old body of Bernie Squires. His belly entered, followed by Bernie himself. Gold-rimmed, light-sensitive spectacles adorned his balding head, setting off the white shirt and red bow-tie of one of East London's villainous sons. Cockney charm oozed from the ex- boxer's gnarled face.

'Sally, don't be silly, treacle. Course I'm here, ain't I? Hello, Mr Stark. How are you? Sorry about that little misunderstand-ing- you can't get the staff, see?' His large hand enveloped Stark's as he warmly shook hands and then Nobby's. 'And Mr Clarke too. My, my, we are honoured. I didn't know you were betting men?' Bernie's furrowed brow and raised eyebrows emphasised the question in his voice. He was a big, powerful man, quite an imposing figure, a hard nut, but now knocking on a bit. Stark remained unmoved by the purposeful pressure Squires applied during the hand-shaking ceremony. Turning around to see that the shop was now empty, he nodded to his DS. Nobby returned to the door, flicked the catch and turned the yellowing cardboard sign, 'Closed', to face the street.

'It's been a long time, Bernie,' said Stark. 'I'm afraid it's not a social call. Can we talk privately?'

Squires adjusted his glasses. 'Yes, sure, but I have got a busi-ness to run, Mr Stark – let's play fair.'

Stark addressed Nobby. 'If you'll talk to the young girl, Nobby, please, and Bernie and I will use the back office.'

Stark followed the by now sweating, Bernie, into the small office and closed the door behind him. It was a very small office for such a big man. A tatty old school desk supported a telephone and a flexible lamp. The only other furniture con-sisted of two PVC-covered chairs and a black plastic swivel office chair, upon which Bernie sat down. A pile of loose papers headed 'Squires Turf Accountants' was strewn mess-ily around the desk. Dusty, wooden-framed certificates hung on the wall next to a picture of Her Majesty the Queen, who looked down regally at her two contrasting subjects. Stark, warm in his grey suit jacket, sat on one of the chairs, aware that Bernie was waiting for him to speak. He took his time lighting his cigar, ignoring Bernie, who could stand it no longer.

'Trouble is it, Mr Stark?'

'You tell me, Bernie.' A cloud of smoke escaped from the corner of Stark's mouth.

Bernie was getting impatient; he fidgeted in his chair. 'Let's not play games with each other – what's the SP, boss?'

'Murder. Bernie. That's the SP.'

'You what? You're joking, right? It's a wind up?'

'I'm afraid not, Bernie. You see, it's Faye Marriott.'

'What about Faye? Here – you don't mean...What it's her... what's been done over?'

Stark studied Bernie's reaction. 'I'm afraid so Bernie. At home – terrible business.'

Bernie got up from his chair and paced the floor. 'Flaming Nora, I don't believe it! She was here only yesterday. I thought she was ill when she didn't turn up today. I've been calling her from a pig to a dog. Bloody hell, straight up?'

Stark nodded and assumed the vernacular. 'Straight up, Bernie, last night, apparently.'

Bernie returned to his chair and buried his head in his hands. He removed his glasses and wiped a shaking palm over his closed eyes. Stark was surprised to see a tear trickle down his reddened cheeks before being wiped away. 'Poor, poor girl. She didn't deserve that. No-one deserves that, but not Faye, Jesus Christ! I can't believe it. Have you got him, the geezer what's done it? Has he been nicked?'

Stark shook his head. Bernie stood up again and pointed at Stark who sat impassively.

'You better had, sharpish, cos if I find the geezer what's done this, you'll be coming for me, cos I will tear that piece of shit limb from fucking limb. That's a promise, not a threat.'

Stark shrugged. 'I need to ask you a few questions, Bernie. Sit down, a minute.' He sat down. Suddenly it dawned on Bernie. 'Here, hold up - you don't think I . . . Nah, listen, just in case your mind is that warped, I can tell you I was with Tommy Slater in his boozer, the Red Lion, till way beyond closing time, we had a lock-in. Then I was straight home to bed,

Shanks' pony.'

'Nobody's thinking anything at the moment, Bernie. I just want to get some background, get to know what I can about the girl. What was she like?'

Bernie started welling up again. 'Fucking diamond, Inspector Stark, salt of the earth. This is fucked up; don't they know who they are dealing with here!' He banged on the desk with his giant fist knocking several papers flying. He stood up and wriggled his trousers up over his belly by the belt. He was restless. He didn't know what to do with himself.
'This'll crack our Sally up. I hope Sergeant Clarke breaks it to her gently!'

'He will, don't worry.'

Bernie lit a Park Drive cigarette with a slight tremble in his hands. He blew out a lungful of smoke. 'This has knocked me sideways, this has. What do you want to know? I want this bastard caught.'

'Did you say "our" Sally?' Stark asked.

'Yes, she's my niece. A nice girl is Sally. She's a student working the holidays. She's stony broke mind, so I bung her a few notes up front and I get the brains where it matters – behind the till. She'll be torn up by this, I tell you. And all the punters love Sally, cos she's a looker.'

'So were they close, Sally and Faye?'

'Course they were, thick as thieves that pair. Two young girls together. Course they were close. We all are here, it's like a family.'

'What can you tell me about Faye?'

'Fifty-two-carat-diamond – straight up, mate, she wouldn't hurt a fly. Wouldn't say boo to a goose, always polite, the punters loved her. Pure gold, she was, straight up.'

'So who might want her dead, Bernie?' asked Stark, fiddling with the stubby cigar in his hand.

'Nobody. Honestly, there can't be. Listen, it must be somebody what don't know her. She was an angel, gospel truth, Mr Stark.'

'Any boyfriends?'

Bernie looked thoughtful, staring at the floor. 'No, I don't think so, all the young lads were buzzing round her, like, but no actual boyfriends, I don't think. Sal will know more about that than me.'

'What about aggro? Do you know if she was in any kind of trouble?'

'No, she wasn't like that; I've told you- she was just a kid.'

'How did you get on with her, Bernie?'

'Fine. We used to have a laugh together, me and Faye, a bit of a mess about, slap and tickle, bit of a cuddle...You know me, Mr Stark, no harm, no foul. I love a bit of a giggle, that's all.'

'Have you had any problems with her, at work I mean?'

'No, none at all. I tell a lie – she had a go at me once, in the shop, packed with customers it was as well. I think it was the wrong time, if you know what I mean. She took exception to my bit of fun. I got a knee in the knackers for my trouble too!' Bernie laughed out loud.

'How long has she worked here, Bernie?'

'About eight or nine months, no more. That was another thing, come to think about it.'

'What's that?' Stark asked, interested.

'Her mum and dad didn't take to her working here. I think they were a bit stuck up, but Faye, she used to love the job, she was a happy girl, everyone liked her.'

'Did she enjoy the attention? From the boys, I mean.' asked Stark.

'What woman doesn't, if truth be told?' Bernie offered.

'How did she get the job here?'

'She just turned up, out the blue.' He laughed to himself as he reminisced. 'She asked for a job and got one. She even brought a couple of references, but I told her I didn't need any: if she worked hard and kept her hands out the till she stayed; if not, she went.'

'Who were the references from, can you remember?'

'Oh Gawd, now you're asking. Let me see.' Bernie put his

thumb and forefinger on the bridge of his nose and closed his eyes to concentrate. 'One was from her bank manager, whoever he was, and let me see- yes, the other from Florence Hodge, one of her old teachers. I'll tell you how I know, because her old man comes in here for a flutter on the QT.'

The telephone on Bernie's desk rang. Bernie quickly glanced at his watch and then scowled. He looked at Stark ignoring the phone. The phone rang twice more. Bernie still didn't move. Stark, puzzled, looked at Bernie, who smiled back at him nervously.

'Aren't you going to answer it then, Bernie?' asked Stark, intrigued by his reluctance to lift up the receiver.

'No, leave it, I'm busy.' Bernie rubbed the flat of each palm over the tops of his thighs, rocking his upper body. The phone still rang.

'You can't just let it ring,' said Stark.

Bernie's voice was louder, annoyed. 'All right then.' He picked up the receiver two inches, then dropped it back down on the cradle again. 'There, that's solved that. Now I hate to hurry you, but I have got a business to run, Mr Stark. Are there any more questions, or is that it?'

'No, I think that's about it, for now, Bernie. You could have answered the phone, you know.'

'That's me, Inspector, I'm reckless like that. If I hear anything about Faye that might be of use to you, I'll be straight on the dog and bone.'

Right on cue the phone rang again. This time the Inspector answered it and lowered his voice. 'Yes?'

'Yes, Bernie, it's me, old son. I've sorted that little problem out for you, as agreed.' Silence. The voice continued: 'Well, aren't you pleased? You're clean now, Bernie?' No reply. The line went dead.

'Interesting call, Bernie,' Stark observed as he put the phone down.

'That's bang out of order, Inspector, you've got no right to do that. Who was it? A crank call? I've been on the operator about them. It'll be some nutter – forget it.' He toyed with his watch.

'Oh, I shan't forget it Bernie. He seemed to know you. Come to think of it the voice was familiar to me... I just can't put a name to it – it'll come to me. You know, it's always amazed me how you ever got a bookmaker's permit,' mused Stark with a wry smile.

Bernie pulled his shoulders back exaggeratedly. 'Upright citizen, Mr Stark, not one conviction to my name. You get problems in this game, of course. I've been in - what shall I say? – some disagreements with a number of hard men, you probably know them, Johnny 'Jack' Dore and Gary Mahew to name but two.'

'I know them, of course.' Stark confirmed.

Bernie continued. 'Yet, never once have I been convicted of a criminal offence. And I'll tell you something else: I'm proud of it!'

'What's your secret, Bernie?'

He smiled and winked at Stark. 'Like all good businessmen – delegation.'

Stark laughed and shook his head as the two men struggled up from the low seating and returned to the betting office proper. Stark was met with the sight of Sally being comforted by Nobby. He held her tight against his shoulder, patting her head as she drew another hesitant, gasping breath, crying incessantly. Bernie eyed him suspiciously.

Nobby spoke to the girl. 'There, there, Sally – it's all right.' He stroked her hair, giving Stark a rueful glance.

Stark slapped Bernie on the back. 'There you are – I told you he'd be gentle with her. Have you finished here, Nobby?'

'Yes, boss, all done. Listen, Sally, don't forget to give me a call in three, or four days' time and I'll take you for a drink and we'll talk some more, OK?'

'Now, just a minute...' started Bernie.

Sally looked up at Nobby from beneath long eyelashes. 'OK,' she sobbed. 'Thank you, Sergeant Clarke.'

'My pleasure.'

A wall of sunlight hit the two detectives as they stepped out onto the hot pavement, and the noise of the traffic heightened their speech into shouts.

'I might have bloody well guessed.' Stark remonstrated.

'What now?' enquired Nobby incredulously.

'You bloody well know what. I leave you for five poxy minutes and you've all but got your cock out.'

'Oh come on, boss – I was only sympathising with the girl.'

The two men, found a gap in the traffic and half-walked, half-ran to Stark's Cavalier across the street.

'Sympathising. That's what you call it, is it? That's a new word for it.' Stark said.

'The girl was upset, for Christ's sake.' exclaimed Nobby.

'Not as upset as she'll be when you dump her in a month's time for some other tart.'

'Now don't be like that, sir. I'm just a caring policeman showing a little bit of empathy.'

'Yes, whose brains are in his trousers.'

Nobby put his arm around the wide shoulders of his Detective Inspector. 'Do I detect a little jealousy?'

Stark shrugged off Nobby's arm. 'Do you detect jealousy? Of course I'm jealous, she's a cracker.'

The two men leaned against the car in the summer sun.

'Some of us have got it and some of us haven't.' Nobby grinned.

Stark laughed. 'Yes, so make sure she doesn't get it, when you give her one.'

'Now, now, sir.'

'I don't suppose you happened to find out anything of use whilst you were snogging Miss World, did you?'

Nobby lit up a cigarette, stepping back to avoid an old dear with a shopping trolley. 'As a matter of fact, I did. Apparently, Faye had a boyfriend, somebody called Charles. I take it we will pay him a visit next?'

'You don't think its Charlie Carter, do you?' They laughed. 'We'll go and see him once we find his address.'

'That shouldn't be too difficult: he should be in Faye's diary so if we shout up happy Jim McIntyre, on the radio, he can give it to us.' Nobby suggested. The two men got into the Cavalier and hastily wound down the windows to get some air into the hot car.

'DI Stark to Control.'

'Go ahead, sir,' came the reply.

'Talk-through with DC McIntyre, please.'

'You've got it, sir.'

'DI Stark to DC McIntyre.'

'Go ahead, David.' The Scottish twang in his voice was evident.

'Yes, Jim. Get hold of Faye's diary – it's in amongst the exhibits. Look for a Charles in it, or Charlie or a Chaz or whatever, and get back to me with his details.'

'Ever heard of please and thank you? Stand by.'

'God, he's a miserable bastard,' said Stark, annoyed at the DC's disrespect, particularly over the radio. He started the car and waited for Jim to get his act together. He passed another observation to Nobby. 'You're a jammy bleeder with women, Nobby.'

'Luck doesn't enter into it.'

'I bet she screws like a jack rabbit.'

Nobby looked sideways at Stark. 'I'll let you know.'

The Inspector confided in his old mate and Detective Sergeant. 'It'd be nice to solve this one, Nobby. It wouldn't do my promotion prospects any -' the crackling of the radio cut him short.

'DC McIntyre to DI Stark.'

'Go ahead.'

'There was only a telephone number for this Charles, so I've had to mess about ringing Telecom.'

'You poor baby,' thought Stark, but he kept his own counsel.

McIntyre continued. 'He lives at 14 Sunrise Cottages, Arnold – it's quite a select area. There's no trace on the Police National Computer for this guy: looks like he's been a good boy. His full name is Charles Edward Lyon.'

'Ten-Four, Jim. Any other news?'

'Negative. Nobody's got back to me yet, but I'll keep you posted.'

Stark nudged Nobby; he was smiling.

'DI Stark to DC McIntyre.'

'Go ahead.'

'Yes – in future use "sir" when you address me.'

There was a pause. Stark could only imagine the cursing and defame issuing from Jim's mouth back at the station. He and Nobby were giggling as would be anyone else in earshot, as they would know what Dave was doing. He wasn't a dick, he was just bringing Jim into line.

'Did you receive, Jim?' Stark wouldn't leave it.

'Yes…sir.'

Stark's smile stayed with him as he pulled away in the car. 'We are going to have to get Bernie looked at very closely. What do you reckon, Nobby?'

'I couldn't agree more. In the mean-time I'll look at Sally in great detail.'

'Oh, piss off!'

*

The detached six-bedroomed house stood palatial in its landscape setting. The imposing white door displayed a large brass horse's head as a knocker. It was too stiff for Stark to use properly, so he merely hammered on the door with his fist. There was a pause. As he reached out to knock again, the door opened. A rather elegant middle-aged woman, wearing a flowery silk scarf and a long blue corduroy dress, greeted the two strangers.

Stark introduced himself and asked to speak to Charles Lyon.

'I'm afraid he's still out with friends, Inspector, but he is due home, imminently. You are welcome to come in and wait. I hope it isn't anything too serious?'

The men didn't answer as they stepped into the hall. The smell of polish on wood underscored the cleanliness of the place. It had a serene ambience which matched that of the lady of the house. The chime of a grandfather clock emphasised the quietness that embraced the cold living-room into which the two men had been ushered.

'We can wait a short while. You are expecting him home soon, you said?' Stark asked.

'Anytime now.' The woman smiled warmly.

The décor was lavish; a cluster of fine-china ornaments were shelved against the oak-panelled walls; a tiger-skin rug guarded the Adam-style fireplace and the furnishings were of the highest quality.

She held out a hand which Stark shook. 'I'm Mrs Lyon, Charles's mother, in case you hadn't realised. Will you take tea?'

'Yes, please,' Stark replied politely.

'Cheers.' Nobby grunted.

'Please, do take a seat.' She offered.

Mrs Lyon hovered out of the room to prepare the Earl Grey. The two men sat down, each in a high-backed leather chair that squeaked at the slightest movement.

'What a miserable place this is,' volunteered Nobby.

'It's colder in here than it is outside,' whispered Stark. 'I'm sure wealthy people don't realise the heating can be turned up. It's always the same.'

'That's probably why they're wealthy. Tight buggers.'

'Still, it's a nice pad.'

Nobby continued to take in the room. 'They haven't got a television in here at all, just a piano – look.'

Stark arched his neck and saw the writing desk overshadowed by the baby grand piano, complete with silver candelabra.

'I bet they have wow parties here, boss.'

'Everybody isn't such an ignoramus as you are; some people live a more sedate and sophisticated lifestyle,' said Stark.

'Boring you mean,' said Nobby.

Stark felt as if he were in the study of his headmaster, who had just left momentarily. He felt compelled to talk in hushed tones. Silence befell the living-room; a far-off chinking of pots indicated the imminent arrival of refreshment. Mrs Lyon glided back into the room and set the silver tray down on the occasional table.

'It is all a little disconcerting. What could Charles possibly do for you, Inspector?' she asked.

'It is to do with his girlfriend, Faye Marriott.'

'I knew she would be trouble. I warned him about her, dreadful girl.' She sipped at her tea. 'I suppose I should be more charitable. I don't want to appear unfair, nor judgemental, but facts are facts, and she is definitely beneath Charles's bracket, if you understand me, Inspector.' She placed the cup and saucer down on the salver.

'I take it you've met her, then?' asked Stark, a little peeved at the pomposity.

'Oh no, I haven't met her, but I told Charles from the beginning not to entertain the likes of her. What is she? Some betting-office lackey, or something. How ghastly. I knew she'd bring trouble. And he has the cheek to call me a snob. I'm right, though aren't I? Aren't I, Inspector?'

Stark didn't offer an opinion but decided on a question of his own. 'What does Charles do for a living, Mrs Lyon?'

She again reached for the bone china cup and saucer. 'He's just started his own business – he can't fail, he's an absolute darling. Sharp as a tack. I just wish he would come out of himself a tiny bit more.'

Stark couldn't avoid the mental picture he had conjured up of Mummy Lyon wetting her handkerchief in her mouth and wiping some imaginary mark off the young Master Lyon's face.

'I think we ought to explain the purpose of our visit. It's about Faye Marriott, as I started to tell you – she's dead. Murdered.' The Inspector's face remained emotionless.

Mrs Lyon raised a hand to her mouth. 'Oh, good gracious! How terrible. That poor girl.'

Stark continued, 'In fact, the whole family have been murdered.'

'Oh, how shocking.' Mrs Lyon stood up. 'Who could do such a thing? When was this, Inspector? Today?'

'Last night, we think. Obviously, we want to speak to Charles as a matter of routine.'

'Of course, but last night he was playing bridge with myself and the Crawford twins – they will confirm that.'

They heard the sound of the front door slamming.

'Tis' only I, Mother,' came the theatrical, high-pitched greeting.

Charles Lyon entered the room in a blaze of glory. Had it been the eighteenth century he could only have been described as a fop. Nobby would have said he was a bit 'light on his feet'. He wasn't a tall man, and he had an immaculately clean look about him, as if he groomed his curly brown hair every hour on the hour. His turquoise crushed velvet waistcoat and gold watch-chain went well with the pink shirt and Chino's. He appeared shocked and stopped in his tracks as he entered the room. 'Good heavens. I see we have company.'

Nobby whispered to Stark, 'Enter Fairy, tripping lightly.'

'Shush!' Stark whispered in return.

Stark rose from his chair with ease and offered his hand. The hand of the former divisional boxing champion met a smooth, well-manicured hand that flapped limply.

'Hello, Mr Lyon. I'm Detective Inspector David Stark, and this is Detective Sergeant Clarke.'

Stark broke the news as gently as he could and watched the devil-may-care cavalier turn into a gibbering wreck. It transpired that Charles had grown to love the betting-shop girl. He'd known her for three months; they had met in the Café Victoria and he had wined and dined her ever since. Embarrassed, he accepted that they had a sexual relationship, although only on two occasions which 'was a disaster.' And which Faye had claimed 'didn't count'.' They hadn't talked about marriage or anything like that. She was a demure girl – but carefree. Charles had stayed in all last night playing bridge, as his mother had said previously. He gave the address of Daisy and Jemima Crawford as alibis. Charles said he saw Faye only two or three times a week, at most. He had last seen her on Tuesday and was supposed to pick her up for a meal tonight at seven o'clock. She had seemed in good spirits when he left her on Tuesday; she didn't appear to have any problems at all. Charles stated that 'of course' he was her only boyfriend as she didn't mix particularly well; she certainly didn't mention anybody else to him. He occasionally burst into full blown tears, proper shoulder heaving stuff, when talking about Faye; he continually mopped his eyes with his white cotton handkerchief. He said that they had discussed spending a couple of weeks in Bermuda next month, at Charles's expense, of course. Faye didn't have many friends – in fact, Charles knew only of a Sally at her work, and another girl whom she mentioned a couple of times. Stark prompted him as his mind fleeted back to Faye's diary, and Charles agreed that Chantelle Naylor indeed sounded familiar. Stark explained that they were trying to track Chantelle down, but Charles couldn't quicken the process as he knew nothing about her, not that he could recall, at least.

Assembled in the cold living-room, they spoke for over an hour. Stark briefly contemplated arresting Charles, to give them something to work on, but Charles's reactions seemed authentic; and more importantly he had a good alibi. Stark wanted something more positive than diving in with both feet. Was Charles capable of staging a burglary? Maybe, but it was a stretch. Stark wasn't feeling it. The fop looked concerned as the detectives got up to leave. 'Does this mean I am a suspect, Inspector?' he asked red-faced.

Stark lied. 'Of course not, Charles. You've been a great help.'

They bade their farewells and the two men walked down the sheltered drive. Nobby grunted out of the side of his mouth.

'Fucking mummy's boy!'

'Seems like a nice boy to me,' Stark replied, 'and nice boys don't commit murder, do they?'

*

Stark and Nobby joined their colleagues and sat around the wooden desks in the CID general office. Everybody had arrived back safe and sound and began to relate their experiences to each other in a loose de-brief. It was strange that Stark was far less affected by a casual and open chat with a group, than when it was more formal and when all eyes were on him. Why was that? Steph and Ashley explained how they had visited Faye's old school as a matter of course, and had in fact already spoken to Florence Hodge, the teacher who had given Faye the reference for the betting-shop job. She agreed with everyone else that Faye was a quiet, fairly intelligent, but quite selfish girl. She often, surprisingly, appeared a trifle 'stand-offish'. A couple of her local school friends had been traced and had told the detectives, that she was a bit of a dark horse. She wasn't one for sharing personal information with others but was often keen to illicit information about the personal lives of everybody else. One friend, Tracey, kept in touch with her occasionally but that consisted of a 'stop and chat' in the street, or if she saw her on her lunch break near the betting shop. Sometimes they might have a coffee. Apart from that very little information had been forthcoming from other members of staff who felt she was one of those children who melted into the crowd, pretty 'non-descript'.

Charlie and Steve told the group that Walter Marriott was a senior bank clerk who had worked his way up through the ranks of banking the hard way. Walter wasn't a particularly interesting person; he had little or no social life and spent most evenings either reading or watching television, apparently. The only incident of note was a recent, out-of-character argument he had with a colleague at the office. He had a full-on rant and rave with one Edwin Cheeseman, but this was just a storm in a teacup according to Edwin. It amounted to built-up frustration by Walter, over an accounting project which was way behind schedule, and Edwin had offered to help him, and he just blew up at him. Walter was yelling at Edwin and repeatedly asking him 'Do you want to do it?' and it was one of those where Edwin was answering in hushed tones to try to calm him down. It was apparent that customers in the front could hear the altercation but no matter what he said to Walter he just kept shouting, in an increasingly louder tone; 'Do you want to do it?' and again 'Do you want to do it? Do you want to do it? Do you? Do you want to do it?' Eventually the Manager came in and broke the weird spell and ushered Walter into his office, but within a few seconds Walter came back out and took his coat and after slamming each door on his way out apparently went home. The Manager could get nothing from Walter other than he was under a lot of pressure and was sick of the likes of young Edwin Cheeseman taking the piss. This all happened about three or four months ago. Something was bothering him, but whether it was just a bit of a mid-life crisis, no-one seemed sure. Enquiries at the bank to see if there were any major customer vendettas had so far proved negative. He did deal with high-value transactions, some mortgages, and business mortgages and so this should remain open until it was 'bottomed out.'

Audrey Marriott was a housewife who buried herself in her work for the Salvation Army, whenever she could, and who doted on her daughter. There were no initial indications that either Walter or Audrey was being, or had been, unfaithful to each other, although it was very early days. There was no apparent reason why anyone would want to kill them, as things stood.

Paul Fisher had been in contact with the Force Intelligence Bureau and glumly informed everybody that within the last year there had been four-thousand-nine-hundred-and-sixty-eight house burglaries in the Nottingham area involving an attack to the rear window of the property; the favoured approach, of course.

Usually the rear of the premises is where there is a garden or fence or hedge to offer some cover for the burglars. The truth was that the last thing a burglar wanted, was to encounter a person on the premises, and that was why most dwelling house burglaries occurred during the day, when people were out at work. A good class burglar would not choose an alarmed house, would not choose a house with no cover at the point of entry, and would always knock-on first to check that there was no-one inside. The first act of a good burglar, once inside the house, is always to open a door and leave it ajar, not to get in, but to get out, should they be disturbed. Nor would they take a bag to the scene, they would use a quilt cover from the house or a pillowcase to put their booty in. They would either live very close to the attacked premises or they would have a vehicle secreted a short distance away. Many burglaries were committed by near neighbours. Stark was, of course fully aware of all of this and that is why he felt that the burglary at the Marriott's was a potential cover-up job. If this burglar was to be believed, then he had done none of the above, having entered a house that had an occupant, not opened a door for an easy escape and seemingly taken the video after deciding to rape young Faye. This was not definitive of course; it could be a novice, or someone on drugs who was not thinking straight or was desperate, or it could have been someone breaking in, to rape Faye and it just went belly-up from there. They just did not know yet.

Paul had tried to identify any burglars who used the same MO and who also had convictions for sexual offences and/ or violence. This, however, was extremely time-consuming and nothing particularly constructive had been discovered. He had issued a tele-printer message with the relevant details on it to all forces and had prepared the basis of a press-release, which Superintendent Wagstaff had then given on the lunch-time radio news. Paul was able to report that there were twenty-eight similar murders in the country as a whole in the previous year, but none of those seemed related as yet.

Jim complained that he was getting swamped with his action sheets and information returns. There was nothing of any great importance from him that hadn't already been said and he couldn't 'bloody wait' for the HOLMES team to set up the computer tomorrow.

Stark told the group about their little adventure at Bernie Squires Turf Accountant, then instructed Charlie and Steve to find out if there were any relations living in the area who could be seen, or any friends of Walter and Audrey. Stephanie and Ashley were to go to see Faye's bank manager and, once they'd done that, to visit as many as they could from those who remained unseen from the list of contacts in Faye's diary. Paul and Jim were to carry on as before, with Jim to type a list of all the names in the diary and make a photocopy of it.

'Would you like me to stick a broom up my arse at the same time, sir?' He emphasised the 'sir'.

'No need for that Jim, how would you be able to talk?' Stark was lightning-quick with his response and caused a raucous wave of laughter from those in the room, much to Jim's chagrin.

They were to re-assemble at 10.30 p.m.

Stark was itching to talk to Chantelle Naylor. She was in the diary, and as the detectives got up from the tables Stark began to dial the digits on the phone in the office.

A female voice answered. 'Hello?'

'Is Chantelle there, please?' asked Stark.

The woman's voice was coarse. 'Hold on a minute, duck... *Chantelle!*' she screeched.

A distant voice could be heard. 'What? I'm watching telly?'

'Telephone call - come on, it's a man.' There was something about a telephone call that demanded a response, as if it could not be ignored and must take priority over anything else.

'Yes, who is it?' He could hear the sound of chewing gum as she spoke and chewed at the same time which was no mean feat.

'Hello, Chantelle. It's Detective Inspector David Stark from Nottingham CID. How are you?'

'All right, why? What's up?'

'Nothing's up, but I would like to come and have a word with you if I can. It's nothing to worry about.'

'Yeah, I suppose. When are you coming around?'

'Now if I can. It is rather important.'

'Yeah, all right then.'

Stark didn't want her to know he did not have her address to hand. 'I'm just trying to read my mate's handwriting, what's the address? Fifty something is it?'

'Eh? Twenty-eight.'

'Oh yes, I can see it now, twenty eight...?'

'Twenty eight, Calladine Court, Crabtree Farm Estate. God, your mate's handwriting must be crap.'

'It is, you're right.' Stark smiled. 'See you in about twenty minutes, Chantelle.'

'OK, Bye.' She hung up.

He turned to his colleague, sitting to his left. 'Come on, Nobby. I want to introduce you to a nice young lady.'

'Oh, goody, another one.'

'She was very calm about a Detective Inspector ringing her up out of the blue.'

'Maybe she was expecting it?'

*

The River Trent cuts through the county and when it reaches the south side of the City, it divides the two famous football clubs; Nottingham Forest and Notts County, which dwarf the occasional passing barge, riverboat and multitude of thin rowing boats. The River grew quiet after dark. The moon was visible as dusk was making a play to ease in the night, and there was a shimmer tormenting the ripples as they swept across the surface of the expanse of water at pace. Despite the lateness of the hour, the handful of faithful anglers were there on the bank, and even on the high concrete steps trying to catch one more fish. As on they stared meditatively at the bobbing floats; they failed to see a shadowy figure creep down the worn track on the far side of the river amongst the trees and bushes offering modest cover for any murderers wanting to go about their business.

There was a slight hum of traffic further along from the road on Trent Bridge, and the headlights of cars would periodically offer brief illumination to parts of the bank.

The killer had had a nightmare of a day; wanting to speak about it, tell someone, anyone, but not daring to. He had been up and down. At one point he had shed a tear, but they were crocodile tears, tears for the predicament he found himself in, and not for the poor souls that he had taken at Maple Close. After a lengthy period of malaise and feeling sorry for himself and smoking drugs and having his dick sucked by a heroin addict, he decided he must do something to get his act together. He thought hard about what had happened, not soul searching, or contemplating whether he should hand himself in, but how he could try to evade capture. He came up with this escapade. His clothes had been burnt; the remnants were now in a large metal tin, which in turn had been placed in a dustbin-liner along with the video and the screwdriver; the bag had been sealed tight. He was wary about burying it in the woods as he had seen on the news where dogs dig up all this sort of stuff and he wanted it gone forever. He felt uncomfortable as he was unfamiliar in these surroundings. He did not know the River too well and had been surprised to see fishermen on the banks. He had not expected it. He had toyed with going further along the bank to see if it was more secluded, but he was concerned that he would bump into other fishermen on his side of the River and once seen, you cannot be unseen. He preferred to stay where he was, unseen, so far, at least.

The splash it made as it hit the water was heard by several anglers. A couple of them craned their necks in an attempt to ascertain the cause; the rest didn't bother, mesmerised by their floats or the tips of their rods. None of them had seen the weighty tin and bag hit the water, nor the person scrambling, somewhat clumsily, up the banking behind the treeline.

He stayed still for a few seconds, protected from view by the bushes, listening hard, trying to get a view. He could feel his elevated heart rate galloping in his chest and he felt his breathing must be so loud that they could hear him. Was anyone coming to investigate? He heard some distant conversation which was incoherent, emanating from the group of men. Were they coming? Nothing. He glanced briefly above the bush. They were stationary. It was a relief. Surely, now he was safe? Surely, it could now all be forgotten. Surely, the police could never find out and never prove a damned thing. Surely, he was in the clear?

4

'The biggest sin is sitting on your ass.'
                                    Florynce Kennedy

The concrete block of flats of Calladine Court, stood three storeys high. Not the sort of place one would choose to live – but, then, the occupants had no choice in the matter.

The metal outer security-door had long since ceased to secure anything. The smell of urine in the corridor was foul and pungent. Stark had learned as a young PC many years ago, not to hold the handrail of steps as you walked up, simply because of the human excrement smeared on it by people with a sense of humour alien to his own. As the two detectives weaved their way up the steps, Stark asked Nobby what motivated people to draw penises all over the walls. Nobby couldn't answer, but then cracked; 'Self-portraits?'

Glancing over the balcony he could see the wasteland carved out by planting this concrete carbuncle on the edge of town. A piece of grass all but rubbed away to a mud pile, which was used by children wearing insufficient clothing, to kick a ball around; fuelled by the improbable dream of becoming a professional footballer. A burnt-out car at the edge of the estate had become a meeting point. A myriad of white goods: fridges, freezers and washing machines were discarded around the periphery of the blocks. Some local mothers had utilised the abandoned settees with upholstery protruding, languishing outside on the grass, as places to socialise. Empty beer cans and bottles, along with hundreds of nub-ends, circled the furniture. A 'poor print', if you like. Toddlers, much too young to be out on their own, ran around the space, some in nappies, some naked, all with dummies sticking out of their mouth, a pre-cursor to the cigarettes that would sooth them from early teens to death. Dogs and their signature, tell-tale lumps of shit, also ran amok and their constant pissing up walls to create boundary lines which they 'owned'. Curiously, un-observed, this boundary pissing was emulated by the crowds of youth-gangs that patrolled the estate vying for their own status on the estate. Their own symbolic pissing competi-tions to display dominance, were met by the level of violence demonstrated or other criminal activity to impress their peers. The futility of it all was lost on them, of course; seek-ing identity, seeking family, seeking what life hadn't given them and who could blame the poor sods? They demanded 'respect', but nobody really gave it them, because nobody had explained to them that respect is earned. They confused 'ci-vility' with respect. No-one really respected them. They were pitied, if truth be told. Feared too, but no-one with an ounce of sense wanted to be them. They confused their interpretation of respect with fear, and so their aim for one was perpetually thwarted by the other.

What Stark found interesting was that there were so many decent law-abiding people who were trapped in this type of housing. Mothers and fathers desperately trying to find a path-way to either get out of the estate and most importantly to prevent their own offspring from becoming embroiled in the gangs or aspects of criminality. Some of the most genuine people Stark had ever met lived on estates such as this. To keep your own moral compass in line with such a backdrop, needed complete stoicism and a real depth of character that should be admired, in his view.

Number 28 Calladine Court had a puce-coloured door with two glass panels, one upper and one lower. Stark noticed that the lower panel had been replaced by chipboard, as had many others in the block. The problem was that it was too easy for the local tow-rags to kick in the lower panel and take whatever they could get their grubby little hands on. These weren't homes: they were just places where people lived.

Chantelle was twenty years old. Her natural blonde hair was permed and fluffed out, away from her head; her blue eyes could melt ice and tug at the heartstrings of any red-blooded male. Her skin had never felt the heat of a tropical sun, but it was tanned, and played its part in emphasising her pearly-white teeth. Her pert, nubile young body fought to get out of the skimpy, one-piece mini dress that she wore most days. Nobby's mouth dropped open as the goddess greeted the two startled detectives. Stark wondered how such beauty could emanate from such a shit hole.

Chantelle had a lot going for her in life, appearance-wise, but elocution wasn't her strong point. 'Eh-up. You're the coppers what rang, aren't you? Come in.

Stark wanted to know how nature, after creating such beauty, could drop it into this environment and allow her to be dragged up in such deprivation. Nobby's eyebrows were raised; his practised eye noticed that Chantelle didn't have any knickers on under the figure-hugging polyester summer dress. Her perfectly formed buttocks displayed not a hint of a line or indentation. That indescribable chemical reaction that has ruined many a happily married man began to stir deeply within Nobby's loins.

Chantelle ruined the moment. She spoke. 'First of all there's no bent gear here, so you've shit out, if that's why you've come.'

Stark laughed. 'You don't think we'd ring up and make an appointment if we wanted bent gear, do you? It's about Faye Marriott. Do you mind if we sit down?' Stark was polite and courteous.

Chantelle extended an arm. 'No, suit yourselves. Mum's out at Bingo. You didn't want her as well, did you?'

Stark and Nobby sat on the worn furniture, the cigarette burns all too apparent. The carpet had a slight sticky feel to it.

'No, love, we don't want to speak to your Mum.'

Stark didn't know which family the coat-of-arms hanging on the wall, portrayed, but it was made of plastic and it had two swords sticking out of it. It seemed like every other flat in the block displayed one on its wall, along with the cheap picture of 'the crying boy' and the over-filled ashtrays.

He went on: 'Chantelle, I've got some bad news for you. It's Faye ...' His voice trailed off.

'Why what's she done?' asked Chantelle.

'Nothing, but I'm afraid she's been attacked. It's bad, Chantelle – it's very bad. I'm afraid she's dead.'

Stark just caught it. A fraction of a second of grief and pain appeared on her face before the years of accepting adversity slammed shut the doors of real emotion.

'I'll go and put the kettle on.' Chantelle left the room wearing the vacant stare that Stark had seen too many times. He could hear the muffled crying in the kitchen.

Nobby's insensitivity rose to the surface. 'You know she hasn't got any knickers on, don't you?' He whispered.

Stark shook his head. 'For Christ's sake, Nobby!'

Nobby protested. 'Oh, come on, boss, she's gorgeous. I'd bet a month's pay that she's got no knickers on and no bra either.'

'All right, I'm not blind, you know. Show a bit of decorum.'

'Why are all these women so damned attractive, for God's sake?'

'Are they attractive, though, Nobby?'

'Yes, they are!'

'But are they, really? They are good time girls, Nobby, it's all they've got, their appearance, but it's on lease, it's not a permanent feature, then what?'

It was a bit deep for Nobby, he shrugged. Stark continued, 'look at their situations. Are their situations attractive? No, I don't think so. Listen to how she talks, she's in servitude, she has been moulded by her upbringing and shaped by her surroundings.'

Nobby grunted. 'And fucked by half of Nottingham, probably. She's still fit though.'

Stark gave up. The two men watched the end of the chat show *Wogan* on the large, rather ancient television set in the corner of the room. Chantelle returned with two white mugs; they had that unmistakeable dried tea-stain on the side, that hadn't been caused by this pouring. Stark explained the sorry tale to a now sullener Chantelle. She had regained her composure after the initial shock. She had only really known Faye as a drinking partner rather than as a close friend. She didn't feel as though she was close to her, but she didn't think anyone was really close with Faye. She gave off many faces and lived many lives. Stark enquired how she and Faye had met; they didn't seem to have a lot in common. How wrong he was.

'I met her at Annabelle's Night Club. It was quite funny, really, because my mate had got off with somebody, and her mate had as well, so we just looked at each other standing there on our own and burst out laughing. Then we got talking.'

Nobby grinned. 'Annabelle's, huh?'

'Do you go?' she asked.

'It's been known.'

'Well, if you see me down there, I might let you buy me a drink, or two.'

'And, if I see you down there, I might just do that, Chantelle.' Nobby smiled.

Stark interrupted the love-in. 'Going back to how you met Faye, did you arrange to see her again or get a phone-number or something?'

Chantelle crossed her tanned, well-defined legs slowly, 'No, we were talking, and these two black guys came up and asked if we wanted to dance, so we did. Before we knew it we were back at a flat at Hyson Green.'

'Then what?' Stark enquired.

'They screwed us, of course. In fact, both screwed me. Faye just had one of them.'

Nobby coughed into his tea, spilling some of it. Was she just speaking like this for shock value? Or was her world so open and so coarse that this was just the norm, and she took the assumption that everyone did?

Chantelle smirked, savouring her audience's reaction. 'Are you all right, me duck, or do you want me to get you a cloth?'

'No, I'm fine.' Nobby said.

The Inspector continued his questioning, noting Chantelle's tendency to seek attention and wondering if she was being one hundred percent truthful in her account. 'Was Faye into that sort of thing then, Chantelle?'

'I don't know. But if she wasn't then, she certainly was from that moment on.'

'How do you mean?'

'She couldn't get enough of it. She's like me.' Chantelle glance at Nobby, who smiled at her.

'So, she used to go out shagging regularly then?' Stark asked, adopting the 'when in Rome' technique.

Chantelle laughed. She lit up a half-smoked cigarette that she had fished out of the full ashtray on the settee arm. 'Not half! She used to give her phone number out like confetti. She used to get more blokes than me, for some reason. We joked once that if I could talk all posh like her, I could become Miss World, but she said "No, you'd be Miss Turkey 'cos you're the best gobbler!'" She threw her head back and cackled like a pantomime witch, drowning out Stark and Nobby's half-hearted attempts to join in the laughter. Nobby's initial attraction to her began to dissipate. There were limits, after all.

'So how long have you known Faye?' Stark asked, amazed at her honesty, but also the crude way in which she spoke. She spoiled herself. She really did.

'About six months, something like that, not that long, really.' Chantelle answered, swirling the tea in her mug and smiling to herself.

'How many times have you been out with her, Chantelle?' Stark asked.

'We used to go out two or three times a week. Sometimes I couldn't afford it, but she would help me out. Apparently one of her boyfriends was absolutely loaded, she had it made, so good on her.'

'Was she on the game, Chantelle?' Stark asked matter-of-factly.

Her mouth opened, aghast. 'Cheeky bleeder! No, she was not, and before you ask, neither am I. What do you take us for?' It seemed Chantelle had no qualms about sleeping with anyone she known for three minutes, but the suggestion she would do this for a fiscal advantage was insulting.

'How many boyfriends did Faye have?' He asked.

Chantelle screwed the cigarette butt into the other nub-ends in the ashtray staining her bright red nails briefly with ash. 'Oh, Christ. Let me think...she used to get-off with someone most nights. She never took them home, though – I think her dad used to give her some grief about going home so late. They weren't good parents like me mam, she lets me do what I want. I don't think her mam even knew she got home late, half the time. Faye once told me that her mam still thought she was a virgin. I ask you!' Chantelle's eyeballs rolled upwards to emphasise her apparent incredulity.

Stark's mind was quick. 'If she went with two men a week for six months, that's forty-eight men. Did she keep any names or phone numbers of these men, do you know? Other than in her diary?'

Chantelle shrugged her shoulders. 'I wouldn't know to be honest.'

'Can you tell us any of the men she went with?' Stark asked.

'I doubt it. These were one-night stands, Inspector, not big love jobs. I'll have a think.'

Nobby asked a question: 'What about drugs?'

'Blimey, it speaks. Come on now officer, would I tell you that?' Chantelle folded her arms.

Nobby tried to reassure her. 'Look, Chantelle, this is a murder enquiry, we need the truth. We aren't interested in doing anything about it. We are trying to catch a killer, here.'

'All I will say is that as far as I am aware, she didn't do any *hard* drugs, she was not a junkie if that makes sense?'

Stark answered. 'I get what you mean. Did she confide in you at all?'

Chantelle nodded. 'A fair bit, yeah, look, I've told you all there is to know, really. There's no big secret or ought like that.'

Stark was persistent. Faye's lifestyle was quite a revelation. Faye was obviously not quite the girl they thought she was, and this investigation had suddenly taken on a whole new angle. 'Did she have any arguments or any enemies?'

'No, I don't think there was anything like that, no aggro. Although thinking about it, she used to complain all the time about someone at work, but I didn't really pay much attention. Works just work, isn't it?'

'Do you work, Chantelle?' Nobby asked.

'I ain't got time to work.' The cackle returned. 'It knackers your benefits up for a start, don't it? What's the point? I don't get it. Why work, when people will just give you money? It's a mug's game, sorry, like I say, I just don't get it, but that's me.'

'Self-respect?' Nobby said with a tinge of annoyance in his voice.

'What was the problem at work?' Stark asked.

'Like I say, I don't know. I can't tell you who it was. Some fucking idiot.'

'A man, or a woman?' Stark asked.

'Man. I think.'

'If she was complaining all the time, Chantelle, surely you can remember something about the nature of it? Was it serious or petty or what?' Stark didn't want to leave this potential line of enquiry, could it be Bernie Squires himself or a punter perhaps?

Chantelle shrugged. 'Soz. Dunno.'

Stark sighed and glanced at Nobby, who grimaced. Stark decided to change tack.

'Did you go out with her last night?'

'Yes, we went out about eight o'clock and ended up at Ritzy's. Faye was worried that her parent's had been visiting relatives out of town, miles away apparently and so would be back late and that they would, you know... give her a hard time for being out late again.'

Stark took the obligatory written statement. Chantelle explained how the two of them had gone out together; they had been to the *Star*, the *Bull and Butcher*, the *Q.E.* for a sing-along; and had completed the evening's festivities at Ritzy's at around eleven o'clock, or just after. They had become split up at around midnight. She had seen Faye smooching with a guy about ten minutes later, and then she didn't see her again. This, however, was not particularly unusual. Chantelle had only briefly seen the man she was dancing with. All she could say was that he was a white man, mid-twenties, dark hair, quite attractive looking, or 'fit' as Chantelle said. And he was wearing a white shirt with collar and possibly grey trousers. She had then seen Faye talking to Winston Kelly, a black guy, whom Faye knew quite well. That was about it.

The two men left the flat, their footsteps reverberating, hollow. As they walked down the corridor and on to the concrete steps. Chantelle's door slammed shut behind them.

'Still want to screw her then, Nobby?' asked Stark smiling.

'What a waste though, isn't it?'

Stark nodded. 'It sure is.'

Nobby stopped in his tracks, suddenly. 'Flaming hell- just look at that!'

Hatred is expressed in many ways, and on this particular occasion it took the form of human excrement, neatly placed, and in fairness, beautifully coiled on the bonnet of the red Ford Escort CID car, which Nobby had parked a couple of hours earlier.

'I'll go and get some toilet paper,' said Nobby, shaking his head in disgust.

Stark also shook his head; he couldn't resist it. He shouted after his colleague: 'Don't bother, Nobby, he'll be miles away by now!'

*

The group of detectives had decided to discuss the day's events in the public house that had been so conveniently built next door to the police station. It had recently had a refurbishment and now matched all the other bland interiors of half the pubs of Nottingham. The cops were stood in the proverbial circle a few feet away from the bar. After Nobby had got the drinks in, he told the others about Chantelle and her 'chapel hat pegs.' The conversation then took a more constructive turn, and the subject of murder took priority. Jim explained that SOU had finally finished the fingertip search and had seized several items: three miscellaneous pieces of paper, two bottle tops, a used condom, six cigarette ends, and a plastic loop thing.

'What's a plastic loop thing?' enquired Stark, understandably.

Jim attempted to describe the object more eloquently. 'If you look at your shoelaces, the ends of them have got a plastic loop thing on them, to stop them fraying. It's one of those.'

'Where was it?' Stark asked.

'Outside the front of the house; near the front door-step, apparently.'

'I didn't see that.'

'I think you would struggle to see it, unless you were on your hands and knees.' Jim offered.

'Is it traceable, do we know?'

'I don't know yet.' Jim said. 'I'll check in the morning; if people stop giving me mountains of work to do.' He couldn't help himself.

'Sip ahoy!' Nobby said as he sipped at his glass of whiskey. It was something he said so regularly nobody acknowledged it anymore. He continued, 'It's an aglet.'

'Sorry?' Stark looked puzzled.

'An aglet. The plastic shoelace thing; it's called an aglet.'

Nobby looked pleased with himself.

The group exchanged glances. 'How the hell do you know that, Nobby?' Stark asked.

'My dad's, dad, was a cobbler.'

'You mean your grandfather.' Stark said.

'Oh yes, I suppose I do.' Nobby said.

'Okay. Wow. At least we know what it is called, the day hasn't been a total waste.' Jim offered.

'What about the condom?' Stark asked.

Jim shook his head. 'That's nothing, it was half buried and perished. It's been there years probably.'

'And these other things are all out the back garden, or front?' Stark asked.

'Back.'

Nobody else had a great deal to say to each other about murder. They were all murdered out from their efforts throughout the day. Such long days usually meant stilted silences, and staring straight ahead, when the pub relaxed the brain. Nobby crudely began comparing Stephanie with Chantelle. Steph joined in the tease and stuck out her chest, which pleasantly surprised Nobby, as there was little difference in the women's proportions. Stark decided it was time to leave and head towards home. Tomorrow would be another long day, and all the unanswered questions were dancing around his head, to the accompaniment of 'Is This Love' by Whitesnake; the loud rock music blaring from the jukebox.

He began to bid his farewells.

'Aren't you stopping behind, boss?' asked Steph.

'No, I'm going to be boring tonight and get off home. Thanks to all for all your efforts today. It might not seem it, but we are making progress.'

'Goodnight, boss.' They shouted in unison.

*

Dave Stark pulled into his drive. He couldn't remember a

lot about the journey; the unanswered questions wouldn't go away. It looked as though Carol was still up. He tried to close the door quietly, and he removed his shoes in the hallway. It was after midnight and he would at last see his wife; his children would be asleep in their beds.

He was proud of his family and of what he had built up. Fleetingly, his mind returned to the first day he saw Carol, seventeen years ago. He was a young Detective Constable, investigating a series of thefts in a large office block. He had to spend a lot of time there in an attempt to catch the offender. The management had given them full co-operation and access to all personal files. A young woman in the Personnel Department was most helpful. Her name – Carol Needham. She was a pretty little thing, who gave out a warmth and genuine kindness. Her smile would light up the office. Her naivety and vulnerability drew Dave to her. He envied her innocence, wanting to protect it for her, wanting to taste it, wishing he still had some left. She wasn't a tall girl – five foot three in her stockinged feet, which was how she chose to walk around the office, casting her high heeled shoes under the desk. Stark liked this quirkiness about her. She was slim and always dressed immaculately. She had short, light-brown hair and wide, sparkling eyes, which never dimmed, like the eyes of a child on Christmas morning. When Carol smiled, nothing else mattered.

Dave first saw her as she sat scrutinising some documents; she spilled some coffee on his trousers – she was most apologetic and embarrassed. Dave reminded her of the accident the following week when he asked her out to dinner. He initially asked her out for a drink, but she said, 'If you are going to ask me out, Dave, ask me out properly.' She had a cheek, but he acquiesced readily, and she couldn't refuse. Dave arrested the office thief – a manager from another floor, as it turned out – and his job there finished, but he knew the affection that had grown for Carol would only grow and it eventually landed him on the steps of Saint Mary's Church two-and-a-half years later.

Today had been a strain for Dave. He stretched and loosened his tie before entering the living-room. Carol was wearing a pair of his pyjamas, the sleeves a foot too long. She got off the settee, standing to greet her husband; she was bleary-eyed and blinked to focus on him. She put her arms around him and kissed him.

'You look as if you were fast asleep, love,'

'I was. How are you?' She rested her head on his chest and closed her eyes.

Stark squeezed her lovingly and drew his hand over her backside. She didn't object. 'OK. How are you?'

'OK, apart from Christopher and Laura messing about all night. They're in bed now.'

'What have they been up to?' asked the vaguely concerned father, his mind crowded with more pressing questions.

Carol said, 'I don't know what the matter is with them,'

Dave released his grip on his wife and collapsed into the soft armchair. Carol continued talking to herself: 'they've been at each other's throats all day long. I'll be glad when the six week's holidays are over, and they get back to school. Are you still taking Christopher to the football match tomorrow?'

'Sorry, love – what did you say?' Stark rubbed his tired eyes.

'You're not listening, are you? I said, are you taking Christopher to the football match tomorrow?'

'No, I can't, I'm sorry, love, I'm going to be tied up at work tomorrow. I did tell you that on the telephone, earlier.' What he wanted to say was – *'Seriously? You think it is possible for me to investigate three fucking murders and poke around the under belly of the lower echelons of society, with hundreds of actions to complete and a team of detectives to sort out. Do you think in any sane world I can take time out to drive home and take my son to bloody football? Are you real?'* He didn't say any of that.

'Oh yes, of course, those murders... You're not even safe in your own home are you? That Mr Wagstaff's dealing with it isn't he?'

'Well, sort of, but in truth...' He was interrupted.

'It's terrible, isn't it? I saw it on television. Does he know who's done it yet?'

'No, not yet. It's going to be an awkward one, I think. Still, its early days. I'm hoping that by the end of tomorrow we'll know exactly where we stand.'

'Are you going to be late again tomorrow, then?'

Stark said, 'It certainly looks that way, love, I'm afraid.' He was tired.

Carol flopped down onto his lap and he let out a gasp. She was sarcastic. 'Oh sorry, I'll go and sit in the corner of the room, shall I?'

Stark was too tired to argue. 'Don't be like that, Carol. I just want some breathing space, that's all.'

There was a pause. Dave put on a silly voice, as if he had a sore throat. 'Do you love me, Carol?'

'What do you want?'

'Charming. Just a little whiskey would be nice.'

Carol screwed her face up. 'Ah, can't we go to bed? I'm tired. I haven't stopped all day, you know.'

'Okay, you go up. I'm exhausted too, but my mind is still going around. I'll be up in a couple of minutes.'

'Don't be long; I want that cuddle you promised me on the phone.'

Carol poured him a whiskey and kissed him before going upstairs to bed. Dave clung on to his crystal glass and closed his eyes. His body had stopped moving but his mind raced, darting and dancing around in a whirlpool of ideas and images, occasionally stopping at incidents that had scarred the tissue: a naked girl brutally murdered; the post-mortem; Paul Fisher's lunch; Bernie Squires; Charles Lyon; Chantelle's breasts; Ritzy's nightclub; Winston Kelly...That name rang a bell...

Eventually tiredness battered down the jack-in-a-box images and Stark struggled upstairs to bed. An hour passed. He snuggled up to his sleeping wife. He thought of his daughter Laura, sixteen next birthday, a young woman now; his son young Christopher, a rumbustious thirteen. He smiled. The image of last Saturday's football together in the park healed the scars in his mind. He had never had that: his father was a bully of a man who had chosen drink and left when Dave was a mere boy. He stroked his wife's slim stomach and thought of Chantelle in that dingy flat, striving to get some cheap bit of attention from anyone and everyone. He had a lot to be grateful for.

5

'Forgive your enemies, but never forget their names!'
John F. Kennedy (1917 – 1963)

Stark sat in Detective Superintendent Wagstaff's office, in the naughty-boy's chair. Although Stark had not been a naughty boy on this occasion; he was there to brief his boss, he still felt his status could change at any minute.

Wagstaff had obviously tried to personalise his working environment. A large trout hung in a glass case on the wall next to another large trout: a photograph of the beloved, but curiously stern-faced, Mrs Wagstaff. An array of group photographs of detectives on various training courses, as well as various commendations, hung on the wall also. The modern grey desk with green trim had a green flexible lamp and matching telephone standing symmetrically either side of neatly placed paper trays and notebooks.

Wagstaff, wearing a blazer, twisted round in his chair; he held on to his lapels, thumbs sticking up, as he concentrated on the rudiments of Stark's account of the progress of the investigation.

'…so that's how the enquiry stands at the moment, sir,'

'Mmm- we need an inroad, a break,' Wagstaff said to the wall.

Stark thought better of saying 'No shit, Sherlock.' but it troubled his mind. 'That's right, sir, we have to make our own luck, of course.'

'What's your plan of attack for today then, David?'

Stark was ready for the question. 'We are getting HOLMES computer set up and then…'

'Yes, I will come to headquarters to do that with you. There is another press conference at midday. It has made the national news and the chief wants me to make a statement. Anything you want me to ask the public, David?'

'Not really. Just the usual "anyone with information..." routine, will suffice for now, thanks.'

'Fine.' Wagstaff pursed his lips. 'I remember, I think it was 71 or 72. I had a child murder in Bestwood and the only reason it was detected was by a member of public who overheard a conversation in a pub.'

Stark began to zone-out and whilst he saw Wagstaff's mouth moving the words were lost on him. It was going to be a boring anecdote and not take them any further at all. After the reminiscing finished Stark continued relating his plan for the day to his Superintendent: 'There's plenty the lads can be doing from yesterday's activities. SOU can continue with house-to-house enquiries: the people that weren't at home yesterday may well be in today. I've got to decide what manpower I will need from sub-divisions and in what way they need to be deployed. I'm going to use my lads for the main body of the investigations; SOU and staff from other divisions can do the slogging.'

Wagstaff made the comment he had been waiting to make. 'Right, David, it looks as though you've got your finger on the pulse. I'll see you in about half an hour. If you sort your men out with various actions, then we'll travel over to headquarters and check out progress together.'

'There is just one thing, sir.'

'What's that, David?'

'I'd like to lead this from the front if I may. I am grateful for you giving me the opportunity to lead the enquiry in real terms, but it's not my style to be stuck in the Incident Room looking over shoulders all the time. Plus, you have the real expertise in command at the Incident Room.'

'Yes, I suppose you are right, David. It's a good suggestion, yes, I will co-ordinate things from the Incident Room for you, once the wheels are in motion with HOLMES. You've got a free rein, as promised.'

'That's great, sir. See you in a bit, then.' Stark left the office.

Wagstaff allowed himself a wry smile as he leaned back in his chair.

*

Stark was in an ebullient mood as he entered the packed CID office. 'Morning, team. Right – where's my tea? Come on, Steve, get your act together. You know the aide to CID always makes the tea for the DI.'

The timid Steve went red. He mumbled, 'Sorry, sir.'

Stark addressed the portly figure in tweed. 'Now, Charlie, what's this about some witnesses?'

'There's basically those who you and Nobby saw yesterday, but having gone through the updates this morning there is someone...would you believe an ex-copper, Peter Glover?'

Charlie announced the name as a question as if to enquire if the name meant anything to Stark.

Paul Fisher, sitting to Charlie's left, jumped in. 'I know him. He should be a good witness. What's he seen, then?'

Charlie stood to hand the papers to Stark. 'Ouch, you bugger!' he said. This exclamation of pain was so regular that nobody referenced it anymore. Sometimes when Charlie stood up or even when he sat down, he would emit the same cry: 'Ouch, you bugger!' They just put it down to his bones aching as he got older as he would often rub his knee as a decoy, Charlie knew only too well what it was: haemorrhoids.

'His Ford Sierra had broken down nearby and as he was looking under the bonnet, apparently he saw somebody running away from the direction of Maple Close.' Charlie said as he returned to his seat.

'Great stuff. He and I joined together,' Paul said.

'Ouch, you bugger!' Charlie sat down and rubbed at his knee. 'They were scraping the barrel that year.'

'They were, Charlie, obviously.' Paul gave a flat, mock smile.

'I knew Pete had left, but he was stationed in the north of the Force and we kind of lost touch, so I don't know the full story. How come he didn't report it at the time, you know, on the night of the murder?' Paul asked.

Charlie shrugged. 'I don't know, it was just a bloke running, maybe he'd had a few sherbets? He had been driving. We will find out soon enough, I guess.'

'Who else?' Stark asked.

Charlie glanced at his note pad. 'There's some bloke called Ernest Gray, and of course, the window-cleaner who found the bodies needs tracking down; the Coroner will want a copy of his statement to open and close the inquest this week.'

'True.' Stark agreed. 'But we know what the window cleaner is going to say. Who's this Ernest Gray character, Charlie?'

'I think he's the local village idiot personally. I knew his brother, Eric; daft as a brush he was. He reckons he's seen something suspicious, but I would take it with a pinch of salt, he's a bit of a daft lad.'

'Let's see what he has to say. Let's keep an open mind, eh?'
Charlie nodded. 'No problem.'

Steve Aston returned with the cup of tea. His brown Hush Puppies made no sound and Stark gave an exaggerated jump as Steve suddenly appeared at his side. 'You must stop doing that,' he said, laughing. Steve lowered his head and gave a sickly grin as he turned away; he wanted to reply, but he couldn't think of anything to say.

Stark spoke to the group. 'Listen, I'm going to have to go and set up the HOLMES computer this morning with old Wagstaff. Jim, you'd better come up with me and bring all the returns you've got so far.' Jim tutted.

Stark continued: 'Paul, if you know this Peter Glover you might as well take the statement off him. Ashley, if you take a statement off Ernest Gray and Charlie you do the window cleaner. The rest of you get a couple of actions off Jim and crack on. I want you to put the word out on the street, use your own informants and keep me posted. From this morning the enquiry will be based in the Incident room at Sherwood Lodge. There is a main briefing at 2.30 p.m. in the parade room, which is next door to the Incident Room for those that don't know: make sure you're there, please. Good luck, and I will see you all later.'

'Cheers boss.' 'See you, sir,' came the various replies, as Stark disappeared out of the room.

Jim spoke: 'Looks like I've got the shit end of the stick, again. I do all the work while the gaffers sit on their arses sipping bloody tea all day in the comfort of the Incident Room.'

'Privilege of rank, Jim,' Paul commented philosophically.

*

The phone rang. Paul Fisher's tight-fitting suit stretched to breaking point as he reached to pick it up. 'CID, DC Fisher,' he answered.

The lady caller spoke from the downstairs reception area in the police station. 'Hi Paul, I've got a Peter Glover at the counter asking for CID, do you want to see him?'

'Yes, Pat, bring him up, love, will you?' He had heard the other more established detectives make such a request of her.

'What do you think this is; the bloody Ritz?' She said curtly. 'I've got five people queueing at the counter. I'll tell him you'll be down shortly.'

'Okay, I'll be down in a minute.' She had already put the phone down. Paul tutted. 'No need to be like that.' He muttered to himself.

Paul found an empty office and ushered his former colleague in and they both took a seat. They chatted about the old days at training school and then the reason Pete was an *ex*-cop surfaced. Six years before, Pete Glover had looked as though he had a very bright career ahead of him in the police service, until he fell-foul of the Police Complaints and Discipline Procedure. He had been in the force only ten months, and was still a probationary PC when it all came tumbling down around him. A young black woman had been caught glue-sniffing; a fad at the time where, mainly kids, would sniff fumes from tubes of superglue and the like, in a plastic bag which gave them a high, and a huge bloody head-ache most of the time, and spots and personality disorders and so on. It was a good spot by Pete; he had clocked her sitting on the wasteland with her back against an old skip. Pete was with a village bobby at the time called Dennis Mannion, who was not known to be an experienced thief-taker and not up to much beyond the odd speeding ticket. The fifteen-year-old girl was at the back of a deserted Victorian warehouse and had made the mistake of sitting against the skip instead of sniffing in the privacy of the decrepit, but deserted building. Pete had done the talking and taken the bag off her as evidence and she gave her details through a fuzzy haze created by the improvised narcotic. Dennis had returned to the panda-car to radio in her details, and do a name check, primarily to see if she was circulated as wanted or missing from home. Pete stayed with her, to make sure she didn't do a runner. Upon his return, only three or four minutes later, Dennis was aghast to see that the girl had a broken jaw and a bruised eye. She made a formal complaint when back at the station, and subsequently produced a mystery witness; a supposed passer-by. The Police Complaints investigators believed her and the witness, and Glover was persuaded, against his better judgement, to resign from the force. He still felt bitter about it. He remained adamant to the very day that he was innocent and that, as he told them at the time; she injured herself whilst thrashing out wildly in a state of mania induced by the glue sniffing. What the witness had seen was not him assaulting her, but him trying to restrain her and stop her injuring herself further. It was two against one, and Pete did not want to risk a court case and a jury and knowing how fickle juries can be; even the risk of prison, so he reluctantly resigned. It was all very unfair and even Dennis who had been duty bound to report the incident, thought Pete had been badly treated.

The incident which created Glover's short-lived police career might have been a blessing in disguise to some extent: he now worked in insurance; he had a very nice company car, a fat salary, perks and was doing very well for himself. He certainly wasn't bitter to the extreme, about what had happened, but it grated. Still, he was public-spirited enough, to report what he had seen on the night in question, when he had heard about the murders on the radio the next day.

'Look at you, Mr Billy Big Bollocks, on the CID.' Pete commented. They sat opposite each other on the plastic moulded chairs.

'I know, who would have thought?' Paul laughed.

'Not me!' Pete joked.

'Ha bloody ha. What about you in your expensive suit and silk tie? Very suave.'

'Things are going well, I must say. I still miss the old days, mind. I fancied CID, one day, myself.' Pete grimaced as the memory of what happened seemed to flash into his mind.

'That was a bum deal, Pete. It was out of order. It could have been any of us.' Paul shook his head as if to underline the comment.

'Of course, but the public don't realise that, and whilst it's not so bad now, at the time, mate, people used to look at me like I was a piece of shit. Even people on the job, cops who should know better, and some of them even perpetuated some of the rumours circulating about me. It was all pretty disappointing and unsavoury.' Pete sighed before continuing. 'My poor old Mum suffered with her health because of it, bless her. She had been so proud. Anyway, that's the past. Life goes on. No point letting it define your whole life.'

'How is your Mum?' Paul enquired.

'We lost her three years ago.' Pete frowned.

'I'm sorry to hear that, Pete.' He paused slightly. 'What have you seen, what's the story from the other night?' The detective was curious.

'It's probably nothing, Paul, but I heard about the murders

on Maple Close on the radio and that it had been a burglar who was disturbed?'

'Sort of. We aren't exactly sure yet, Pete.'

'Well, I had been out at a club and was driving home, it was late, about half one, something like that, when the motor started flashing a warning light, so I thought I had better pull in. I thought I had left the petrol cap open or something, so I got out to have a look. As soon as I got out, I heard an almighty bloody scream, which as you know is not that unusual at that time of night...' He laughed. '...and I thought it was probably a domestic.'

'OK. Carry on, mate.' Paul scribbled on the lined witness paper.

'A minute or so later, I saw some geezer running down the opposite side of the street; towards Hucknall.'

'What's the description, Paul?'

'It's not going to help, much I'm, afraid.'

'It all helps, mate.' Paul smiled at his old friend.

'Let's think. About six foot, dark - longish hair, black jacket and jeans, trainers.'

'Was he white?'

'I'm not sure, mate. He could shift though, so he must be young-ish I would say; teens or twenties. I shouted to him, but he was gone in a couple of seconds.'

'You didn't fancy a chase then?' Paul grinned.

'Not really I didn't have time to lock my car and...'

Paul looked up from the statement. 'And?'

'Don't quote me on this, but I'd had a few beers, so I thought best to keep out of it. There's no need to put that in the statement is there?'

'It's your statement, Pete, it's not really relevant. You have been good enough to come in and tell us, so no need to complicate matters.' Paul reassured him.

The snag was that Paul was inadvertently allowing his affection for his old friend to colour the way he was dealing with him and that was always a mistake. Of course, it was relevant that he'd had a drink. R v Turnbull 1977 was a stated case and whilst not specific to alcohol consumption it was relevant to establishing factors which illustrate how well the witness had perceived the event in question. If a witness states they had seen an offender commit a crime, for example, R v Turnbull stated that it should be ascertained how far away they were. How long did they observe for? Was their view obscured at all? What was the weather like? What was the overall visibility like? All of those things which would enable a jury to decide on the credence of the witness's testimony, and the accuracy of the description, or indeed recognition of the offender. The fact that Pete Glover had drunk six pints would go some way to determining that.

'Was he carrying anything?' Paul asked.

'Oh yes, erm, he was, thinking about it.'

'What was it? What was he carrying, Pete?'

'A black bag, quite big, it looked quite heavy.'

'But he could still run at speed?' Paul asked.

Pete shrugged. 'I guess so.'

'What sort of bag?'

'I think it was a bin-liner, something like that. Not a holdall.'

'So what did you do, Pete, anything?'

'Yes. I walked to the petrol station to get some bloody petrol!' They both laughed.

He signed the statement. They said their goodbyes and shook hands. Despite the promises to keep in touch, Paul didn't expect to see him again. Peter had moved on, moved up a notch in the social bracket, and whilst they were friendly, they seemed more distant now than ever.

*

In the room adjacent to Paul Fisher and Peter Glover sat Ashley Stevens and Ernest Gray. Two more different men you couldn't imagine.

Ashley was probably the most handsome and best-dressed

CID officer on the division. Ash, did not need the wage of a CID officer, his extremely wealthy father gave him a private income, but in fairness to Ash; he did not just sit on his backside and be a playboy, he took it upon himself to do a dangerous and difficult job as a detective...and also be a playboy.

Sitting opposite him across the wooden desk was a man about forty years old, maybe slightly older. He needed a shave – in fact both of his chins needed a shave. His unkempt, straggly hair hung limply over his long-out-of-date 'Elvis' sideburns. The oily stains visible on his stubby fingers had not been acquired that day, but served to disguise the nicotine stains, which were being reinforced by a Park Drive cigarette, spewing out smoke that irritated Ashley's eyes.

He explained his story to a man who never had, and never would have, oily hands. Mr Gray had finished work early for once. on the night in question. Early for him was about twenty-five to one in the morning. He worked nights at the pit boiler room. He started the trek home, through Maple Close and up to the council estate perched at the top of the hill, where he lived. As he turned into Maple Close he heard a scream: 'Don't! Please, I'm begging you, please, no!' He, like the ex-cop Peter Glover, had assumed that it was a couple arguing and paid it no heed. A minute or so later he saw a man running full pelt along the back of Maple Close, away from Hucknall, towards Bulwell. He had only seen him from behind, but he appeared to be carrying something as he ran. He couldn't see what it was. The man was about six feet tall with a slim build.

Ashley finished off the self-description form, a standard for all witnesses in murder enquiries, with great relief and opened the door to let some oxygen into the, by now, smoke-filled room. He bade farewell to the dirty man and watched him as he coughed his way out of the main door of the police station.

*

Paul and Ashley compared notes and passed the information through to the Incident Room at Sherwood Lodge.

'At least it looks as if we've got some witnesses who have actually seen the killer,' said Paul.

Ashley replied thoughtfully. 'Yes. The problem is, Pete Glover and Ernest Gray say that the man was running in two different directions.'

'That's for Stark to sort out. Anyway, I know who my money's on,' said Paul.

'Hello, here's happy Charlie,' said Ashley. Paul turned to see the dishevelled detective shuffle in with a long face.

'Piss off about happy. I've just spent over an hour with that prat of a window-cleaner. What a miserable bleeder he is.'

'What did he have to say?' asked Paul. 'Anything sparkling?'

'No, not really, he found the bodies and phoned the police, that's about it. He reckons he might have touched some of the things in the hallway, but he's not sure.'

'Did you take elimination prints?' Ashley asked.

'Of course, but I had to wait twenty minutes as the water from his bucket had shrivelled his finger-tips. They should be fine.' Charlie dropped into a chair 'Ouch, you bugger!' and lit a cigar. He blew out his cheeks and rubbed at his knee. He wasn't getting any younger.

'I take it you told him he wasn't getting his money for doing the Marriott's windows?' Ashley said.

'Ha bloody ha!' A spent match bounced off Ash's head.

*

Ernest Gray lived quite a solitary life. He spent most of his time in the boiler room at work looking at old newspapers and drinking tea. If ever he had a visitor it was a major deal for Ernie. He would suffer periods of boredom for several hours and for days would suffer from a form of depression. Being left alone too long with his thoughts can make a man crawl too deeply down the hole, and flirt with, not necessarily insanity, but an odd persona, a quirky point of reference. There was no doubt his workmates and others in the town saw Ernie as an oddity, and in truth he did nothing really to dissuade them from this viewpoint. He spoke monosyllabically, gruffly; a trait he got from his drunken and violent father, who was a bully. An obnoxious bastard, who beat his wife and his children and thought, like the ignoramus he was, that it made him a man, or at best that this was what a man should be like, as the figure head of his family. Almost inevitably Ernie had ended up being a carbon-copy of his only male role-model.

His wife Violet, of similar demographic standing, had put up with a lot, and only her lack of self-confidence had prevented her from leaving him, which she should have done years ago. She knew what Ernie was, and what he got up to, and when she spoke with acquaintances in the town would say; 'you don't know the half,' when they mentioned her husband. Other phrases she used, was 'he's daft as a brush' and 'he's harmless enough'. Only Ernie was not harmless, if the truth were known.

Ernie felt quite pleased with himself as he walked home. He had a strange walk, like a half-run, half shuffle as if he was perpetually hurrying across a zebra-crossing with a car approaching. Who would have thought that one day he would be the police's star witness in a murder case? He couldn't wait to tell the lads in the Newstead Abbey pub; which he frequented most days.

Violet was a buxom woman; she wore a small apron, her 'pinnie,' short for 'pinafore dress', something of a misnomer but a regular colloquialism for women of her age in the locale. She screwed her mascara'd eyes up at Ernie; it was the only make-up she used, other than the occasional bit of lippy, as he bounced into the house. Any love she'd had for him was long since gone; her contempt for the forty, fat and fusty man, ate away inside her. She greeted him with more than a hint of acid in her voice: 'And where the hell have you been?'

'Here we go. Do you mind if I get in the house first, before you start?' Ernie protested.

Violet over-emphasised her banging around of pots and pans and cupboard doors. She scowled out another sentence. 'I'm asking you an honest question, Ernest Gray, and I would like an honest answer.' The two of them were always a whisker away from heated exchanges, Violet deciding years ago that attack was the best form of defence and both of their lack of communication skills meant that discussions were always arguments, within seconds.

Ernie was still flushed with excitement. 'As a matter of fact, it's got absolutely nothing to do with you and I'm not sure I should tell you with a gob like yours. It's confidential.'

This was like a red rag to a bull with Violet. She was annoyed. She stood in the doorway which separated the kitchen from the living-room. 'Do you know, in eighteen years of marriage you've never once volunteered to tell me what you're doing or where you are going? There's always this bloody big secret. Ernie, you're a boiler-man at the Pit. Don't you think that a man and wife should be able to talk about what the hell they are doing? Don't you think that's the norm? Not that you are bloody normal, half the town know you're a...'

Ernie interrupted her tirade. 'I shouldn't have to report to you every verse end – I'm a grown man, for Christ's sake!'

'A grown man. Ha. That's a bloody laugh.'

'Eh, pack that in.' Ernie shouted.

Violet continued. 'If you are such a big man, why do you scurry about like an insignificant bloody nobody? Why does half the town, including me, think you are one big joke?'

Ernie's fists curled tight. 'Oh, hark at the big words. Well, Madame, this nobody has been to see the CID.'

'You've done what?'

'I've been to the police station and given a written statement to the CID. Some nobody, huh?' He picked up a newspaper from the worn table at the side of the threadbare armchair.

'Statement about what? What have you given them a statement about?' Violet folded her arms, her concern rapidly increasing. 'I'm serious, Ernie, I want to know!'

Ernie spoke into the open newspaper which he scanned but was not really reading. 'About the murders on Maple.' He was smiling, pleased with himself, like the simpleton he was.

'What can you possibly know about the murders, Ernie?' She sighed.

'*Ernie* now is it?

She was losing patience. She barked at him, 'Stop being so bloody stupid. I'm being serious!'

Ernie leaned back into the armchair, 'I've seen the killer!'

'You've done what? Seen what?' She was flustered. 'Our sort doesn't get involved with the police, Ernie, it is always trouble, they can't be trusted, and they will twist your words, sure as mustard. What have you seen, anyway?'

Ernie put the paper on his lap and looked her in the face. 'I've seen the killer. I didn't know it was him at the time, but it's him all right.'

'Where exactly did you see him, you daft bloody oaf?'

'The CID treated me like royalty, they did. "Anything we can do for you, Ernie," they said, "just let us know."' Ernie clasped his hands behind his head.

Violet persisted. 'I said; where did you see him, Ernie?'

'That night, of course, just as I was coming home. I saw him run off towards Bulwell town centre, down Maple Close. Carrying something he was, too.'

'Which way was he running?'

'I've told you, towards Bulwell. Why? What's it to you?' He released his hands and let them rest on the paper in his lap.

Violet rose from the chair and shouted at her bemused husband. 'You never get anything right, do you? You are the most stupid, ridiculous person I have ever met, or ever will meet.'

'What have I done now?'

Violet picked her thin jacket up off the chair back. 'I'm going to my mother's. You can get your own bleeding dinner.' She stormed out of the room and slammed the door shut behind her.

Ernie tutted. 'Bloody women. They're not right in the bloody head.'

*

Steve's stomach churned as he sat in the Parade Room at headquarters, next to the Murder Incident Room. Here he was just two weeks into his aide-ship, part of a murder investigation. He couldn't help but feel slightly uncomfortable as he looked around the crowded briefing room, surrounded by a wealth of experienced officers. There were more than twenty detectives, two units of SOU, and two Detective Sergeants hovering near the front. There were no tables in the room, which had a glass ceiling, only plastic chairs loosely organised into rows, one behind the other. Everybody was chatting excitedly, and sporadic bursts of laughter would erupt from time-to-time. Steve hadn't had time to forge any friendships within the department, and if it hadn't been for Paul Fisher, sitting to his left, who had taken him under his wing, he would have felt even more uncomfortable.

Paul sensed his uneasiness. 'All right, Steve?'

'Sorry, Paul – I was miles away. What's the set-up with the briefing, then?'

'We get briefed from Wagstaff or Stark, make relevant notes and wait to be allocated our tasks. That's about it.'

'Okay, thanks.'

Paul added. 'Oh, and by the way, don't ask any questions at the end. Leave that to the others. We don't want you getting in a muddle. Ask me afterwards, if you want to know anything.' He smiled. Paul had been there before, and the simplest of questions suddenly turns into gobbledy-gook, when the dawning realisation that all eyes are on you, suddenly hits you. You can make a bit of a fool of yourself if you are not careful, and now was not the time to do that.

Steve got the message. 'How do you think it's going so far? The case, I mean.'

'OK, but I can see it dragging out at this rate.'

Steve laughed quietly and gave the response he thought he should give. 'There will be a lot of overtime going, then, if it does drag on.'

Paul felt protective towards Steve; he thought he was a nice lad, but also felt he might struggle on the department. 'You've done well getting involved in a murder case on your aide, haven't you?'

Steve shrugged. 'I suppose so. I don't think I'm on the official head-count, a bit of an add-on, but it's great for the experience. There's nothing like being thrown in at the deep end, is there?'

'You'll be fine.' Paul said.

The two men's conversation was interrupted by a loud, deep voice. It was Wagstaff. 'Right gentlemen, and ladies...' He peered out at the room, hand above eyebrows, as if a look-out on a ship. 'I think we have some ladies, ah yes, I can see one or two. Can I have your attention please?'

'*Quiet!*' shouted Nobby. The room got the message and silence prevailed. Wagstaff continued his address, with Inspector Stark looking on. 'Thank you, Sergeant Clarke.' Nobby acknowledged the thanks with a nod of his head. Wagstaff, in blazer and razer-sharp grey flannels, only needed a yardstick and a drill square and he was away. He paused and waited for the room to settle and the murmurings to die down.

'For those of you that don't know me, you should. I am Detective Superintendent, Wagstaff,' His moustache twitched. 'I'm heading the murder enquiry, but in my infinite wisdom I've decided to allow Detective Inspector Stark, a free run at cracking the bloody thing.' There were some mutterings. 'Under my discerning eye of course.' He added. 'I am going to be in and around the Incident Room while Mr Stark gets involved in the exciting bits. Now, because of this it will be Mr Stark who gives you the briefing this morning. All I will say is this: in an investigation of this sort, any one small piece of information could be crucial...' Steve Aston heard Charlie mutter 'Really?' And he smiled. Wagstaff continued '...once it's married up to the full facts of the case. It only takes one irresponsible officer to overlook it and we're in shit-street. Make sure you are not that officer.' Steve swallowed hard. 'Now I'll pass you over to Mr Stark. Happy hunting.'

Stark stood six foot one, and his broad shoulders strained at his grey suit. Inside he was a gibbering wreck. This was like hell on earth to him. He clutched a swathe of papers rolled up in his hand. A small bead of sweat trickled down the side of his face from underneath his brown hair, which was smart, cropped short. During Wagstaff blabbing on, which was just a blur to him, Stark had concentrated on his breathing and tried to surreptitiously fan his reddened face with the papers, hoping no-one would notice. He replaced Wagstaff at centre stage and took a deep breath which broke into a jagged dozen pieces, before commencing his monologue. He was conscious that his hands were trembling slightly, and his chest felt tight.

'Good morning gentlemen, for those that don't know me, I'm Detective Inspector Stark.' He paused and swallowed hard, clamouring for breath. He glanced at the paper in front of him, the words on the page appeared jumbled and he couldn't focus. His head was searching to land on what to say next. 'Say something – anything' he thought. The pause was too long, and a slight mutter was growing. 'You should all be in possession of a typed briefing sheet and some photographs.' He was off again. 'These will give you the whole scenario of events in its entirety, so I want you to read it, and soak it all in. I'm going to be highlighting the salient points and tell you some recent developments; these may well be of use to you as the investigation continues.' He paused for a sip of tea from the mug he had placed on a chair to his right, his hand seemed to be trembling as he reached for the mug. Focus on the content! He rebuked himself inwardly.

'At approximately 1 a.m. on Thursday 16th July 1987, Walter and Audrey Marriott and their nineteen-year-old daughter Faye were brutally murdered. If you glance at the photos they will show you the position of the bodies and the state of the room when it was discovered.' He continued. 'The Marriott's lived at 43 Maple Close, Nottingham, this is a nice, quiet residential area, for those that don't know it. Walter and Audrey went out that night with friends, out of town, and were late getting back home, while daughter Faye went into Nottingham, finding herself at a night club called Ritzy's, some of you may have heard of it?'

There were cheers, as Ritzy was a regular venue for detectives and various CID 'groupies', ladies who had a particular penchant for the CID officers, for whatever reason.

He sounded a little out of breath. 'We have some enquiries to do at the club, but the CCTV is notoriously shit, but let's see what that brings. The house appears to have been broken into, the rear kitchen window having been forced with a blunt instrument, approximately half an inch wide. Faye Marriott has come into contact with the burglar at some stage; whether she was in when he entered, or whether she disturbed him, we don't know yet.'

Paul Fisher asked, 'Is there definitely only one burglar, sir?'

'Yes, only one man at the scene, forensic are certain of that. As you can see on your hand-outs...' All heads bowed to look at the photographs on their laps. Stark quickly wiped his upper lip. '...Faye was semi-naked when she was found, and she'd had sexual intercourse. We can only assume that the burglar raped her, or it is feasible that there was a third person present before the burglar struck. Whoever had sex with her didn't ejaculate.' 'Where were you, Jim?' Charlie asked. There were some giggles.

Stark paced slowly from one side of the room to the other as he spoke, his hands animated in a subconscious attempt to express himself more articulately and to get the blood flowing. The audience were a blur. He was talking to a mosaic of shifting, coloured sand.

'At some stage Faye was asphyxiated to death. Audrey and Walter Marriott, we believe, had bad timing and returned home, disturbing the burglar-turned-killer. He appears to have heard their imminent arrival and we think he lay in wait behind the front door. He killed Walter with a single blow to the back of the head with a fourteen-inch-long, ornamental brass clown. It's likely he then went to attack Audrey, who had walked in first, culminating at the top of the stairs, on the landing. Audrey was then strangled to death manually; no ligature was used. Seemingly he used his bare hands. It was at this point that the killer began acting irrationally. He went to the foot of the stairs, retrieved the clown ornament and proceeded to club the already dead Faye and Audrey, in an obvious, if naïve, attempt to disguise the cause of their death. He then unplugged the video-cassette recorder and left, taking it with him. At some stage he wiped the clown ornament on Audrey's dress, presumably to remove his fingerprints. Two witnesses have come forward, both having seen the man running along Maple Close, carrying the video, possibly in a plastic bag. No definite direction of travel is known due to contradictory accounts. He is described as six-foot-tall, slim build and dark clothing.'

'That's a big help.' Muttered Jim, loud enough for Stark to hear. Stark ignored the comment.

Stark went on: 'There are no alien fingerprints in the house...'

Jim immediately thought of a quip but bit his tongue. Charlie beat him to it. 'E.T. Phone home...' Stark continued.

'...There was no sign of a struggle. The hi-fi was still switched on upon our arrival, which tends to indicate that Faye was at home prior to the burglary taking place. This, of course, could be another ploy by our killer, who is obviously trying to throw us off the scent. Scenes of Crime have detected some red woollen fibres on Audrey's clothing, and the living room carpet. The video recorder is still missing. We have found the manual for it in a cupboard at the house: it's a Matsui VHS; the serial number is on your sheet. There were no other burglaries that night. Incidentally, Faye's handbag contained the usual make-up, purse and several small sheets of paper with

"Squires Turf Accountants" on them. The money - £12.64 – was still intact. We have found a personal diary on Faye's dressing table containing a whole host of names of men, who we need to trace and eliminate.'

Stark paused for another sip of tea which was by now lukewarm. He wiped a film of sweat from his forehead. Nobody in the room was particularly aware that he was feeling uncomfortable, it seemed magnified to Stark, however. 'Faye Marriott was seen smooching with someone at Ritzy's night club; a white male who is unidentified with a fairly vague description and clothing. She was also seen talking to one of our ethnic cousins, somebody called Winston Kelly.'

Charlie commented. 'Not that evil, bleeder! I take it you know he's a pimp, boss? He's got a load of form.'

Stark nodded. 'There is quite a bit on his record and lots of intelligence from the Vice squad accumulated over the years. For those of you that don't know this man, I'll give you a potted history, Winston Samuel Courtney Kelly is a West Indian male. His previous convictions are numerous. They include wounding, supplying controlled drugs, living off immoral earnings, possession of firearms and police assault. He's a bad bastard. He's thirty-three years old and drives a red BMW car, C489 FTO. Now at some stage he's going to be arrested: it's the only way we have a chance with him. I'd like a bit more first, but he will come. We might get lucky with the video being at his house, or forensic on clothing, and all that sort of stuff. When he does get nicked, I want it doing right because this man enjoys hurting people, including policemen. His arrest will be organised at the right time, and we will use the SOU.'

The muscular police officers in uniform and a belt full of various implements, smiled at each other. They liked a challenge. Paul again asked a question- Steve marvelled at his confidence. 'Has he got any form for burglary, sir?'

Stark pointed the now rolled-up briefing sheet at the young man. 'Good question, Paul. Only as a fourteen-year-old; nothing for burglary since then. He doesn't need to – he's earning enough as it is.'

Stark continued. 'Faye worked for a betting shop called Squires Turf Accountants. Hence the headed notepaper in her handbag. It's run by one Bernard Squires. I'm convinced that both he and his whole set-up are bent, but whether he would stretch to murder, I'm not so sure. It's too early to say. There's a stack of intelligence for this guy, but he has no previous convictions at all; he pays others to do his dirty work for him.'

Stark continued. 'The next man who is up with the front runners is Faye's main boyfriend-cum-sugar-daddy – Charles Lyon. This man is a major wimp. He owns his own business, called Foibles; it's a clothes shop on Maid Marion Way in the city. I don't know how to start to describe this bloke to you.' He laughed and looked to the ceiling for inspiration, which was a mistake and made him step backwards as he was unsteady on his feet. 'He's twenty-three years old and a mummy's boy. He hasn't got any form for criminal activities and he was born with a silver spoon rammed up his backside. He has been seeing Faye for about three months and claims he didn't see her the night she was murdered. He has an alibi, but he will be spoken to again, soon.'

Stark threw the briefing sheet on to the floor, but then regretted it, picked it up and fanned himself again with the notes, his shirt now wet-through with sweat under his suit jacket. He was speaking off the cuff, unable to make sense of his notes with the stress of his ordeal. 'I've only just found out, before the briefing, that on the night of the murders, at about midnight, one of the uniformed lads stopped a gentleman who was walking home along Nabbs Lane, at the back of the Nabb Inn, which for those who aren't local, is about four streets away from Maple Close. The man stopped by the young officer was Stanley George Tindle, nicknamed "Jobber" Tindle. He is a prolific burglar and always will be, it's in his blood. For those that don't know Jobber, he earned his nickname because he would do any job, and also for his rather distasteful habit of doing "jobbies" – i.e. defecating on people's carpets whilst burgling their house. Jobber isn't a particularly violent man, but there were no other burglaries that night apart from Maple Close, and he was clocked close-by, so it would be re-miss not to build him into the picture. He will be coming in for a chat later.' He paused again to gather his thoughts the best he could. 'I want DC's to pair up wherever possible. For those of you doing house-to-house, make sure that you see every member of the household and complete the pro-formas accurately and don't forget to check the occupants against the voters register, in case someone is a little shy to talk to us. The killer may well live in the locality, so be careful. Your own Ser-geants will de-brief you. Any questions?' There was a pause. 'Right, see your Sergeants and get your actions. Good luck.'

Stark turned away from his audience and the chatter quickly resumed. He flopped into the chair and pretended to study his notes, working hard to regulate his breathing. He wiped at the sweat which had re-formed on his top-lip. His hands were clammy and still trembling. It was his little secret, but how long could he keep it that way?

Paul Fisher stretched and made a yawning noise without ac-tually yawning. 'I suppose we had better see Nobby and get our actions.'

Steve stood up and looked around the room. 'Yes, we can find out who our partners are.'

The two young men joined the short queue that led to DS Clarke. Paul was handed his action. 'House-to-house enquir-ies; Torkard Terrace, rear of Maple Close.'

'Bloody hell, I bet most of these have been done already. I'm with PC 2407 Jones. What's your action, Steve?'

'General enquiries at Ritzy's Night Club.'

'Shit. You jammy bugger. You don't want to swap, do you?'

Steve looked worried. 'I don't think we ought to, Paul. I'm sorry, but we don't want to get in the shit, do we?'

'I suppose you're right.' Paul tutted and walked away in search of his partner, shaking his head.

A civilian clerk entered the room. He shouted: 'DI Stark?'

Stark craned his neck to see who was calling him. 'Yes?'

'Telephone call for you, sir.'

Stark excused himself and followed the callow youth into the HOLMES room. He picked up the phone. 'DI Stark.'

He recognised the voice immediately. 'Hello, Detective Inspector Stark. It's your darling wife here. Do I qualify for an audience with you, oh great one?'

Stark glanced at his watch. 'Of course, you do. What's the matter?'

'Does there have to be something wrong before I speak to my husband?'

Stark sighed inwardly; this, he didn't need. He tried wafting himself by flapping his suit jacket, which he could not take off as his shirt was still wet through. 'No, don't be silly of course not. How's it going?'

She was smiling. 'I'm fine. Missing you, of course.'

He sat down and his body became tense. 'I'm missing you too...' He glanced around the Incident Room; everyone seemed to be busying themselves, but he knew they would be listening in at the boss's conversation, albeit one-sided. '...are you on your own?'

Carol sighed. 'Yes. The kids are out. I'm going to go and see Mum, later.'

Stark tapped at the desk. 'Good. Give her my love, won't you?'

His wife was smiling as she spoke. 'What do you want for dinner?'

He couldn't hold back any longer. 'Look, Carol, I'm not being rude, but it is slightly awkward to talk to you at the moment, my love. You know I won't be home for dinner. I did tell you.'

'All right, grumpy, I know I shouldn't have called you, I'm a pain in the arse, I get it. I'm sorry.'

'Don't worry about it. Listen, I'm going to have to get back to work now. I'll hopefully see you later.'

'So I am a pain in the arse?'

'Carol.'

'OK, I get it. How much later?' He again looked at his watch, as if that was going to help him get a feel for when he got home. 'I've no idea. Probably the same as last night. It might be later, there's a lot happening today, Carol. You don't have to wait up, you know.'

'I am tired. I think I will go to bed tonight, if you don't mind. It's been a busy day, I did some of the ironing earlier...'

Wagstaff came into the HOLMEs room. Stark turned away from him, the coil lead on the phone stretching against his arm. Stark spoke in more hushed tones. 'Of course I don't mind. You go to your Mum's and have a good time. I'll be thinking about you, OK?'

Carol felt a bit better. 'OK, I'm sorry for ringing. I just felt, oh, it doesn't matter, I love you. Bye.'

Stark looked up. His eyes met Wagstaff's, twitching his moustache: 'Tell her you love her, then.'

Stark whispered into the phone. 'Love you too. Bye.' He quickly replaced the receiver. 'I'm sorry about that, sir,' he said apologetically.

Wagstaff looked stern; he appeared annoyed. 'Don't you ever apologise to anyone again for caring about your family. Understand? They've all we've got.' Wagstaff's face resumed its smile and he smacked Stark's back with a strength that surprised his DI.

Stark felt churlish, he knew his boss was right. 'Thank you, sir. You're right.'

6

'A kleptomaniac is a person who helps himself,
Because he can't help himself.'
Henry Morgan

Stan Tindle hadn't made much of himself. He was a scruffy forty-three-years-old and he was knackered. He sat in the dimly lit vaults of the Bull and Butcher pub. His balding head sporting a 'comb-over.' He had a walrus moustache; the remnants of his breakfast were clinging to the hairs for dear life. It was fifty-fifty whether they would cascade down into his mouth, past the yellowing teeth and into his bulbous belly which was swilling with stale ale. He wore a tatty grey jumper underneath the thin blue anorak that served as both winter and summer wear; and had more years' service, than Paul Fisher had. Stan coughed into his pint of 'Mild'. The ash from his rolled up cigarette had fallen onto the mahogany table, despite his efforts to guide it into the yellow tin ashtray bearing the brewers name.

From the age of twelve, Stan had been breaking into houses. He always did it the same way – nothing sophisticated: he would just force open the rear kitchen window and he was in. Even though he was much less nimble nowadays, the adrenalin always somehow got his bulk inside. He would only ever steal three things: cash, jewellery and video recorders, these being the items that were easily saleable in the pubs and working-men's clubs in and around the City. Unfortunately, Stan was the nervous type; whenever he burgled a place, nine times out of ten he would feel a stirring in his stomach, and he would have to empty his bowels. He didn't like doing it – he just couldn't help it. It was an occupational hazard to him, others may have to drive through traffic, or work late; he had to crap on people's living room carpets. He never allowed himself to think too much about the disgusting sight that would greet the householders upon their return. If he needed money, he would get it the only way he knew how – burglary. He always blew the money on fags, booze and the odd bet on the horses. Sometimes he would treat himself to a fry-up at Piccadilly café of a morning.

Stan had been in Her Majesty's Prisons on seven occasions throughout his life. The Theft Act 1968 gave burglary a maximum sentence of fourteen years, but it was rare that anything like such a sentence was ever passed. His last stretch had been his longest: four years – two years were actually served, with remission. He didn't fancy a return visit any time soon and he was nervous. Why had that bloody copper stopped him? He appeared from bloody nowhere, sneaky bastard. No way was he doing time again, he couldn't hack it.

Stan was so engrossed in his own thoughts that he didn't notice the two tall men standing at the bar, drinking. The vibration in a pub always moved up a couple of notches when the CID were drinking in it. The Bull and Butcher was no different. Pretty much everyone knew who they were, that was the point; they weren't supposed to be undercover, not many people walked around in suit and tie, after all. It was to demonstrate that they could, and would, walk into any pub, at any time, and nowhere was completely safe from them. Which was fine if you were minding your own business and making your way in life, but if you were up to no good, it might make your bum-hole twitch a little. Paranoia and mistrust amongst criminals were rife. 'Honour amongst thieves', was a myth of monumental proportions. Whilst Stan was too distracted to notice the cops, they had noticed him, and Charlie Carter and Nobby Clarke walked towards him. Stan was oblivious to them until they sat down next to him, one on each side.

'Hello, Stan. How are you, my old mucker?'

Stan jumped, spilling some of the mild on to the round wooden table. His eyes widened; he was swept with fear. 'Jesus Christ! What is it with you lot, sneaking up on people?'

'You were miles away, Stan. I mean, how can you miss us?' Charlie grinned.

'Before you start, I've done nowt. I've done fuck all.' He raised his hands as if in surrender.

Charlie reassured him. 'Nobody said you had, Stan. We just want a cosy chat, that's all, my friend.'

Stan was literally in a corner. He hit back, conscious now that all eyes on the pub were on him. He did not want to be seen as an informer; a grass, even though he was at times. He needed to put on a show. 'Cosy Chat. Get fucked. Coming sitting next to me. What the fuck? I know your lot, none of you can be trusted. Why don't you just piss off?' His voice was raised.

Nobby heard his cue. 'Listen, my friend, watch your fucking tone. The nice Mr Carter and I want a chat, but if you want to turn it into something else, we will be happy to oblige, pal.'

Stan remained unconvinced. 'Well, I don't want to talk to you, thanks for the offer.' He smiled sarcastically but couldn't meet Nobby's piercing stare.

'What were you doing when you were pulled by that copper the other night?' Charlie asked.

Stan's mind was whirling. 'I haven't been pulled by any copper. What copper? I don't know what you are going on about.'

Charlie remained patient, he knew Stan was a big bag of wind behind the bluster. 'We're talking sometime around midnight, up on Nabbs lane.'

'I was in all Wednesday night, ask our Marg.' He stammered.

'Who said it was Wednesday?' Nobby grinned.

'You did.'

'No we didn't.' Nobby said.

'Yes, you did.'

'Oh, for fuck's sake, Charlie let's just nick the prat.' Nobby didn't like being messed around and he too had a reputation to uphold.

Charlie endeavoured to explain. 'Look, Stan, we're not talking about some lame burglary, or crapping on someone's Axminster...'

Nobby interjected with a glare. 'Dirty cunt.'

'...we are talking about something a lot more serious.' Charlie finished.

Stan didn't listen. He folded his arms. 'Talk about what you want. I've told you I don't know what you are talking about, you must have the wrong bloke. Not me, officers.'

Nobby had heard enough. He stood up. 'We're not pissing about, Stan. You're under arrest!'

'What for?' Stan protested.

'Try murder.' Said Charlie.

'You what? Here hold on a minute – I was only joking. Of course, I'll talk to you.'

Nobby smiled. 'Too late Stan. You've failed the attitude test. Drink up –we're going.'

Stan drank up and reluctantly got to his feet. As he did, he pulled a strange face. 'Oops!'

Charlie looked at Nobby. 'What's up, now, Stan?'

Stan looked like a four year old child, as he announced. 'I've had an accident. It's in my pants!'

The smell of excrement permeated the nostrils of all in the vicinity.

Charlie looked at Nobby and grimaced. 'Oh fuck.'

*

It turned out Steve Aston's allocated partner had gone sick so he was on his own for this particular enquiry. Steve pushed the front door of Ritzy Night Club. To his surprise it was open, and so of course he strolled in. The smell of stale ale, and nicotine, filled his lungs. He winced. The reception area was small; a counter carved into a wall with space for coats behind it. No one was there, it was four hours before it opened to the public. It was unclear what magical process would convert the yellow-walled, stench filled, club into an attractive beacon for the population. A population willing to pay five pounds entrance fee, perhaps a combination of darkness, bright disco lights, wall-to-wall people, music and alcohol as well as the draw of the opposite sex, were contributory factors to the illusion.

Steve pushed at the heavy double doors and he was inside the huge space that was the club itself. He became more conscious of the sticky carpet than he ever had on the numerous occasions he had visited as a punter. Over the far side of the football-pitch sized room, was the raised podium used by the DJ who would be selecting dance tunes from his play list, which that night would include recent favourites such as: I Wanna Dance With Somebody by Whitney Houston / When Smokey Sings by ABC / Reet Petite by Jackie Wilson and bizarrely the recent number one – Star Trekkin by The Firm. The periphery of the large gloomy space was dominated by bar space running the lengths of all the walls. Hanging from the ceiling were three large cages, currently vacant, but which would be populated by female dancers, skimpily dressed, come eleven o'clock.

'Yo!' A voice shouted and Steve scanned the dimness to discover its origin. A small guy with a big gut and a pony tail, appeared from near the DJ area and marched towards him. 'We aren't open yet, my friend.'

Steve had already reached for his wallet as the man strode purposefully towards him. By the time he arrived the wallet was raised. 'CID' Steve said, which stopped the man in his tracks, and instantly changed his expression from challenging, to acquiescent.

'Okay, Cool. How can I help?' He offered his hand, and they shook their greeting.

'Are you the manager?' Steve asked.

'Owner, for my sins.' The guy threw his hair back unnecessarily.

'Is there anywhere we can talk privately?' Steve asked, conscious now that people had emerged from the shadows; workmen, dancers, bar staff and hangers-on.

'Sure there is my office. Follow me.' They returned the way Steve had come; back through the double doors and into the reception. 'Pony-tail' lifted the countertop and they walked through the cloakroom space and opened a door at the back wall. The room was surprisingly large and contained all manner of stock; crates of drink, various feathery-type pieces of clothing, a myriad of coats seemingly uncollected, unidentified cardboard boxes, and empty bottles yet to be cleared from the four desks pitted around the large space. At the far end of the room a large muscular gentleman and a heavily made-up lady dancer seemed to untwine themselves from a passionate embrace. The young woman was correcting her attire and fussing with the hem of her short skirt and bra strap.

'Hi Barry.' The bouncer said, he was a little out of breath, but polite, as he nodded to the two men as they entered.

Barry and his pony-tail thought he ought to mention to the bouncer that his need for privacy with the detective, trumped his own, albeit arguable. 'Can we have some privacy, please, Jakub?'

Very matter-of-factly, Jakub, the bouncer, pulled the zip up on his trousers, and the girl covered up her bouncers, and continued to pull at her skirt. After what seemed an age, the two walked in silence past Steve and Barry, Steve's mouth agape, the dancer avoided eye-contact, but Jakub again nodded as they got close. He put out a hand to Steve as greeting. 'Nice to meet, you.' Steve settled for a thumbs up rather than shake the likely soiled hand. Jakub shrugged, and continued out the door.

'Sorry about that, officer. Things get a little wild in here sometimes, naturally I didn't know they were in here. Sorry.'

Steve, still a little shocked, shrugged. 'Hey, it's your place. Live and let live, I say.'

Barry sat on the corner of the desk and lit a cigarette from an open packet he found amongst the invoices on top of it. 'How can I help? No problem is there?'

'No problem. I am investigating a murder.' Steve felt so proud saying those words.

*

Charlie and Nobby had the somewhat unpleasant task of supervising Stan in the Gents toilets of the pub as he washed himself down at the sink. It wasn't a pretty sight. Nobby sagely advised him to sacrifice his off-white underpants to the bin, rather than try to make anything out of the mess that was inside them. The funk was awful. Nobby gagged a couple of times and lit a cigarette to mask the smell, it didn't really work. They eventually got him into a sufficiently acceptable state to put him in the car.

Charlie tried to strike up some conversation with Stan on the way back, but Stan just stared into space with a vacant look on his face. He was never going to live this down.

Charlie and Nobby led him through a maze of corridors into the cell complex at Nottingham Central Police Station. The Custody Sergeant was just placing the set of large cell keys on the desk as the three men arrived. The cell complex consisted of a high counter, behind which the Sergeant stood on an elevated platform; behind him was a wall of clipboards with various 'custody records' on them. To the Sergeant's right was a Perspex board with the names of the prisoners listed against a cell number.

Tom had been Custody Sergeant for a number of years. He wore thin, gold-rimmed spectacles and had rather overly bushy eyebrows. He was a quiet, serious man who didn't suffer fools gladly; he had seen a lot of criminals walk through that door, and he wasn't impressed with Stanley Tindle.

'Not another one.' he sighed.

'I'm afraid so, Tom,' Nobby replied.

Tom reached underneath the desk and produced various sheets of paper. He began filling out the custody record. His voice was a monotone. 'Name?'

The prisoner knew the position and answered quietly: 'Stanley George Tindle.'

'Date of birth?'

'8.6.47'

Tom glanced over the top of his spectacles at the dishevelled state of the prisoner. He muttered to himself: 'Male, white, five foot six inches tall. What's your address?'

Stan's throat was dry. He croaked out a reply: 'Number 284 Radcliffe Road, West Bridgford.'

'Reason for arrest?' Tom looked at the two detectives.

Nobby answered. 'Suspicion of murder.'

Nobby thought Tom would miss the correct space on the form, because as he wrote it, his eyes looked at Nobby throughout, rather than the piece of paper he was writing on. He finally returned his gaze to the booking-in form. 'Officer, arresting?'

'Me, Detective Sergeant 1312 Clarke.'

'Time and place of arrest?'

'5.12 p.m. The Bull and Butcher pub.'

Tom looked at Nobby. 'Don't disappear, Nobby. I'll have a word with you in a minute. Is the officer in the case DI Stark?'

'Yes, it is.'

Tom began the spiel that he must have said a thousand times; he was on autopilot. 'Mr Tindle, I'm the Custody Sergeant. I'm here for your benefit. Whilst you are detained here you are entitled to certain rights. These are: the right to have someone informed of your arrest; the right to consult with a solicitor of your choice; and the right to consult the Codes of Practice relating to your treatment whilst you are detained. You may do any of these now or at any subsequent time while you are being detained. Do you understand all of that?'

'I should do – I've heard it enough times.' He was beginning to adjust to his environment. Tom gave him the piece of paper that spelled out his rights. 'I don't want you to tell anybody I'm here and I certainly don't want a brief, not after last time.'

Tom continued. 'Right then, Stan, empty your pockets. You know the routine.' Stan placed his wooden tobacco box, which he had made in prison, on the desk. This was joined by a box of matches, cigarette papers, a comb and £7.48 in cash. Tom returned the tobacco box and cigarette papers to him.

'Don't forget your shoelaces and belt, Stan,' Tom reminded him. Stan dutifully removed them, clutching extra hard to the waistband of his trousers, the fibres of them already irritating his bare backside underneath.

Nobby had a look at the shoelaces which had been placed on the desk. They were intact.

'Just check him over, will you?' Tom asked Charlie.

Charlie searched him, tentatively, bearing in mind his earlier 'accident'. 'He's fine. Eh-up, what's this?' Charlie retrieved a screwdriver from the lining of Stan's coat.

'Oh dear,' said Charlie.

'Oh dear,' said Nobby.

'Oh fuck,' said Stan.

He was taken down into the cells and the door slammed shut behind him. Nobby explained the circumstances to Tom and told him that if Stan suddenly decided to contact anybody, family or a solicitor, they would make an application to delay such a process, at least until Stan's house had been searched. Tom agreed and asked to be kept informed on progress before Stan's first review in nine hours' time.

*

Steve Aston peered at the small television screen in the counter area of Ritzy Night Club. The images were in black and white, and a white band of distortion repeatedly rose up the screen; obscuring much of the images being portrayed. It was due to the tape not being replaced regularly enough. The owner – 'Pony-tail' Barry had to agree to the CCTV system being installed at the Club when he renewed his licence, due to the level of violence and anti-social behaviour in the area, notably at the weekend. The provision did not stipulate that he had to manage it effectively however, and the bouncers were nervous being on CCTV, for obvious reasons, so it was pretty much ignored. It suited them that the picture was obscured but it did not suit Steve Aston. Barry was peering over his shoulder and Jakub had returned, concerned when he realised that Steve was a detective. Jakub had been told many times that he needed to calm down when dealing with the drunks but it never seemed to penetrate his very thick, bald, misshapen skull.

Steve had discovered that the timer on the screen did not match real time, and was one hour twelve minutes behind. He had managed to find images of Faye entering and leaving the Club. She entered with another female, presumably Chantelle Naylor, but she did not leave with her. She left early, around 12:15 a.m. It was impossible to tell if she was on her own, as the small foyer was so crowded, with people coming and going. From what he could tell she was not clinging to a man or apparently with someone; but the three seconds that she appeared on the screen was inconclusive. Regardless, had any of the thirty or so others milling about, actually been in her company it seemed unlikely that they would be able to get a positive identification from the ghostly images on the screen.

He decided that the best approach was to just seize the video tape and take it back for others to look at and to see if the Technical Unit could manage to enhance the images sufficiently to make sense of it all.

*

Stark was busy at the computer terminal, tapping away at the keys. The green screen had white letters on it. No mouse was evident, the 'enter' key as it was known, was the main one used, along with the shift key, and arrow keys to navigate around the designated, bracketed, spaces for data to be inputted.

Several detectives and officers were milling around the room, some staring at computer screens, others reading statements and some just chatting.

'DI Stark?' The question was shouted from a PC clinging on to a telephone just behind Stark.

'Hello?' Stark spoke into the handset.

'They've got Stan Tindle, David.' It was Wagstaff. 'He's being held at Nottingham Central. Nobby and Charlie nicked him at the Bull and Butcher. It's quite amusing, apparently, he literally shits his pants when they lifted him.' Wagstaff was cheerier than usual, probably due to the potential break-through.

'Nice.'

'That's not all, David, he had a screwdriver in the lining of his coat.'

'Did he really?' Stark stood up and put his hand to his head and scratched at his hair, despite there being no itch. He was thinking.

'Do we know what size it was?'

'No idea, David, you'll have all that once you get over there, which I suggest you do pronto.'

'Okay, I'm going straight over. I don't want any interruptions unless absolutely necessary, if that's okay, sir.'

'I'll cover for you this end, David. Good luck.'

'Thanks.' He put the phone down and grabbed his suit jacket off the back of the chair.

7

'Two things are infinite: the universe and human stupidity; and I'm not sure about the universe.'

Albert Ein-stein

Stan Tindle sat on the wooden bench in his cell that passed for a bed, his beer belly straining at his tight-fitting grey jumper. The room measured sixteen feet by eight; it had a concrete floor and a small area with a toilet in it, which was not obscured from the watchful eye of the 'cell man'. Stan clung to a coarse grey blanket. Throughout his criminal career he had been in this position many times. It didn't get any easier. His fellow-criminals often bragged that being locked-up did not bother them; in fact, Stan had said it himself – 'I can do two years standing on my head' was the regular phrase used – but they all knew it wasn't true. That's why they ran away from the cops and informed on others to get reduced sentences. He wondered how long he had been there – perhaps an hour? Two hours? He pressed the buzzer and waited for the approach of the heavy footsteps behind the thick metal door.

Tom slid open the square metal spyhole to cell number 9. It created an opening in the body of the door, which remained closed; about the size of a paperback book.

'What's up, Stan?'

'Give us summat to read, boss.' Tom didn't speak; his leather boots audible as he walked away; twenty-three steps to the counter, and curiously twenty-four steps back to the cell. Stan was counting them. A paperback book flew through the square opening and landed on the floor at Stan's feet. The spy-hole shutter slammed shut.

'Cheers, boss.' Stan shouted gratefully. He picked up the book and read the title; *Wuthering Heights by Emily Bronte.* Stan frowned. *'Have you got anything by anybody famous?'* He shouted. There was no reply. Stan glanced through the pages; he couldn't make head nor tail of it. He pressed the little metal buzzer button near the door again.

Twenty three steps later, Tom slid open the spy-hole again. He was not pleased. 'You know if you keep pressing that buzzer you will get sod all.'

Stan was apologetic. 'Sorry, boss. Can I go into the exercise yard, please?'

'I've just given you a bleeding book.' exclaimed Tom.

Stan tried to look sheepish. 'Yes, and I am looking forward to reading it, but I would love a roll-up. I'm desperate.'

Tom sighed. 'Come on, then.' He led Stan to the exercise yard, bundled him in and gave him a light, before slamming shut the large metal door.

Stan examined the exercise yard. It was about twenty feet long and ten feet wide, enclosed by high walls that reached up to a metal grille where fresh air could be found; the grille only partially obscuring the sky above. Hardly enough for a game of tiddly winks, never mind exercise, but then no-one wanted to exercise in the exercise yard; they only want to stand in the corner, and smoke as many cigarettes as they could, and delay going back to their cell for as long as possible. Stan sucked on his roll-up cigarette and a quarter of its length turned to ash, he had learned to use his baccy sparingly. He busied himself reading the graffiti scratched on the wall by previous occupants who were seemingly just as pissed off as he was, going by the words they had etched.

Stan began to think out loud. 'Murder. They're bleeding mental. They are not pinning this one on me. I'll just deny it out right. Should I get a brief? Why bother? They never do bugger all. "Say nothing." Fucking brilliant. Four years at law school and they all say the same. Wankers the lot of them. What are the coppers playing at? What are they pissing about at?'

He was getting nervous; he wanted to go to the toilet again and he reluctantly pressed the buzzer. Tom escorted him back to his temporary abode. Stan knew never to waste an opportunity, the Sergeant seemed a reasonable bloke and his paranoia was building, he needed reassurance.

'Eh, boss. What are they playing at? I mean what is taking them all this time?'

Tom smiled: the age-old question, the need to know that it is all going to be okay in the end. 'You know better than to ask me that, Stan. Just try to get your head down. They will be with you soon enough, then you'll probably wish they weren't.'

Stan was alone again. He went to the toilet, then lay on the hard wooden bench and covered himself with the thin grey blanket. He closed his eyes.

He heard a young voice from the next cell shout to another invisible cohabitee of the cell block: 'What you told them, Bog?'

He got a reply. 'I've told them nowt, mate. They're trying to say we've nicked a car, an XR2, but I've told them that we were in the Wagon pub until about ten, and then we went…'

The shouting between the two lads prevented Stan from getting his beauty sleep. He stared out into the semi-darkness and swore under his breath at his own carelessness. 'That bloody screwdriver.'

*

'A bloody screwdriver!' said Charlie excitedly. 'It would be great if it matches up forensically with the marks at the murder scene.'

'Yes,' Nobby replied, 'but you know how long forensic takes. It'll be two or three days, even if we hurry them up, and we've only got thirty-six hours at the most before we've got to charge him with something.'

Charlie put a question to his younger Sergeant: 'Do you think Stark's jumped in a bit with getting us to nick Stan?'

Nobby protruded his bottom lip in thought. 'No, not really. He's out of the way for the search; he can't contact anyone and if we find nothing at the house it's got to be done through interviewing anyway. If we hadn't nicked him, we wouldn't have that screwdriver, would we?'

'Yes, you're probably right. Stan, raping a young girl though? Really?' Charlie seemed unconvinced.

Nobby shrugged. 'I know what you mean, but this job teaches you never to second-guess anything, Charlie. Anything is possible, you know that.'

'I know. What time does the chinky open?'

Nobby looked at his watch. 'About six o'clock, I think. I must admit I am hungry – I think I shall have to sample some chicken fried rice.'

Stark arrived at the station and Nobby explained the situation to him. Stark decided that he and Nobby would interview Stan, while Charlie and Ashley would search his house. Charlie knew Stan's wife, Marge, well. Stark and Nobby began the pre-interview analysis. They contacted officers who had interviewed Stan before to try to understand his strengths and weaknesses, what strategy they might employ and any plan of attack they might try. Stark studied Stan's previous convictions: he was particularly interested in an ABH three years ago, it was the only hint of violence on his previous convictions, but it was relatively recent.

*

Charlie and Ashley stood in front of the distressed grey door to 248 Radcliffe Road. The door of the terraced council house was opened by Marge, a middle-aged woman with badly highlighted hair, heavy make-up and a cigarette hanging from her mouth. The cigarette looked in jeopardy as she spoke.

'Eh-up, Charlie. Come in duck. What's he been up to now?'

Charlie was honest in his reply. 'To be fair, Marge, I can't really say.' The carpet in the hallway was threadbare.

Marge cackled. 'Top secret is it? He's never started working for MI5 has he?'

Charlie joined in her laughter. 'No it's nothing like that. It's MI6.'

Marjorie threw her head back and hit Charlie's upper arm. 'Oh, you silly sod. I'll put the kettle on, duck. Aren't you going to introduce me to your dishy mate?' She flashed her eyes at the man in the expensive-looking suit.

Charlie apologised and easily switched in the vernacular; 'duck' being a colloquialism, a local term of endearment. 'Sorry, duck – this is Ashley Stevens, my partner in crime for today.' He put his back against the wall so that she could have a better view of the dashing young man in the crowded hall-way. Ashley smiled coyly and somewhat self-consciously at the narrowing eyes of Marjorie Tindle as she looked him up and down. Again, she smacked Charlie on the arm. 'He'll do!' and she cackled. 'I don't know – they get younger, Charlie!' She tried to put a posh accent on. 'How many lumps of sugar do you require, Ashley?' She reverted to her broad Nottingham accent. 'Ashley's a posh name, are you not from round here, me duck?' She tittered.

'One please, Marge.'

Charlie said. 'She only said lumps because she hasn't cleaned the sugar bowl for months.'

'Cheeky sod.'

Both Charlie and Ashley followed Marge into the kitchen-cum-bombsite. Charlie's comment about the sugar had been quite correct. Ashley looked around: there were pots all over the place and nobody had ever cleaned the oven rings, which had long been suffocated by the overflow of Marjorie's cu-linary delights. The chip pan that took pride of place was covered in fat, and mould had formed on two plates on the cheap wooden table. There was an overwhelming smell of stale fat permeating the kitchen as well as the whiff of something indeterminable, but rotting. Cabbage? Ashley regretted agreeing to the cup of tea.

Marge spoke with her back to the two men, while she rinsed some mugs under the sink tap. 'You can't tell me what it's about then, Charlie?'

'No. It'll be nothing, I bet – don't worry about it.'

Marge laughed. 'Worry? I've long since stopped worrying about Stanley bloody Tindle. What have you come for? To search the place?' She asked.

Charlie smiled. 'You've got it right in one, Marge. Is there anything here?'

'No. Bloody hell, Charlie, he might be thick but he's not that thick.' Marge reached for the teapot and Ashley spotted the torn, off-white underskirt beneath her flowered polyester dress.

'Why do you put up with it, Marge?' Charlie asked.

'Oh, I don't know. I still love the daft old bugger, I'm too stuck in my ways at my age, Charlie.'

'Has he brought any gear back lately? It's important that we know from the start if he has, we don't want you getting dragged into it for handling, do we?'

Marge turned around from the worktop and looked Charlie in the eye. 'Eh, Charlie, how long have you known me – ten years? More maybe? I wouldn't have it in the house, duck, and I'll tell you straight: I don't want to know where he is, where he's been or what he's done. I'm not interested. As long as he behaves himself while he is in this house, that's all I need to know.' She continued to prepare the tea. Ashley noticed the pile of potato peelings that lay rotting in the sink.

The three eventually adjourned to the sparsely furnished living-room and made small talk. Charlie reminisced with Marge about the time that Stan had hidden in his attic and they had sent a police dog in after him. She laughed, 'Soft old bugger – he should have come down. I've never heard him squeal like he did when that bloody great dog sunk his teeth in his backside.

He's still got the scars you know.'

After Marge had enquired about DI Stark's health and one or two of the other lads at the nick, the two detectives finished their tea and commenced a search of the Tindle household. Marge knew the routine: she'd been done a dozen times or more. She didn't protest – what was the point? Anyway, she felt certain there was nothing at the house. Stan had a cut-out section in the loft where she would hide stuff for him if he had a successful night, but she knew that had been emptied two or three weeks ago so that wouldn't be a problem.

Ashley, of course, had drawn the short straw. He pulled himself up into the darkness trying to avoid the insulation covering, which would always cause a rash against the skin. Charlie was shouting encouragement from below and Marge was puffing on her cigarette, dropping ash on to the floor as second nature.

'Shit.' Ash cried out.

'What's up?' Charlie asked.

Ashley's muffled voice came out of the darkness: 'I've caught my trousers on a bleeding nail. Bloody hell!' His troubled face peered down on Charlie and Marge who were shaking with silent mirth. 'Thanks very much for the sympathy.'

The search eventually drew to a close. Much to Marge's surprise and inward cursing, they had seized a chisel, a pair of gloves, three necklaces and a gold bracelet.

'Thanks a lot then, Marge,' said Charlie as they left the house. He appreciated a good working relationship.

'Don't forget, I want that bloody jewellery back!' She said.

'You'll get it back if it isn't nicked,' Charlie assured her.

She waved. 'I believe you, thousands wouldn't.'

'Likewise.'

Ashley was still cursing and complaining about the two-inch slit at the side of his trouser leg as the two men loaded the property into the car.

The two men waved at Marge as they drove away, as if they were relatives on a visit, instead of two murder detectives trying to catch a killer.

*

DI Stark asked the Custody Sergeant for four sets of tape for the tape recorder, as he stood in the cell complex. Tom handed him the tapes and noted them in his log.

Stark gave his instructions. 'Fetch him up, Tom, please. Let's have a word with him.'

Tom disappeared down the corridor, returning a short time later with Stan Tindle, whose shoulders were hunched, the grey blanket still around them. 'What took you so bloody long?' he asked Stark and Nobby.

Stark beat Nobby to the reply. 'It's taken us so long to sort through all the evidence we have against you, Stan.'

The three men went into the interview room, off a corridor adjacent to the cell complex. The room contained a grey table, which was screwed to the floor, and four chairs; two each side of the desk. On top of the desk stood a large tape recorder.

Nobby sat opposite Stan, across the desk, with Stark positioning himself at Stan's side, at a slight angle to him.

'Have you got an ashtray?' Stan asked, already starting to shake.

'You'll have to use this bin.' Stark placed the metal wastepaper bin on the floor next to him. He touched the prisoner's arm. 'Have you been interviewed on this new tape system before, Stan?' He shook his head. Stark explained. 'It's very simple: as soon as we press "record" there will be a loud bleep. Then I will introduce myself and ask you your name and stuff, then we can talk properly and forget all about the tape recorder. OK?'

Stan still hadn't looked at the detectives; he appeared moody. 'OK, but I'll tell you now I've done nowt.'

'Nobody ever has, until they have, Stan.' Nobby retorted.

Nobby undid the transparent seal on the tapes, inserted them in the recorder and pressed the 'record' button. The bleep lasted only twelve seconds, but it seemed a lot longer as Stark and Nobby sat looking at their dishevelled quarry.

The bleep came to an end and Stark commenced. 'I am Detective Inspector David Stark of the Nottinghamshire Constabulary, presently stationed at Nottingham Police Station. The other officer present is …' He paused; Nobby was ready for his cue.

'John Clarke, Detective Sergeant 1312, of the Nottinghamshire Constabulary, stationed at Nottingham Police Station.'

Stark continued. 'Can I have your name and date of birth, please?'

Stan muttered into his walrus moustache. 'Stanley George Tindle, 8.6.47.'

'And your address?'

'248 Radcliffe Road, West Bridgford, Nottingham.'

Stark smiled inwardly to himself. It was always at this stage that he felt like Magnus Magnusson on the popular high-brow quiz show *Mastermind* and he had to refrain from saying, 'And your chosen subject is…burglary. You have sixty seconds on burglary starting…now.' Instead he kept rigidly to the Police and Evidence Act 1984 Codes of Practice.

'We are at Nottingham Central Police Station. It is Friday 17th July 1987, and the time is now 6.14 p.m. I will remind you Stan, that you do not have to say anything unless you wish to do so, but anything you say may be given in evidence. Do you understand that?'

Stan nodded; he felt sorry for himself.

'I'll have to ask you to speak up, Stan, because the tape can't hear you nod.' Stark smiled.

'Oh, right, I forgot about that – yes I understand, yes.'

'At the end of the interview, I'll give you a notice which tells you what happens to the tapes, OK?'

Stan nodded again but remembered and said 'OK.' He was still avoiding the gaze of both detectives. He looked submissive and patted some imaginary dust off his dirty trousers by brushing at them with his hand.

Stark began the interview proper. 'Now then, Stan, I've not met you before. I think I've seen your Mrs; Marjorie, a couple of times, years ago. I am the Detective Inspector at this police station. Did you kill the Marriott family?'

Stan's eyes widened. 'What? Eh? Bloody hell, you're having a laugh. No, of course I didn't!'

'I like to know who I am talking to, Stan, so tell me a bit about yourself. Do you come from this area?'

'Yes, I was born and bred in Nottingham.' He stared at the table.

'Do you work at all, Stan?' asked Stark, lighting up his cigar.

'No. I've been in and out of work all my life. I've done the odd job here and there, you know.'

Stark lit Stan's cigarette for him. 'The odd job?' he repeated.

'Yes, a bit of brick-laying, a bit of lawn turfing, that sort of thing, you know.' He glanced at Stark.

'Doesn't bring much money in, though,' the DI observed.

Stan sighed. 'It's a struggle to make ends meet, at times.'

'I bet.'

'That's what sent me out thieving in the first place. We never had a penny when I was a kid. My Mum was always trying to make ends meet, and so what can you do?'

'I don't suppose it's been easy for you then, Stan,'

'You can say that again. I mean, them youngsters in the pub, you try and tell them what it was like years ago, but they don't believe you. They don't know they're born, half of them.'

'I'm just trying to work it out, Stan: you weren't a war baby were you?'

'No, my dad was in the army, though – Sherwood Foresters.'

'Sherwood Foresters, eh?' Stark sounded impressed.

'Yes. He got to the rank of Corporal until he came out in 1948.'

'Pretty good. What did he do when he came out then, Stan?' asked Stark, interestedly.

'He went down the pit – Babbington. That's when it was rough down the pit, mind.'

'I bet it was. Didn't you ever think of following in your dad's footsteps?'

Stan's arms unfolded as he leaned back in his chair. 'No way. You wouldn't get me working down that bloody great hole.'

There was no light shining in Stan's face, there were no detectives leaning over him menacingly; it didn't work like that. Stan was loosening up: he was doing what everybody likes doing- he was talking about himself. Stark was just fuelling the fire. There was plenty of time to put him under pressure.

*

Ashley was annoyed with Stark and Nobby as he walked into the CID office. 'You'd have thought they'd have waited, Charlie,' he said as he dumped Stan's belongings on the desk. 'How are we going to tell them about the jewellery and jemmy that we found at the house? They've started interviewing and they don't even have the full facts. We can't interrupt them while they're interviewing, can we?'

'No.' He picked up the phone and dialled four digits.

'Cell block.' It was Tom, the Custody Sergeant.

'It's Charlie upstairs, Tom. How long have Dave Stark and Nobby been interviewing Tindle?'

'About twenty minutes,' came the sullen reply.

'How many sets of tapes has he taken in?'

'Four.'

'Oh shit. OK, Sarge, cheers.' Charlie replaced the receiver.

It was Nobby, rather than Stark who noticed the 'enquiry' light come on above the interview room door.

'DS Clarke leaving the interview room. The time now is 6.37 p.m.' he announced to the tape recorder. Nobby closed the door behind him and appeared a trifle annoyed at the interruption as he met Ashley in the corridor.

'Sorry to disturb you, Sarge, but we thought that you should know what we seized from Stan's house,' Ashley spoke in a whisper and passed Nobby a piece of paper with the details of the search written on it.

'Has he said anything yet?' Ashley asked inquisitively.

'We've only just started. Stark's into all this psychology bit, so we could be here till next bloody week at this rate.'

'You don't want anything from the Chinese takeaway, then?' asked Ashley.

'Yes, get us something and get something for Stark, will you? We'll warm it up in the microwave later. I'll give you the money in a bit. What have you done to your trousers?' Nobby asked, puzzled at the untidiness of the usually immaculate DC.

Ashley shook his head. 'Don't ask. It's a long story.'

Nobby looked at the piece-of-paper supplied by Ashley as he walked into the kitchenette to prepare plastic cups of coffee before returning to the interview room.

Stark glance at the paper that Nobby handed to him. He supped at his cup of coffee; he had created an air of affability in the room. He continued the interview.

'It's fair to say you are a burglar, isn't it, Stan?'

'It's fair to say that, I suppose, but it's only cos I'm skint half the time. I have to put food on the table.' There was a pause. 'Here, can I ask you a question, Mr Stark?'

'Yes, of course you can, Stan. I can't guarantee an answer though,' he smiled.

Stan asked, 'Why the hell have I been nicked for murder? It's a joke isn't it? You know full well that I'm just a run-of-the-mill burglar. I wouldn't hurt anyone, it's not my M.O. – honest.'

'Well, your name hasn't been picked out of a hat, Stan. We've got our reasons for believing you could be involved,' Stark replied honestly. 'So you accept that you're a burglar then, Stan?'

'Yes, but that doesn't mean that I've done any burgling jobs lately, though.' Stan grinned uncomfortably, for the first time.

'How would you describe the way you do your jobs, Stan?' asked Stark, leaning back in his chair.

'Always the same way: back kitchen window, or back window with transom, big screwdriver, reach my arm in and open the bigger window, sorted.'

'Do you do it that way without fail?' Stark asked.

'Without fail,' Stan confirmed, with a definite nod of his head.

'What sort of stuff do you take? Do you nick to order or what?'

'Depends, I sometimes get people asking me to get them certain stuff, otherwise I nick owt that I can get rid of easy. We're just talking generally here though, right?'

Stark nodded. 'We're just talking, Stan. What sort of stuff is it that you take?'

'Video's, cash, sometimes a bit of Tom, the normal, that's it. Easy to get rid of, good mark-up. I wouldn't nick owt else, you end up with stuff you can't get rid of and that's when you can have problems.'

'Who are you knocking the gear out to, Stan?' Stark raised his eyebrows in expectation.

'Come off it, Mr Stark, I'm not that daft, and anyway it's a lot of different people. But as I've told you, I've done nowt lately.'

'So how are you living then?' asked Stark.

'How does anybody live nowadays?'

'Have you been doing any brick-laying lately?' Stark puffed out another cloud of smoke from his cigar.

'No, there's plenty of casual work about but I've been having back problems,' said Stan.

'Yes, you can't get it off the bloody bed.' said Nobby, unable to resist it. He instantly regretted the unprofessional interruption.

'A minute or so ago, you said that you don't hurt anybody, is that right?

'Absolutely.'

'That's not true is it?'

'It bloody is.'

'It bloody isn't. What is on your form sheet, Stan? Actual Bodily Harm? What was that all about?'

'Oh, that was years ago. Some stupid tart caught me in her kitchen, she grabbed hold, so I just gave her a backhander, what else could I do? That's all. She reckoned I'd knocked a tooth out, the lying cow.'

Stark allowed himself a glance at Nobby.

*

The telephone in the CID office was answered in mid-ring.

'CID, DC Stevens,' Ashley's well-spoken voice greeted the caller.

'Hello, mate. Is Nobby Clarke there?' said the gruff unannounced voice.

'He's here, but he's interviewing at the moment.'

'Is he likely to be long?'

'Probably quite a while yet. Can I take a message?'

'No, leave it. I tell you what, you might be able to help me. You've got Stan Tindle locked up, haven't you?'

'Can, I ask who's calling, please?'

'Sorry, mate. I should have said. It's Dave Saunders, from Regional Crime Squad speaking. Can I ask you what Stan's in for?'

Ashley thought the voice was familiar. 'Yes: murder.'

'Murder. Stan?' He laughed. 'You're joking!'

'That's a coincidence, it's just what *he* said.' Ashley retorted.

'It's not that triple killing on Maple Close, is it?'

'You've got it in one.' Ashley toyed with the pliable telephone cord as he sat at his desk.

'Bloody hell. Look, Stan's been doing a bit for us lately and there's an armed robbery that's due to go down next week and we could do with him being out. He's not seriously in the frame for this, is he?'

'He's in the top three or four at the moment.' There was a slight pause.

'Listen – do us a favour. If you kick him out, tell him it's because I gave you a ring, will you?'

Ashley knew how the game worked. 'Yes, Dave, of course.

Consider it done.'

'Cheers, Ash.'

'Cheers.'

*

Stan was sweating profusely in the interview room and the questions just kept on coming. He felt trapped; he was uncomfortable. The build-up of the interview had thrown him into turmoil and the pressure was getting too much for him.

Stark continued the barrage. 'If you haven't done any jobs lately, what were you doing with the screwdriver in the lining of your jacket?' His voice had become considerably harsher.

'I always carry it,' answered Stan, wiping his forehead with his sleeve. The sweat left a wet mark on it.

'Bullshit, Stan! Now I want some answers. What's all this crap about you being with Marge the night you were stopped?' Stark leaned forward, resting his elbows on the desk.

'I didn't know what to say to you. I panicked.' He looked at Nobby. 'So, I was stopped – so what? I was clean. I didn't get nicked.'

'Yes, but why lie to Charlie and this officer about it, Stan?'

'I don't know, I just did. It's awkward, everyone looking at me in the pub, what do you expect? I'm telling the truth now, aren't I?'

Stark pursed his lips. 'I don't know, Stan – are you? What were you doing on Nabbs Lane?'

'Nothing.'

'Nothing. You're just bloody lucky that it was a young copper that stopped you, otherwise you'd have been searched properly and you'd have been nicked, Stan, wouldn't you?'

Stan had his answer. 'I didn't have the screwdriver on me, did I?'

'More bullshit! You've just bloody told us you always carried it. Which is it, Stan?' Stan folded his arms; his fists had become clenched tightly. Stark went on. 'Because a couple of streets away a whole family were wiped out, Stan; murdered by a burglar who'd been disturbed, just like you were disturbed three years ago and who is the only burglar rocking the streets that night? Stanley bloody Tindle! It's you isn't it, Stan?'

'Bloody hell. Honest I have not – listen.'

'Listen? Listen to what? Guess how the burglar got in, Stan? Was it with a crow-bar? No. Did he kick the door in? No. Did he break the glass and reach in for the key? No. Was it a side window? No. Was it the main window that was forced? No. Let me tell, you, Stan. He got in through the back transom window, Stan; using a bloody great screwdriver, just like yours. What would you think, Stan? What would anybody think? And there you are two streets away. It's you, Stan.'

'I wouldn't hurt people like that.' Stan had been fidgeting in his seat throughout the accusation. 'I wouldn't...' His eyes were darting between Nobby and Stark, looking for a sympathetic response to his claim. He didn't find any.

'But you've just told us you hit a woman who disturbed you last time.'

'Yes, but that was a mistake, it just happened, on the spur of the moment. I don't normally do that, you know that, Mr Stark.'

'This was on the spur of the moment too, wasn't it, Stan? Or do you know something we don't?'

'I've told you I didn't do any jobs that night. That young copper scared me off.'

'Guess what was nicked, Stan?'

'How should I know?'

'A video was nicked. What an amazing coincidence. What was the very first thing you said when I asked you what you stole?'

'A video...but...'

'Get it off your chest, Stan, - you know you want to – it's not worth all this aggro is it?'

Stan didn't answer. He just shook his head.

'That screwdriver is going to match up with the marks on

that window, Stan, and you know it,' said Stark, leaning back into his chair again confidently.

'I know it won't.' .

'Stan, nobody's saying you meant for it to happen. It was probably all an accident – a spur-of-the-moment job, like you said. You were there, Stan. We've got a policeman who can put you there an hour before it happened. The same M.O, the same stuff nicked – it's too much of a coincidence: it's got your name written all over it, Stan. It's down to you. We've even got your gloves you were wearing that night, Stan. Give it up, mate – we all make mistakes.'

Stan stared at the table silently. It was relentless.

'I know you're not vicious, you're not a killer. It might have been an accident – I don't know until you tell me, do I?'

Silence.

'I can't say it was an accident for you, can I? It's down to you. You're not helping yourself here. You're making yourself out to be worse than you are.'

Stan shook his head slowly, still not speaking.

'What's the court going to think, Stan? Was it an accident, or did you go in there intending to kill them? You were there, weren't you…weren't you, Stan?'

The onslaught continued for a further quarter of an hour. Before Stark went into an interview he tried to get his mind right; he would tell himself that the person he was about to interview had done it, there was no doubt about it – he'd done it and that was that. He had learned the hard way; he had sympathised with suspects in the past, when he was a young copper. He would never apologise for doing his job to the best of his ability, because if that person had done it, he wasn't going to admit it in a nicely worded letter to the Chief Constable, was he? The CID deal with the evilest people in society. The mothers of children who have been sexually abused. Elderly ladies who have been brutally raped are hardly going to thank you, if you merely have a cosy, comfortable chat with the perpetrator and, if he says he hasn't done it, just accept it and let him go. Stark was paid to do a job; he wasn't paid to make friends. He was paid, in this instance, to find the murderer and that's just what he intended to do.

Stan still wasn't having it, but he had plenty to think about. Stark and Nobby took him back to the cell block and the loving arms of the Custody Sergeant. Stan had his hands in his pockets and his head was bowed. He didn't speak; his face was flushed and his palms sweaty. His ordeal was over, for now. 'Just have a think about what's been said,' Stark shouted to Stan as he was led down the corridor. 'We'll speak to you again later.'

The cell door slammed shut behind Stan. He turned and pounded the wall repeatedly with the side of his clenched fist. 'Bastards...Bastards...Bastards...' with every strike.

*

Nobby placed the chicken fried rice in the microwave in the brightly lit kitchen. 'What do you reckon then, boss?' he asked, pressing the digits on the control panel and watching the turntable burst into life.

'No idea, Nobby. What about you, what do you think?' Stark plonked himself down at the white table.

'I don't know. It could be him, but I'm not really feeling it, I tend to think it's not his style.'

Stark grimaced, '"Could be", isn't going to be enough. It's the rape thing that bothers me.'

'If it was a rape.'

'You think she consented to Stan Tindle. I can't see that. We are making it fit, Nobby.' Stark said. 'And that doesn't feel right.'

'More than one offender, perhaps?' Nobby offered.

'We need a lever on him, Nobby. We've got him overnight at least.'

The kitchen door opened and a man asked for Detective Inspector Stark.

'That's me.' The microwave pinged.

A callow-looking youth of about twenty-one in a Summery shirt introduced himself. 'I'm Pete Bloomfield from Scenes of Crime. Do you want the good news or the bad news?'

'Give me some good news,' said Stark, 'I could use it.'

'Your man Tindle isn't the murderer, I'm afraid.' It was a bold statement to make and he appeared almost apologetic as he blurted it out.

'You what? And how do you know that, might I ask?' Stark enquired.

'The report from forensic – they did it as a rush job, it doesn't take long if it's a negative. It's categorical. There was no break-in at the house. The murderer had chipped away at the window while it was open. It was a set-up. Forensic have studied the plaster cast and photos of the mark. The window was not forced. It's definite.'

'Give me the report.' Stark barked. He studied it and got to the findings at the foot of page four. 'Well, shit a brick!' He handed the report to Nobby who was busy serving the Chinese meal up.

Bloomfield continued his explanation. 'So, the murderer was either invited in or he conned his way in; he certainly didn't force any windows or doors.'

'That doesn't mean Tindle hasn't done it.' Stark's determined interviewing mode was still switched on and hadn't returned to normality.

'Come on, boss,' said Nobby. 'Tindle didn't even know the Marriott's. It's not his way, and the rape thing, let's face it – he's just a piss-pot burglar.'

Stark conceded. 'All right, but bail him to come back to the nick in a couple of months' time. I still want his gear forensically checked. And get the jewellery checked out – it's bound to be nicked.'

Nobby went out the room to give his instructions; he wasn't going to do it person – his Chinese meal would get cold.

Stark muttered under his breath. 'Right, Winston Kelly,

you've got some questions to answer.'

Nobby returned to the kitchen and joined him at the table. The two men ate in silence, their eating habits indicative of their personalities. Stark toyed with the food, deciding which morsels he wanted on his fork, teasing the ingredients with his knife before carefully and steadfastly placing it in his mouth. Nobby, however, used only a fork, shovelling large quantities in as if there were no tomorrow, the occasional pea or piece of rice falling on to the table or floor.

Nobby spoke with his mouth full. 'What are you thinking, boss. Kelly?'

Stark nodded and swallowed before he spoke. 'Kelly.'

8

'The only normal people are the ones you don't know
very well...'

Joe Ancis

Violet Gray hadn't gone to her mother's at all. She had told another lie to Ernie, it was getting easier to do so. For the last week she had seemed to do nothing but lie and cover her tracks. She wore a grey mac and a headscarf despite the sultry air. Once inside the red telephone kiosk at the corner of Main Street, she felt more at ease, and she leaned with her back into the corner, in order that any passers-by wouldn't recognise her. She fiddled in her brown faux leather shopping bag and pulled out a small red purse with a clasp fastener, which she twisted to reveal the stack of coins she saved for moments like this.

She deposited ten pence in the slot of the call-box at the second attempt, her hands were shaking. From the same purse she opened a folded scrap of paper and dialled the unfamiliar telephone number. A man's voice answered. 'Hello?'

'It's me.' Violet spoke with a voice that was quavering and uncertain.

'What the hell are you doing ringing me here?' the man whispered in a panic.

She closed her eyes and sighed. It was the reaction she had expected. 'Can you talk?' she asked, the adrenalin pumping through her veins, she was scared, out of her mind with worry.

'No, not really. You never know who might be listening, for Christ's sake! Don't use names.'

Violet responded meekly. 'I won't.'

'I have told you never to ring me here, so what do you do? You ring me here. Thanks. Thank you so bloody much!'

'I'm sorry. I would never have rung you unless I had to. I'm sorry, all right?'

'No it's not all right.'

'Look, I am in a telephone kiosk. It's the only thing I could think of. Just listen to me.' Violet was trying to control her breathing and disguise the rising panic. 'Ernie's been to the police and given a statement about the murders. He's seen you running away.'

There was a silence, born of disbelief.

'He's done what? Don't say the name again.'

'He's been to the police.'

'You are joking. What kind of a moron is he? What is wrong with the man?'

She continued. 'I know. He's going to ruin everything. Don't worry – he's not named you, but it could mean trouble for us. I'm scared.'

'Have you disposed of the evidence?' He asked.

'Of course, I have. . . Oh I nearly said your name, then.'

'Please don't'. There was a further brief silence. 'Let me think.'

'Trust me, I've been doing nothing but think. Can't you try and get an alibi for the time and if anybody asks about it just deny all knowledge, no matter what they say. No matter what. Do you promise?' She waited for a response. 'Promise me you won't, please.' She begged.

There was a pause. 'You have my word.'

'Say "I promise".'

'I promise, OK? Look, sorry I was sharp with you. I'll be in touch when things calm down. Don't worry it will be fine, things will blow over. Just don't panic. OK?'

The man put the receiver down as Violet said 'Bye.' After taking a few seconds to gather her thoughts, she hurried out of the telephone kiosk, keeping her head down, beginning to regret ever getting involved.

*

Paul Fisher knocked on the door of Number 6 Torkard Terrace, one of a row of several two-bedroomed terraced council houses. The small front garden consisted of tidy shrubs and some carnations, standing out from the other gardens, which were barren. He already had his warrant card in his outstretched hand and held it there, as the elderly lady partially opened the door, her wrinkled face staring out suspiciously from the gap she made between door and frame. She seemed a little unsteady on her feet. A friendly expression met her doubting glare.

'Who is it?' She shouted, her voice a little croaky. She hadn't spoken to anyone all day.

'Hello, love. I'm from the CID ... from the police. I'm making some enquiries about the murders across the road the other night. Have you heard about them?' The lady opened the door slightly wider.

'Yes, I have. It's awful, isn't it?' she replied.

Paul agreed. 'Yes. Has a policeman spoken to you about it at all?'

'No, they haven't, love.'

'Do you mind if I come in then, and have a chat?'

The elderly lady pulled Paul's hand towards her and scrutinised his warrant card. 'It doesn't look like you,' she said, her deep-set eyes examining the young detective's face warily.

'I'm starting to realise that.' His memory fleeting back to the morning of the murder and his house-to-house experience with the pungent Mrs Lewis. 'It was taken a long time ago,' he smiled.

The woman relented. 'All right, you had better come in.'

It wasn't long before it became apparent to Paul that the lady, Mrs Charles, had some information that could be of great use to the enquiry. She gave an account of her activities on the night of the murders.

'You see, I can never get to sleep, so I usually don't bother going to bed until one or two in the morning. I reckon to have a bowl of cereal about 12. Both my children live away, now, so I don't see so much of them. I don't mind, they have busy lives, it's not easy for them, bless them. We talk on the phone, but it's not quite the same. I'm grateful to hear from them but it's not the same. I'm not complaining, mind.' Mrs Charles had the verbose habits of someone who did not have a lot of company and subliminally was now making the most of it.

'Of course not,' Paul said sympathetically. 'But could you just explain to me again exactly what you saw?'

'I was putting the milk bottle out, now, I never used to have a bottle delivered every day, but I've taken to having a bowl of cornflakes at night, like I said. I never want a full dinner nowadays. It must be down to old age.' She laughed, before continuing, 'So that is the only reason I had to put my bottle out, if it had been a few weeks ago I wouldn't have seen anything.'

Paul tried again. 'So what happened, Mrs Charles?'

'I use it for tea as well, during the day, the milk I mean. What did you ask me?'

'Just what happened, that's all.'

'He nearly knocked me flying, he was running like Billy Whiz. You have to question people nowadays, I mean, when we were young, and I'm going back a bit, we were taught to have respect for your elders, but they don't seem to bother nowadays. I had just put the bottle on the floor, I have to take my time because I can get dizzy spells when I lean over; which is something to do with blood pressure, I think, but I am on tablets.'

Paul smiled. 'That's good, so then what, happened?'

'He nearly frightened me to death, running like the clappers he was, I don't think he was looking where he was going.'

'Who was it? Do you know him?'

'I've lived in the town for over seventy years, so there aren't many I don't know, certainly around this neck of the woods.

I've lived in this house for over thirty two years, can you believe it?' She laughed again. 'Before you were born probably. Both my children were born in this house.'

'So did you know the man, Mrs Charles?'

'Same as I say, I know most people around, here I've seen them all grow up. Of course, I know him. It's Elsie Markwell's eldest lad, Colin.'

'Sorry, who was it?'

'Elsie's lad; Colin Markwell his name is. He's always been an odd bugger, he has. You know the row of garages at the end of the road?'

Paul nodded.

'He use to climb on to the garage roof and just sit up there for hours when he was a lad. One time he fell asleep up there, it was when we had that really hot summer, and they had to throw stones at him to wake him up. Daft bugger.'

'Are you sure?' Paul asked.

'Of course I'm sure. I saw it with my own two eyes. My lad tried to climb up after him, but I shouted at him and told him to get in the house.'

'No, sorry, my fault. Not the garage thing. Are you sure it was Colin Markwell who ran past you?'

'Of course I'm sure. He's at church most Sunday's with his wife and those two brats. Oh, what's his wife's name?' she asked herself.

'Do you know where he lives, Mrs Charles?'

She screwed her eyes up to concentrate. 'Let me see... somewhere on that new estate – it's the corner house. It is either Charnwood Grove or Ellis Avenue. It's the corner house, anyway.'

'That's fine we will find it. Did you notice if he was carrying anything?'

'I only saw his face as he ran at me. He was running really fast and, in a panic, I would say. By the look on his face, he looked as if he'd seen a ghost.'

'So you didn't see if he was holding anything, then?'

'I didn't say that. From behind, I would say that he probably was carrying something, yes.'

Paul asked the obvious: 'Did you see what it was he was carrying?'

'No, I didn't. Aren't you listening, young man? I've just told you that.' It wasn't a nastiness, just that matter-of-fact way of talking which some elderly people can adopt, often out of frustration.

Mrs Charles couldn't give any further information, particularly as to what the thing was that he was carrying, which troubled Paul slightly, but he communicated, by radio, the interesting snippet back to the Incident Room. It was a good lead and it didn't take long for Colin Markwell to be located at 23 Charnwood Grove by one of the uniformed computer operators using the voters register. Stark had instructed Charlie and Ashley to bring him in to the station to 'help with their enquiries'. Paul had been told to continue house-to-house and to meet Charlie and Ashley to hand over the witness statement. Paul was a little deflated that he seemingly had not been trusted to do the interview by Stark. He knew he was young in service in the CID, but there was sometimes a feeling that during murder enquiries all the old favourite Detectives would be asked to do the important bits, and it was something of a closed shop for the others. Stark just saw it the same way as a football manager, who chose his players according to their known strengths. His job was to detect a murder, not worry about gossip. Paul's turn would come.

Stark had told Charlie and Ash that he would speak to Markwell later, but they were to 'invite him in' and start things off, and if it looked promising, they were to contact him immediately. Stark and Nobby were in the process of drawing up plans to arrest and interview Winston Kelly who had been with Faye at Ritzy's Night Club, and they only had 'two pairs of hands.'

*

The cellar of the house was pitch black. A total black-out. Not a sliver of light from anywhere. He lay on the old settee, his eyes closed, but awake; the underground room was warm and his 'special place' where he could be alone with his thoughts; away from all the distractions and aggravation he seemed to attract. Why was it always him that was so unlucky?

He was enjoying the feeling of being lost in the darkness; sensory deprivation with just the tiniest hum of noise, from where, he knew not. Periodically he would open his eyes; no change to when they were closed. It was a very strange sensation and one which thrilled him a little, but also slightly disconcerted him at the same time, as he was afraid to let his mind totally relax. Too many demons to totally let them loose, untethered. The initial disorientation 'the happening' caused him, a few days ago had started to ease. He had called it 'the happening' in his own mind as he really didn't want to call it murder, or killing; that would make him, by association, a murderer or a killer and he wasn't ready to accept that was who he was. Nor would he ever be ready for that acknowledgement. It was too simple to label people like that and life was anything but simple and in any case what happened was just something unavoidable really.

He stretched out his arms and legs and made that guttural noise that accompanies such a stretch, followed by a gasp of releasing air from his lungs, which threw him into a coughing fit. He sat up on the settee, still blind and oblivious to his surroundings. He nodded to himself, smirking, he was going to get away with it. If he did, he promised himself he would sort himself out, this time. It would never happen again; that was his vow. He had spent his life making these promises to himself and then bubbling away under the surface, was his temper, and the slightest crack to the surface would make him erupt. Everyone deserves a second chance though, don't they? Why not him? It just happened. It wasn't even pre-meditated for God's sake. It was a shame they are all dead, of course, but also, fuck them. The evidence had been disposed of. It was safe. He was going to get away with it, particularly knowing the jokers who were investigating it. That Wagstaff geezer on the news looked like something from the bloody 1940's. What chance did he have against him? They had no clue who they were dealing with and what he was capable of. The police were pathetic. They think they know everything, but they know fuck all. Even the press was starting to ask questions about them. 'No definitive lead'. He laughed out loud, again, the cellar ringing like an echo chamber to his mania. 'No definitive lead'. What a fucking joke! He was no stranger to the police giving him a hard time. He could see the desperation in their eyes. He wanted to rub their noses in it. Make them suffer for a change. He felt invincible. Superior. He should take his time, keep tabs on what was happening and then he would be able to change his ways. It was no good starting right now. Now wasn't the right time. Timing was everything. Once he knew everything was going to be okay, then he would seek the help he desperately needed. That way he would know he wouldn't kill again.

*

Charlie and Ashley heard the strains of a James Bond film issuing from the family focal point as a young girl, with a bow in her black hair, opened the front door and greeted them. They explained who they were and expressed their wish to speak to a Mr Markwell. The girl cocked her head back and shouted: 'Dad? Dad!'
There was no reply.
  'Anybody know where Dad is?' She tried again, directing the shouted question to the house in general.
  'No,' came the chorused reply from the living room.
  'What? Who is it?' came the irritated questions as Colin Markwell appeared from the hallway in a fluster. He was a man of about forty; his black sideburns were turning grey, he had a tanned complexion and wore a smart, casual beige shirt with

off-white trousers.

'It's the police.' His daughter said, the concern evident in her voice as she nodded towards the door.

'The what?' Colin looked beyond her to the smiling gentleman on the doorstep.

'Oh. All right, leave it with me.' His daughter stayed where she was.

'Go on nosy, off you pop.' It wasn't open to debate and his daughter begrudgingly slouched back to the living room. Colin seemingly looked puzzled, his heart was pounding when he saw it was the CID and he was short of breath, and bleary eyed. 'What can I do for you, gentlemen?' he asked.

Ashley produced his warrant card. 'Did we wake you up?'

'No. No, I was just busy out the back, there. What's the matter?'

'I take it you are Colin Markwell?' Ashley asked.

'Yes. There's nothing wrong, is there?' Colin asked, already knowing the answer and he pushed his hands deep into his trouser pockets.

Ash explained, albeit not entirely truthfully. 'No, there's nothing wrong, Colin, but we'd like to have a chat with you at the station, if you don't mind.' Colin retreated a few steps and surreptitiously closed the interior living-room door and Roger Moore's rhetoric faded.

Colin protested mildly. 'It isn't the best time, it's a bit awkward…I mean what do you want to talk to me about, for heaven's sake?'

Ashley cautiously explained, not really wanting to give the game away; 'I'd rather not discuss it on the doorstep, but it involves your being seen in very suspicious circumstances at the rear of Maple Close, the other night.'

Colin grimaced momentarily and his lips tightened. 'Oh God. I've been dreading this. I'll get my coat.' Ash glanced at Charlie.

He closed the living-room door behind him as he re-entered the room; it didn't totally disguise the conversation which took place behind it.

'What do you mean you're going to the police station?' asked a concerned Mrs Markwell as she rose from her seat, her portly body clad in a green leisure suit.

'They want someone to help them with an identity parade and I said I'd help, as a stand in on the line-up, a volunteer, you know. They give you a tenner. I shouldn't be more than an hour, two at the most.'

She was not amused. 'Whatever possessed you to agree to that? Tell them to go away. It's family time for God's sake.'

Colin passed over the remark and struggled with himself to remain calm. 'I've told them I'd do it now; they're waiting outside. Do you want some chips bringing back?'

This seemed to placate her. 'No – er, yes, OK, just bring me a bag of chips, nothing else, apart from a battered sausage and some mushy peas. Don't be too long, will you?'

Colin kissed his wife, attempting a smile that wrinkled into a frown. He really didn't want to leave his family to go with the two strangers outside. He had a bad feeling in the pit of his stomach. Why did he have to do it? Why had he ever set foot on Maple Close? This was God punishing him.

He took a deep breath and addressed the two solemn men on his doorstep. 'Sorry about that, gents. Right – shall I follow you in my car?'

'Do you know where Nottingham Police Station is?' Ashley asked.

'Yes, of course.'

'In that case, we will follow you then,' said Ashley with a wry smile.

'Fine . . . fine. . .' Colin's voice trailed off as he trudged to his car.

*

The operator answered the police-station switchboard. The female caller's voice was low and sensual, despite the distortion of the telephone.

'Can I speak to Detective Sergeant Clarke, please?'

There was a pause and some clicks before the deep raspy voice answered, 'CID DS Clarke.' Nobby and Stark had been busy discussing Winston Kelly and his voice betrayed slight irritation at the interruption.

'Hello, its Sally.'

'Hello, Sally?' Nobby tried to mouth to Stark, 'Who is Sally?' Stark looked puzzled at him.

The lady was a trifle embarrassed. 'You don't remember me, do you?'

Nobby hastily searched his memory. 'Sally. Of course I do, Sally.' he lied, 'hold on a minute, I'll come clean, it has been a long and busy day; it's slipped my mind, I'm sorry.'

'That's OK. I'm the girl from Bernie Squires' betting shop, re-member? You were kind to me when I was upset about Faye.'

Nobby remembered. 'Oh, *that* Sally. The beautiful young woman of my dreams. How could I ever forget you, Sally? How are you? Hey, I'm going to send you the bill for my jacket – your mascara wouldn't come out.' he joked.

Stark scribbled on a piece of paper and held it up for Nobby to read 'You dirty bastard'. Nobby smiled and displayed his middle finger to Stark, in best American tradition.

Sally was oblivious to the malarkey. 'I'm fine. I'd like to apologise for breaking down and crying like that – you must have been really embarrassed. I feel really silly now.'

Nobby put on his best sympathetic voice. 'Don't feel silly – it's completely understandable. Have you got over it a bit more, now?'

'Yes, there is no point in worrying about things that we can't change. I would like to thank you for being so kind, if you'd let me?'

Nobby smiled and looked over at Stark before giving his reply. 'That's nice. What did you have in mind? How are you going to thank me?'

Stark screwed up his face and groaned. 'It's pathetic.'

Sally continued with her rehearsed conversation; things

were going well, it had taken a lot of courage for her to make the call. 'I thought you might like to come over to my flat and I'll cook you a nice dinner.'

'It sounds absolutely terrific, but it would have to be quite late, if you mean tonight?' Nobby said with a grin. Her sensuality travelled through the phone into Nobby's nether-regions.

'Sounds interesting.' A little giggle followed her observation.

'About ten-o'clock-ish?' asked, Nobby.

'Great. How does Chicken Tikka grab you?' The excitement in Sally's voice was apparent.

'That sounds absolutely mouth-watering, *and* the Chicken Tikka. I can hardly wait.'

'Cheeky! I'll see you later then: ten o'clock.'

'*Wait!*' shouted Nobby.

'What's the matter?' asked Sally, concerned he might have had second thoughts.

'I don't know where you live.' The two laughed.

'Oops, sorry. Number 12 Sunderland Court. It's off Mapperley Plains – do you know it?'

'I know it very well. It's quite a select area, too select for the likes of me; I'm impressed.'

Sally offered a word of caution. 'Don't build your hopes up too high. Have you ever been in a student's flat?'

'Would I admit to it if I had?'

'It's a date, then.'

Nobby agreed. 'Yes, I'll be there. I take it you're on the phone?'

'Yes, it's 309569.'

He jotted it down on the 'You dirty bastard' piece of paper. 'Got it. I look forward to seeing you later, Sally. Take care,'

They said their farewells, and Nobby spoke aloud as he replaced the receiver. 'Well, Clarkey, old son, you've done it again.'

Stark spoke. 'I think it's pathetic, a man of your age taking advantage of a poor defenceless girl. I think I should go in your place for the sake of the reputation of the force.'

Nobby laughed. 'Defenceless young girl? She rang me! Anyway, you're only jealous, boss, and it is an inroad into Bernie Squires' activities.'

Stark shook his head. 'You're so full of sh-'

Nobby raised a warning finger. 'Now, sir, don't be like that.'

*

Ashley explained Colin Markwell's rights to him as he and Charlie prepared to 'chat' with him in the interview room.

'You are not under arrest, Colin. You are free to leave the police station at any time, and you can consult with a solicitor at any time.' Ashley then cautioned him, but it was Charlie, standing near the door, who started the questioning.

'Right, Colin, what were you doing at the back of Maple Close the other night?'

Colin sat on the black plastic chair, staring at the floor. 'I can't remember being at the back of Maple Close,' he said.

'I take it you've heard all about the murders on the news?' asked Ashley.

'Yes, but what has that got to do with me?'

Ashley continued. 'You were seen running down the back of Maple Close around the time of the murders being committed. All we want to know is why, Colin?'

Markwell appeared very uncomfortable; he was lying, and Ashley and Charlie knew it, but he continued the charade. 'To be honest with you, I don't even know myself what I would want to be doing at the back of Maple Close!'

There wasn't a tape recorder on and Colin wasn't under arrest, but Charlie endeavoured to explain. 'Well, my friend, you'd better think and think quickly, because you may not be under arrest at the moment but you're a gnat's bollock away from it!'

'Who says I was there?' Colin enquired, with a quick glance at Charlie.

Ashley, however, replied: 'A witness.'

'Yes, but who is this witness?'

Charlie interrupted. 'Look, pal. We ask the questions here, not you! Just take it from me that somebody who knows you, has seen you running along Maple Close, all right?'

Ashley contributed, in a slightly friendlier tone. 'Colin, we don't have time to randomly pick people off the street to ask them questions. You are here because a witness, who we don't wish to name just yet, has seen you. It's dead simple.' Ash thought that Charlie was being a bit too old school and had jumped in too early with the aggressive approach leaving them nowhere to go. He tried to offer an olive branch. 'Colin, nobody is saying you've done anything wrong, necessarily, but we have to understand what you were doing there, if only to eliminate you from our enquiries, and if we can't, then you remain a person of interest.'

Colin paused slightly. He was chewing on his fingernails.

'Well?' Ashley encouraged him.

'I...I...'

'Yes?' Ashley was trying to help him get there.

Colin blurted out: 'I cannot give you an answer to that question, I just can't.'

*

DPW Stephanie Dawson walked into the Royal Oak public house alone, her long flowing hair cascading over the purple, clingy dress that emphasised the curves of her figure. She seemed out of place in the 'drinkers' pub'. It wasn't personal, but she had been 'paired up' with a young copper and she didn't want her 'snout' scared off by some spotty-faced youth, straight out of training school. Similarly, she didn't want the youth's confidence shattered by some embarrassingly accurate insults from the tactless petty criminal she had arranged to meet.

Benny Willows had been informing on his friends to Stephanie for nearly two years, quite a long time. Usually something goes wrong with an informant within a year or so, particularly if they are an active criminal, as they re-offend or want some impossible favour, or they over-step the mark in their relationship by being too careless or 'gobbing-off' when drunk. Benny was in his late thirties and scruffy. He stood at the bar of the seedy joint, where sticky bare floorboards welcomed all visitors and ancient pictures of trains inexplicably hung on the walls, in a vain attempt at decoration by the clueless landlord. The pub must have been ten miles from the nearest train station, but the pictures were going cheap in a job-lot, offered under dubious circumstances, by one of the regular punters. The pub was almost empty. The closest Benny had ever come to the big time was agreeing to drive for an armed robbery a couple of years ago. He'd bottled out at the last minute and had contacted Steph. All his mates had got nicked and had been charged with 'conspiracy to rob'. They received between 3 and 5 years at the Crown Court. Benny got a suspended sentence as he was 'removed from the violence', which was enough to distract his friends from questioning the leniency he was given. The judge had been sent a letter in private explaining that Benny had co-operated fully, and the arrests were because of this. It was code that he had informed on his friends.

Beyond that case, Steph had used her sensuality to cultivate Benny, she knew he fantasised about 'having' her and she just kept him hanging on a thread, with a hint that she might one day let him. Ridiculous though, that premise may be. It was a dangerous game, but a lot of the policewomen did this, in fact so did some of the male detectives with female informants. She always paid Benny in cash for any good information he gave her. 'How much if this info comes off, Steph?' Benny was quick to enquire; his toothless grin supported the question.

'What did you say? How much will I take off? Cheeky, bugger.'

'Not take off, I said if the info comes off.' Benny laughed like a hyena, a saliva string stretching from his top gum to the bottom.

'Okay, I believe you. You never know, Benny, you never know.' She winked at him.

Benny laughed. 'No, I said, how much will I get paid, if this comes off, the info, like?'

'Oh, I see. Me and my dirty mind. It must be the effect you have on me, Benny. I like a bit of rough.' She sipped at her drink. 'Now, let me see, if it's any good, and we get him charged, you've got to be looking at five hundred, something like that.' Steph knew he would probably get more, but £500 to Benny was a fortune in his current financial state. She would have to apply to Headquarters for that sort of money and get it all witnessed, but it would be worth it.

Benny asked another question: 'Do I get a thank-you kiss if it pans out OK?'

Steph shuddered at the thought. 'Oh, you're making me go all funny at the mere thought of it. Of course, you do. You'll get me into trouble, you will, Benny.' They both laughed.

'Chance would be a fine thing,' he said.

Steph made sure that her ample bosom brushed past him as she leaned over to pay the barman. 'It'd better be good, Benny. How do you know about the murders?' she asked

'I don't know about the murders, but I know about her.'

'Who?' Steph asked.

'That tart, Faye. She's been about a bit, she has, Steph.'

'What about her?' she asked, sipping at her gin and tonic.

'Five hundred?' Benny smiled.

'Only if it comes to something, Benny, I'll put in for six hundred, so I should get five. You know I can't be precise about figures. Don't go building your hopes up, it has to solve the case in the end, don't forget.'

'I know, I know all about that. I will take you for a candle-lit dinner when I get it,' said Benny as he wiped his nose on the sleeve of his jacket.

'I'll look forward to that,' said Steph with a straight face.

He lowered his voice and leaned in towards Steph. 'Does the name, Winston Kelly, mean anything to you?' He gave a sideways glance around the deserted bar.

'It might do.' The verbal fencing had begun. Steph knew she had to be so careful not to feed him anything that he didn't already know.

'He was trying to get her on the game, you know.' Benny's mouth widened to give her yet another view of his three stubby teeth, joined together by a chain of thick, clear saliva.

'How do you know that?' asked Steph, closing her eyes momentarily to shut out the ghastly image.

'I've been out with them loads of times. She didn't want to know, about going on the game, I mean, so he beat her up.'

'When was this, Benny?'

'About a month ago in the Florin pub. He punched her full on, right in the stomach, he did. He's a mental bleeder, you know. Be careful around him, Steph, he's a fucking nutter.'

Steph nodded solemnly. 'I know he is, Benny. What else?'

'He threatened to kill her, Steph. He told her straight out that if she wouldn't go on the streets, he'd kill her. Now here she is, dead. He's capable of it too, Steph, trust me.'

Steph was cautious. 'People are threatening to kill each other all the time, though, Benny.'

'Not people like Winston Kelly. When he says it, he means it.'

'Who else witnessed the fight and the threats?' asked Steph, seeking corroboration.

'Everyone. Harry, the landlord, you know, Harry Dennis? Well, he saw the whole thing. Threatened to throw him out, he did, but he didn't 'cos he's shit scared of Winston Kelly, just like everyone else is. He never threw him out. If that had been me. I'd have been out on my arse.'

She had enough to go on. She tapped Benny's forearm. 'Thanks, Benny,' grabbing at his grubby hand and squeezing it, before hurriedly leaving. Benny felt as if he had been paid already, missing the fact that she wiped her hand on the side of her dress as she walked out.

Steph quickly checked the information out with Harry Dennis the landlord, who was going to tell her about it, 'honest', but he'd been too busy. He thought he would wait until the CID came in for a drink next time. Steph was straight on to Stark with the information, who immediately laid down plans to contact a magistrate to swear out a warrant, to 'do the business' on Winston Kelly. This additional information added to the preparation they had been doing to try to get Kelly arrested. This was the break-through in getting a proper job done on this violent criminal.

*

The interview of Colin Markwell continued.

'What were you carrying that night, Colin?' Ashley asked, hopefully.

'I've told you, I wasn't necessarily there that night,' Colin persisted, with his ridiculously worded answer, his confidence waning.

'In that case, where were you?' Ash asked.

'In town, I think, round the pubs.'

'You think! Which pubs?' Charlie asked.

Colin moved the plastic chair towards the desk. 'I don't know. I can't remember. The Crusader, I think.'

'Who with?'

'I was on my own...wasn't I? Yes, that's right. I was on my own.'

There was a pause. Charlie sighed somewhat dramatically and 'laid it on the line'. 'Colin, we talk to dozens-upon-dozens of people a year, like this. Do you honestly expect us to believe this bullshit? My grandmother, who still believes in fairies, wouldn't believe it. I don't think you even believe it yourself.'

'Well, it's all I can say.'

'What is it that you are hiding, Colin?' Ash asked. 'Whatever it is, it can't be worth all of this; becoming a suspect in a murder enquiry. You need to tell us the truth, Colin, while we are still prepared to listen.'

'I'm not hiding anything, nothing. I just can't tell you that's all. It doesn't make me a murderer.'

Charlie was becoming impatient. 'Have we got to arrest you? Is that it, Colin? Have we got to burst in your home, with your Mrs and kids there, and search it? Have we got to do it the hard way? Are we being too reasonable with you, eh?'

'There is no need for that.' Colin squirmed in his chair, thinking of the reaction of his wife and children to any such scenario.

'Why did you say you'd been dreading us coming?' asked Ashley.

'What? I never said that.' Colin, not quite as confident as before, had a whole host of thoughts jostling for space in his mind.

Ashley was certain. 'Yes, you did, Colin, you said it to us as we spoke to you at the door.'

'I didn't. Stop putting words in my mouth.' He turned in his chair to face away from the officers so that he was sideways on to them.

Charlie sneered. 'We aren't going to go away, Colin, because you've moved your chair three inches. This is a murder enquiry, pal. If you think that by just saying nothing, that we can just give up and send you on your merry way, then you are much misguided, my friend.'

Ashley sighed. 'Look, we are going around in circles, here. Do you accept that you were at the back of Maple Close?'

'No.'

'For God's sake!' Charlie was getting irritated by the ridiculousness of the conversation.

Ashley continued. 'What were you carrying, Colin?' He asked again.

He stared blankly at the wall. 'I don't know what you mean.'

Charlie clenched his fists with tension, not as a threat, but he appeared just as menacing and walked up to Colin who immediately reacted and put his hands up to his face, to protect himself, his actions full of melodrama. 'Stop threatening me, or I shall shout for help! I can leave, you know, you told me at the start that I could leave anytime. I would like to leave, please.'

'You can leave, if you wish, Colin,' said Charlie, 'but get one thing straight: if your arse leaves that chair, it ends up in a cell!'

*

Nobby had set off dutifully for his rendezvous with Sally, with Dave Stark's blessing. Stark had traced the 'magistrate on call', and Cyril Forsythe was the Justice of the Peace who welcomed the Inspector into his large, detached house.

It was perhaps little known that out-of-hours, when the Courts were closed, that police officers could, in urgent cases, contact the duty Clerk-to-the-Court and if they could pass muster with his or her questions; then he would arrange for them to visit the on-call magistrate at their home address, to make the application proper. If not, the application would not go ahead, and the magistrate would not be disturbed.

Forsythe was a man in his late forties; he wore well-pressed trousers, a shirt and tie, and a fawn cardigan with leather covered buttons that looked like little brown footballs. He was well groomed and spoke with an authoritative air.

Stark was on his best behaviour. 'I'm sorry to disturb you at this time, sir, but I'm sure you will understand the urgency of it, once I explain.'

'The clerk who rang me informed me, Mr Stark, that it's regarding the Marriott murders. Absolutely awful.' He shook his head in disbelief. 'How can a family in their own home be attacked, for no apparent reason and killed? It is unbelievably abhorrent to even contemplate it.' Observed the JP.

These were all good signs to Stark. Forsythe led the Detective Inspector into his old-fashioned study and handed him a small black Bible from his large oak bookcase. 'I suppose we ought to get the formalities over with,' he said.

Stark hated this part of the proceedings. It was all right in court, but it felt so silly when there were just two people present in somebody's living-room. He looked past his attentive host as he gave the slightly different oath, necessary to tender evidence for a warrant to be granted: 'I swear by almighty God that the information that I lay before the magistrate is the truth, to the best of my knowledge and belief.'

Forsythe retrieved the Bible from the embarrassed Inspector. 'Thank you, Mr Stark. Now perhaps you will relate to me the basis of the application?'

Stark explained the details over a cup of coffee brought in by Forsythe's lady 'helper'. He explained why he suspected Winston Kelly: the sighting of him with Faye on the night in question at Ritzy Night Club; the recent assault and threats to kill in the Florin Public house, now corroborated by Harry Dennis; Kelly's previous convictions; and the general background to the relationship between the two. Stark added that he would like the search warrant to search for the video recorder removed from the scene, an item of clothing - red in colour, which may have left the fibres on the deceased and also for a screwdriver used to gain access to the premises. It was necessary to request the warrant as it was likely that entry to the premises would be refused if requested, and that such a refusal would delay access to the premises and jeopardise evidence, as it may enable disposal of same. It was not necessary to request a warrant for Kelly's arrest as this would be done once he was discovered, on reasonable grounds, as it would with any other case. The likely issue was going to the house; and if there were no reasonable grounds to suspect that Kelly was inside the premises, then they could not enter *without* a warrant. Contrary to popular myth, however, if there were grounds to suspect that Kelly were on the premises: if he was seen at the window for example, or his car was outside; then forced entry could be made, and if he was on the premises, he would be arrested and under section 32 of the Police and Criminal Evidence Act 1984, they could search the premises for the evidence, without the need for a search warrant. Stark did not want to take the chance that they would visit and he would not be there, and his neighbours alert him to the fact that they were on to him and give him a head start.

Forsythe asked a few token questions, some of which had been fed to him by the Clerk on the telephone, before Stark arrived. Once these were answered Forsythe leant over his desk to sign the already prepared warrant and the written information that accompanied it, typed by Stark himself. DI Stark thanked him and said farewell. As he stepped on to the magistrate's drive, Forsythe said, 'Oh, just one other thing, Mr Stark.'

Stark groaned inwardly. 'Now what?' he thought to himself before asking 'What's that, sir?'

'Good luck.'

Stark shook his hand. 'Thanks.'

*

Ernie Gray was out when the knock on the door came. It was expected. Violet had been sitting in the armchair in silence, with only a ticking clock for company. Grudgingly, Violet forced herself to answer it. Her feet were like lead weights as she trudged to answer the door. She was sick to the stomach with guilt, and recrimination.

'Is it Mrs Gray?' Paul Fisher enquired.

'Yes,' she croaked. Her dry lips were exacerbated as she bit at her already chipped varnished finger-nails.

'I thought so. I'm DC Fisher from Nottingham CID. Your Ernie's been up to the station earlier, hasn't he?'

Violet nodded. 'Yes, so he tells me, but he's out at the moment.' She swallowed hard.

'That's OK I've been doing house-to-house enquires and I notice that you haven't been seen yet. We've seen Ernie, of course, but not your good self.'

Violet bit her bottom lip and said, 'That's OK. I was going to come and see you anyway. There is something you need to know. You had better come in.' Despite her best intentions she couldn't carry the secret anymore, she felt that she was going out of her mind with worry and had been for days. Paul cheerily accepted the offer to come inside and also for a cup of tea although the length of time it took Violet to make it, he almost wished he hadn't. It was like she was dragging the chains of Jacob Marley around with her. Chains which she needed to shed.

'So what did you want to tell me, Mrs Gray? Something about Ernie?'

'No, not really. Well sort of. It is something and nothing, really, but it's been on my mind.'

'Mrs Gray spit it out, my love. If there is something that has been bothering you, then you need to tell us. It's better out than in, so they say.'

'I know.' She took a deep breath and it all came flooding out.

Violet Gray revealed all to young Paul Fisher, her involvement in the activities of the fateful night and how it had all started. The phone call she had made from the telephone box, and how ashamed she felt for allowing herself to be involved in something so terrible.

Tears were shed and explanations given. At the end of it all, Paul stood on the doorstep of the Gray household and put his hand on her shoulder.

'Do I have to come to the station? Are you arresting me?'

Paul laughed. 'No, of course not.'

'Oh, thank heavens, I thought I might go to prison, you see I have never had much to do with the police. Why would I?'

'Don't worry, Mrs Gray. You have done the right thing. My Inspector will be more than interested in what you have told me. We will be in touch.'

Violet summoned up a tired smile for Paul. 'You have been very kind and understanding. I'm glad it's over, in a way. Thank you. Thank you very much.'

*

Charlie was pacing the interview room floor, impatiently, refusing to sit, partly for effect, and partly to ease his niggling haemorrhoids. 'What were you doing running around Maple Close like a headless chicken in the early hours of the morning?' he asked for the fifth time.

Colin was stuck in a groove of denial. 'I've told you all I can tell you.'

Charlie sighed. 'What were you carrying?'

Colin made his declaration. 'Look, I am getting just a little pissed off with this. OK, I was in Maple Close, but I honestly cannot tell you anymore. I am a Christian man. If I could tell you, I would. I know you're getting mad with me, but I don't know what the answer is.'

'I don't care if you are Christian, Hindu, Muslim, China-man, Red-Indian or Tibetan bleeding monk. What's the bloody story, Colin?' Charlie explained.

The door to the interview room opened and a beaming Paul Fisher stood on the threshold. 'Sorry to interrupt. Can I have a word with you, Ashley?'

'Yes, sure.' The two men went out, leaving a bemused Charlie alone with Colin Markwell. Charlie could see Paul and Ashley in hysterics outside, through the frosted toughened glass panel of the interview room. Ashley returned to the room alone and spoke to Colin.

'The game is up, mate. We know all about what's been going off. I think you'd better confess all to DC Carter.'

'What do you mean?' Colin asked nervously.

'It's not difficult, Colin. It's time you told DC Carter the whole story about you and Violet Gray.' Ashley spoke with great confidence.

Colin's head fell into his hands. 'Oh God! How do you know?'

'Violet's told us everything,' Ashley assured him.

Colin finally felt free from his promise to Violet, to explain to the detectives how he met his unlikely consort at church. He admired her strength of character for putting up with a brute of a man like Ernie Gray, and the fact she had taken him into her confidence, and over time they had fallen in love. The affair had been going on for two years now, and he had thought that each of their spouses were oblivious to it. Ernie was on regular nights and his wife was dead to the world and snoring by 10pm. How could he suspect? On the night of the murders, Colin, had been in bed with Violet when they heard a spine-tingling scream. They had both rushed to the window and looked out. Violet had to then stop herself from screaming, when she saw Ernie staggering towards the house only a matter of a hundred yards away. Unbeknownst to the two adulterers, Ernie had suspected the long-standing affair and, been wrangling with what to do about it. With the bravado of several pints of beer swirling around his belly, Ernie had set off home to confront his wife and her lover. He had subsequently been surprised to find her alone in the house. In the panic that ensued on seeing Ernie returning home, Colin hadn't had time to put on his jacket or shoes and it had been these that he was carrying as he sped down the road, almost knocking the elderly Mrs Charles over as he dashed along, not daring to look back.

Charlie refrained from laughing until the story drew to a conclusion. It was at that point that he exploded into a huge guffaw. 'Why the hell, didn't you tell us, you daft bugger?' he laughed.

Colin stared at the floor. 'I gave my word, never to tell a soul.'

'You bloody idiot! What a waste of time.' Charlie wasn't laughing so much as it dawned on him.

DC Carter showed Markwell to the door, assuring him that they were not at liberty to tell his wife, and where the nearest chip-shop was.

Charlie returned to the office. Paul had rung the Incident Room so that Stark would be made aware. Paul was feeling pleased with himself that he had got the breakthrough with one of the main suspects. 'I told you Pete Glover was right. That was why there was a mistake with his and Ernie's observations that night, why they said that the man they saw was running in different directions. Ernie was pissed and got it round his neck. Ernie was wrong, not Pete.'

Ashley agreed. 'Markwell said that he was running in the same direction as described by Pete Glover, didn't he? So, was it him that Pete saw, or the actual offender?'

There was a momentary silence, before the three men simultaneously burst into laughter. 'Poor old Ernie, anyway, get your coats gents. It's pub-o'clock.' Ashley said. 'I think we've all earnt a pint.'

*

Ashley, Paul and Stark met in the pub next door to the station. It was packed. Charlie had gone for a drink too, but he had made prior arrangements with an ex-DC colleague he knew from way back, to meet up at the Miners' Welfare.

As always, the three stood close to the bar, the odd men out, in their suits and ties; like creatures in the zoo; their every move was assessed by those around them. A clandestine, almost subversive crowd, glancing at the detectives, angling for a better view in the sea of bodies, ebbing and flowing with ripples of movement here and there. There was a hum of noise in the soup of chatter which was a pitch or two above comfortable for the conversationalist. Periodic shouts and spasms of laughter would inject stridence into the wall of noise, which persisted as tenaciously as the blanket of smoke, floating like halos above the heads of the revellers. The three were in a jovial mood, they were used to the sneaky attention from onlookers and they laughed and joked amongst themselves. The pub was particularly thronged, yet Stark couldn't help noticing a bronzed, blonde-haired beauty, wearing a tiger-skin summer dress. She was standing at the end of the bar. Unfortunately she appeared to be in male company. He pointed her out to Ashley and Paul, who were far more likely to do anything about it than he was. He was an admirer from afar of such sirens, and it amused him to see the younger unmarried detectives, jostle for position during the mating season, which seemed to run from December to November each year. The two young detectives studied the girl and then her man friend.

'Eh, that's Pete Glover!' Paul declared.

Glover, wearing a rather loud, summery shirt, had noticed the detectives, he waved and started towards them. Paul introduced Stark to Peter, who ordered a round of drinks.

Paul was chuffed to see him again. 'Marvellous. I don't see you for years, and then twice in a couple of days.'

'Weird, huh?' Peter said sipping at his pint of lager.

'What brings you in here?' Paul asked.

'I thought, I would try it for a change. What brings you reprobates in here?'

'Well, it is next door to the police station, Pete'. Stark observed.

'True, fair point. So, what's happening? How's the investigation going? Obviously very well, if you are in here boozing.'

Paul laughed. 'Everybody has to wind down, Pete. It's going OK. No confessions yet, unless you want to admit all to us, Pete? How are you fixed?'

Pete put his hands out, wrists together. 'OK, I'll come clean. Take me away, officer.' The men laughed.

Ashley was interested in other things. 'Screw the investigation, who's the lovely lady, if you don't mind me asking?' Ashley asked.

Paul beat him to the answer. 'He probably doesn't even know her name, the number of women this guy gets through.'

Pete smiled. 'Now, don't be like that – you'll get me a reputation.'

'You've already got a reputation,' Paul laughed.

'I tell you what, Pete, she can give me a bad reputation any day of the week.' Stark said.

There was a pause. Stark's attention was drawn to the doorway. 'Look what the cat just dragged in.' He nudged Ashley.

The heavily muscled body weaved through the crowds towards the bar. The man was at least six feet three, and certainly stood out in a crowd, with his broken nose and short-cropped hair, towering well above everyone else and immediately catching the eye of the bar man. Thirty-two years old, wearing jeans and a tight-fitting, light –blue collared T-shirt, the well-known criminal was smiling as he made a wake through the punters. He would nod, occasionally at people he knew, which were many. Everyone wanted to be seen to know him, reflecting in his notoriety.

'Isn't that Terry Banner?' asked Paul, butterflies starting in his stomach.

Stark was ready with the reply. 'It sure is. I'm surprised to see him in here, the last intelligence we had on him said he was down the smoke. Maybe he prefers being a big fish in a little pond.'

Pete Glover turned round to see who they were talking about and promptly trod on Banner's soft grey shoes. The hard nut's smiling face turned to anger and his eyes flashed wide.

'What the fuck do you think you're doing?' he barked at Pete, who had turned white. The noise of the crowd dimmed and all eyes fell upon him. Banners fist clenched, but relaxed when he saw Stark.

'Everything all right, Terry?' said the DI, a slight challenge in the question, his chin raised in defiance.

The cogs in Banner's brain were whirring. This would go one of two ways. His voice was gruff. 'Evening, Dave. Everything is just fine. It's all good.' He raised his glass as a sort of salute and turned away continuing over to a group of youths near the slot machine.

On hearing the reluctant greeting, something that had been niggling him was resolved; a memory came searing through from Stark's subconscious: the voice on the telephone in Bernie Squires' office!

*

Nobby's red BMW pulled into the kerb adjacent to Sunderland Court; he was five minutes late. Nobby peered through his car window into the darkness and studied the spooky looking house, built in Victorian times. It was three storeys high, with a dirty grey, pebble-dashed façade. The large oak front door was barely visible in the darkness of the shadow cast by the stone archway which surrounded it. Nobby alighted from the car and his heels clicked on the large paving slabs, the metal 'Segs' sometimes known as 'Blakey's' he had hammered into his leather souls, being the cause. The slabbed path had become uneven with the ravages of time. It dissected a garden of overgrown shrubs and trees, and incongruously a plastic gnome holding an electric guitar, and wearing flared trousers which guarded the doorstep. The shadowy surroundings influenced his approach and he tried to soften his step. He was a little tentative as he pushed open the exterior door, which led into a somewhat dingy and dusty entrance hall which was dimly lit. The fusty smell was overridden by the familiar odour of cannabis. A corridor peeled off to the left, revealing four bare wooden doors, all were even numbered; generous wooden stairs faced him. He began to climb, disturbing a ginger tomcat who leapt on to the bannister and eyed the stranger suspiciously. Nobby found himself in a ridiculous stare-off with the domesticated animal, before realising the absurdity of it and concentrating on his tentative climbing of the stairs. The effort added to Nobby's sticky feeling. Sweat had formed on his forehead in the mugginess of the late-summer evening, and he was concerned that the deodorant he had squirted on himself earlier that morning might just be losing the battle. It was a quiet building, too quiet for a student house, and Nobby began to feel strangely uneasy, as he found Number 12 in the far corner of the landing. Perhaps he should have brought Stark, or one of the lads, after all.

He tapped on the blue-painted door, not wanting to disturb the quietness of the sleepy building. There was no reply. He knocked again, only harder, straining to hear any noises from behind the door. There were none. The silence was becoming unbearable. He checked his watch: surely, she would wait five minutes or so? His heart began to beat faster; he was becoming slightly concerned. He banged on the door a third time with the side of his powerful fist. Still nothing. He tried the door handle: it was locked, a Yale lock. He placed his ear to the door: still nothing. He banged again: quiet.

He had a choice: either he walked away, or he put the door in. The simpler option of knocking on a neighbour's door, happened to escape the limits of his often binary approach to problems. He shouted 'Sally?' loudly, his voice reverberating around the rafters in the eerie silence.

He thought aloud. 'She knew I was coming, oh fuck it!' He stepped back three yards to get a good kick at it, leaning his large frame back to gather momentum for the kick, his right boot raised. It was at this point that the door opened. Nobby became unbalanced as he stopped his kick in its infancy and he stumbled to the right, grabbing the bannister of the landing with both hands. His Blakey's scored the wooden floor and lost their purchase, throwing his legs out from underneath him.

Sally's happy face suddenly became troubled at the weird and comical image of a dishevelled Nobby Clarke, clinging to the bannister and on his backside, tie askew. 'You're not drunk, are you?' she asked, removing her stereo earphones on her portable Walkman, and pressing the 'stop' button.

Nobby was embarrassed. 'No, no...sorry...er, how are you? I've been knocking ages.'

'Sorry, I had my ear-phones on. Erm, do you want a hand up?'

Nobby pulled himself up and straightened his tie, regaining his composure, but not quite fully his dignity.

Sally was wearing tight-fitting jeans and a loose white T-shirt; her young breasts free and moving independently, without the support of a bra, but with the full support of Nobby Clarke. Her jet-black hair shone in the new brightness emanating from her room.

'You've been knocking ages?' She giggled. 'I never thought – sorry.' She threw her ear-phones on to the floor just inside the doorway of her flat and continued with the explanation: 'It's old grumpy next door. She's about ninety, so I have to resort to those…she goes to bed about nine-o'clock.'

'I thought it was all students in the house,' Nobby said.

'Mostly students. Come in.' she beckoned.

Nobby stepped into the flat at Sally's invitation. The open-plan kitchenette was to his right, its lino floor giving way to allow an old carpet to lead into the living area. There was a large, soft brown settee and two armchairs, both of which looked as though they were straight out of an old people's home, with high backs and wooden armrests. A rectangular glass coffee-table, dead centre, strained under the weight of numerous books and some fashion magazines. Black-and-white framed pictures of moody coastal scenes adorned the white woodchip wallpaper. The flat was a mixture of furnishings owned by the previous, now deceased old lady, and the frills of Sally's somewhat naïve attempts at personalisation.

Nobby feeling slightly awkward, stood on the lino as Sally closed the door behind him. She asked, 'What do I call you? Sergeant, Mr Clarke or what?'

'Everybody calls me Nobby.'

She giggled. 'OK. I'd better not ask why.' The two laughed nervously. Nobby decided not to explain that it was an old tradition to call somebody named Clarke – Nobby. He left her supposition uncorrected.

'Something smells nice. What is it, did you say, Chicken Tikka?'

Sally nodded, her hands behind her back, swinging her torso with her pert breasts trying to keep up.

'I hope you like it?' She smiled provocatively.

Nobby was hypnotised. 'I love it.'

They sat down on the chairs, and made small-talk for around half an hour, before Sally served up the meal. She apologised for their having to eat it off a tray. Nobby shook his head and waved a dismissive hand. 'Don't be silly – it's the only way to eat.' He was glad he hadn't brought Stark after all.

At the end of the meal they sipped at their coffee. The conversation had relaxed, and Nobby asked her about her uncle Bernie, the bookmaker.

'You don't think I like the fat arsehole, do you?'

Nobby shrugged his shoulders and laughed. 'Say what you think, Sally, don't hold back.'

'I know what he is, you know. I won't have anything to do with his underhand, dodgy dealings. I only work there for the money. He pays well for people who work hard, don't ask questions and keeps their mouth shut.'

'And look gorgeous to attract the punters.' Nobby added.

Sally blushed slightly. 'I don't know about that. Maybe.'

'And that's what you do is it?' Nobby asked clumsily.

'What?' Sally looked confused.

'Don't ask questions, and keep your mouth shut?'

'I suppose it is, yes.' There was a momentary pause. Sally swirled the dregs of her coffee around the base of the plain white mug.

'Is something the matter, Sally?'

'It's probably nothing, I'm being silly, and I wouldn't want to accuse anybody, I mean, much as I dislike the man, he is my uncle,' Sally shared her thoughts quietly, her voice soft and uncertain.

Nobby's experience had taught him that often the best way to get information was not to ask for it. 'Listen, Sally, you don't have to tell me anything, you know. I've come around as your guest...'

Sally plucked up the necessary courage. 'No, I will tell you, Nobby – you seem a genuine person, trustworthy and genuine.' He smiled but didn't interrupt. She stared at the coffee mug. 'You see, Faye and Uncle Bernie had a love-hate relationship. He more or less ignored me, but he was all over Faye. He fancied her something rotten, randy old bugger. Obviously, she didn't fancy him.'

'Hence the groping sessions I've heard about?' Nobby took a punt.

'You've got it. How did you know that?'

'I am a Detective.'

'I'm impressed. She suffered the groping, but I walked in on them once, in his office. Faye was in the corner of the room and Uncle Bernie stood in front of her with his arm resting on the wall, as if blocking her path, you know?' Nobby nodded. 'They looked startled as I came in. I apologised and left, but not before noticing the fear in her eyes. She was scared, Nobby. Really scared, terrified in fact. When I got outside, I listened at the door. I was worried for her. I could hardly hear anything, but I could tell that Uncle Bernie was angry, like I had never heard before.'

'What was he saying?'

'I couldn't hear what was being said, it was the tone of the voice. He sounded full of hate, full of anger.'

'When was this?' Nobby asked.

'Only about a week ago. We'd just closed, I think it was a week last Thursday.'

Nobby persisted. 'Did you hear anything at all of the conversation, even if it was just one word?'

Sally shook her head. 'Sorry, I couldn't hear what was actually being said. That's all I can tell, you.'

Nobby smiled. 'That's interesting, obviously, Sally; thanks for mentioning it.'

They chatted for another hour at least. Nobby felt sorry for Sally; she was a lonely kid, and as he went to the door, she grabbed his arm. She fell into his strong arms. 'You don't have to go, you know.' She stroked at his sharp stubble chin and moved her hand down his chest and down to his manhood. He didn't stop her. She had only been with young lads and had not been with a mature man, and she gasped as she felt the thickness and the length of his cock and she moved her hand slowly up and down it. It began to swell and pulse, surprising her even more and she went to kiss him.

Nobby sighed. 'Shit.' he thought. He stopped her by placing his hand on her neck. Her pants were wet as she yearned for him, and her head grew limp yielding to his strong hold on her.

'I'm sorry, Sally I can't. You might be a witness in a bloody murder case. Trust me I want to.'

She took hold of his strong, hairy forearm and he loosened his grip. She leaned upwards and kissed him, her tongue filling his mouth as she hungrily devoured him. He kissed her back, just as passionately.

9

'If called by a panther, don't anther.'
Ogden Nash (1902 – 1971)

Carol turned over, the quilt her cocoon of warmth. She reached for her husband across the double bed: he was gone. He stood at the bedroom door, sounding like a music-hall ventriloquist, as he tried, in vain, to make her understand him from behind the froth that he'd created as he brushed his teeth.

Carol grunted some fragmented words in a sleepy daze. 'Time? What?'

Stark rinsed his mouth out and teased her. 'Me no sleep. Carol sleep!' He kissed her. 'Good morning, darling.'

'Bog off. I mean good morning darling.' They embraced but Carol had no strength in her arms, and she flopped them around his back.

'Get back to sleep, Carol. Don't get up.' Dave caressed her pixie-like short hair.

Carol forced herself onto her elbow and rubbed her face with her hand. 'It's fine. It's the only chance I get to see you. What were you saying when you were brushing your teeth?' She asked, wearily. Dave sat next to her on the bed, her prostate figure looking tiny amidst the bedraggled quilt and sheet.

'I was saying, don't get up, it's too early.'

She slapped his back. 'You woke me up, to tell me not to get up! Really?'

Stark leant down and kissed her again, the smell of sleep emanating from her. She had yet to open her eyes. 'I'll come back to bed in a bit.' She muttered. Hugging her pillow again. She then began kicking out at the quilt and somehow, with the strength of Hercules, forced herself to sit up on the edge of the bed, eyes still closed. 'Most normal people are in bed at this time.'

'Who wants to be normal?' Stark replied, despite knowing that he certainly did.

'I do.' Carol mused. 'I'll go and put your breakfast on.'

Carol put her dressing gown on and staggered downstairs, eyes still mostly closed, knocking into doorframes, her head lolling and her arms flapping around limply.

Dave stepped into the shower cubicle and relaxed as the powerful jets of water cascaded on to his muscular, but aching body. 'This life cannot be good for you.' He thought. His head had a crevice of pain traversing the length of his skull, brought on by his tiredness. This type of headache was too frequent a visitor to the Stark skull. He often struggled to sleep very well when he had a big case on. It went with the territory.

Stark was reticent to get out of the shower; the heat was wonderful. He washed his nether-regions thoroughly, getting a good foam up. He thought about it but couldn't be bothered. He forced himself to turn off the shower, dried himself, and put on his towelling robe. He tried to go downstairs quietly so that he did not wake his children, but there was always that fourth stair that creaked. He hurried past it and down into the hall and then the living room and collapsed on the big chair. He pressed the button that created images of annoying people talking heatedly at stupid o'clock in the morning. He turned the sound down and blew out a sigh. The noise from the television could not be heard upstairs, where his daughter Laura continued the dreams that her parents wouldn't let her watch if they were a movie.

Carol walked in with a plate and a mug of tea. 'I've done you some bacon sarnies.'

'My hero.' He said.

'Heroine.' She corrected.

'No thanks, I'll just have the sarnies.'

It was quick for that time of the morning. He ate the sandwiches heartily, pausing only to thank Carol for the effort she had put in to making them, he was grateful. Dave stared vacantly at the television, but the images he saw were those created in his own mind. He pondered the forthcoming day's events. He knew that Winston Kelly had access to firearms; in fact, word had it that he might have one in his flat. Unfortunately, rumour alone didn't qualify one to draw on the glorious resource of the armed-response teams to execute the warrant. The best he could do was arrange for an armed-response traffic car to be 'in the area' at the time of the raid and take a dog-handler. It was a strange bureaucratic policy that the office Walla's thought to be justifiable in case of accidental discharges and the subsequent enquiry that would follow. Allowing armed police in a confined space was a recipe for disaster, when based merely on rumour alone. Quite what they thought the police were to do if the criminal intentionally discharged one, remained a mystery. One of these days, the rumours were going to be justified; and another needless police widow would receive the knock on the door.

'Penny for them.' Carol said.

'Sorry?'

'Penny for your thoughts.' Carol smiled.

Stark mirrored the smile. 'Oh, just enjoying my sandwich. My brain is still struggling to piece together a whole thought,' he lied.

'Have you got a shirt ironed?' Carol asked hopefully.

Stark glanced at the clock on the brick fireplace. 'I don't know, have I? I hope so, Carol.'

Carol disappeared but returned with a clean but un-ironed white shirt. Stark sighed. 'Bloody hell, Carol, I've got to be going in ten minutes.'

Carol remained unflustered. 'It won't take a minute.' She scurried to the ironing board.

Dave could feel himself becoming agitated as the 'minute'

turned into five. Carol followed him upstairs and lay on the bed. She watched him dress. He was a big man and he had kept his strong muscular body despite approaching middle-age.

'What are you doing today, Dave?' Carol asked.

'We're going to try to nick some scrote and see if he would be kind enough to have a little chat with us.' He spared his wife the less glamorous aspects of the proposition.

'I thought I might take the kids to Wollaton Hall, if Laura hasn't planned on seeing that boyfriend of hers. Have you had that talk with her about going on the pill, yet?' Carol asked.

'Isn't that your territory?' Stark said, as he buttoned up his newly ironed, and still warm, white shirt, whilst looking in the full-length mirror.

Carol threw a pillow at him playfully. 'You said you would do it!'

'Was I drunk?' He smiled at himself in the mirror.

'She's fifteen, think about what you were doing at that age?' she asked.

Stark threw the pillow back. 'I daren't think about it – it frightens me too much. I will have a word with her when I get time, which is precisely what I don't have right now. Anyway, there is only a three-minute window in any one day when she is either not in bed or talking on the phone to you-know-who.'

'We have to face facts, Dave, that's all I am saying, and we don't want a pregnant fifteen-year-old on our hands.' She fiddled with the cord of her dressing gown. 'What time will you be back today?'

'I don't know, late, probably.'

She sighed. Dave kissed her, as she got off the bed to bid her farewell. He held her tightly in his arms as they embraced, squeezing hard, closing his eyes and caressing her hair. The danger of the day ahead flashed across his mind. He had a bad feeling about it for some reason. Just the usual nerves with such an operation, probably. He spoke softly to her. 'I love you, darling. You know that, don't you?'

Carol was oblivious to his private fears. 'Of course, I do.

What's the matter with you?'

'Nothing, love. Can't a man tell his wife how much he loves her?' Dave took a deep breath and released his grip. 'Listen, I'll try to be home as soon as I can. Enjoy Wollaton Hall if you go.' He walked down the stairs to the door.

'Give the kids a kiss for me.' He kissed her again briefly and he was gone. Carol spoke. 'See you...' the door slamming shut behind him. '...later'.

*

Time was running out for Winston Kelly. Those officers present in the briefing room were after him, and they were determined to get him. Stark had explained the plan of attack. He and Nobby would go to the front door accompanied by a dogman, Steph, and two SOU men with a sledgehammer and crowbar to affect a forced entry, if required. There were no back doors in the flat complex and at six stories up, the windows seemed less of an attractive option. They didn't know how many men would be inside the flat; there could be just Kelly, or there could be half a dozen – there was no way of knowing. Not if they wanted to do the warrant that morning, anyway. The armed response traffic car was only allowed to tour the area, low-key. They would use a separate radio channel to ensure that there would be no routine transmissions at the crucial time of the mini operation. Everybody was to bring their truncheons and handcuffs. Many CID officers didn't bother with their handcuffs, some hung them off the back of their trouser belt, in the small of the back, not visible under their suit jacket. It helped with the slow dances at Ritzy's Night Club, that's for sure. No-one in CID ever had a truncheon with them; where do you put it when you wear a suit? It is a fourteen inch piece of wood, for heaven's sake. If it was thought there was going to be some aggro at a specific job, some would insert their wooden 'peg' up their suit jacket sleeve, and hold it in place with the palm of their hand, making it pretty invisible to passers-by and anyone silly enough to have a go. If there were any females on the premises, they were Steph's business, Stark ordered. Once captured, Kelly would be handcuffed and searched immediately. SOU would remain behind whilst they searched the flat; any outhouses allocated to the flat and his car.

Stark gave them a potted history of Kelly and his capabilities, and warned them about his extremely violent nature. The interminable rumours that circulated about his behaviour indicated that he had 'disposed' of a 'Yardie', a fellow West Indian gang-member, in Birmingham three years ago. Some fall-out about prostitutes, apparently, and his jurisdiction, which was being encroached upon. These rule-breakers didn't like it when their rules were broken. The hope was that after being up most of the night, doing his nefarious activities, Kelly, would be too disorientated to put up much of a fight before the handcuffs were on him.

Stark was a little apprehensive about what might lie ahead of them, as always, but in truth he would sooner face a hardened criminal than speak to a room full of people. To Stark the worst bit of the day was over by completing the briefing! He breathed a sigh of relief.

'Right,' said Stark, 'let's go. Pull into position out of sight first, then I'll give you the word to strike over the radio.'

*

The small bedroom was dirty. It was furnished by a solitary item: a bed. No wardrobes, no drawers or dressing tables, no pictures on the walls, just a bed. The bed was surrounded by a myriad of clothes, strewn around by their unfastidious owners. The ashtray on the floor at the side of the bed was overflowing with roll-ups and reefers. The sweet, pungent smell of marijuana hung in the air competing with the stench of sweat and body odour.

The quilt had been thrown off as the two people became

active on the sheets, which were covered in dry semen stains. Kelly made the skinny young peroxide blonde squeal as he entered her from behind, as she positioned herself on all fours on the bed. She wasn't ready, but he would take her whenever the mood suited, and it did frequently. He grabbed at her hair and yanked her head back as he tried to get himself fully inside her, using his other hand to assist his efforts. She let out a muffled squeal. She had been hoping that the session they had in the night had satisfied him; but no, he wanted more. He thrusted into her. She tried to stifle the whimpering which the pain at her hair-roots and vagina were forcing out of her, as she knew this would make him go harder. She clawed at the sheets, his Rastafarian dreadlocks tickled the side of her face whenever he lowered his head to bite at her neck, grunting and salivating as he did. He was getting some momentum going and he pummelled into her with great force and speed which caused a dull pain in her stomach. She tried to wrest free his grasp from her hair, but she didn't dare protest to the eyes that stared at her so wildly. He was strong and he liked hurting people. She was only young and confused this type of casual sex with love. It wasn't.

The pain grew as the relentless onslaught continued, and she yelped at each thrust. Her strength fading, she grew courageous, spurred on by the pain. 'Stop! Stop! Please!' she begged, her speech distorted by the pounding of bone into bone, jarring her body. She was wasting her time and he continued, until her pleading turned into sobs. The crying seemed to stimulate Kelly, and the rush of orgasm forced his long length of penis into her, nearly up to the hilt. The arms that had been supporting her buckled and the girl collapsed forward, her face crashed into the headboard with Kelly falling onto the bed with her, staying connected, his throbbing penis emptying into her. Her head was now between mattress and headboard as she felt her own orgasm gush from her, the waves and contractions, sucking the final juices from his thick member. Kelly had finished. He withdrew the now softer wet cock slowly from her and she gasped with the release. It slapped against his thigh and as he lay on her, she felt it resting, reaching nearly halfway down her skinny thigh. The girl was in a sexual whirlwind, confused about her emotions. 'That fucking, cock!' she panted to no-one. 'My God!' They lay together for a while, their gasping and panting slowly subsiding. Having arranged themselves more comfortably. Kelly reached for a cigarette.

Kelly claimed to be a Rastafarian. True Rastafarians are mellow, peace-loving people, often zoned out on marijuana, of course, but nothing to be feared. Kelly was a violent, evil, obnoxious criminal. He ran prostitutes and dealt in drugs; he was interested only in money and power and emptying himself into the nearest woman when the mood took him. He was a big man, six foot three inches tall and powerfully built. He tied his long dreadlocks back over his shoulders and strode around the Hyson Green area of Nottingham as if he owned it. He was a bully; he gesticulated aggressively and spoke in a loud, challenging voice. If it suited him, he could use a normal, reasonably educated voice; but to keep his street credibility on a high, a strong patois, such as many young Rastafarians speak, was his usual tongue.

Despite his aggressive persona, Kelly was not an unintelligent person, and it was his clever manipulation of people that had gained him false standing among his 'brothers' in the community. He had been arrested by the 'Babylon' several times and charged with only one offence on each occasion. Kelly didn't talk to 'filth'. Because of course, the police were filth weren't they, not him? He claimed to be oppressed by authority, but he wasn't a tenth as oppressed as the poor young girls he had taken advantage of, the girls who in their innocence became enslaved heroin addicts by the ingenuity of his sheer evil cunning. Once he had put the girls on the street as prostitutes, he would ensure that he had complete control over them. If there was a hint or a suggestion that they had withheld money for food or cigarettes, or for their children, or if they tried to return from whence, they came, he was not averse to punishing them. Usually forcing them to sit naked in a bath of bleach, until their private parts became swollen and sore, causing agonising pain.

Kelly abused women's vulnerability; he abused the children he had spawned around the place; he was all powerful. That was about to change. It was soon to be his turn to be bullied, his turn to know what fear is; his turn to do what he was told.

*

Stark had seen Kelly's BMW car parked in its usual place in the street, outside the entrance to the block of flats. It may as well have a 'reserved' sign up, as no-one in their right mind ever parked in it. The three cars and a transit van pulled slowly into the kerb, out of sight of Winston Kelly's flat on the other side of the block.

Stark spoke into his radio: 'Is everybody fully clear about their jobs? If not speak now.' There was a silence, followed by his command: *'Strike! Strike! Strike!'*

The vehicles sped around the corner and screeched to a halt. Their occupants jumped out and raced to their positions. The adrenalin was pumping, hearts were beating fast and senses strained to the limit. Every second was a second for Kelly to dispose of evidence.

Stark had felt the burn on stairway four, when he knew there were two more to go, but on he raced to the sixth floor. Stark arrived, somewhat out of breath, at the dirty grey door and hammered on it. *'Police – open up!'* He could only guess at the pandemonium inside. He hammered on the door a second time. *'Open up! Police!'* Neighbouring dogs began to bark, and curtains twitched; the police dog, Goliath, joined in the ca-nine chorus as he strained at his leash, his large fangs exposed and dripping saliva.

Stark stepped aside. 'Right, I'm not waiting all bleeding morning – hit it!'

It took one well-practised blow from the sledgehammer by the burly SOU officer to split the door almost in two, as it crashed off its hinges. Stark burst in first, followed by the rest.

'Police!' Stark shouted as they quickly checked the rooms, which were empty until he and Nobby together attempted to open the door in front of them. It moved a couple of inches only, then slammed shut again. Obviously, the occupant did not want to let the nice policemen in.

Stark shouted through the wooden door, now a barrier: *'Don't be a prat. Don't make it worse than it has to be, Winston!'* The attempted platitude was ignored.

Nobby was on an adrenalin high. He succinctly explained the position to the occupant. *'Move out the way of the door, Kelly, or the sledgehammer's going to smash it down and you with the fucker!'* The aggressive tone set the police dog off and it began barking and snarling ferociously. Nobby had a very persuasive way with words, and his impassioned plea obviously had a good effect: the door opened. The group burst in.

The skinny white tart lay curled up on the bed, the quilt pulled over her, only partly concealing her naked body. Kelly stood in the far corner of the room in his baggy brown underpants. The knife he was holding was a large one – the blade itself was five inches long, and all eyes focussed on it.

Stark spoke, an immediate conciliatory tone in his panting voice, restraining the adrenalin coursing through his veins. 'Woah, hold, on, Winston, drop the knife, pal!'

'Fuck you, Babylon!'

The dog man had subconsciously unclipped the lead and held the heaving mound of teeth and muscle back by the collar. It was taking a great deal of strength to do so; it was in a frenzy of barking and snapping at the obvious aggressor in the room; W. Kelly, esquire. Kelly did not drop the knife; he began walking towards the group with his arms outstretched, trying to angle for the door. He waved the knife from left to right, his feet catching in the filthy clothes discarded on the floor. He was smiling maniacally, and his eyes were wide and desperate.

On police open days the public applauds with great enthusiasm the way in which police dogs majestically attach themselves to the outstretched padded arm of the fleeing 'villain'. That is not what always happens in real life. The police dog often bites the first thing it focuses on as soon as it is released by the handler. Police dogs can be evil. Goliath was the evillest. The first thing Goliath focussed on as he was released was the contents of Kelly's underpants.

Even Nobby winced. The knife went flying, and there was an indescribable scream of pain from Kelly. The girl's hand went to her mouth and her eyes widened. Kelly's eyes widened too.

The girl saw Kelly in a different light as all his bluster was stripped bare, and he cried and whimpered like a small child, pleading for mercy, as Goliath began to twist like a crocodile grabbing a bison at the lake side.

The dog-handler bellowed: *'Leave!'* Goliath's ears went down; he released his grip and returned to his handler with his head down and the whites of his eyes displayed sheepishly as he glanced up at his master. Kelly rolled on the floor screaming and crying, clutching between his legs.

Nobby thought he could see blood. He patted the dog: 'Good boy.'

Kelly was handcuffed. He had been lucky. Later that day the police surgeon would note bruising to the testicles and blood emanating from small cuts on his lower abdomen, just above the pubis.

SOU stayed at the flat and searched it. They seized two Bowie knives; one flick knife: a woolly red, yellow and green 'Rasta' hat; four reefers; and some tiny plastic transparent 'dealer bags', some of which contained a vegetable matter that was undoubtedly cannabis.

Stephanie ascertained that the girl was only fifteen years old and had been reported missing from one of the local children's homes. She was returned, quite the worse for wear, and not on the pill. Stark thought about his daughter, Laura.

The girl went missing from the children's home again later

that night.

*

Carol Stark lay on the settee, still in her dressing gown, telephone in hand. The kids were still in bed. She would speak with her friend and confidant most days. It 'kept her sane'. Her friend, Sandra, was in a similar position to her, with her husband being a long-distance lorry driver, and so not at home as much as she would like. You could argue that it was worse for Sandra, as at least David came home every night for a few hours. His absence was only temporary, in cases of great importance. Sandra's husband was often away three or four nights in a row.

Carol had prepared herself prior to making the call. She had a mug of tea and two digestive biscuits which she would dunk in her tea during those longer exchanges when Sandra went into a diatribe about how badly the world was treating her.

'I haven't seen him for days. Not properly anyway.' Carol said.

'What is he doing?' Sandra queried.

'That murder case, have you seen it on the news?'

'Which one. The family one? The one in the house up on Maple Close? Do you mean that one?' Sandra asked.

'That's the one, but it makes me laugh, he reckons he's really busy, and he probably is, but he doesn't give a thought to what I have to do all day.'

Sandra agreed. 'None of them do, Carol, they haven't a clue.'

Carol continued. 'It's not as if they have caught anyone, and anyway he's supposed to be the boss, so you are not telling me that he couldn't come home earlier, at least one of the nights.'

'It makes you wonder, doesn't it? I mean, if they actually want to be at home or if they are just in the boozer with their mates, half the time.' Sandra offered.

'That's the other thing, when Dave gets into bed, I can smell booze on him. It's bloody awful. He stinks. It goes to show that he must have some time to spare, so why not come home to his family?' Carol's lips grew thin as they pursed together, and she shook her head.

Sandra sighed. 'I don't know, Carol, my Barry came in the other night. He sat his fat arse in his chair filling his face with a pizza watching telly and never said a bleeding word. Never asked how my day had been? No, because he is the only one that does anything, obviously.'

'I know.' Carol said, dunking her biscuit.

'He never thinks that perhaps someone has to run the home, whilst he's off gallivanting around, someone has to do the cooking and cleaning. It doesn't clean itself does it?'

Carol swallowed a mouthful of biscuit. 'I know. They're selfish, Sandra, that's their trouble, and then they expect you to wait on them hand and foot when they get in. Oh, his Lordship has arrived, let's drop everything and tend to their every need.'

Sandra laughed. 'They've got it too easy. Does Dave snore?'

Carol agreed. 'They've got it way too easy. No, Dave, doesn't snore, why does your Barry?'

'He snores like a pig. The times I have to elbow him in the night. It's getting beyond a joke, and then he says *he's* tired!'

Carol laughed. 'At least I don't have that with, Dave.'

'Well, think yourself lucky then, Carol. Sometimes I pray that he isn't coming home.' Sandra confessed.

'I know what you mean.' Carol said.

There was a pause. 'What are you up to today, Sandra? Another busy one?' Carol asked her friend.

'Pretty busy, as always, I've put the washing on. I've got an appointment at Shelly's; just a cut and blow dry, and then I said I would meet Joanne at Victoria Centre for a walk round, and a bit of lunch. The washing will be done by the time I get back. Join us if you want.'

Carol thought about it. 'Ah, thanks chic, but I told Dave I would take the kids to Wollaton Park for a couple of hours, later.'

'You work too hard, that's your problem, Carol.'

'I know.' Carol said.

*

Winston Kelly, of course, has asked to see a solicitor; a Mr Bard from Kirkham, Turner and Ross. The better criminals usually asked for him. Stark had initially attempted use the PACE Codes of Practice, to delay Kelly's access to a solicitor, but the station Chief Inspector, Brian Turley had insisted they play safe. They had already executed a warrant at the address, so there was no viable reason to delay legal access to avoid potential destruction of evidence.

Stark entered the interview room with Nobby. Winston Kelly sat next to his solicitor, looking moody. Mr Bard was good at his job. He was a small man with a thin face and wispy moustache; he wore the almost obligatory pin-striped suit and carried a black briefcase that appeared to be a little too heavy for him. Stark and Nobby sat down on the other side of the table, dominating the room. Three suits and a shiny black tracksuit manoeuvred for position in their chairs. Stark turned on the tape and went through the routine.

Stark began the interview. 'Have we met before, Winston?'

Kelly leaned on the desk with his arms folded and stared at Stark unflinchingly, his dreadlocks hanging limply on his shoulders. He did not speak. Stark had encountered this manner with criminals many times before. Stark was certainly not going to be intimidated, nor was he going to go away.

'What were you doing in the early hours of Thursday 16th July? It's only a few days ago, Winston.'

Silence, just staring.

Stark continued. 'I see, it's going to be one of those jobs, is it? Well, we've got plenty of time.' He leaned back in his chair. He went on: 'What were you doing the other night, Winston? You might be an innocent man for all I know. Oh, by the way, I almost forgot, consider yourself under arrest for possession of cannabis with intent to supply, resisting arrest and unlawful sexual intercourse with a girl under the age of sixteen years – in addition to murder, of course.'

Kelly began to shake his head. He tutted and began to sing-cum-chant; 'Babylon is burning... Babylon is burning... Babylon is burning...'

If nothing else it was a reaction. A strange one, but a reaction none-the-less. Stark pondered. He elevated his voice over the chanting. 'Are you a true Rastafarian or just playing at it?'

Kelly stopped his chanting and just said 'Whiteboy!' in an almost indiscernibly heavy patois. He continued his staring.

Stark looked at Nobby who was grinning like a Cheshire cat. 'What did he say, Nobby?'

'Something about Whitby, I think.' Nobby looked at Kelly. 'I've only been once, and it rained. Are you thinking of going there on your holidays, Winston?'

Mr Bard spoke up. 'Officers...'

Stark ignored the lawyer, still looking at Nobby smiling. 'I think he said Whiteboy,' he looked at Kelly, 'which is very observant, Winston, but not particularly relevant. What is relevant is your involvement in the murder of three innocent people, and instead of farting around, trying to be some sort of hard-nut, all you have to do is tell us, give us some proof it wasn't you involved, and we can all go home.'

Mr Bard was in again. 'I think it is your job to find proof, Inspector.'

It was Kelly's turn to grin like a Cheshire cat; continuing his unblinking stare at Stark.

Stark returned the smile and received silence in return. Dave had agreed with Nobby beforehand that he would lead the questioning.

'Were you with Faye Marriott the other night, Winston?'
Silence.

'Of course, you don't need to ask us who Faye is, do you, Winston, because you know her very well, don't you?'
Silence.

'We know everything about you, and your little girls, who

you seem to be able to bully and abuse. That's hard, isn't it, Winston? You are so tough with those little girls, aren't you?' Stark was trying to elicit a response.

Mr Bard spoke. 'Can we keep to the issues at h...?'

'Bumbaclart!' Kelly shouted. Stark was well aware of the Rastafarian derogatory term meaning something you wipe your posterior with. A bit rude.

'So, come on, Winston, I'm all ears, tell me all about your innocence, how it can't be you involved and we'll go out and get the bloke who has done it. Only you can't, can you, Winston? Because you were there, weren't you?'

Silence.

Mr Bard piped up again. 'I'm sure it is apparent even to you, Mr Stark, that my client is taking advantage of his legal right, which he is fully entitled to do, just as you told him at the start of this interview, to say nothing. I can hardly see the point in continuing.'

Stark smiled and acknowledged the solicitor for the first time. 'That is true and whilst your client can take up his right to silence; I also have a right to ask your client questions. I am sorry if this makes you uncomfortable, but ask them, I will, Mr Bard. I will remind you this is a murder enquiry.' He looked into the eyes of Winston Kelly. 'All right, Winston?'

Kelly shrugged out a laugh. 'Checkout da bigshot.'

It's going to be a long day, thought Stark.

*

Charlie Carter watched Ashley Stevens scribbling on a piece of paper at his desk in the CID general office. Steve Aston was in the far corner, wrestling with a huge amount of papers and statements. Ashley's gold bracelet was scratching on the table as he wrote. He had the telephone handset trapped between his ear and his shoulder.

'All right, cheers.' He said, and replaced the telephone. He lit up a Benson and Hedges Gold cigarette, only the best for Ashley. He continued writing onto the piece of paper, recording the information he had just accumulated.

'Interesting.' He mused and began tapping his gold pen loosely onto the desk in between puffs on his tobacco sticks.

Charlie's curiosity got the better of him. 'Who was that, Ash? Something to do with the murder case?'

Steve Aston looked up, but Ashley didn't; he resumed scribbling again, but answered his friend. 'It was the Forensic Science Lab at Huntingdon, giving us an update on their work so far.'

There was silence as he continued writing and smoking. Charlie looked over at Steve who shrugged.

'Well, come on then. What did they say?' Charlie was impatient.

'Yes, come on Ash, let's hear it.' Steve said.

'Hold on. Let me write the bloody thing down, before I forget.'

Charlie laughed. 'Looks like they told you a lot.'

Ash completed his notes with a flourish and an exaggerated final full-stop. 'There, now, Detective Carter and Detective – ish Stevens, what do you want to know?'

'Ooh, naughty. Steve is a Detective, aren't you mate?'

'Trying.' Steve said, embarrassed and colouring up.

'I wanted to know what the lab said, but I think I've lost the will to live, to be honest. What's the news, Ash?' said Charlie.

Ashley swivelled his chair to face his older friend. 'It turns out the plastic shoelace loop. . .'

'The aglet.' Steve interrupted.

'Yes, the aglet. Funny, the scientist called it a shoelace loop, never mind. Anyway, the one found in the garden comes from shoes made by Clarks. It's used only in their grey-coloured ones, and there's eight different styles of shoes that they used the loop on.'

Charlie raised his eyebrows, 'It's a start, I suppose.' He looked thoughtful. 'There's going to be an action to track down all the bloody sales of those shoes, you know that don't you? They will want to know how many were sold in Nottingham and who to, and when, and all that shit.'

Ashley grinned. 'Apparently, there are two hundred and fifty thousand such shoes on the market. The different models have been on sale for six and a bit years.'

'Ah.' Charlie said.

'Oh, dear.' Steve commented.

Ashley continued with the good news. 'Yes. The red fibres are from a crimson-red jumper or cardigan which is approximately eight months old and made of wool and cotton. Possibly made in India.'

'Brilliant. What would we do without them?' Charlie asked sarcastically, his momentary optimism dissipating. 'This case is going to be a runner, I'm telling you.'

Ashley was philosophical. 'Come on, be fair. It's not one piece that completes the jigsaw, it's the whole lot put together.'

'Thank you, Sherlock, for those pearls of wisdom.' Charlie said.

'How are you getting on with your actions, Steve?' Ash asked.

'Just checking through all the witness statements, it's an action that HOLMES has spat out.'

'And?' Charlie asked.

'They seem sound enough, Ernie Gray had told us what he thought was the truth.'

'What, that his missus had been shagging someone from the bloody Church.'

Steve shook his head. 'No, well Violet told us that, but you know what I mean. He did see someone running, it was just Colin Markwell running with his dick in his hand.'

Ashley blew smoke out his mouth as he laughed. 'What about Paul Fisher's old, mate, that ex-cop? Pete is it?'

'Pete Glover.' Steve corrected him. 'He's given a good account, his story checks out, apparently Paul Fisher checked out the garage and he did buy a gallon of petrol as he said, so that is legit.' Steve dropped a couple of papers onto the floor and stooped to gather them up. Then there is Norman the window-cleaner, he rang the police in the first place. He had collected his money off his customers, both before, and after finding the bodies, and he was hardly dripping with blood, so there is nothing that stands out as odd in all that. What do you think, Charlie?'

Charlie nodded his head. 'Sounds about right.'

'Ash?' Steve asked.

'Yep, seems fine to me, Steve.'

Steve smiled. 'That's great, I don't want anything to come back and haunt me, not on my first murder case.'

*

Stark had never agreed with the ethic employed by some detectives, that if a suspect remains silent, all you can do is ask him the relevant questions, return him to his cell, and try to prove it some other way. They were already trying to prove it some other way, in any case. He felt that it was not only defeatist, but it was also the easy way-out. Anyway, fuck him! He would talk to Kelly and he would ask him questions; he didn't need a reply to motivate him, because he knew that no matter what antics Kelly did, whatever bravado he showed, he couldn't help but listen. In fact he wanted to listen. He was desperate to listen. Hanging on Stark's every bloody word. Kelly wanted to know what the police had to say. What evidence had they got? Each question would have an impact on him regardless of what he did. Kelly couldn't escape and, if nothing else, it put him under that bit more pressure – which, despite his dramatics, he was undoubtedly under. Stranger things had happened, he might give up and admit it, or have an outburst, or make some mistake, or contact someone to make a move on his behalf, which would reveal his guilt.

'How long have you known Faye Marriott?' Stark asked.

Silence.

'Months, years, or what?'

Silence.

'Have you had sex with her?'

Silence.

The pause after each question would be elongated, maybe five seconds of silence, but no longer. Stark knew that after that amount of time, human nature, even if the subject is aware of what is happening, dictates an overwhelming sub-conscious urge to say something, especially if the question is directed at them personally. The slow questioning and wait after each question, allowed the recipient to answer the ques-tion, albeit in their minds, which was nigh on impossible to avoid doing. Stark knew that Kelly was under pressure, be-cause a couple of seconds after each question he would shift his position in his seat. It's hard to keep totally silent, when it's your turn 'in the barrel'.

'You have been seen with her at Ritzy's, Winston. Do you go there regularly with her?'

Silence.

'Remember we are asking questions, many of which we al-ready know the answers to, Winston.'

Silence.

'What's the problem? Why wouldn't you tell us all about it, if you had nothing to hide? Why, Winston? It's because you have something to hide isn't it? Isn't it?'

Silence.

Kelly glanced at the tape machine. Stark knew he was look-ing for the time indicator to see how much longer this might go on for.

'For example, we know about you hitting her in the pub last week.'

Kelly began rocking his upper body backwards and forwards.

'Don't you like the tape recorder, Winston? Don't you like its honesty? Are you scared? Are you frightened?'

Kelly sneered at Stark and gave him a mock smile and began drumming the table with the flats of his hands. Another re-action; the need for the body to displace stress.

'What are you scared of, Winston?'

Kelly continued his drumming on the table and resumed his chant. 'Babylon is burning... Babylon is burning... Babylon is burning.'

Stark continued, his voice raised. 'I'm not asking for an admission, Winston, just where you were, stuff like that. It's dead easy.'

Mr Bard butted in, much to Stark's annoyance. 'My client doesn't want to tell you, Mr Stark.'

Stark remained emotionless and ignored the solicitor, leaning forward on the table, closer to Kelly's face. 'Yes, you do, Winston. You don't want to be in the frame for Murder if you haven't done it, now do you?'

Silence.

Kelly looked down at his shiny tracksuit trousers and brushed some imaginary dust off them; the commonest stress displacement of all. He was feeling the pressure all right.

It was getting on towards lunchtime and Stark knew only too well that the law dictated that Mr Kelly must have his refreshment at the appropriate hour. He decided that at the end of the tape he would adjourn proceedings. In truth it was going pretty much as he had expected it would.

'You were trying to get her on the game, Winston. She didn't want to know, so you punished her, Winston, but you went too far, didn't you? You killed her, didn't you?'

Silence.

'But, unfortunately, Mummy and Daddy came home early and caught you, didn't they?'

Silence.

'So you killed them, didn't you, Winston?'

Kelly shook his head and looked down at the desk in front of him.

Stark continued. 'You've even been seen running away from the scene, Winston. You see, it's got to be you. Of course, it is. You were the last person to be identified as being with her. The next time she was seen she was lying dead. Killed in cold blood. Killed in cold blood by you, Winston Kelly!'

Silence.

The interview went on along much the same lines until the end of the tape.

'Do you wish to clarify anything you have said, or do you wish to add anything?' Stark was laughingly compelled to ask, even though Kelly had said nothing at all.

Still silence.

The time is now 12.40 p.m. and we'll stop the tape.' Stark pressed the button and the whirring tapes clunked to a stop. He opened the tape drawers on the machine and removed the tapes.

Kelly looked at Stark with pleading eyes. 'It ain't me, Babylon.'

10

'All truths are half-truths'
Alfred North Whitehead. (1861 -1947)

Stark and Nobby sat at the table in the station kitchen, discussing what the hell to do with Winston 'bloody' Kelly. Nobby tucked into his fish, chips and mushy peas. He didn't refrain from talking simply because his mouth was full. 'I tell you what I think, his big black arse wants kicking all around the station, the leery bastard.'

Stark nodded. 'I couldn't agree more, but that isn't going to help us prove murder is it?'

'It might.' Nobby offered.

Stark grinned. They discussed the options open to them.

The murder evidence was pretty non-existence, certainly somewhat thin: yes, he was violent, and used women, and was violent to women, even violent towards Faye, and importantly had threatened to kill her.

He had supposedly murdered before, and yes, he was seen with Faye at the club on the night in question. It was all of great interest. He was the number one suspect, of that there was no doubt. But ... there was no forensic, nothing to put him at the scene. It just wasn't enough. It was not 'beyond reasonable doubt'. They knew it, Mr Bard knew it, and Kelly knew it.

Stark decided that if the stalemate continued, they would charge him with unlawful sexual intercourse, resisting arrest, and possession of cannabis, and apply to the Magistrates Court for him to be detained in police custody for a further three days, or to be remanded in prison. They would then seek fur-

ther evidence and apply for three days interviewing at a police station at a subsequent remand hearing, when they had
more evidence to put to him. He would have to stay in the cell
block here, until the next remand hearing. The benefit of that
being that while he was locked-up here, he could not warn off
potential witnesses or informants. It was a potential opportunity to find the missing piece. Stark wanted to maximise
this opportunity and get back to some old-fashioned policing.
Perhaps it was time to knock peoples' heads together, in a
metaphorical sense. He would order his men to go out on the
streets and get some evidence on Kelly. People might be a bit
more willing to talk if they knew he was locked up. It was time
to get his detectives out on the streets to shake the bag and see
what fell out.

*

The woman on the street corner wore a string top, to display
her tattoos on her forearms, and an artistic, but common,
swallow flitting across her exposed shoulder blades. At thirty-
two years old, she knew the ropes. She had remained rather
trim through the exercise that her employment gave her. Her
bleached blonde hair was offset by heavy mascara, recklessly
smeared around her eyes. She didn't like working in the afternoon, but times had been hard. Kelly hadn't had sex with her
for a couple of weeks and she felt that she was falling out of
favour. She wanted to impress him with a higher income this
week and so avoid the beating that she felt was only a wrong
word away.

She was growing disgruntled, business had been slow; all her
regular punters were obviously night crawlers. She noticed a
blue Vauxhall Senator drive slowly past her; she wasn't sure
if he was interested or just a 'gawker'. Usually she could tell
straight away. She smiled at the driver anyway, just in case,
he seemed a little tense. Maybe a first timer? Things were
looking up. Maureen had her usual working clothes on. Tight-

fitting top, no bra, and a black PVC mini-skirt which was so short you could see what she'd had for dinner. She was not an unattractive woman, but her attempts to look more so had spoiled the original specimen, and she was beginning to look old beyond her years.

The Vauxhall Senator reappeared and drew up alongside where Maureen stood. The man looked apprehensive and offered a nervous smile. He was middle-aged, balding, and shaking like a shitting dog. Maureen confirmed that she was doing 'business' and informed the prospective purchaser of the rates: fifteen pounds for straight sex, twenty pounds for nude sex, and anything – and she meant anything- was negotiable for the right price. The man nodded and opened his passenger door to allow the tart access. Maureen made small talk with the punter as she directed him to her flat. His eyes kept flicking to his rear-view mirror; Maureen reassured him in her broad Geordie accent: 'Don't worry, pet, I've not seen no vice squad all day.'

The man glanced down at Maureen's firm, tanned thighs, the tops of which were exposed above her stockings as her mini-skirt rode up towards her crotch. He was beginning to enjoy his little adventure. Maureen rubbed his inner thigh and pointed out the 'maisonette' at the end of the block in front of them.

Maureen noticed the net curtains twitching at two of the adjacent flats. The women in both flats either side, had complained to the council about her on a couple of occasions, but she was fucking both their husbands at twenty quid a time, so hey, who's the fool?

The punter went to open his car door. 'Hang on.' She took hold of his arm. 'Money first, darlin', them's the rules!'

'Oh right. Fifteen, yes?'

'If that's what you want.' She smiled as he handed a twenty-pound note over. 'Sorry, pet, I don't have change.'

'Okay so. . .' he paused. 'Okay, so make it nude sex.' The man might be an idiot, but he was not a complete idiot.

Maureen couldn't have cared less, all she knew was that it was an extra fiver for her.

The man could hear a television on in a downstairs room, as he was ushered immediately upstairs; he also heard a child's voice as he pushed open the bedroom door, which had a fist-shaped dent punched in it. The room was unkempt and tawdry. The wattage of the unshaded bulb was inadequate, but the punter seemed comforted by this, as he undressed and revealed his plump white body. Maureen, as always had hidden the twenty-pound note in the vase on the stairs as she walked up. 'Get on the bed, pet.'

He complied and started to get under the blankets.

'No, on top of the sheet, pet.'

'Oh, sorry.'

She took off her clothes as if she was in a cubicle at the swimming baths rather than putting on any sort of show. She couldn't be bothered to take her stockings off, so she left them on, hopeful that he wouldn't quibble over the 'naked' part of the verbal contract. She was well trimmed, loosely hung, with big nipples. She joined him on the bed but as he tried to kiss her, she pushed him away, explaining further rules, none of which he had signed up to. 'No kissing, I'm afraid, pet.'

'Oh, that's a shame.' He muttered disappointedly. Definitely his first time.

She began massaging his genitals methodically and mechanically without interest or emotion. She was confident that it would all be over soon, and she could return to her 'beat'.

Surprisingly his penis was large and as he grew erect she masturbated him with two hands, one on top of the other. The man groaned. If she timed it right, he wouldn't be inside her for long. She didn't like the big ones, few though they were. She carried on as if plunging a sink, and threw in a groan herself, making it sound as realistic as possible. The man had his eyes closed and he began stretching his pelvis up and down in slow thrusts. 'Nearly there.' She thought. The act would hold no such excitement for Maureen; she was simply interested in performing a physical act, for the purpose of obtaining money, completely aloof from what she classed as 'real' sex. Maybe she could get him to return for more though? She groaned again. 'This is a big fucking cock!' She gasped, glancing at her watch. The man smiled and she felt him begin to pulse.

She reached over to the bed side table, for her work tools; quickly smearing some lubrication on herself as a precaution. She then rolled the customary sheath on to the man's penis, giving it an extra few tugs so she didn't lose him.

'Come on.' She said.

He rolled on top of her and began clawing at her breasts. 'Mmm!' she groaned. He had to raise his backside high in the air to give him room to manoeuvre his weapon into a position to enter her. This he did slowly and deliberately. He puffed and panted away; Maureen felt obliged to let out some further grunts and groans, to hurry him up. The punter was not having it, however, and ten minutes became fifteen, and fifteen became twenty. She was getting quite uncomfortable as he ploughed into her. She had totally misread this geezer, there was no sign of it ending. He obviously wanted his money's worth. Maureen reached down and gently squeezed at his testicles to try to hurry him up. This did the trick; he moaned loudly and pumped his seed into the prophylactic. He withdrew quickly and rolled off, much to the relief of Maureen, who this time let out a genuine groan, as he disengaged. The man's pink face betrayed the fact that it had all been rather a strenuous effort for him. To be fair, it had been for Maureen.

She got off the bed to put her knickers on, while the punter sat in a daze on the edge of the bed holding the used condom, not knowing quite what to do with it. Suddenly there were raised voices downstairs. Men's voices. 'Who's that?' The punter asked worriedly.

'I'm not sure.' Maureen said, biting her lip nervously.

*

DPW Stephanie Dawson knocked on the double-glazed windows of the UPVC door. It was a semi-detached house on Vaughan Estate, not a bad area at all. The police didn't have occasion to visit it that much. It was a bit of a sleepy hollow.

She was feeling a bit tired. It had been a long haul. He was the last of the 'unknowns' on her diary list, so she could seek solace back at the station once he'd been done. She knocked again. She could see some movement inside but couldn't make out quite what it was. After a short time, a well-built man of around thirty answered it, in a white vest and summer shorts.

'Yes, my love, what can I do for you?' He smiled a toothy grin. He looked a bit full of himself, a bit over-confident for Steph's liking.

'Hello. I am Detective Policewoman Dawson from Nottingham CID. Are you Dennis Jones?' She asked.

'Yes, but people call me Den.'

'OK, Den. May I speak to you in private, please?'

The smile faded. 'Yes, sure, we can talk here, what is it?'

'I am making enquiries into a murder. You may have seen it on the news?'

He shrugged. 'I don't tend to watch the news, it's boring.'

Steph continued. 'Your name has been found in the diary of a young woman - Faye Marriott. You must know her, she's a regular at Ritzy's Night Club.'

The man didn't have time to reply before his two-year-old boy appeared between his hairy legs, and a woman's voice could be heard in the background. Stephanie could see the panic in his eyes. She raised her eyebrows and a thin-lipped smile landed on her face. She could see the situation he was in. The man looked at Steph open mouthed, words failing to emerge.

Steph looked at the man, she was waiting. 'Well?'

The man leaned towards her and spoke to her in a whisper. 'Come and see me at work, McInley's Engineering, 210 Mapperley Plains.' He didn't give her time to answer, he slammed the door in her face.

'A little bit rude.' She thought. 'Cheeky sod.' She raised her fist to knock again, but hesitated. She had a decision to make here: did she ruin a marriage or not? Is he being discreet to save his marriage, or is there something in the house that he doesn't want the police to see? Stephanie shrugged her shoulders and muttered to herself: 'You made the choice, pal. You should have kept it in your pants.'
She knocked again, loudly on the window of the UPVC door.

*

Charlie had known Maureen for the three years she had been a prostitute on the streets in Nottingham. She could be a wildcat at times, and her 'faggot' brother Reggie, was just as bad. This was how Charlie, and indeed her brother described himself- 'I'm a fag, get over it!' It was Reginald, who opened the door, in his off-white, baggy silk shirt and floral neck-scarf, Ashley asked, 'Is Maureen here, Reggie?'

'No.'

It was only Charlie's size elevens that prevented the door being slammed in their faces, and it was his shoulder which forced it to be slammed back towards Reggie's'. After jumping backwards, the wiry youth camped up his protest. 'How dare you. Bitch!'

'Thanks for inviting us in Reggie. You don't mind if we check do you?' Charlie's question did not beg an answer, although Reggie gave a desultory 'Just come right in, why don't you?' his initial confidence waning.

As they walked inside Reggie began his tirade, screaming and shouting, effing and blinding, as Charlie and his companion checked the downstairs rooms. Reggie had hoped the furore would alert his sister, busy upstairs with a client. It did. Pandemonium broke out in Maureen's bedroom. She hastily began putting her knickers back on, whilst the rotund punter, his dream turned nightmare, struggled to his feet and hopped around the bedroom with new-found energy in an attempt to put a sock on. An experienced punter might have started with his pants rather than his bloody socks!

Charlie told Reggie to put a sock in it, as he threw open Maureen's bedroom door. The comical pair inside froze, momentarily, in their various stages of undress. Maureen was the first to move. She flew at Charlie with fingers outstretched and nails exposed, like a cat landing from a very high jump. Charlie caught her wrists, and bare bosoms swinging, he threw her onto the bed.

'Now, don't be naughty, Maureen. We only want a chat. No point getting nicked, now is there?' Charlie said.

Maureen was breathing heavily and quickly, her chest rising and falling, attempting to keep pace with her diaphragm. The punter, meanwhile, had escaped, scurrying under Ashley's arm, as the detective leaned against the door. Ashley turned his head to see the man's large pink bottom wobble down the stairs, and away out the front door. Reggie raised an eyebrow as he craned his neck to follow the fleeing punter's naked form, disappearing out on to the street.

'What the pissing hell do you want, Charlie Carter?' Maureen asked, reaching for her cigarettes on the bedside table. She lit one up and exaggerated her exhale, unashamedly making no attempt to cover her heaving breasts.

Charlie explained the reason for his impromptu visit. 'Sorry to burst in uninvited like this, Maureen, but the shit has hit the fan.'

'Why what's up, now?'

'Your pimp, Winston Kelly is locked up for murder, and you need to start telling us about his exploits. That's what.'

'First of all, he ain't my pimp, and secondly he . . . well, I've got nothing to say. I'm not a grass.'

'Put your top on, Maureen.' Charlie instructed.

She picked it up off the floor and pulled it over her head.

Charlie asked. 'What is the story with this Faye Marriott, girl, don't tell me he hasn't mentioned her?'

'Charlie, you know I can't go there, pet, it's more than my life's worth; even if I knew something, which I don't, by the way.' She busied herself by squirting a cleaning agent on her hands and rubbing them together.

'Maureen, love, this is not something that is going to go away, it's the biggest murder case we've had for many a year, so pretty soon we are going to have to start fucking people's lives up.'

'What do you mean by that?'

'Yeah, what?' Reggie decided to join in.

Charlie sat down on the bed at the side of her. 'Ouch! You bugger.' He said, rubbing at his knee.

'That's piles.' Reggie said.

'Oh, that's what it is.' Ashley said.

'Shut up, Reg. Just because you are an expert on arse holes.'

'No, I'm not, I don't know anything about you.'

Even Ashley laughed. 'Good come-back, Reg.'

Charlie covered up a smile himself, 'If you don't mind, I'm talking to Maureen. I've lost my train of thought now, oh yes, what I mean by that, is that people need to realise that we too can be. . .what's the word... cunts. If necessary.'

'You already are.' Reg said.

'What do you mean?' Maureen asked.

'Let's see, maybe I should get the vice car to park up outside your flat for three weeks, it might cause you a bit of an issue, mightn't it? How would our Mr Kelly like that?'

'It's a maisonette, not a flat.' Reggie said.

'You wouldn't do that, Charlie, would you?' She said.

'Unless this gets sorted, soon, all sort of shit is going to happen. There will be a right clear out, people have been having it too easy, for too long. So, get your thinking cap on, Maureen.'

She sighed. 'Look, Charlie, there are things I could tell you about him, that would get him sent down for years, but he has friends. Just 'cos he's locked up, it doesn't mean he can't hurt me bad.'

'I know, but people say things and they don't carry them out, it's all talk, love.'

'Not with him it ain't, Charlie, and you know it. I know I have a pretty crappy existence, but it is an existence, and I would like to keep it that way, plus I have little Joel to think about.' She reached for another cigarette.

'Sure?' Charlie asked.

'I want to help, Charlie, you know I've always had a soft spot for you, since you helped us with Reggie's trouble that time, but I know what he's capable of. One of the girls, I'm not saying who, once told Winston that he didn't own her, do you know what he did?'

'What?'

'He fucking branded her with a hot knife, carved his initials in her arse cheeks. She was screaming the place down and all he did was laugh his fucking head off. He's a psycho, Charlie. And you keep this to yourself Reg, as well, do you hear me?'

'Course sis. I'm not stupid, am I?' Reggie said.

Charlie sighed. He knew it was a long shot. 'What about on the QT? Off the record? Just between us?'

She too sighed. 'I'd love to Charlie, I just can't, pet.'

Charlie put his hand out for her to hold, which she did. She leaned forward and kissed him on the cheek. 'Sorry.'

'Don't worry about it, kiddo.'

*

Charles Lyon was a sucker for a sexy voice; that's what he had liked about Faye. Detective Policewoman Stephanie Dawson sounded incredibly sensual to him as he spoke to her over his marble-and-brass telephone. It was a re-visit action kicked out by HOLMES to speak again to Charles, to see if he had anything more to say, or indeed, if he changed his story after Stark and Nobby's previous visit. He had agreed to talk to her about Faye. He had felt terribly wicked, and not a little bold, in suggesting that the meeting take place at the Chateau Restaurant.

He explained that his initial shock on hearing the news about Faye, had waned, and anyway, he felt more relaxed entertaining over a glass of claret than a mug of tea. Steph had been reluctant at first, but on reflection she relented and said, 'The Chateau would be perfect.' They had arranged to meet early at around 6.30pm.

The task Steph was arranging with Charles was just one of scores of minor foot-slogging tasks referred to as 'actions'. Despite all the activity there was still no sign of a result. The detectives working on Bernie Squires, after Stark inputted recognising Terry Banner's voice into HOLMES, had thrown up a few minor illegal practices, but no connection to murder. The mysterious call from Terry Banner to Bernie, which Stark had intercepted while in his office, was so ambiguous that it could have meant anything. It was something of a coincidence given the timing and the circumstances, however.

Stanley Tindle, the 'jobbing' burglar was out of the frame, and they were struggling now with Winston Kelly, but he seemed the best bet they had. How to turn that into something tangible was proving more difficult than they had hoped, with no-one prepared to talk, despite detectives like Charlie and Ash 'shaking the bag' as directed by Stark. It had filtered back that Kelly was not amused, even whilst waiting for the next remand hearing, word had got out about the police 'Harrassin' me brethren.' It would impact on his business with police officers crawling all over it, and his associates in that seedy world were already lying low until it eased off. Kelly was in a cleft stick, he refused to be seen to cooperate with the police, but he would be losing money hand over fist, with all the heat they were applying. Meanwhile, he languished in a cell. He had to get out, or somehow steer the 'Babylon' away from him.

The murder team needed a break, some luck, a new line of enquiry. Stark was hopeful that Steph's meeting with Charles Lyon would throw some light on the current impasse.

*

Charles was most impressed with his first view of Steph as he walked from the car-park towards the red awning which surrounded the main entrance of the Chateau. At least he hoped that was her. The delightful Stephanie was standing waiting underneath it, as arranged. His excitement grew as he approached her; her slender figure and large, firm breasts were more than satisfactory to the lascivious eye of the odd Mr Lyon. She clutched her plain white handbag, and her long hair waved gently as the slight breeze blew through it. A perfect vision of beauty, Charles thought.

They greeted each other politely and shook hands, Steph made a point of loosening her grasp of Charles' hand in a slow, deliberate manner. As their hands parted, she noticed a glint of gold cuff-link beneath the sleeve of his blue suede sports jacket. After Charles complimented her on her appearance; the two made their way into the subtly lit entrance hall of the chic restaurant. Charles was greeted personally by the Maître D and they were shown to a private bay.

After they had sat down, Steph explained that she might have to ask him some awkward, if not embarrassing questions. Charles told her to relax and that he would answer all her questions with the utmost candour. She wasn't quite sure what that meant, but it sounded hopeful. He summoned the alert waiter standing nearby, and ordered Camembert Rochelle to start with and Chateaubriand, for two. Steph met his questioning glance with a nod of her head, agreeing to the choice. Charles was at home in these surroundings, he was relaxed, and that was how Steph wanted him.

He summoned the sommelier to the table. 'A bottle of Lanson Gold champagne, preferably 1972, please.'

'Excellent choice, sir.' He bowed and backed away, still bowing as if Charles was the King of Siam, although Steph had him down as more of the Queen of Sheba at this stage. Maybe both?

'I want to celebrate the honour of being blessed with such charming company.' He said. Steph feigned a blush and lowered her gaze more than adequately, looking up at him with her long eyelashes. The fact that she could snap him like a twig, if she wanted to, seemed lost on Charles.

After ten or fifteen minutes, their slight awkwardness and over-polite pleasantries subsided a little, and the conversation flowed more readily. Charles answered her questions and explained that after meeting Faye on their first night, he took her to the Dans le Club Casino. He took her home in his Daimler and the two of them had become 'amorous,' as he put it.

It was exactly where he put it that Steph wanted to know. She asked point blank: 'Did you have sex with her on that first night, Charles?'

'Erm, OK, that was unexpected.'

'I did say I would have to ask you some personal questions. I've heard it all before, don't worry.' She said.

'Goodness me.' Charles repeatedly folded and unfolded the immaculate white napkin. 'No, in fact I did not. She stopped me at the final hurdle, if you please.' Steph nodded. He continued. 'Infuriating it was – she was a real tease. I never saw that in her.'

'Were you expecting more then, Charles?' She asked.

He dabbed at his upper lip with the screwed up napkin. 'I was, shall we say, a little pent up. Still, she must have given me her telephone number, although I don't remember her doing so. I found it in my jacket pocket the next day on a piece of paper.'

The sommelier arrived with the champagne and Charles examined the label. The sommelier opened the bottle with a flourish and Charles took a sip to ensure it had not corked, before their glasses were filled a little more, and the bottle was left in the silver bucket on the table.

Charles raised his glass and there was a chink. 'Cheers.' They said in unison before each having a sip of the delightful sparkling wine.

'Mmm lovely. Very nice, thank you. So, did you call her?' Steph asked casually.

'Of course. I rang her that day. She appeared really excited that I had done so. So we met again, I brought her here in fact, to the Chateau, and then our relationship seemed to blossom and we saw each other all the time.'

'All the time?' Steph queried.

'Well, a couple of times a week at least.' He clarified.

Steph sipped at her champagne and formed the words of her questions slowly with her blood-red shiny lipstick, unsullied by the drink. 'Did you meet her parents, at all, Charles?'

'No, she scarcely mentioned them. On reflection it was I who did most of the talking about pretty much everything, she seemed a little shy, I thought.'

'What made her shy, do you know, Charles?' Steph asked, lighting a long menthol cigarette which she held at the tips of her long fingers.

Charles finally placed the napkin on his lap in anticipation of the first course arriving, attempting to smooth out the creases in it as he replied to the question. 'I think the main problem was the difference in our upbringing. It didn't matter a jot to me, of course. My friends are mainly public school, hers were predominantly comprehensive, and with the best will in the world, that's a hell of a chasm to cross.'

The first course arrived, and the two fell silent, whilst the fussing around by the waiters took place. Steph extinguished her cigarette, regretting the timing of her lighting it. She was un-phased by all the cutlery laid out in front of her. Her Grandma had always told her 'outside-in'. She still waited for Charles to grab his, before copying him, just to be on the safe side.

He had just about got the first forkful to his mouth as she asked, 'I take it you had a sexual relationship with her, then? Eventually, I mean?'

He put the food in his mouth to buy a little time with the answer. He was secretly enjoying the tingle the intimacy of the questions was giving him. It was a strange conversation for two strangers to be having, but he quite liked it. After six chews, a swallow and a dab with the napkin, he decided to answer. 'Yes, we did. After two or three weeks I think it was. We stayed at the Major Oak Hotel for a weekend. I think she told her parent's she was staying at a friend's house – Sandra? Samantha, something like that?'

'Chantelle?'

He pointed his knife at her. 'Chantelle. Fuck. You know more about it than I do, Stephanie.' He snorted out a laugh.

Steph laughed too, not so much at the observation, more at her surprise at the expletive and the way he pronounced it. 'Fock!' She imagined her regaling the story to Nobby in the pub later. 'Focking hell, Nobby! I think I need a focking drink!'

Charles continued, 'It was fortunate, actually, because when I invited her to the hotel, she was, you know. . .'

'No, I don't know?'

'Well, a little, you know, she was a little bit down in the dumps. That's it. Down in the dumps.'

'Why was that?' Steph asked.

'Something about her car, or her father's car? She needed two hundred pounds, well, I was only too happy to help.'

'Ah, now, I see.' Steph was starting to feel sorry for the chump.

'Anyway, as soon as I said that I would help, she jumped at the chance for a get-away for a couple of days. You know, to cheer herself up, I should think.'

'Yes, I know, exactly what she was thinking.' Steph observed, tactfully.

Steph ran her finger around the top of the Champagne flute. 'This is another tricky, Charles.'

'Fire away, we're all friends here.'

'So how was it? Did things go well?'

He snorted again. 'Oh, rather!'

'I see. This is a little awkward. But I have to ask, did she do anything unusual, or did either of you do anything, shall we say, a bit more adventurous?'

'No, not really, it was all a little understated really, she had a headache for most of the time we were there. The worry about the car issue, I shouldn't wonder.'

'But you did actually do it?'

'Oh yes, bless her it was her first time, so she asked if we could just have sex, no build up, if you know what I mean.'

Steph smiled sympathetically. 'I know what you mean. Her first time you say?'

'Absolutely.'

'That's nice.' She smiled again.

'It was all rather romantic, she explained that she preferred just lying on the bed together, cuddling, bless her, she was sweet. So sad she's gone.'

'Any arguments or fall outs?' Steph asked.

Charles began to smile as it was his turn to play with the glass. 'Only once. It was a dreadful business. She accused me of being useless in bed, so I gave her a whack!'

Steph was taken aback. 'You hit her for saying that?'

'No, I hit her for knowing the difference!' He began to laugh.

Steph looked puzzled.

'It's a joke. Don't you get it?' laughed Charles.

Steph's initial shock turned to a smile and the two laughed together. After the laughter subsided Charles apologised. 'I'm sorry for teasing you. I suppose it was in bad taste, given the circumstances of our little chinwag. No, we didn't argue at all, it was all very civil and very quiet and very sweet.' His face suddenly became serious and his lips pursed. He took another sip of his champagne and averted his gaze from Steph. He knew she wasn't buying this rubbish.

*

Detective Charlie Carter was struggling; he was getting nowhere fast; he was running out of ideas. Nobody was prepared to talk to him about Winston Kelly. It was a wall of silence. His patience was wearing thin. He and Ashley decided to go to see Kelly's parents. Why not?

'If these don't want to play ball, we are totally scuppered.' Charlie seemed more tense than usual, he had hoped for more from Maureen or even Reggie, but was that fair? Was he going to be able to offer them protection twenty-four-seven? No, was the quick answer.

'I hope to Christ they don't give us any lip, I'm not in the mood. Don't take any shit from them Ash. We can drag their arses down to the nick to talk to us, if we have to.'

Ashley shrugged. 'Sure.'

He was expecting aggro from the Kelly household, if they were anything like their obnoxious anti-police son. Charlie hammered on the varnished wooden door of the ageing town house. It was a statement-of-intent type of knock. It was quickly opened. A tall, slender, middle-aged West Indian man presented himself. 'Good evening, gentleman.' He was softly spoken but assured, and he smiled in welcome, as he invited the two men into his humble abode. Charlie glanced at Ash, disarmed by the gracious welcome.

They sat down. The living room was incredibly tidy, with everything in its place. The television surround and wall-unit were of a dark teak; there was a beige standard lamp and a faux sheepskin rug in the centre of the room. There were too many ornaments, cheap stuff, collected over the years and crammed on to the unit, which curiously had a picture of the Queen at the side of it. The room was clean but quite dated. Charlie suspected it had been like this for many years.

'This my wife, Louisa.' She shook hands politely with the two detectives.

The years of bringing up the feral Winston Kelly had left its mark on his father's face. The trauma, the worry, the conflicting emotions and the disappointment had wrought the man a sad expression, weathered, but bathed in a calm wisdom and a shadow of sadness shrouded his eyes. Yet, his watery eyes hadn't totally succumbed, despite all of that, he retained a sparkle in the depths, which had attracted the young beauty, Louisa to court him in Albert Town, Jamaica, in the summer of 1957. Louisa had stayed with Samuel ever since, and had been overwhelmed with joy when she gave birth to a boy. It completed their lives. All the hopes and desires for their new-born were a blanket of warmth to them and they saw a new future in a place called England. Samuel related the story to the two detectives with a far-away look in his eye, as he recollected happier times. The boy had been given a rather grand name – Winston Samuel Courtney Kelly. 'A proud name!' Samuel said. Their dreams began to turn sour when Winston started to kick back at much of the racism and injustices that he faced in England in the 1960's and 70's. Samuel had tried to get him to channel his anger down the right path, for good, for progression. Winston wasn't up to it though, and he stole a watch out of the kitchen of an elderly black man, three streets away, known as Grampa George, who Samuel knew well and respected. He was so ashamed and dragged Winston down to the house to apologise, when the watch had been discovered under his bed. Winston had been arrested for burglary, and so the train tracks switched towards a cloudier sky. The arrest suddenly gave the young Winston a bit of status at school, once word got around, and a bit of, what Winston interpreted as respect, instead of a feeling of rejection and ridicule. He liked that feeling. For once he could hold his head up and he became notorious, chasing that feeling evermore. The fights and confrontations at school and in the street stopped, girls became intrigued, and somehow, he became the school hard man. So he thought he had better live up to the legend. He enjoyed the attention and the status, a big fish in a small pond, the celebrity, the pride, all of which had a pay-off. He had to maintain the myth. He couldn't go back to the old place, when he was looked at like a piece of dirt on somebody's shoe. He clung on to the status and began to get embroiled in all manner of nefarious crimes. He was locked into the lifestyle, and then locked-up. Whilst living up to the reputation, he was bringing down the family name. This was the beginning of it all.

As Samuel graciously related the story to him, Charlie felt a little ashamed of his ignorant comments on the doorstep of the Kelly household. Louisa, in a baggy flowered frock, and bobby socks, brought tea in her best cups and saucers, and offered biscuits to her guests on her best china plate. The Kelly's were a quiet, proud couple who knew how to behave with a polite dignity, despite the shame that their wayward son had brought to them.

Samuel explained that in between his personal problems and working 12-hour days at Calverton Colliery, he had taken stock of the boy. He had talked, he had lectured, he had explained, he had shouted, and yes, eventually he had fought with Winston, all to no avail. As time passed, Winston became more slippery, avoiding contact with his parents, dropping out of school, staying out all night. For large periods Winston only really saw them when Samuel dutifully trooped to the police station, to try to help his boy. Winston was an ungrateful little shit and cared not a jot for the pain he was causing the very people who loved him the most. Samuel explained how it all came to a head one Sunday lunchtime when the boy had grown into a young man. Winston was about nineteen years old. Samuel had been playing dominoes in the Afro-Caribbean Club, at the Marcus Garvey centre. One of his friends had passed a comment, about seeing Winston showing 'the beat' to a girl in the red-light area of Hyson Green, and that 'him a gallist'; a Jamaican word for a pimp. There had been a fight, and Samuel had fought like a tiger for his son's honour; he had lost and taken a severe beating. Upon his return home, Louisa had bathed his wounds and Samuel confronted the now Rastafarian Winston. The boy didn't admit or deny the accusation; he just said, 'it is time for me to leave.' And with that he left the household for good. Samuel hid his tears, but they silently rolled down his cheeks as he held Louisa in his arms. She was distraught, heaving and sobbing and blaming herself. From that day to this, Samuel had turned his back on his son. Winston occasionally visited the house but would remain in the kitchen and talk to Louisa; and every time he visited, twenty-eight years of emotion would well up inside Samuel.

Charlie didn't like asking the questions he had to, regarding the murders, but he phrased them tactfully so that the true inference, he hoped, was disguised sufficiently, whilst still getting to the truth. Louisa hadn't seen Winston for over a week. He had seemed troubled, but he didn't give any reason for his consternation, telling Louisa that it was 'just street, Momma'.

Samuel asked the detectives their names again. 'Charlie Carter.' Samuel repeated, nodding. 'I've heard of you at the club.'

'All good, I hope.' Charlie grinned, a little nervously.

'Actually, yes. I remember about ten years ago. . .'

'Blimey, ten years ago.'

'I have a good memory, Mr Carter. You helped a young boy, name of Leroy Smith?'

Charlie shook his head. 'Sorry, Samuel, I deal with so many people, I don't remember them all.'

'He was a young Jamaican boy from Radford. Anyway, he was going down the same path as Winston, and you helped him.'

Charlie's eyes lit up. 'Oh little, Leroy! Yes, tiny little lad he was. Got you now.'

'You gave him your football ticket to see Forest play, didn't you? Told him if he stayed out of trouble, he could use it. In the fancy seats, with his Dad.'

Charlie smiled. He remembered it well. 'Oh, I don't know, it's a long time ago. Anyway, you have been most gracious, Mr Kelly, Mrs Kelly. Thanks very much for the tea.'

The two detectives rose from their chair to leave, and Samuel offered his hand. 'Any time you are passing, officer, call by. You are welcome in my house.'

Charlie accepted the hand of friendship, readily, and with respect.

*

Charles Lyon swilled his brandy around the glass, as he puffed away at a large cigar that appeared too big for his little face. The conversation with Stephanie had momentarily ceased. Lyon stared at his drink, then raised his eyes towards Steph. Something was clearly on his mind and had been for the last few minutes.

'I owe you an apology, I'm afraid.' He said.

'Why?'

'Because I have been a little economical with the truth, I'm afraid.' He frowned

'Do you think I don't know that, Charles?' She smiled softly.

'Of course, it's your job to know, I suppose.'

'So tell me the truth about you and Faye, Charles, I'm going to give you a free pass, but this is your last chance. Don't spoil it!'

He sipped at his brandy and took a deep breath. 'I knew what Faye saw in me, Stephanie: my wallet. I may be a lot of things but I'm not completely stupid.' He hesitated slightly, trying to formulate the words, he didn't know where to start, how to explain. 'I needed her company, that's the truth of it. Up to the time I met Faye, my idea of a good night was a game of bridge or a night on the piano. She gave me a whole new aspect to my life. The women I know are all wrinkled or naïve, Faye was different. She was beautiful, she was coy, but she gave me everything in bed, she taught me, she recognised my needs, it was a beautiful experience. It may sound crazy, but she made me feel like a real man, at last. So, she took me for a few quid, so what? Who am I to judge someone for that? I've never wanted for anything. I have always been able to buy anything I want. It has never entered my consciousness that people have to go without. I can't begin to imagine what that must be like. I did not judge her too harshly for that.'

'Sounds reasonable. I understand.' Steph smiled.

'I knew I could never let her go.'

Steph's stomach took a leap when she heard those words. Was he about to confess? She pondered.

'Then the problems started, the nightmare began.' He sighed heavily. 'She started being cruel, nasty, taunting me incessantly, Stephanie. It's a little embarrassing.' He lowered his gaze and began to look at the candles, rather than meet Steph's sympathetic expression. 'She used to tease me and ridicule me, constantly criticising my manhood and sexual performance. Even when I was actually doing it with her, you know, making love, she would often laugh out loud.'

He dared a quick glance at Steph, examining her reaction meticulously. She appeared to be understanding, she was a woman of the world. 'Things deteriorated, I started gambling, as a distraction, but that just made me more and more depressed. Mother kept asking me what was wrong, but how do you tell your Mother, or worse, your father, that you are rubbish in bed?'

'No, *Faye* said you were rubbish in bed. That doesn't make it true, Charles. She may have just been saying that. People say things they don't really mean, for a whole host of reasons.'

'That's what I tried to tell myself. I asked her to stop, but she couldn't resist her quips and comments, and then it started happening when we were with company, and I knew that was the end.' He sipped at his brandy once more. 'I lost what bit of confidence I had and became all but impotent. She was cruel to me, Steph, hurtful, and when I couldn't perform at all, that just made her worse. I wanted to finish with her, but I just couldn't bring myself to do it. Much as I hated what was happening, the thought of becoming boring old Charles, again; playing bridge with mother and the wrinklies was just too much to bear. I didn't kill her, Stephanie. God knows that if I had, it would have been a long time ago.'

The two had scrutinised each other in the dim light of the restaurant. Steph thought about his alibi, and the way he had spoken to her and told her private things, which he didn't have to. 'Do you know something, Charles?'

'What?'
'I tend to believe you.'
Charles sighed. 'Thank you.'

11

'If you aren't fired with enthusiasm,
You will be fired with enthusiasm.'
Vincent Lombardi (1913 – 1970)

Stark sat at his kitchen table in a daze. His brain cells were misfiring and struggling to get purchase on the day ahead. Another day at the office lay ahead for the Detective Inspector. Many people count the days to the weekend and the blessed relief from the drudgery of their bean-counting job or whatever the hell they do. Stark felt that he was fortunate, as he was doing a job which he enjoyed. He didn't work for some multi-millionaire chairman of a conglomerate, where all his efforts were merely to add to their bank balance, with them throwing some miniscule crumbs his way so that he could struggle to survive. He had met people who endured such careers, many times. These were often frightened men and women who were just as trapped by the prospect of losing their lifestyle, as a heroin addicted prostitute was. Sacrificing their dignity and moral compass for sycophancy and an Audi A5. Stark, in this sense, knew he was lucky, although he had worked hard to get to where he was. He was appreciative that he was in such a position, because while he, of course, had a boss to work for, his activity was helping the general public and impacting on their lives to a huge extent. They were his raison d'etre. He was saving lives, and protecting people from criminals, psychopaths, sexual deviants, maniacs and killers. It mattered that he had been on the planet, because he had done his bit.

He still felt tired, and irritatingly he had a softly whirring clamour distracting him from afar at the back of his mind. The clamour in his brain was the sum of all the questions and activities that needed to be answered and completed on the murder case. Floating around, incessantly trying to land in the right place, and failing. This was frustrating because it was a puzzle that he could not yet solve. He was somewhat disheartened because it felt like he was going down a rabbit hole with this damned murder enquiry. He couldn't yet see the end game.

He felt Winston Kelly was where he needed to put his focus, and that was what he was doing, but he kept hearing the words Kelly said to him at the end of the interview. 'It ain't me, Babylon.' He seemed genuine and annoyingly he tended to believe him. That was confusing. It was confusing because he knew that all the 'evidence', albeit circumstantial, pointed to Kelly and he had to go with that. It was a niggle though. What else was there? What was he missing? He needed some clarity. The forensics hadn't come up with anything. Why was that? Surely, if, as he suspected, the burglary was a put-up job then there would be fingerprints in the house. Someone goes in there as a friend and comes out as a killer; he is going to leave a trace. Unless it was more pre-meditated than he thought? Or there was some other reason that there were no fingerprints. What though?

'David! Tea or Coffee? For the third time. You are clearly not listening; I don't know why I bother.' Carol stood facing him with her arms folded.

'Sorry, Carol. I was miles away. Coffee please, love.'

In Stark's home, bedlam reigned as it creaked and groaned with the weight of the family waking up. Dave liked to start the day gently, building up to some semblance of normality. He could normally manage stupor to fully awake, in around twenty minutes; if coffee was on tap. His record was fifteen. Today was not a record breaking day.

His children, Christopher and Laura were the opposite, or

were when they were younger. They seemed to wake up at full pelt and work backwards, winding down from there. They were less enthusiastic now, his daughter, Laura certainly was. At fifteen she was starting to become the victim of 'foggy brain', first thing in a morning, accompanied by aches and pains as her bones and muscles stretched her upwards and out-wards, and her body went through changes. Dave could sense an argument brewing as he and his family sat at the pine break-fast table.

'Oh, grow up Christopher!' Laura exclaimed.

'You are the one pretending to be grown up with that poofy boyfriend of yours. "Oh, Laura, I love you, let me give you a big kiss!"'

Stark laughed at his young boy. 'Don't encourage him, Dad.' Laura barked.

Christopher started making kisses, pursing his lips exagger-atedly, towards his sister.

'Shut up, little boy. He's more of a man than you will ever be!'

Carol interrupted. 'Will the two of you please eat your break-fast quietly? It's too bloody early. Jeez!'

Christopher put his tongue out at Laura.

'Pathetic.' she muttered, irritated.

Stark tried to adjust the blinds at the window, twisting that fiddly stick thing, as the sun was shining on the television in the far corner of the room. It was the television that the kids tended to use for watching videos, but it would do. He wanted to see the news. The volume was down low and inaudible.

Carol shouted over from the sink area. 'Do you want toast, David?'

'Please. Will you pass me the TV remote, Laura, please?'
He turned the volume up, as the weather report was closing, and the lead report was on the latest outbreak of Salmonella at a local food chain-store. He then saw the story he guessed would be near the top of the news.

'*Quiet, everyone!*' Stark shouted.

'We weren't saying anything!' Laura protested.

'Shush!' He put his hand on Laura's arm to back up the shushing.

'Police are hunting the killer who savagely attacked a family in their own home in Nottingham. The Marriott family were brutally murdered in the early hours of Thursday 16th July on Maple Close. A man is said to be helping the police with their enquiries. Residents have expressed their horror at the news.'

Stark shook his head. 'What the hell has he released that for, without discussing it with me? A man is helping us with our enquiries. Everyone will think we've solved the bloody thing!'

The newscaster continued *'. . . Detective Superintendent Wagstaff, who is leading the hunt, has said that significant inroads are being made to track the killer down. Our reporter, David Smith, spoke to Mr Wagstaff at Police Headquarters. . .'*

Carol passed her husband a mug. 'Here's your coffee, Dave.'

'Shush! Just a minute.'

'Thank you, Carol.' She said to herself.

The slightly windswept journalist spoke to Mr Wagstaff, who was a policeman, not a television presenter, and it showed. The reporter was wearing his concerned face as he asked. *'Can you give us any more information on how the investigation is going, Chief Inspector Wagstaff?*

'Superintendent.'

'Sorry, Superintendent. How's it going?'

'Fine, thanks.' Stark nearly choked on his coffee.

'Sorry, I meant how is the investigation, going?'

Wagstaff stumbled through a robotic reply, turning into a caricature of himself, resorting to police speak, when under pressure. 'The investigation is one of a protracted nature, and enquiries are continuing as expeditiously as possible.'

He sounded like who he was; a policeman on television; untrained in the subtle art of televisual communication. Stark laughed. 'Hah! He sounds like PC bloody Plod. He sounds like someone from another planet, for Christ's sake.'

Carol slid a plate of toast in front of him and he began devouring it.

'What arrests have been made, Mr Wagstaff?'

'Careful, Waggy.' Stark said through a mouthful of toast.

'I cannot divulge the full details of the case but suffice it to say that a gentleman is helping us with our enquiries, as such, in so much as he has been arrested, yes.' The words were a grammatical wasteland.

'Oh, my God.' Stark laughed out loud. Carol put her coffee down on the table; her laughter had almost caused her to spill it.

The journalist pressed. *'Is there any sexual motive behind the killings?'*

Stark shouted at the screen. 'Waggy!'

'I would prefer not to be specific in the divulgence of information, otherwise the enquiry could be severely hampered.'

'Phew.' David said.

Wagstaff tried to look into the lens of the television camera but couldn't hold it, which made him look weak to the viewer, his camera shyness rapidly becoming apparent. He had become red with embarrassment; it seemed that every time he opened his mouth, he said something increasingly more farcical.

'Are you still appealing for witnesses to come forward?' The reporter asked.

Wagstaff pushed his foot further into his mouth. 'Yes. If there is anybody out there who feels that they might have any information which may be of direct, or indeed indirect, use to the enquiry, they should contact us, in confidence. Their call will be treated confidentially...' It looked as though he was going to continue.

'For Christ's sake stop. Somebody stop him. Kill him, anything!' Stark shouted at the screen, his children looking on bemused.

The reporter beat Wagstaff to it. *'I'm afraid we are going to have to stop you there, Chief Inspector Wagstaff...'*

'Superintendent.'

'... This is David Smith for the East Midlands News, handing you

back to the studio.'

Stark was smiling as he turned the volume back down. He shook his head. 'If I ever start talking like that, Carol, I want you to take me outside and shoot me.'

'You are rotten. I felt sorry him at the end. I like him, I do. He's sweet.'

'Sweet? We're trying to catch a bloody murderer!'

'You know what I mean.'

'He is a one-off, is old Waggy. I shouldn't criticise him really, I mean, he has given me a chance to prove myself with this case. I am doing far more in leading the investigation than I would normally, it's all down to him.'

Carol put her arms around David and hugged him. 'It's because he knows how wonderful you are.' She kissed his forehead.

'You are quite astute, aren't you?' said Stark wryly.

Carol's smile turned to puzzlement. 'Why didn't he mention the sexual side of it, David?'

'We don't want that released yet. No end of problems arise when you start telling the public too much.'

'Why? Surely it can only help?'

Stark grabbed the hand of his wife. 'You're right, sometimes that's true, but what can, and has happened in the past, particularly with notorious cases, is that an array of lunatics turn up confessing to the crime.'

'OK. Strange.'

'Don't ask me why, they obviously have problems, or want to be famous, or whatever, but you can spend weeks, or even months, doing enquiries on the wrong person.'

'I still don't get why you can't tell them everything?'

'So, erm. Let me think.' He gathered his thoughts. 'In a case where there are no forensics, sometimes all you have is a confession. So, the only way to test if that confession is accurate, is to go into the nitty-gritty details of what happened at the crime. Details only the perpetrator would know, and if all the details are available on the news, well, then anybody could confess to the thing and give quite a bit of detail about the crime, even though they haven't done it. Do you get what I mean?'

'I get you. It seems weird that someone would admit to things they haven't really done.'

'It is, I agree, but it's happened lots of times, it has also happened the other way around where you get a genuine confession from the offender and then a clever barrister starts knocking out all the pieces of a confession by showing clips of newspapers and television released to the public. It lessens the strength of the admission to the jury and they end up walking.'

'Blimey. I get it now.' She kissed him on the lips. 'Mr Wagstaff has obviously got the cleverest detective, running the case.'

Stark grinned. He was starting to have doubts about that.

*

As Stark watched Wagstaff pacing up and down his office, it became apparent that his Superintendent was looking for a scapegoat. His embarrassment during the television interview had fuelled the anger within him. Stark sat looking up at the new television personality, who was now in full –tantrum mode, like a spoilt child.

'I have spoken to the Chief today. He is not a happy man. He wants this detecting, like, flaming, yesterday!'

'I want it detecting as well, sir.' Stark said matter-of-factly.

'Don't you interrupt me, David. I've given you a chance on this one, and yet nothing has happened.'

'Nothing has happened? We've been working balls out!' Stark protested.

'David, I won't tell you again! I am talking. Now I thought you were up to this – perhaps you are not. From now on I want to know everything you are planning on doing, and when you intend doing it. I want to know when you intend wiping your bleeding arse!'

Stark protested. 'Or indeed wipe it for me, no doubt. I cannot do an investigation under those terms, sir, I mean'

Wagstaff cut him short. 'David, all I am saying is get me something tangible, a lead, anything, otherwise I'm not going to be able to keep you on it.'

Stark was beginning to get a little peeved. 'What is that supposed to mean? Look, sir, I have busted a gut trying to sort this out.'

'Well, you will just have to bust another gut, otherwise I'm going to have to take over the investigation in its entirety.'

There was a pause. Wagstaff felt that he had probably overstepped the mark with his reprimand: he had mistakenly thought that Stark needed a kick in the relevant area. Stark felt that the onslaught had been unwarranted. It was he who broke the silence.

'Let me ask you a question, sir.'

'Very well.' Wagstaff sat in his chair.

'Is there anything that I've done, that you wouldn't have done?'

Wagstaff thought for a moment. 'Well, Lee Mole, the DI at Carlton, thinks we should be pressuring Lyon a bit more.'

'Fucking Lee Mole! That's what this is all about, is it? What has another DI's opinion got to do with this? Sneaky fucker!'

'He is not being sneaky, David, we were chatting that is all. He happened to call in.'

Stark was pissed. '"Happened to call in." I fucking bet he did. What did he "happen to drop in" for exactly?'

'I can't remember, now.'

'No, because it's bollocks! He's just come over to stir the shit, as he always does.'

Wagstaff grinned. 'David, everyone isn't out to get you.'

'No, but that prat is, if it meant he got promoted.'

Wagstaff shook his head. 'It was all very innocuous, David.'

'I bet it was.' Stark was tight-lipped. They fell silent again.

After a few moments Stark spoke again. 'Look, sir, Lyon has been seen twice, it could be him, but we aren't feeling it at the moment. I am more interested in Kelly now. There is something he knows, but daren't say for some reason, I'm sure of it. I'd like to know what that is.'

'Mmm.' was all Wagstaff could offer.

Stark couldn't resist. 'It is important that Kelly is helping us with our enquiries, in so much as he is arrested.' He was laughing inwardly as he mocked Wagstaff's televisual terminology. The Superintendent's eyes narrowed as he looked for a hint of sarcasm in Stark's face. He found none.

*

Two other men were in the midst of a heated debate: Simon Derwent and Mr Bard of Kirkham, Turner and Ross. Winston Kelly sat impassively in the dock of the Guildhall Magistrates Court, Number One.

The clean-cut Mr Derwent had completed his rhetoric on behalf of the Crown Prosecution Service. His application to remand the prisoner in custody, with the full rationale had been based on a quick perusal of the lengthy report forwarded to him, by the stubby fingers of Nobby Clarke. Mr Bard, defending Mr Kelly, rose to his feet, full of self-importance, smiling at the three magistrates on the elevated bench in front of him. Bard wore the same pin-striped suit he had worn at the police station, when representing Kelly at the interview with Stark. His hands rested on his lapels, occasionally leaving them to move the array of papers on the desk in front of him. He had a brash, confident air and he spoke very loudly.

'Your Worships,' began Bard, 'the prosecution has mentioned that my client *may* commit further offences, if he were released on bail. I ask the court what further offences exactly? My client has only been charged with three disparate and heavily disputed offences, which are totally unconnected and relatively minor in nature.'

He paused for an exaggerated cough, before continuing at his own pace. 'Let us deal with the first – unlawful sexual intercourse with a girl under sixteen years. Your Worships, the woman in question gives the appearance of being at least twenty years old. My client has no previous convictions for any similar offence, and of course it was a one-off incident, the details of which are hotly disputed. My client strongly denies the charge; he is categorical that full sex did not actually take place despite the girl's advances toward him. The girl was immediately returned to the home from whence she came, no doubt to be advised about her sexual proclivity. My client who is most upset to learn of her age, and holding that knowledge, he is now no danger to her.'

Bard paused to let it sink in.

'He has been charged with unlawful possession of cannabis. Again, my client vehemently denies this. He was oblivious to its existence and can only assume that it came from that poor misguided child, who he had kindly given shelter to, purely out of his own good nature.'

Bard sipped at is water.

'Finally, he has been charged with resisting arrest. Your Worships, my client has been in fear of his life for a number of months since a threat was made to him by a former business associate. When he heard his front door being smashed to pieces, he naturally assumed it was a group of aggressors breaking into his flat to attack him. He was terrified, poor man. Who wouldn't be?'

Kelly tried his best to give the bench a 'puppy eyes' look, but this turned into a bit of a sneer.

His solicitor continued. 'He was most concerned for the safety of his female company, whom he nobly felt obligated to protect. How would any of us feel, in the belief that you were in danger of immediate and serious harm? Before he realised that the plain clothed officers, were indeed police officers and not attackers he picked up the nearest thing to him, to defend himself, and was then immediately attacked by a vicious police dog. He was not resisting arrest, your Worships, he was resisting attack! There was no intent to harm the officers. The only person injured because of this ill-judged approach by the police was my client! Indeed, he is still in pain for an attack by the police, who misguidedly tried to arrest him for an offence, which, importantly, he has not even been charged with!'

Bard paused and sipped at his water again, to underline the impact of his case. He placed the glass delicately on the table and looked thoughtful in the silence he had created. All eyes were on him. He spoke loudly and with enthusiasm as he continued into the next phase of his plea.

'Your Worships, the word murder has been used in this courtroom today. Let us be clear, my client has not been charged with murder. It is preposterous and designed merely to mask the heavy-handed way in which the police have decided to approach Mr Kelly, for whatever motivation.' He fell short of saying racism. Bard waved a dismissive hand. 'I am confident that the magistrates will understand that such a suggestion, without charge, is both underhanded and irrelevant, and should form no part of their considerations, sticking to the facts of the case alone, and not unsubstantiated tittle-tattle. There is no suggestion that there are any third parties involved in any of this who might interfere with evidence, not that there is any of course. What evidence? Your Worships, I ask again, what evidence? Your Worships, my client has always dutifully attended previous court cases, and he was not on bail at the time the police burst into his home. There is no outstanding property to be identified.'

He sipped at the glass delicately for a third time, before continuing.

'Despite my client's previous convictions, and the police hounding him at every turn, he is trying to make a fresh start in life, which, I hope you agree, should be encouraged. He has co-operated with the police regarding these matters. He tells me that he has the prospect of a labouring job in the very near future, which could be the catalyst needed to help him on the right path, which he is desperate to do. He pays regular visits to his mother to care for her, as she is not in the best of health, and it is with this in mind, that Winston would accept any conditions imposed, should you think that appropriate. Such conditions would enable my client to continue with his recent impeccable record, start a new job, treat his mother's illness and prepare for his defence to the grossly inaccurate charges mistakenly laid on him by the police.'

Bard sat down with a 'this is all crazy!' look on his face.

The magistrates left the courtroom to discuss the issue. Those who remained in the well of the courtroom chatted in hushed whispers. Mr Bard and Mr Derwent laughed, in a re-strained way, at an apparently witty comment one of them had made. Then the usher's booming voice barked out the order, 'All stand!'

The magistrates had been deliberating for only nine minutes. The Chairman of the Bench was a man of about forty years, with a greying beard and a suede sports jacket. He spoke: 'Would you please stand Mr Kelly?' The accused obeyed the instruction slowly, his police escort standing alongside him.

'We have considered the applications made to us this morning, and we have decided that you should be bailed to return to the court on 28th September 1987 at 9.15 a.m. We do, however, impose certain conditions, and these are that you reside at your current address at 16 Chard Court, Nottingham, and that you report to Hyson Green Police Station at 4pm every Friday. You are free to leave the court, Mr Kelly, and I hope that your endeavours to find suitable employment are successful.'

*

Ashley handed the telephone to Stark who was chatting with some of the lads in the general office.

'Stark.' He announced into the handset.

'Boss, it's Nobby, he's walked.' Nobby had been assigned to monitor events at the remand hearing and assist the prosecution solicitor with any questions.

'He's walked. You are joking!' Stark exclaimed which, when

heard by the detectives in the office created a series of groans and 'Why do we bother?' style comments.

'It's no joke.' Nobby confirmed.

'How the hell did that happen?' Stark queried, leaning back in his chair, seemingly less concerned than his junior colleagues.

'You had to be here, boss, in fairness Bard walked all over our guy.'

'Brilliant. I had a feeling he might.'

'Looks like we will have to go to plan B.' Nobby said.

'Yes, we will.' Stark agreed. 'What is plan B, exactly?'

'I was hoping you would tell me, boss.' Nobby seemed exasperated.

'There is one, definitely, it's just that I don't know what it is yet.' Stark was strangely frivolous given the circumstances.

'Oh.' Was all Nobby could say.

Stark grinned. 'I'm kidding, Nobby. Listen carefully. Don't balls this up: Go to the front steps of the Courtroom, blow your nose and then drop your handkerchief, and immediately pick it back up.'

'Sorry?'

'You heard, Nobby. Drop your handkerchief once you've blown your nose. It's a fairly easy one to remember, Sergeant.'

Nobby was stammering. 'Yes, but, what, why. . .' Suddenly the penny dropped. 'Here, hold on, have you got RCS doing surveillance outside?'

'Bang on, Nobby. Sergeant Sammy Bates is hooked up and as we speak is outside the court, waiting for the signal.'

'Wait, is he that fucking tramp holding the polystyrene cup out?'

'Probably. Who knows?' Stark said smiling.

'Bollocks, I gave him a quid.'

'Very generous, Nobby, you will go to heaven after all. If you can give him the handkerchief sign. He will know that he has got the go ahead. The Regional Crime Squad are going to do a surveillance on the fine upstanding citizen that is young Winston.'

'So, there is a plan B. I love it. You cunning bleeder, sir.'

'See you later, Nobby.' Stark put down the telephone and lit a cigar, putting his feet up on an adjacent chair.

'So, this is how you catch a murderer, is it?' Detective Inspector Lee Mole walked into the office with his skinny Detective Sergeant alongside him.

Stark rolled his eyes and spoke exaggeratedly. 'Thank God you are here, Lee. You can save us all and give us your superior wisdom. Thank you, God.'

Mole sat on the desk ignoring Stark's sarcasm. Stark was still aggrieved by Mole talking to Wagstaff, behind his back.

'All right lads?' Mole said to Starks team. No-one replied to the ferret faced, double-dyed, troublemaker, who was well known for shit stirring, and trying to score points over both Stark and his team, at any given opportunity.

'So, how's it going, David, any closer?'

'Did you want to chat in my office?' Stark asked, knowing that it was likely to be testy. It always was.

'No, not at all, you can speak openly, I don't hide anything from my team do I, Carl?'

Detective Sergeant Carl Davidson stood at the door, leaning against the frame. He looked like he had his father's suit on. 'Absolutely not, boss, we are very open in our team.'

'Please yourself.' Stark shrugged.

'So, any progress, or is it still all a bit much for you?' Mole asked, looking around the office for some reaction.

'I thought you would know how the case is going, or couldn't you hear the update with your nose being too far up Wagstaff's crack?' Stark replied. There was some giggling from Paul Fisher, Charlie and Ash. Steve Aston wasn't used to the bitchiness and didn't know quite how to react.

'Now, now, don't be like that, David. Just offering a valued opinion to an old colleague. Mr Wagstaff did ask for my expertise, after all.'

'I bet he did.' Stark said disbelievingly.

'I wondered, if you wanted my team to give you a little assistance?' Mole asked.

'Why? So that you can come in when all the leg work has been done and try to take all the glory. I think I will pass but thank you so much for a very considerate offer, Lee.' Stark gave him a false smile. He knew it was killing Mole that Stark had effectively been given control of such a high-profile murder case.

'Okay, but my boys know a lot of snouts on your patch, and they are hearing some strange things.'

'Two things Lee: One, if you have any info, feed it into the HOLMES room for allocation, and two, keep the fuck off my patch.'

Mole got up off the desk and joined his sweaty DS at the door. 'Don't say I didn't warn you.'

'I won't. Bye.' Stark was narked, as Mole and his side kick strolled out of the office.

He stretched his leg out and kicked the door, which slammed shut behind them.

*

The team of Regional Crime Squad detectives were the go-to-guys for work of this nature; they were the best in the force at surveillance operations. They had undertaken such work time after time and were experienced in using both technical equipment and boots-on-the-ground. There was often a bidding war to get your case accepted, as there were only a finite number of them. This meant that they ended up only being involved in murders, kidnappings, blackmail and the odd armed robber. They were expert in adopting disguises such as tramps and road-workers for static surveillance. All of them also had to have passed the police advanced drivers course for those vehicle follows which would require a huge amount of resource to avoid compromise by the target. This would often throw up a strange mix of smart, short-haired trainee road traffic officers sitting in a Ford Granada taking a police driving course with a smelly foul-mouthed hairy individual with a ring through his nose. Sometimes it was a female with a low-cut top with a ring through her nipples, and tattoos. Police-women were used frequently by the RCS, as a couple in a car, or in a pub, attracted far less attention than two men, of course. They had to be prepared to play any role and this might involve 'snogging' a male colleague and groping each other just to keep up appearances, so to speak. It sounded more glamorous than it perhaps was, with many hours of nothingness followed by short bursts of activity. It was also often very intense and de-briefs at the end of the day would be at best tense, and at worse, almost come to blows. Their standards were so high, as were the stakes, that they were constantly seeking perfection.

Thankfully, today was a warm sunny day. Sunny, but a little windy, as became apparent when Detective Sergeant Nobby Clarke stood on the court steps and dropped his handkerchief, which then blew down the steps just out of reach, as he repeatedly tried to stamp on it, until it landed right in Sammy Bates' polystyrene cup. Nobby, tried to recover the situation by retrieving the handkerchief and throwing another pound coin into the cup. It wasn't the best of starts. Sammy was two pounds up on the deal, however, so all was not lost.

They had given the 'off' from the Court when Winston Kelly came bounding down the front steps, without a care in the world, about forty minutes later. Kelly had taken a taxi to his flat, which was the easy bit, because the driver was DC Tom Skerrit from Regional Crime Squad, complete with genuine cockney accent and a 'cut-here' tattoo around his neck. Kelly stayed at the flat for just over an hour and a half, he was desperate for a decent shower, and a puff of weed. He then drove his blue BMW car to the red-light area of Hyson Green. He surreptitiously collected some cash from two girls on Southey Street, giving one a cuff around the head and a kick up the backside. He then went to the Cricketers pub on Radford Road.

Such a location was always difficult, as the surveillance commander had to decide quickly whether to follow inside, or
merely surround the building. It was tricky, because it was a
pub of locals, mainly West Indian youths. If a stranger walked
in, it would almost certainly make the pianist stop playing,
the bar tender close the hatch, and the poker players to tilt
their Stetsons and reach for their Smith and Wesson .45's. On
this occasion they decided to put a circle around it and wait. It
looked like it was going to be an active surveillance for the Regional Crime Squad.

*

Stark peered at the piece of paper on his desk. It was a list he
had scribbled down in desperation – a compilation of all the
relevant features of the case reduced to basics. Now, fired up
by the gloating Lee Mole, he re-visited it. The top part of the
list was headed *'Points of Interest'*, and the lower part *'People
in Direct Contact with the Circumstances'*. The lists looked like
this:

Points of Interest

1. 3 murders – 2 fatal asphyxiations, 1 fatal head
   wound – attempts to disguise same.
2. Offender fakes a burglary.
3. Hi-Fi still switched on when police arrive.
4. Sex act.
5. Red fibres at the scene.
6. Bronze clown ornament wiped clean of fingerprints.
7. No alien prints at the scene.
8. Video removed after the murders.
9. Shoelace loop in rear garden.
10. Man seen by Gray and Glover running away.
11. Parents, respectable; Faye promiscuous.
12. Faye in the Florin pub with Kelly–arguments/as-

sault/threats to kill.

13. Faye in numerous pubs, before Ritzy's, on night of murders, seen with Winston Kelly and mystery man smooching.

14. Employed by dodgy bookmaker – Bernie Squires – cryptic phone call implying the 'job had been done'.

15. Charles Lyon sexually ridiculed by Faye and in front of his friends.

People in Direct Contact with the Circumstances

Norman Price (window cleaner)
Ernest Gray   (saw man running away)
Peter Glover   (saw man running away)
Bernie Squires (betting shop)
Terry Banner   (voice on phone at betting shop)
Chantelle Naylor (friend of murdered girl – Faye)
Winston Kelly   (seen with Faye; punches her, threat to kill her)
Charles Lyon   (sugar daddy boyfriend – humiliated sexually)
Stan Tindle   (prolific burglar, in the area around the time of the murders)
Colin Markwell   (ran away from Gray's house)
Violet Gray   (wife of Gray, and Markwell's lover)
Maureen Ross   (Kelly's prostitute)
Reginald Ross   (Maureen's gay brother)
Sally Lawrenson (Bernie Squires' niece; Faye's workmate)
A.N. Other   (involvement of a third party or stranger?)

As it stood at the moment, one of these people must be the murderer. What about the diary? All the men had been traced and eliminated from the enquiry. Stark pondered the problem. The only other possibility was a complete stranger. Stark remembered his motto, the same motto he had been told as a young DC: 'Go on what you know.' He drew a circle around the name Winston Kelly.

*

Winston Kelly's bravado was an offshoot of a crash-course in survival on the street. He might behave like an animal at times, but inside his brash persona, he was a very worried animal. He had to get out of this mess. He knew Stark wanted him, and he had to use every ounce of his intelligence and street-smarts to throw him off the scent.

Kelly spoke to an old tramp in the alleyway at the side of the Cricketers Arms public house. The ageing West Indian man had seen better days; his donkey jacket was scruffy, his pork-pie hat stained with years of sweat. The two men spoke with heavy Jamaican patois accents.

Kelly stood menacingly close to the man and gesticulated in his usual aggressive manner. 'Two G, Pop, cash!'

The old man shook his head. 'Me not know, boy.'

Kelly reached into his track suit pocket. 'Rasta man' and produced the money in twenty-pound notes.

The old guy, well known to Kelly, was in a corner and he knew what Kelly was capable of. He stared at the litter-ridden floor. The old guy shook his head. 'Me not know, boy. Risky mon.'

Kelly was insistent. He had thought out the lie. 'Why, mon, I was wid you all night, mon, checking out da cards, blood.'

The man blew out a heavy sigh. He tapped the leather pork-pie hat to the back of his head and let out a sigh. 'Me hear bout you, boy. Me hear some *serious* shit. Me hear word of murder!'

'Pop, check dis, or betrayal, brethren.' Kelly was almost pleading.

The old guy shook his head again, but he was scared. He apologised, in the vain hope that Kelly would understand. 'Sorry, boy, me not trust Babylon, me no hot stepper.'

Kelly punched the old man hard in the face and watched him collapse on to the floor in a heap. He thought about cutting him, he had tooled up at his flat, but settled for a kick in the ribs instead. Kelly scurried away, leaving the old tramp semi-conscious and whimpering, like a starving puppy, in the deserted alleyway.

RCS dropped a man back to monitor the old man's progress from afar. After a couple of minutes, the old man struggled to his now unsteady feet, a cracked rib for refusing Kelly was not a bad result, in the big scheme of things. The injury would never be treated. He'd had a lucky escape. RCS had a bigger prize at stake than a cracked rib, so the officer didn't 'show-out'; instead he reconnected with the surveillance team. The coded babbling on their radio by each subsequent 'eyeball' told them that Kelly was at Maureen Ross's flat. Shouts could be heard from inside.

*

Maureen Ross's camp brother, Reginald, stood limply in front of Stark's desk, his hands on his hips. He wore a multi-coloured knitted tank-top with no shirt and tight-fitting trousers. He was vehement in his protestations. He was camping up the conversation.

'It's the truth, Mr Stark. No way could Winston Kelly have killed that family.' Reggie was frightened. No, he was terrified. It was written all over his face.

Stark zig-zagged the smoke issuing from his cigar by the slow shaking of his head. 'I'm sorry, I just don't believe you, Reggie.'

Reggie sighed and transferred the weight from one leg to the other. His hands remained glued to his bony hips. 'I should have told Charlie Carter when he came to see our Maureen.'

Stark laughed. 'Told him what, exactly?'

Reggie moved a hand away and started gesticulating, twisting his hand at the wrist as he explained, as if this might help to make the point more believable. He wasn't looking at Stark, he stared at the ceiling and spoke his lines. 'There was me and Winston at Maureen's maisonette all night, watching videos. *Predator* was one, and then we played cards for a bit and then we watched another video, *Running Man* with Arnold Schwarzenegger in it.'

Stark had been updated by RCS that Kelly had holed up at Maureen Ross's flat prior to Reggie's crusade at the police station. 'What time did Kelly get to your flat that night, then, Reggie?'

'It's a maisonette actually. He got there about five past eleven, and he didn't leave until twenty past five in the morning.'

Stark tapped his cigar butt into the ashtray on his desk. 'What was he wearing?'

Reggie counted out the description on his long bendy fingers, 'A green T shirt, jeans, Adidas trainers and his Rasta hat.'

'What card game did you play?' enquired Stark, as he put his hands behind his head and leaned back in his chair.

Reggie was quick to answer. 'Nine-card brag. He took ten quid off me.'

'How long did you play cards for?'

'About an hour and a half.'

'Did anyone else see you with Kelly all night?'

Reggie's hands returned to his hips and he stuck his neck out. 'Of course not! I've just told you it was just me, our Maureen and Winston.'

Stark had heard enough, he leaned forward, his elbows resting on the desk. 'What were you doing two nights before the killings, Reggie?'

Reggie seemed surprised. 'What?'

'I said, what were you doing two nights before the killing?'

Reggie was confused. 'What has that got to do with it? How the hell do I know? You want to know about this night, don't you?'

Stark wasn't satisfied. 'All right, what were you doing the night after the murders? The Friday night?'

Reggie shrugged his shoulders. 'I went out. No, I didn't. Sorry, yes, I did. I went to the boozer for a bit.'

'Which boozer?' Stark asked.

'Florins, I think. Yes, Florins.'

'They've got CCTV there haven't they, Reg?' Stark asked, knowing the answer.

'Erm. Yes, that's true, but it could have been somewhere else.'

'Like where?' Stark was grinning.

'Anywhere. This is ridiculous.' He stamped his foot like a petulant child.

'How long were you at the pub for, Reggie?'

Reggie puffed his cheeks out, his face reddening. 'Bloody hell, I don't know.'

'OK. Then what did you do?'

'What's this got to do with the price of fish?' Reggie flounced.

Stark ignored the question. 'I said, then what?'

'I don't know. I went to our Maureen's, I think. . . No, hold on, I went to the chippy first. Or was that Saturday night?'

Stark was unrelenting. 'See, it's got a lot to do with the price of fish.'

'Not funny, Inspector.'

Stark was laughing. 'What did you do at Maureen's?'

'I don't know, watch telly I suppose. I'm not sure.'

'What was on?'

Reggie put his finger to his mouth and thought hard. 'I don't know – er, a film.'

'What film?'

Reggie was becoming impatient. He was worried for his sister. 'Look Mr Stark, please. What has this got to do with why I'm here?'

'It's got everything to do with why you are here. Goodbye, Reggie.'

Desperation clouded Reggie's eyes. 'Please, Mr Stark, I'm telling the truth.'

Stark explained the position. 'You've got a choice, here Reggie. I can send you back with some of my men to arse Kelly out of Maureen's flat,'

'Maisonette.'

'Or you can go back and tell Winston Kelly that the nice Mr Stark believed every word and took a statement from you.'

Reggie was puzzled. 'How did you -?' He didn't bother finishing the question; he didn't want to know. He breathed a sigh of relief. 'Cheers, Mr Stark, I owe you one.'

Stark felt obliged to ask, 'Will you give us a statement about what Winston Kelly is doing at Maureen's flat? Trying to frighten you into giving an alibi?'

Reggie gave a helpless, somewhat pathetic look. 'I'd rather cop for his murder charge than do that, sorry, Mr Stark.'

Stark nodded his head towards the door. 'Go on, piss off, Reg, and don't say I never do anything for you!' He waved a dismissive hand at the camp figure, who scampered away out of the building. The exchange had elevated Stark's concerns about Winston Kelly being involved. If he was going to such lengths to create an alibi, he was on the back foot. Why do it, if you've got nothing to hide? As for Reggie, he now owed Stark a favour, and he would be glad to collect, when he needed some information in the future.

*

The Regional Crime Squad officers observed Kelly, as his large gangly gait carried him from Maureen's flat to his car. He seemed to have a spring in his step after Reggie's return. They followed him, using their interchangeable manoeuvres, the complexity of which would send a stage-musical choreographer into apoplexy. Twelve cars were involved and two motorcyclists; that sort of complexity. They were intrigued as they watched and logged his every move. He went from house to house, flat to flat, person to person, like a profligate bumble bee collecting nectar in a blossoming garden. Eventually, he ended up in the vicinity of Ritzy's nightclub; old habits die hard. It was a bar opposite the club. He was seemingly well known by the customers in the bar, as he flitted from one person to the next, each time receiving a 'hail-fellow-well-met response.' It was a microcosm of his earlier activities, around the various locations of Nottingham. What was he doing? Socialising? Seeking further favours? RCS sent a couple in, but the bar was rammed with people, and it was impossible to get close enough to hear the conversations he was having, apart from when he came near the bar. He was talking about weed and something to do with a barber shop that many West Indians go to. As the RCS couple apparently spoke to each other, they were not really talking to each other, not having a proper conversation. They had small state-of-the-art microphones inserted in their clothing, and they were repeating the conversation they were hearing. The loggist listening in on the radio, switched them to another channel, and took his notes. In truth, there was nothing that was of any great interest, but it was all logged. The wider surveillance team were then able to use the main radio channel to set up their vehicles and footmen accordingly, in a pattern that would take him from the bar to wherever the next location might be. After an hour and ten minutes, Kelly left the premises, followed by his invisible entourage.

*

The only light in the corridor emanated from DI Stark's office. He sat at his desk and supped at the glass of whisky he had allowed himself, and stared at his lists. He had told the rest of the gang to finish at 9 p. m. and they had trooped out for a beer. Stark had declined the offer to join them; he needed some time alone with his thoughts. He began to write another list entitling it: '*Questions Arising from Facts Known.*' On completion the list looked like this:

Questions Arising from Facts Known

1. Why disguise the way they were murdered?
2. Why disguise the entry to look like a burglary?
3. Who had put the Hi-Fi on, Faye or the killer?

4. What implement was used to cause the marks on the window and where is it?
5. What was the killers' motive?
6. If not burglary, what was he doing at the house?
7. Had he gone there specifically to rape or murder Faye, or her mum or dad?
8. Why no struggle by Faye?
9. Why no fingerprints if a visitor was at the house at the height of summer – no gloves?
10. Why hadn't the offender ejaculated? Condom?
11. Why remove the video after the murders?
12. How did the killer gain access to the house?
13. How did the killer actually get to the house - transport?
14. Is the shoelace loop the killers'?
15. Are the red fibres the killers', the smooching man, or some other person's from a previous night?
16. Who is the smooching man?
17. Can every person's account be trusted on face value, and if not, who cannot be trusted?
18. Did the killer know Faye?

Stark was certain that the sum of the answers to these questions added up to the killers' identity. All he had to do was fill in the gaps.

12

'Do not insult the mother alligator
Until after you have crossed the river.'
Haitian proverb.

The Boxer public house derived its name from the fact that it was across the road from the historic gym used by Nottingham's finest pugilists over the decades. It had been quite a sleazy pub at one time; the underworld's connections with the boxing scene dictating that its patrons often consisted of those owing a debt to society; but it had changed over the years. The 'spit and sawdust' image had been replaced by beautifully decorated walls and sculptures. The clientele had become huddles of friends, encircled in the warmth and patronage of those they knew. Anybody who accidently knocked into someone carrying drinks would now have their apology readily accepted with a smile, rather than a right cross to the jaw. Since the Boxer had been re-furbished, no separate lounge or bar existed – just one large room with a circular shaped bar and various groups gathered together around it. All sorts were there – young, old, male, female, miners, and 'yuppies'. A 'yuppie' being the relatively new buzz-word for someone being 'young and upwardly mobile.'

The group of detectives were so engrossed in their conversation that they hadn't paid any attention to the five or six West Indian youths standing behind them. It was almost 11 p.m. and Paul Fisher had consumed more alcohol than his brain cells could cope with. 'Stark's a bit miserable, not coming out with us, isn't he?' he said in an over-loud slur of alcohol induced bravura.

Ashley agreed. 'Yes, it is a bit off. I don't know what is up with him. He usually likes a drink; I think Lee Mole wound him up earlier. That's probably it.'

Charlie, uncomfortable in his surroundings, contributed to the small-talk. 'I think he's bottling it a bit with the Marriott murders, mind.'

Paul gave his opinion. 'He reckons its Winston Kelly, and I've been thinking about it.'

Ashley warned his colleague, jokingly, 'don't you go and detect it, Paul, and stop the bloody overtime supply.'

The detectives laughed. Steve Aston wanted to join in the banter, but still felt a little self-conscious, slightly alienated and unqualified to contribute. He had tried to chip in once or twice earlier, but had been shouted down by his loud, confidant colleagues. He took another sip of his orange juice and started to wonder if he would ever really fit in.

Paul continued his drawl, alcohol continuing to loosen his mouth. 'No, hear me out. It's obvious that there was no burglary, right? So, whoever killed her had to know her, otherwise she would never have let them in.'

Charlie tried to rebut the suggestion. 'He could have conned his way in, Paul. Do you think all of this has not been considered?'

Paul took another large swig of his pint of bitter before answering. 'Yes, granted, but why at that time of night? And, can you see Faye Marriott opening the door to a stranger? We are forgetting that she was pretty streetwise.'

'Someone call Dr Watson, Sherlock has had a thought.' Charlie said laughing.

Paul continued unabated. 'Ha, ha. There wasn't a struggle. She must have *known* the killer – that's why the burglary was staged.'

Ash nodded. 'You are probably right, Paul.'

Paul was still slurring. 'Of course, I'm right. It's got to be. I reckon it is the bloke who was smooching with her at the club.

We need to find out who it was, and we have him. I want to have another look at the CCTV tape we got from Ritzy's when I get to work tomorrow.'

Ashley nodded again. 'You aren't going to lose anything, Paul. Why not?'

'How long are RCS going to be following Kelly around?' Paul asked nobody in particular.

'I don't know. . .' Ashley's answer was interrupted by Charlie Carter. 'Oi! Shut it! Keep your fucking big mouth shut, Paul.'

'I was only asking. Keep your hair on.'

'I don't give a fuck what you were doing, zip it. If you can't take your ale, piss off home, kid.' Charlie was succinct.

The detectives instinctively looked around them after Paul's, over loud faux-pas, and it was then Charlie saw the West Indian youths, giving him the thousand-yard stare, at twenty paces.

'That's going to set the jungle drums going.' Charlie said underlining his curt response to Paul.

'Keep it down, Paul.' Ash said. Paul was oblivious, as he could not focus more than two feet in front of him, everything was a blur.

There was an awkward silence. 'Time for bed.' Ashly announced.

'It's about that time, I suppose.' Steve muttered.

Charlie was still glaring at Paul, who asked, 'Is anyone coming over to Ritzy's? The night is still, young.'

They all declined. 'I think you have had enough, son.' Charlie said to Paul. 'Why don't you get yourself off home, instead of going over to Ritzy's?'

'Home? I'm a twenty-four-hour party person.' Paul raised his glass in the air. *'Party! Party-person!'* His friends walked past him towards the door. Two of the West Indian youths went out the same door, to find Winston Kelly.

*

Kelly had returned to his flat and had stayed there a good half an hour. The RCS had been called away to a firearms incident and had been replaced, by the newly formed Force Surveillance Team. The team had been seriously depleted and were at half-strength in order to cut down on overtime payments and to keep some senior officer in the police authority's good books.

Kelly took them all by surprise, when suddenly he ran at full pelt from his flat towards his car. His dreadlocks flying in all directions as he raced along the pavement in the shadows, which the yellow street lights and the large trees conspired to create. He was in a big hurry. The police radio crackled with urgency as Kelly's BMW was fired into action. The powerful car quickly generated enough speed to cause the surveillance team great difficulty in keeping close enough to him, without showing out. Kelly's car raced onto the M1 motorway, came off the southbound carriageway and doubled back on to the northbound track, going around the traffic island four times. The team knew that this was a tactic to discover if he was being followed and indeed dispose of any such followers. It didn't mean that he knew he was being followed; he could just be taking precautions. His car roared around the streets of Nottingham for twenty minutes before he abandoned it near the city centre and took off on foot, leading those pursuing a merry old dance.

After a further ten or fifteen minutes Kelly ran into the Bell Inn public house and through to the back toilets. The surveillance team lay in wait trying to decide whether to send someone in after him. Was it a trap? He was behaving irrationally. After three or four minutes they sent three men into the Bell. Thirty seconds later, the scruffy men ran back outside and garbled into the miniature transmitter: 'You're not going to believe this. The guy we have been following is a Rasta in Kelly's clothes, but it is not Kelly! Repeat, *not Kelly!*' They had been duped.

*

The killer had seen a drunken DC Paul Fisher leave Ritzy's night club, and watched him devour a kebab outside the late-night chip shop next door, the last bastion of the unsuccessful bachelor. It was 2.10 a.m. The killer was hidden in a shop doorway a hundred yards away, along the pedestrian area. He watched the inebriated detective slowly stumble towards him, away from the dispersing crowds, and dutifully dump the polystyrene tray into a bin. The killer checked for passers-by: there were none; it was deserted. He lay in wait to the detective's left as Paul approached. He toyed with the four-inch bladed knife, switching it from one hand to the other. The killer was sweating profusely and had to make a conscious effort to avoid his quickening breath being heard in the now quiet street. He knew what he had to do. His heart was thumping as Paul slowly and deliberately meandered down the street towards him without a care in the world. He was singing to himself softly.

It took a couple of seconds for Paul to register what had happened. He thought someone had punched him in the chest at first, and it was only as the man, now in his blurry vision, drew back the knife for a second blow that Paul realised the danger he was in. He twisted slightly to the left, as the second blow struck him to the right side of his chest. He was too slow. Paul was a strong young man who had looked after himself many times during his police career, against some very hard men. But on this occasion, he had lost the edge and had been completely surprised by the unprovoked attack. Terror crashed into his brain as he looked into the killer's frenzied eyes, and realisation chased away his intoxication. Paul staggered backwards – half as a reaction and half with the force of the blow. The attack took seconds, but it seemed to Paul as if it were in slow motion as adrenalin pumped through him. He ducked, bending forwards to avoid the third blow. He tried to summon up enough strength to save himself, but the message sent to his right arm to strike out at the man, got lost in the shattered nerve ends slashed by his attacker's first strike. His punctured lung limited his shout for help to a gargle as the blood rammed up his throat. Paul was defenceless and crashed on to the un-relenting paving slabs face down, his nose cracking because of the unprotected fall. The next blow, intended for his neck, missed, and cut into his face, his left cheek, knocking a tooth out with its force. The killer momentarily got the knife stuck in Paul's face, between the teeth, and had to slash upwards to release it.

Paul realised he was going to die and a calmness swept over him – the calmness that would bring eventual unconscious-ness. Paul looked up at his murderer sweeping blows upon his own helpless body; the assailant was now kneeling alongside him for extra purchase. Paul felt an immense sadness as he thought of his mother and father's reaction to the news of his own death. He also thought of the horror his detective friends would feel at investigating the crime. He imagined himself naked on the white slab, dead, with Tony the mortician tell-ing jokes at his side. He had to give his friends a chance to catch his killer. He used every fibre of his being to reach out at the head of the killer with his left hand; he scratched at him as hard as he could, pulling at his hair and scalp. Paul recog-nised the final blow as it powered into his back. It cut straight through the muscle and punctured his heart. He felt his heart explode and a searing pain scorched into him. Three or four seconds of a terrible sense of doom overwhelmed him as his heart sputtered to keep going, it failed, and his breath quickly expired from his lungs, none would replace it and then the black shrouded over him. It was all over.

The killer scurried away into the darkness of a nearby alley-way. Detective Constable Paul Fisher lay dead in the gutter, in the warmth of his own blood, a clue to the killer's identity in his own fingernails which he had known would be scraped and clipped off during his own postmortem.

*

Stark's fists, like his eyes, were screwed up tightly. He stood over the body of the twenty-six-year-old man lying on the cold pavement. He instinctively wanted to throw a blanket over him to warm him, but of course that was futile. He couldn't stop the tear trickling down his cheek, which he immediately swiped away. His breathing was short and stilted. He stood over the body of Paul Fisher, glistening in the morning dew. Death had caused Paul's facial features to relax and Stark had to look twice before confirming the worst. A fleeting glimmer of pure joy had soared through him when he first saw the cadaver. It's not Paul! It was. His appearance, without his life's' blood coursing through his veins, made Paul look older, his features misshapen and unfamiliar. Paul had gone, shedding the carcase of his former self.

Scenes of Crime were fussing around the scene. Stark's voice was shaky as he gave out his instructions. 'Once the . . . erm, photos and video are complete let's . . . let's just get the body removed as soon as we can. The undertakers will be arriving any second, according to Control.'

The SOCO officer nodded. 'I'm pretty much done, sir. I'm sorry that it's, Paul, sir.'

'We all are, Terry. We all are.'

Terry shook his head in a mixture of sadness and disbelief. 'The rest can be done at the morgue, to be honest, sir. Just the blood on the pavement to capture, once the body is removed.'

'I will want a search done for the, erm, murder weapon, and a team seeking out any CCTV footage, the rest is for the Post mortem. SOU are on the way to make a start.' Stark sighed. 'Thanks for all you have done, Terry, I'm grateful.'

Everybody had finished the preliminaries and the undertakers, newly arrived, picked up the body to take to the mortuary for Tony the mortician to put in a drawer; just as Paul had envisaged in his final moments. Paul's body was rock solid, frozen in time by rigor mortis. Stark instinctively looked away, as they picked up the mannequin set in grotesque pose. The muscles in Stark's neck tensed, and he swallowed hard. He felt sick to the pit of his stomach. Wide-eyed and red faced, Stark ridiculously tried to meander around the scene as he always did.

'Are you OK, sir?' The SOCO asked.

Stark answered softly. 'Of course, I'm not, Terry.' He shook his head. 'I am, however, the DI running the Marriott murders, and until we know Paul's death is unconnected, it is my job to deal with this murder as well.'

'Not DI Mole?' Terry asked.

'No! Not DI Mole. *We* are Paul's team and *we* are going to find the low-life bastard that did this to him!'

First Stark had a task to perform that he hoped he would never have to. He would have to tell Paul's parents. Bad news always arrives unannounced, and their world was about to be changed forever. This would destroy them. Death not only devours its prey, but it rips away those invisible strands of affection, which, in life, connect the victim to their loved ones, tearing holes in the soles of those left behind.

*

Michael and Sonia Fisher had got up at the usual time, to the accompaniment of Radio Nottingham. They were a fine couple, married some thirty-two years. Michael, a school-teacher, on the cusp of retirement, was a complex, sensitive man. Now his balding head was buried in *The Guardian*, newspaper, his pen scribbling away at the crossword. Sonia had always been a housewife and mother to their only child, Paul. Her greying hair, neatly pinned back, and pinafore were synonymous with the cosy feeling of home that she created all these years for her policeman son. Friends, neighbours and even slight acquaintances, could testify to the pride that Sonia felt in the son for whom they had waited so long in the early years.

She hummed to herself in the kitchen as she began to cook bacon and eggs, then she went to knock on Paul's bedroom door. There was no reply, so she went in: the bedroom was empty, and the bed had not been slept in. She returned downstairs; her husband remained rooted in the living room chair.

'He's not been in all night, Michael.' Sonia told him.

'Well, he's old enough, love – he's stopped out before. He's obviously picked up some woman and gone back to her place or stayed at a friend's.' Michael was smiling, basking in his son's ability to be 'one of the lads', something he himself had never quite mastered as a younger man.

Sonia was unconvinced, always fearing the worst. 'But he usually rings home if he's going to be out all night. He could be lying in a gutter somewhere.'

Michael laughed and again tried to reassure his wife. 'You can't expect the lad to break off from a young woman, to ring his mummy up, love, he's twenty-six years old, for heaven's sake! He's not our baby anymore.'

'Yes, he is.' Sonia said smiling.

She busied herself with the breakfast, the butterflies now twirling in her stomach. She knew Paul was a grown man, but to her he was still a boy and the tinge of paranoia, that at times haunts every parent, bit into her. She knew everything would be OK, but it was only natural to worry a little bit.

'Well, I hope he is being careful, then.' she shouted aloud.

Terry tore himself away from the crossword and came into the kitchen and they ate their breakfast in near silence. They were just returning to the living-room when there was a knock on the front door. Sonia darted a glance at Michael. 'Who's that at this time of the morning?'

Michael laughed. 'There's only way of finding out, my love. It's probably the window-cleaner wanting his money.'

Sonia was shocked and her face reddened when she saw a sullen faced man in a suit accompany Michael back into the room. Michael managed a nervous smile to accompany the introduction. 'This is Detective Inspector Stark, Sonia –love, the one that Paul's told us so much about, his boss. He says he wants a word with us.'

Sonia scrutinised the well-dressed man. His face looked drawn and ashen. Her hand went to her mouth. 'There's nothing wrong is there?'

'I need to have a chat with you both,' was all he said.

'My God, there is something wrong, Michael!' She was already trembling as she clung on to her husband, as they sat down together on their settee, feeling like strangers in their own home, consumed by the worry of the intrusion.

Stark sat in the armchair. He sighed heavily, leaning forward, resting his forearms on his knees. 'As you know, I am Paul's Inspector, and that is why I have come to see you.' His voice was low and strained and he could not yet look the doting parents in the eyes.

Michael tried to stop himself shaking so that he could support his wife. 'Paul's not in any trouble, is he?'

Stark shook his head. 'No, of course not, but I'm afraid I do have some terrible news.' He glanced quickly at the quivering couple on the settee, clinging on to each other for dear life.

Sonia felt she could not move, her thoughts had flipped from considering the worst to trying to find something that could be bad but bearable. She dare not ask the question she kept landing upon. Michael did it for her. 'He's not been hurt, has he, Mr Stark?'

Stark had to reply honestly. 'I'm afraid so, Mr Fisher. . .' Sonia let out a sob. Stark continued. 'It's worse than that, I'm afraid.'

Michael's grip on Sonia tightened and his voice trembled. 'So he's been seriously hurt? How seriously?'

'I'm afraid there is no easy way to say this. . .'

'Oh no, please don't!' said Michael, shaking his head, fighting off the realisation as it seared into his mind.

'What's he saying, Michael? What's he saying to us?' Sonia felt she would vomit; she closed her watery eyes and her chest began heaving.

Stark went on. 'I'm afraid it is the worst possible news. Paul has been attacked. He has been stabbed. I'm afraid he has lost his life in the early hours of this morning. I'm so sorry.'

There was a stunned silence. Michael had blocked out the phrase. 'Sorry, he's lost his, what?'

Stark leaned forward. 'He's lost his life, Mr Fisher. I am afraid he has died from his injuries.'

A wail emanated from far down within the mother's breast. The two had lost part of their very soul and they wept. Stark felt helpless and struggled to control his own emotions. He wanted to tell them everything would be fine, he wanted to comfort them; but he couldn't. He got up out the chair and went into the kitchen, unsure what he should do. He paced around momentarily, welling up with emotion.

In a daze of blunt emotion, Stark put the kettle on and turned the gas off the stove, that had been cooking bacon. He had no control over the tears falling down his face. He could hear the wailing and the sobbing and had to force himself to go back into the heavy air of the pain-filled room. He felt like an intruder, but there were things he wanted to tell them. He stayed with them for most of the morning, and told them what he and his colleagues thought of Paul as a man and as a police officer. He wasn't sure if they heard him; there would be plenty of time to tell them again in the future. He explained the practical arrangements to Michael, who nodded, and he gave them his card. They could call him whenever they wanted to; he had scribbled his home number on it too.

Stark left the house, feeling pretty drained, as he flopped into the driver's seat of his car. His hands gripped the steering wheel tightly. 'Fuck this!' He took a long deep breath, the exhale faltering, he tried to compose himself and failed. Grief was turning to a wave of anger that lipped at the sides of his restraint. The tyres screeched as he drove away at speed.

*

Stark stood, looking out of the window, waiting for Detective Superintendent Wagstaff to return to his office. He had been told he was on his way. His mind was full of thoughts, emotions and questions. He couldn't understand why the lads had left Paul to go to Ritzy's on his own, particularly when he was so drunk? Hindsight is a wonderful thing. If only he had gone for a drink with them that night, maybe he would have stopped Paul going on his own? And maybe he wouldn't. There was no point asking the 'what if?' questions; he needed to be concentrating on the 'what now'?

Wagstaff walked into his office. 'Ah, sir.' Quickly following was DI Lee Mole, who spoke to Stark as he entered.

'Hi David, I will need a statement off you about your attendance at the Paul Fisher scene this morning.'

'No, you won't.' Stark said abruptly.

'Yes, I will, it has happened on my patch and so I will be dealing with it.'

Wagstaff sat at his desk and put his head in his hands.

Stark addressed the Superintendent. 'Sir, can you please explain to DI Mole, that I will be dealing with the murder of one of my own DC's.'

Wagstaff took his hands away and sighed. 'Oh, David, Lee has a point, it was on his patch.'

Starks eyes widened. 'Sir. You had better explain to DI Mole that *I will be dealing with the murder of Paul Fisher!*'

'David, it is on Lee's patch.' Mole sat in the chair with an insipid grin on his thin features and folded his arms. Was he enjoying this?

Stark spoke to Mole. 'Lee, can you give me a couple of minutes with Mr Wagstaff, please?'

Lee shook his head. 'Absolutely not. We need to get an update on what is happening, so I can continue the investigation of a murder *on my area.*'

Stark went back to Wagstaff. He was furious. 'Sir, this is non-negotiable.'

Mole interjected. 'You are right, I will be dealing with it. You told me only the other day to keep off your patch, so I suggest you follow your own advice, and keep off mine.'

Stark ignored the jibe. 'Sir, it is one hundred fucking yards on his patch.'

Wagstaff appeared torn. 'I understand why you would want to deal, David, of course I do, but with issues like this I have found it is better to stick to procedure and I can see right here in the policy manual that. . .' He began reading aloud. '"*The Detective Inspector responsible for the area where the crime has been committed has sole overall responsibility for the investigation.*" It is quite clear.'

Stark approached Wagstaff's desk and swiped the manual and all other papers off it, and they flew at speed into a heap on the carpet. Stark then picked them up and threw them towards the wastepaper bin at the side of the desk, knocking it over.

'Whoah!' Mole said laughing.

'*This is what I think of the fucking rule book!*' Stark bellowed.

'David!' Wagstaff stood up.

Stark stood in front of his Detective Superintendent, only the desk separating them, his eyes were wild and he was breathing heavily, his fists clenched.

'Sir, this is my DC. It's Paul, for fuck's sake! His murder is undoubtedly connected to the Marriott murders. . .'

'You don't know that.' Mole shouted from behind.

Stark glanced over his shoulder. 'Shut the fuck up, Mole!' He continued addressing Wagstaff. 'This is going to be connected to my case, *our* case, and putting all emotion to one side, we are best placed to deal with it. Paul deserves that. He deserves your call on this one, sir, and believe me, I am willing to walk, over this. I *will* resign! I fucking mean it, sir.'

'Let him walk then, who cares.' Mole shouted. 'He's lost the plot.'

Wagstaff sat down again. 'Sit down, David.'

'I will not sit down.'

'*Sit the hell down, Inspector!*'

Stark reluctantly returned to the seat and sat down. Wagstaff puffed out his cheeks. 'It is a tricky one.'

'Sir. . .' Mole started up again.

'Quiet, Lee!'

Stark shot a sneering glance at Mole. 'Cunt!' he muttered in utter disdain.

Wagstaff eventually spoke. 'OK. I don't need to empty the waste-bin to continue reading the quote from the policy book. I know it off by heart. It goes on to say: "*in the event of extenuating circumstances, investigations may be dealt with by a Detective Inspector who is appointed, at the discretion of the CID Commander, with overall charge of the Division.*" As you know, at least last time I checked, that is me. I have seen David's understandable passion, and I agree with him. David and his team will continue with the investigation into Paul Fisher's death. . .'

'Sir, I must. . .' Mole interrupted.

It was Wagstaff's turn to cut him short. 'Lee, please! I am talking. It is not open to debate, and it most certainly is not a reflection on you. If the murder of Paul Fisher is not extenuating circumstances, then I don't know what is.'

Stark got up and put his arms around Wagstaff and hugged him. 'Get off! What are you doing, man?' was all Wagstaff could say, as he wriggled to break loose from Stark's embrace. Mole got up and walked out the office, slamming the door shut behind him. Stark shook Wagstaff's hand heartily. 'Thank you, sir. It is the right decision. Thank you!'

*

The next few days flew by for Stark. Both he and the team were on over-drive. They refused all over-time payments and worked day and night to avenge their friend. All the usual procedures for a murder hunt had, of course, triggered into action. Stark had not asked any of his DC's to do the postmortem, that was just too much, but he forced himself to attend, and it was the most horrific thing he had ever done. He did it for Paul; he wanted nothing missed, and he wanted to make sure that the idiot mortician did not make any smart comments. He didn't. Overall charge had been transferred to Detective Chief Superintendent Davies, Head of CID; with it being the murder of a police officer. Stark was pleased with this, because it meant that all the responsibilities, press, and internal politics were under control and he could get back to be a detective and doing the job his way, out on the streets.

Paul Fisher had been stabbed eleven times in total, all wounds were in the thorax and face. The insertion of a ruler into the wounds, by Professor Disney-Hargreaves showed that the murder weapon was a four-inch-long blade, which at its widest was an inch. Stark felt quite emotional when it became apparent that Paul, bless him, had given his clue from underneath his fingernails. 'Good lad.' Stark muttered to himself. The blood, skin and miniscule hair samples, Paul had ripped from the killer, were being hurriedly tested at the Forensic Science Laboratory at Huntingdon. Once the killer's body samples had been processed, any suspects could be checked using the DNA genetic profiling system, which was still in its infancy. It was the best clue they had. All they needed was a match. Kelly?

The murder weapon had been taken away from the scene by the killer; at least none had been found in the vicinity by the Special Operations Unit, when they did the bins and the fingertip searching.

The enquiry had been directed on the correct assumption that Paul's death was connected with the Marriott murders, and the investigation into them. Scores of police officers had been drafted in to assist and it was quickly becoming the largest enquiry undertaken in the Nottinghamshire Constabulary for over seven years.

Kelly had been re-arrested and behaved in an identical manner, apart from his readiness to co-operate in providing a blood sample for comparison. He was bailed pending the DNA comparison with Paul's clue. The surveillance team remained Kelly's unseen companions. Since Paul's death, the surveillance team had been given an infinite amount of resources to ensure that they did not lose Kelly again. The surveillance photographs taken by the RCS team had been perused by Charlie, Ash and Steve Aston and they identified several as being from the group of West-Indian youths, who had been loitering near them in the bar, before Paul staggered off to Ritzy's. This could be significant. Charlie felt that they had overheard Paul's over-loud comments about his views on the case and notably Kelly being surveilled; Ash and Steve were less certain.

Stark had revisited the Fisher household and tried to console them in the best way he could. He made absolutely certain that they knew that Paul hadn't stood a chance and that his courage and strength had left the legacy of an important clue. It was little solace, and it wouldn't bring Paul back, but Stark felt it might be a crumb of comfort to them in years to come, when in the later stages of grief. The coroner's inquest had been a traumatic experience for them. Stark had told the Fishers that there was no obligation on them to attend, but they had insisted. He understood. It had created a lot of media and public attention. The public gallery was standing room only. Subsequent CCTV viewing of those entering the Coroners Court, showed that a West Indian couple had attended and enquiries revealed the male to be the brother of one of the gang in the bar. All were associates of a certain Mr Winston Kelly, but then, he did have a vested interest in the case. Martin James, the coroner, was sympathetic to the sensibilities of those attending and made special mention of the presence of Mr and Mrs Fisher and expressed his sincere condolences. The unlawful killing verdict would inevitably come later; the coroner had gone through the motions, opened the inquest, taken evidence of identification, released the body for burial and adjourned the hearing pending police reports. The funeral had been set for the afternoon of Thursday, 6th August at St John's Cathedral, with a private more intimate burial service afterwards.

13

'The reverse side also has a reverse side.'
Japanese proverb.

The diminutive 12 year-old Jamaican boy should have been tucked up in bed at 1.20 a.m. but his parents had long since given up on him. He could scarcely reach the counter of Nottingham Police Station and it was by standing on his tiptoes that he placed the envelope on to the counter. It lay there for quite a while as the boy had not been visible, it was as if the envelope had appeared from nowhere. The young female receptionist glanced at the envelope: it simply read 'STARK'. She shouted through the plastic hole. 'Hello? Anybody there?' With no reply forthcoming she tentatively opened the window and took hold of the envelope.

She shrugged, and threw the envelope into one of the twenty pigeon holes screwed to the wall. Each pigeon-hole had the name of the intended recipient stuck underneath it with embossed tape. Stark's was hanging off and was askew, so she got out the weird piece of machinery from the drawer. This was one of those tasks for the night shift. The Dymo label embosser had a roll of plastic tape and an alphabet wheel over the top of it. You set the letter you wanted, by turning the clicking wheel and squeezed the handle. It would indent the letter into the plastic, also stretching it so that the letter was paler than the background. You then squeezed the cutter and you had a label; that is once you had peeled the fiddly backing strip off. She stuck the new label 'DISTARK' onto the bottom of the pigeonhole. 'That's better.' she said to herself, feeling somewhat pleased. She had forgotten the spacing, but she couldn't be bothered to do it all again. She felt as if she had achieved something. It felt good. It's all relative.

She glanced again at the envelope. She was curious. It was never expressed to her that they *couldn't* open envelopes, not that she could remember anyway. Better leave it. She sat down at the desk. It was quiet. She doodled on the blotting paper that filled the square mat on the desk; there was scarcely room for another one, but she managed it. She then tapped her fingers on the desk and looked again at the DIS-TARK hole. It was beckoning her. There was no way she was going to last the next four hours and forty minutes. She returned to the envelope. It was thin but had a small piece of paper just visible inside with typing on it. She held it up to the light. No good. She put it back in the pigeonhole and then took it out again, hastily ripping the envelope open and shaking the contents out on to the desk. She read the note. 'Weird.' She said to no-one. 'Some nutter.' She sealed it back into a new envelope and wrote 'DI Stark' on it and put it back from whence it came. Mr Stark would see it in the morning. She had written the contents of the note on to the blotting paper, next to her dog. It was a riddle or some cryptic message. It would give her something to do.

> THE WARM BRIDE WHO WOULD HAVE FAME WITHOUT ME,
> WHIRLED AND JIGGED IN BLACK,
> WOULD TAKE WITH HER A SIGH, THE NIGHT SHE LEFT.
> WITH OPEN ARMS, SHE WELCOMED THE COVERED HAND
> THAT SMITE HER DOWN,
> THE TRUSTING EYE LOOKS OUT NOT IN.
> SIGNED.
> THE FATHERS SON.

*

Stark knew that one of his officers needed him. His shirt was

drenched with sweat from the exertion of running flat-out;
he'd got to get there before it was too late. He chased around
the side-streets by the Victoria Shopping Centre and across
the road, dodging the late-night traffic, as the horns, distorted
in motion, blared angrily at his crazed figure. The flashing of
the lights illuminating him, exposing him. He was exhausted;
he'd been running a long time, now. He heard the scream; a
man's voice, and struggled to quicken his pace. Not far now –
the next street. So, he would run and run, and he would arrive
on the next street, to find it was the same street he had just
run from. Not far now – the next street. Again, he was back
where he started. He saw an alleyway, was he lost? Think man!
He dodged down an alleyway and watched in horror as the
stooped figure delivered the final blow. 'Somebody help him!'
he beseeched the crowds of people, but they were laughing
at him mockingly. Lee Mole and Carl Davidson were amongst
them. Even Wagstaff was there pointing at him and laughing
uproariously. 'Fucking idiots – ignore them.' He tried to run
the final hundred yards to get to the killer, but he couldn't.
His feet were stuck to the floor. Still the crowd continued
to scoff. Stark shouted at the killer desperately; 'I know who
your Mum and Dad are. I know where you live!' The dark figure
scurried away. Once out of sight, Stark's feet were released,
and he ran as fast as he could until he reached the lifeless body
on the pavement. It was lying face down, it seemed familiar.
He had a sense he knew him. He turned the body over and saw
the glazed eyes of his own face staring back at him.

He heard a voice a few streets away. A woman's voice. 'David!'
Again, he heard the voice, but this time louder, above him. He
looked to the sky. 'David, wake up!' Carol pushed and pulled at
his sleeping body writhing on the sheets. 'David, you're having
a nightmare.'

David's sub-consciousness eventually received the message
and he began to awaken from his deep, disturbing sleep.

He was bathed in sweat and was panting, his heart racing.
'Bloody hell! Sorry love.' He sat up and Carol, now kneeling on

the bed, put her arms around him. 'No need to apologise, are you OK?'

'I think so, Christ! That was terrifying.'

'What were you dreaming about, for heaven's sake?'

'I was being chased, I think, no I was chasing someone and couldn't get to them. I kept getting lost. Jesus! It was just so bloody real.'

Carol stroked at his matted hair, 'Are you OK now?'

Stark laughed. 'Yes, Mummy, can I have a glass of water, please?' It was typical of Stark to make a joke out of it. He looked over at the liquid crystal display on the clock: 4.13.

'It's not funny, I'm worried about you, Dave. You have had a bad dream every night since Paul died. You've got to come to terms with this, David, love.'

'I know, I will-it's just so . . . oh I don't know. It just takes time I guess.'

'It has been nearly two weeks, since Paul was killed. Can't you get a day off, you need some rest. It's too much.'

'Day off?' Stark laughed. 'No days off until I've caught Paul's killer. Then I can rest.'

'What if he's never caught, love? You can't carry on like this.' She was worried for his sanity.

'He'll be caught, don't worry about that.'

Carol brushed her fingers through his hair and recoiled. 'Ergh! It's wet through.'

'Sweat.' Stark confirmed.

'Your pillow is soaked.'

Dave turned it over.

Carol was still worried. 'Are you sure you are all right now?'

'Yes, I'm fine honestly.' He kissed her and gave her a hug.

'Are you sure?'

'I'm sure. Thank you. Come on let's get some sleep. It's four in the bloody morning.' He said, reassuring her.

Husband and wife cuddled, Carol with her back to him, and he spooned her, their bodies close together. Carol closed her eyes. Dave stared into the darkness – the same darkness that allowed the devils of self-doubt and recrimination to escape again inside him. Later he fell into a twitchy, stunted, troubled sleep; the sort of sleep where every noise sends consciousness racing to the surface again.

The alarm woke Carol at 6.45 a.m. She could smell breakfast cooking downstairs and she sleepily felt for Dave next to her, he wasn't there, the sheets were still wet with sweat. She bit into her bottom lip. She was afraid, afraid for Dave and afraid for her family. She felt completely helpless; she could only pray that things would improve and try to put a brave face on things.

'Morning, chef.' She said cheerily as she landed in the kitchen.

*

The Forensic Science Laboratory at Huntingdon was overwhelmed with work, emanating from hundreds of different cases in the region. The staff were constantly bombarded with human samples; hair, blood, semen, skin, fingernails, toenails, teeth, excrement, body parts, clothing, bits of wood, glass, car-parts, footwear, soil and so the list goes on and on. You name it, they examined it, everything but the kitchen sink, as they say, although in truth, they had three kitchen sinks to examine. To their credit, the scientists more often than not, came up with the goods, and their efforts were vital in the fight against serious crime and locking up the most dangerous criminals in society. The legacy of Monsieur Locard, of course. It was always the process of scientific examination, or more usually, the chain of evidence that would be attacked in courts by defence lawyers whenever forensic evidence was produced at trials. The issue as to whether it was true, or whether the person standing in the dock had actually committed the crime was often not the issue; it was merely sufficient to raise a sliver of doubt to get them acquitted, or a point of law, and if there was a difference in times in a cop's notes versus the exhibit label, you could wave goodbye to a conviction.

Daniel Katuna BSc (Hons) was alone in his own silent world. His laboratory was completely sealed. The room had separate ventilation to prevent cross-contamination from the outside world, or indeed from other laboratories in the complex. He wore a white coat and skin-tight rubber gloves as he stood at the high table, his left eye concentrated over his microscope, watching the strands of DNA dancing with the enzyme he had introduced to the sample. This new DNA 'fingerprinting' was only known by a handful of scientists and was a long and laborious process with a lot of waiting time involved with each sample.

There are only two pieces of evidence which are irrefutable proof of guilt, in given circumstances; good old fashioned fingerprints, and genetic DNA profiling. There was an irrational fear amongst some police and scientists that it was all too good to be true, and that in the years ahead, there would be some discovery that would expose DNA fingerprinting as flawed in some way. More importantly there had been a reticence to use it in the courts as it was felt that it would either be too complex for a jury or that its accuracy would be doubted. If they were to lose a case and at the same time lose this amazing new process to a stated case, it would be catastrophic for law enforcement. It was only a year ago in 1986 that the police first asked microbiologist Alec Jefferys from the University of Leicester to use DNA in a murder case which was to become famous with DNA 'fingerprinting' proving Richard Buckland as innocent, and Colin Pitchfork as guilty, of the rape and murder of two teenage girls in neighbouring villages in 1983 and 1986. It had previously only been used for paternity testing and first tested in the courts with an immigration case. Mr Jeffries and team, had only made the discovery in 1984. Of course, there was no DNA database at this time and so it was used as a strict comparison of one sample with another. The DNA database was slow to get moving and

KEITH WRIGHT

not even given the go ahead for another eight years in 1995. There were human rights issues to consider, and politicians were nervous, as were, amazingly, some senior detectives. It could retrospectively show that a person convicted was innocent. Samples could only be obtained from suspects by their consent, and they were always blood samples that were taken. The Midlands was fortunate that it was at the heart of the new world changing discovery and Stark, in particular was happy to forge the pathway of new technology.

Mr Katuna BSc (Hons) was compiling a DNA profile from Winston Kelly's blood sample, but such is the complexity of the process that it would be an absolute minimum of two weeks before the result could be forwarded to a Detective Inspector Stark at Nottinghamshire CID. It had been 12 days since he began the process.

*

Stark was concentrating hard at the piece of paper on his desk. The envelope, merely had the words 'DI Stark' on it. It appeared to be a female's handwriting, which confused him slightly. Chantelle? Sally? A thin line of smoke headed skywards from his cigar as he scrutinised the riddle.

> THE WARM BRIDE WHO WOULD HAVE FAME WITHOUT ME,
> WHIRLED AND JIGGED IN BLACK,
> WOULD TAKE WITH HER A SIGH, THE NIGHT SHE LEFT.
> WITH OPEN ARMS, SHE WELCOMED THE COVERED HAND
> THAT SMITE HER DOWN,
> THE TRUSTING EYE LOOKS OUT NOT IN
> SIGNED.
> THE FATHERS SON.

Stark pondered over who could have sent it. He had been studying it for quite a while and his mind was starting to wander. He felt it could be Charles Lyon or Winston, or even the mystery smoocher seen with Faye at the club. He felt that the tag 'Mystery Smoocher' did not quite have the same ring to it as The Boston Strangler, Jack the Ripper or Night Stalker. 'Mystery Smoocher, strikes again!' – Perhaps not. Yes, his mind was wandering. The fingerprint department had found nothing on the paper and only a smudged print on the envelope with insufficient loops and swirls to make any sense of it. The mark was not sufficient to be identified, but apparently it did not look like Kelly's or Lyon's. Stark was annoyed with himself for not having solved the riddle yet. If it was Kelly who had sent it, he thought it would be somewhat crude; and Lyon – well, he had more money than brains. Stark felt sure that Winston Kelly had sent it, because apparently it was a young black lad who was seen edging along the wall of the station trying, unsuccessfully, to avoid the CCTV camera. He felt he was getting to know what was making Kelly tick. The boy was a hint for Stark to know that it was Kelly that was making him sweat, that he had the answer and he was going to make Stark work for it. Kelly needed a way out and Stark felt that this was his sadistic way of doing it, albeit quite unexpected and elaborate. It could be a hoax. The publicity around Paul's death had caused a number of crank calls and misdirection's by various non-entities with too much time on their hands. He thought not; it was worth looking at it closely, but with an open mind.

He read it out aloud to himself for the twenty-eighth time.

THE WARM BRIDE WHO WOULD HAVE FAME WITHOUT ME,
WHIRLED AND JIGGED IN BLACK,
WOULD TAKE WITH HER A SIGH, THE NIGHT SHE LEFT.
WITH OPEN ARMS, SHE WELCOMED THE COVERED HAND
THAT SMITE HER DOWN,
THE TRUSTING EYE LOOKS OUT NOT IN.
SIGNED.
THE FATHERS SON.

*

The funeral was to be a full police affair, with a private family burial. Stark had declined the invitation to be a pallbearer and stepped aside for Paul's closer working colleagues, whom the tragedy had hurt just as deeply.

He stood outside the crumbling old cathedral. He was twenty minutes early. He had nodded to several people as they approached the entrance but did not hold their gaze sufficiently to indicate a stop and chat. There were going to be a lot of people attending. The whole of the road surrounding the cathedral had been coned off, with 'No Waiting' the most popular instruction. Police dress was best uniform, white gloves, no medals, and canes for senior officers. It was the white gloves of the non-attending officers that waved frantic directions to the car drivers trying to gain access to park, under the watchful eye of the Divisional Chief Inspector. A couple of traffic wardens hovered in the background to ward off any other cars. Several PC's were patrolling the perimeter to deter any idiots who wanted to shout abuse or mock those attending.

The cathedral was almost three hundred years old and overgrown bushes sheltered the cobbled path which was now lined with a uniformed guard-of-honour. As Stark entered, two PC's muttered his name into a 'memo-cord' recorder. Sounds came from the wall of pipes that was the organ, the keyboard and the organist invisible behind it. Several heads turned as he stopped and looked around; he had that sort of presence about him. He was then ushered into the main part of the cathedral by a uniformed Sergeant.

From the moment that the Fishers had accepted the option of a full police service, the planning had been intricate. The cool air inside was charged with emotion and whispers, from the hundreds already inside the huge space. The police attendees occupied the main blocks of pews at the back and the right-hand side, which stretched all the way up to the altar. Police were also crammed into the rear pews on the far left, the front of that block reserved for the pallbearers and other officiators. The Fishers and a remarkably small amount of civilian mourners, maybe only twenty or thirty family and friends, appeared dwarfed by all the pomp and circumstance. Some of Paul's other friends from college and his time in the service were among them, including Pete Glover who waved shyly at Stark, who nodded in return; Stark's vision then moved beyond him to Mr and Mrs Fisher at the front. Sonia was crying, whilst Michael tried to be stoic. Stark went over and shook Michael's hand and whispered his condolences before taking his seat a few rows behind the civilian attendees. In front and to one side, were Police Federation representatives and the top brass; The Chief Constable, the Deputy Chief Constable, an Assistant Chief Constable, three Chief Superintendents and a gaggle of Superintendents and Chief Inspectors. Mere Inspectors were forced to squeeze in as and where they could find a space. Even the Chairman of the Police Authority and the Civilian Force Administration Officer attended; neither had ever met Paul, but were there to pay their respects.

Stark reached down to the white piece of card in front of him. It was headed 'Service for Thanksgiving for the Life and Work of Paul Fisher – Nottinghamshire Constabulary'. He glanced over the Order of Service. There would be two hymns, a lesson read by the Chief Constable, and address by Detective Chief Superintendent Davies -Head of CID, and one from the Reverend Alan Marsden, the Force Chaplain who had been cursed by ill-health recently, but he insisted on contributing.

Stark and the congregation rose as the Chaplain's voice broke into the hushed assembly, startling them by quoting loudly from the King James Version of the Bible, John 11: 25-26: *'I am the resurrection and the life. He who believes in me, though he may die, he shall live. . .'* Stark's men solemnly carried the coffin of their dead friend and colleague into the aisle of the cathedral behind the chanting cleric. The coffin was draped in the flag of the Nottinghamshire Constabulary. The video cameras secreted outside searched for the face of the killer amongst the crowds and passers-by. Did the killer have the gall to attend, urged by some sort of macabre curiosity?

Stark stared blankly at the wooden coffin, envisaging Paul's body inside it. In his mind's eye he once again saw the image of the undertakers picking him up, stiff and grotesque in death and then worse at the postmortem. He quickly tried to shake the thoughts from his mind; they were persistent, however. All eyes flickered between the coffin and the Fishers. Sonia held a white handkerchief to her mouth, her eyes closed tightly; squeezing tears out of the corners, her shoulders shrugging as she sobbed. Michael had his arm around her. He had aged; it was apparent that he had not slept, his face was drawn and white. Stark was angry – angry at the bastard that had caused this; angry at the people that call our society civilised; angry with himself for not solving the case. He felt helpless and somehow responsible with the killer still at large. He would get him, but right now, there was not a thing he could do about the situation. He could swear vengeance, he could thump his desk another ten times, he could even catch the killer, but Paul would still be dead. He shook his head as the strangers pontificated on the dais. It was all so pointless; he had been a mere boy, really. It was too late to do anything for Paul, other than catch the killer and make him face justice. It was a personal and professional intent.

The Last Post stirred Stark's thoughts and he looked around him at the congregation standing alongside him, for the minute's silence. The optimistic notes of Reveille echoed from the rafters and Paul Fisher was taken to his place of rest. Stark had heard little of what the speakers had said; his service had been a private one – he didn't need anyone to tell him who Paul was, or how to feel.

After a while he slowly filed out of the stone building and into the heat and brightness of the day. He put his sunglasses on to shield the sun and to hide the tiredness he felt. The last white-gloved salute of Chief Inspector Turley shone in the sunlight as he bade a respectful farewell to the cortege. The hubbub of traffic quickly resumed after its temporary pause. Groups of mourners were now talking and smoking and even laughing in their little groups. The world would continue, for the fortunate ones.

Stark shook the hand of Chief Inspector Turley and accepted his condolences, before he left for the police station and a swig of his desk whiskey. Something was niggling at him, tapping away at his brain. Something was wrong.

*

The Reggae Beat Club was a writhing mass of sweaty bodies and screamingly loud reggae music. People from all over the region would come to the club, particularly if they had managed to get a live act to perform. The place was bursting at the seams when they had some of the top Reggae artists such as; Dennis Brown, Barrington Levy or Sugar Minott. Tonight, however it was just records; no live entertainment, apart from the unusual sight of the ebullient Winston Kelly, who was stepping out boldly around the dance floor to the rhythm of Gregory Isaac's 'Night Nurse.' His exaggerated motion was causing quite a stir. Kelly didn't usually get involved with dancing, other than a nodding of his head to the beat. The Reggae beat Club was well known around the East Midlands and beyond, sometimes visitors from farther afield would sample it, or even 'Yardie's' from Jamaica would occasionally check it out. There could be trouble when such visits occurred, it was all about reputation or drugs or old scores to be settled. There had been several stabbings and a couple of shootings in the last ten years at the place and several different 'owners'. The only white man ever to set foot in the place, bizarrely, was DC Charlie Carter, about four years ago. The benefit that Charlie had was that pretty much everyone knew him, and who he was, particularly in the black community. He was given a free pass by Elroy Smith, the guy running the club at the time. Charlie had known Elroy as a kid. One of the teenage street lads Charlie was engaging with; a boy called 'Buff'; named after Buff Bay, the part of Jamaica his parents came from, had negotiated his visit. Buff and his family were poor, and Charlie had spent time trying to get his father a job, on his recommendation. Buff had nothing to give as a thank you, but he insisted on taking Charlie in and when the boy explained to Elroy who it was, and why; he allowed it. Buff wanted to show Charlie what it was like to be the only person of a different colour in a crowded room. Charlie didn't stay long, but he learned a lot. It was a thoughtful gift.

There was no Charlie Carter this night. The dense smoke in the darkened room was penetrated by Kelly's flailing arms. His gold necklace was flapping, and the gold rings on his fingers glistened in the murky haze. He held a can of Red Stripe lager, the contents of which spilled out, because of his loose grip on it, and his jerking body. He captured some of it in his mouth, scooping up the leaking beer from the aperture of the tin. The substantial residue soaked into the bare wooden floorboards, amongst the reefer butts. The noise of the reggae sound caused parts of the furnishings, scant as they were, to vibrate. The crowd, mostly black people from the local community, with the occasional white woman, revelled in Kelly's antics. They mimicked his movements and started to chant cries of support for their latest anti-hero, a certain, Mr Kelly. They were close to fever pitch, the chanting so loud it overwhelmed even Mr Isaac's best efforts: 'Babylon burn! Babylon die!' the West Indians shouted in unison, the wave of noise growing as others joined in, some slipping and falling on the wet floor in the melee as they jumped onto each other, whipping up a frenzy. The funk of sweat was beginning to overtake the Ganga. Kelly whirled around the room, his smile as wide as his face. Kelly was overjoyed. Liberated. He had asked a question of the questioner. 'Irie!'

*

It was 10 p.m. Stark sat behind his desk, his feet perched on top of it; the numerous balls of screwed-up paper betrayed his endeavours at solving the riddle. He couldn't rest. The day's events danced around his mind: the funeral, the desolate grief of a family. He remembered his vow to track down Paul's killer. He tried to expel his emotions and concentrate once more on the job in hand. He cleared his mind and stared down at the piece of paper with the riddle on it for the umpteenth time. He began to think aloud: *'Fame without me . . . fame without me . . .* Of course you idiot! *Fame without me* is "Faye"! He straightened himself in the chair and became a little excited. He was focussing, he was getting on to the right wavelength. 'They are using phonetics.' He mumbled. He began scribbling on a bit of paper and continued talking to himself through the riddle. *'Warm bride. . .* Cold veil?' He tutted and shook his head. 'No that's not it. *Warm bride . . .* Hot. . .' The realisation hit him. 'Oh, Winston, that is so crude: *Warm bride,* hot marry.' Stark laughed. '"Marriott"!' He continued; he felt he was on a roll. *'Whirled and jigged in black. . .* Danced, spun, hopped in black? I'll come back to that. Hold on.' His mind went back to Chantelle Naylor. 'Faye was smooching with the guy at Ritzy's, could that be it? He went on *'Would take with her a sigh. . .* A sigh? God knows what that is . . . *The night she left?* The night she left Ritzy's? The night she left – died? Come on, Winston, give me more than this. . . *Would take with her a sigh, the night she left . . .* Oh Winston, that is good, for you. That's clever. Take the comma out of it, phonetically . . .: *"Would take with her a scythe the night she left!* A scythe – the sign of death. That has to be it. Winston is saying that Faye Marriott has smooched with the guy at Ritzy's, and he eventually killed her. I get it, but tell me something I don't know, Winston. Who the hell is he? I know I'm close, Winston, just give me a tiny shove. *With open arms she welcomed the covered hand that smite her down. . .* With open Arms? So what are you saying: that she asked for it? Could be. *She welcomed the covered hand that smite her down. . .*

Well, there were certainly no fingerprints. .. *Covered hand that smite her down* . . . Just a minute! Bloody hell. Christ. No. It can't be him, Winston, surely!'

He was feeling more than pleased with himself. He took another sip of whiskey, his mind elsewhere, certainly not in his office. He had some calls to make, he would start with Waggy; he reached for the handset, when the phone rang.

Stark jumped. 'Oh shit!' as he spilled his whiskey.

'Stark.'

The man on the other end seemed surprised it was answered. 'Oh, Hello, is that DI stark?'

'Yes, Stark, speaking.'

'Hello, sir. I wasn't sure whether you would be in at this time, but I thought I ought to try. I'm Sergeant Doug Baxter from the Police Liaison Office at Huntingdon Forensic Science Lab.'

'Hello Doug. Any news?'

'We've got the final analysis on the Winston Kelly DNA fingerprint comparisons you asked us to do, you know, from the debris in Paul Fishers fingernails.'

Stark leaned forward. 'Excellent. It's not Kelly is it? Am I right?'

'No it isn't, how did you know that?'

Stark didn't answer the question. 'So, just to confirm, you are telling me that Kelly did not murder Paul Fisher.'

'No, that is not my job, sir, thank God. I am just reporting to you the outcome of a scientific test and that result states: the samples sent from Paul Fisher's fingernails do not match the DNA of the sample of Winston Kelly's blood.'

'Same thing.' Stark was blasé.

'I'm afraid we still don't know who killed Paul.' The Sergeant said cautiously.

Stark sipped his whiskey. 'I do. I know exactly who killed him!'

14

'When ideas fail, words come in very handy.'
Goethe (1749-1832)

Dave had stumbled into bed at 2:50 a.m. Since his unravelling of the riddle, he had been busy organising a rapid response while the going was good. Despite his excitement, the exhaustion that the whole investigation had brought him had been finally released by his discovery and he collapsed into a deep sustained sleep. There were no nightmares. So dense was the veil of black that engulfed him that it was only Carol shaking him vigorously, and her raised voice that dragged him awake.

'Dave, its eight o'clock!'

'You what? Bloody hell! Why didn't you wake me earlier?'

Carol gave her honest answer. 'You were fast asleep for a change, and you've been so tired lately I thought an extra hour would do you good. I mean what time did you get in, the early hours again? Anyway, you are the boss – who is going to mind?'

Stark staggered into the bathroom, followed by Carol. His tiredness caused the inevitable irritable response. 'Carol, Bosses have bosses. I am going to arrest Paul's killer today, for God's sake. The one day I need to be up early you let me rot in my pit.'

Carol was hurt. 'I don't care about any of that. I just care about you. It'll wait, won't it? If you won't look after yourself, I will have to do it for you.'

Stark turned on the shower and placed his hands under the jets of water. 'Carol, I am going to be late!'

She sat on the covered toilet seat. 'Stop panicking. It'll be fine.'

His hand remained cold as the water streamed out. 'There is no bloody hot water now.'

Carol stood and put her hand under the water. 'Oh. Sorry. I could have sworn that there would be enough. Mind you, you usually beat us to it: now you know what it's like to have a cold shower.'

Dave threw himself in and quickly washed his hair and at record speed, amidst jerks and shouts had a swill around. He emerged covered in goose-pimples and shivering. He grabbed at a towel to cover his embarrassment and to rub some warmth into his muscles.

Carol put her hand to her mouth to stifle a laugh. 'I bet you're awake now!' Stark dried himself in silence. They returned to the bedroom, Stark still annoyed.

'That was very amusing, Carol, and do you mind not following me all over the damned place! I'm not in the mood, OK?'

Carol's face dropped. 'God, you're a bloody mardy sod at times, Dave. A bit of cold water and we all have to suffer.'

He was fuming. He knew inside how petty he was being, but he was tired, very tired, and no matter how hard he tried, his nastiness seemed to increase. 'I am not bloody mardy. I just expect basic household necessities to be sorted out properly. I don't go to work every day to end up having a cold shower.'

'It's probably a good job, you'd come home wet.'

'I didn't mean that. You know what I bloody meant!' he barked.

Carol sat on the bed. 'Don't be like that, love, it's only a bit of fun. I am just happy you had a good night at last.'

Stark was sarcastic. 'Sure, let's all be nice and cosy and happy and have lots of fun. Well, I don't feel happy. I'm fed up with you assuming all the time. It's not that long ago I was threatening to discipline Nobby for his lateness, and I have detectives waiting for me at the station and I'm here dancing in the bloody shower.'

Carol bit at her lip, stifling a grin.

'I am investigating a murder; I could be disciplined myself by the hierarchy. I *should* be disciplined. You should have woken me up, that's all there is to it.'

'Here we go,' said Carol sighing.

Stark dressed in the uneasy silence, as his wife sat on the bed watching. He turned towards her and she offered a hesitant smile, which he ignored. Once he was dressed, he gave her a frosty kiss. 'See you later, don't wait up.' He thudded down the stairs and slammed the door shut behind him.

Carol had her hand in the air to wave. 'Bye.' She said to the door.

*

Nobby's carotid artery stood out at the side of his neck as he paced the CID office. He was impatient. 'What sort of a carry-on is this eh?'

Ashley tried to appease his Detective Sergeant. 'Sit down, Nobby, he will probably be here soon.'

His advice was ignored. 'Has anyone rung his house?'

'We thought you might do that, Nobby. It's not for us to ring the gaffer at home.' Ash said.

'I'll give him another ten minutes, but this is ridiculous.' He continued to pace the floor restlessly. He raised the piece of paper he was holding in the sir. 'Have you seen this note he left for me in the diary?

Charlie moved his head to one side, as his feet resting on the desk were obscuring the view of his animated DS. 'Yes, we've all seen the note, Nobby.'

He carried on his trek up and down the office. Nobody spoke, the level of expectancy immense, and the tense atmosphere was not helping them gather their thoughts ahead of what was obviously going to be a big day. Despite Charlie's assurance, Nobby decided to read the note aloud as Steph groaned. '"Nobby. I've cracked it! I will be a few minutes late, I've got a call to make on the way in. Don't let anybody go out, we will need a posse. Cheers, Dave.'" He threw the note on to the desk. 'A few minutes. I mean what sort of a carry on is this?' he repeated.

Charlie was irritated. 'Sit down, Nobby, you're making us all feel bloody dizzy.'

Steph tapped at the seat next to her. 'Sit down, Nobby, he knows what he's doing, I'm sure he will be here soon.' Nobby grudgingly sat down, muttering about 'lack of communication skills.' Steph exchanged glances with Charlie and smiled at him. Steve Aston handed out mugs of steaming tea and coffee. There was a silence, then Nobby blurted out: 'I hope he has cracked it, because I want to get my hands on the bastard that did Paul!'

'Don't we all?' asked Charlie.

'We still have to be professional, for Paul's sake.' Steph said.

There was another lengthy silence. Nobby shook his head disbelievingly. 'Yes, but what I want to know is what sort of a carry-on is this?' He ducked to avoid the barrage of paperclips and rubbers.

*

Wagstaff and Davies had been elated by Stark's call in the early hours. They had fully agreed with his analogy of the evidence, particularly when he explained how he found further evidence beyond the silly riddle, Kelly had sent. Stark had set the wheels in motion to build on that evidence and he had instructed the Special Operations Unit to mobilise immediately, despite the lateness of the hour.

It was as a result of Stark's detailed instructions that the telephone rang and rang in the house. It rang for a full four minutes without answer. There was nobody in. The house was in quite a remote location and it was easier to call first, rather than have headlights going down the country lane towards it and spooking the occupants. The instructions were clear. SOU had their warrant; they were to gain access to the house with the minimum amount of force and search the place thoroughly.

The men forced the front door by smashing a small pane of glass in the door and releasing the Yale lock inside. The damaged piece of glass was replaced while the officers searched inside. The first job for the support officer was to photograph all rooms on the digital camera so he could check that they appeared unmolested once they had finished. They were in their boiler-suits and were careful to replace anything they moved back to its original position. Sergeant Tuckworth's balding head bobbed through the doorways of all the rooms, checking on his officers. This made the search much longer than normal and they had positioned a couple of men on approaches to the house as a crude warning system and a traffic car lay in wait to pull the house owner before he got home, should he get the shout that he was returning.

They made good progress and within an hour and a half Sgt Tuckworth called it as complete. The check of the rooms checked out and all appeared well. He shouted on his radio for DI Stark to be informed that the search was a success with significant finds. As he cleared the team out of the house, Sgt Tuckworth complied with the letter of the law by leaving a copy of the warrant in a 'prominent position'. He unfolded the blue piece of paper and placed it on the Adam-style fireplace. The warrant fell down the back of the mantelpiece, hidden from view. Unfortunately, Tuckworth did not notice this, otherwise, of course, he would have retrieved it. He closed the rear door. It was as if nobody had been there.

*

Stark moved the indicator stick in his car upwards as he waved to Samuel Kelly. Stark was smiling, his faith in human nature restored.

After Charlie's visit a number of days ago, Samuel had spoken to Winston for the first time, man to man. He had asked his son to comply with one wish for his mother's sake: that was to clear the Kelly name, which was now attached to a tragic and awful set of circumstances with the Marriott family murders. Winston had been quiet, as he listened to his father thoughtfully. He then explained what he knew. Winston had kept his promise to his Dad. Stark's subsequent reflections had been right about Winston, and the chill he felt when he looked him in the eyes, at the end of that interview and told him; 'It ain't me, Babylon.' His assumption that Winston had arranged for the riddle to be sent was also correct. It was the only solution Samuel could think of, as Winston had been resolute that he did not, ever, want to be seen as a grass. The conversation would never be mentioned again, but Kelly had cleared his name and vicariously assisted the police in finding the identity of the real killer.

Stark was still grinning as he climbed the steps and walked along the corridor where his men were engaged in a heated discussion.

Charlie was confidant. 'I'm telling you it is that wimp, Charles Lyon. It's the oldest motive in history – sexual ridicule.'

'I've got to go for Winston Kelly,' said Nobby.

'I'm with you, Nobby.' Steve Aston chipped in.

Steph shuffled her backside further on to the desk she was sitting on. 'Yes, but, it's all guess work. How can we prove it?' She asked.

Stark's large frame filled the doorway of the office and the talking stopped. Nobby was the first to speak. 'Where have you been, boss? It's a bit naughty, keeping us in suspense like this.'

Stark threw the piece of paper on to the desk. It was Kelly's riddle. 'It's all in there,' he said.

The detectives all gathered round and Nobby read the riddle out. Stark explained the meaning behind it, line by line. Groans and comments of agreement emanated from the group, then Stark asked the sixty-four-thousand-dollar question. It was so easy it was hard. Who killed Faye Marriott and both her parents? Stark explained.

'I couldn't believe it at first. You see, *the covered hand that smite her down.* The covered hand killed her; don't you get it? What's a covered hand? A glove. Glover killed her.'

The group was startled. Ashley thought aloud, blurting out: 'I don't believe it. Bloody Pete Glover... It can't be Pete: he's an ex copper!'

'That's just it,' Stark said. 'You see, *the trusting eye looks out not in.*'

Nobby's scepticism rose to the surface. 'That is what the riddle says, but who says the riddle is right?'

'I do, Nobby.' Stark said.

Ashley asked the important question. 'Who is the note from?'

'Winston Kelly,' said Stark.

Nobby scoffed: 'You're taking the piss, aren't you, boss? He's just messing with us to throw us off the scent, surely.'

'Don't you think I've thought of all this, Nob? The checks have been made; we've found evidence. SOU have even done a warrant and found further evidence. I can prove it, Nobby. He's the bastard that killed the Marriott's, and he killed Paul!'

There was a stunned silence, before Ashley asked how they could prove it, what was this evidence? Stark explained. 'Glover said in his witness statement that he had broken down on the way home from the club, on the night of the murders.'

Charlie agreed. 'That's right. It was Paul who took the statement off Glover.'

'He lied. He then says that he saw a figure running with a bag. That he had too much to drink, so he didn't give chase. He then went on to the nearest garage and bought some petrol. He put the petrol in the car, which did the trick and so he was able to drive home.'

'I've got the receipt somewhere,' said Nobby.

'No, you haven't, mate: its here.' Stark produced the receipt, which had been recovered from the garage, from his pocket. He handed it to Nobby. 'See anything unusual about it?' he asked.

Nobby studied the small square of paper. He shook his head. 'No, not at all.'

'One pound eighty-eight for a gallon of petrol?' Stark hinted.

'What's wrong with that?' asked Nobby.

Stark smiled. 'Nothing, apart from the fact that on the night Glover bought the petrol that supposedly fired his car into life, diesel from that garage was one pound eighty-eight: petrol was one pound *ninety-four!* His is in a petrol driven car, not diesel. He'd put the wrong sort of petrol in his can, so he couldn't have put it in his car. His car couldn't have been driven away, because it had never broken down!'

There was another pause.

Charlie made a sensible comment. 'It could be a mistake by the garage.'

'They don't think so, Charlie, it's automated anyway. This is just the starter for ten. I've got a list of evidence here to choose from. Mistakes that prove Glover is our man.'

Ashley looked puzzled. 'Why on earth would Glover want to kill the Marriott's and then Paul, for God's sake?'

Stark surmised. 'I don't think that Glover intended to do anything untoward. I think events took over. What makes somebody become a killer? It is apparent now that Peter Glover met Faye Marriott in Ritzy's Night Club. He is the mystery smoocher. He smooched with her, and she promised him more, so he took her home. She, of course, invited him in for coffee and played soft music on the hi-fi. The kissing turned to groping, Faye teasing and getting Glover wound up like a watch spring. He was so into it, he obviously did not want to stop. Faye decided to play one of her old tricks and tried to stop Glover at the last moment.'

'Dangerous.' Steph said.

'Talking from experience, Steph?' Nobby grinned.

'Yes, every time I bend down in front of you.'

'True.' Nobby gave her that one.

Stark continued. 'Glover no doubt thought she couldn't

mean it; having let him go this far and so he carried on. She started to protest as he began sexual intercourse, so he covered her mouth with his hand.'

'Probably thought her parents were upstairs in bed.' Ash commented.

'Maybe so.' Stark agreed before continuing. 'Remember there were no strangulation marks on her neck. Unfortunately for her, he had covered her nose also so that she couldn't breathe. He must have noticed that she had died before he ejaculated.'

'Death is a big passion killer.' Steph said.

'Talking from experience, Steph?' Nobby asked again.

'Yes, anybody ever told you, you look like death every morning?'

Stark continued. 'He had killed her, he hadn't meant to, but he had. He began to panic, and it was at this time that the unfortunate Walter and Audrey Marriott could be heard hastily approaching the door on the gravelly path. Instead of running out the back, or maybe the door was locked, who knows? He grabbed the brass clown ornament in the hall and hid behind the door. You know the rest.'

Ashley was amazed. 'Surely, he could have just run out of the door, either front or back. Why make it worse?'

Stark replied. 'Is a man who has killed a girl by accident just thirty seconds before, thinking straight? Was the door locked? Not only that, Glover obviously has some issue with his temper and losing it, look at why he was kicked out of the force, breaking a woman's jaw.'

'He said that was a stitch up, though, Paul was telling me.' Ash said.

'Did he really, oh, well that must be true then, Ash, eh?' Stark was being sarcastic. 'I've dug a bit deeper in all that to understand, what is the truth, and what is rumour? The woman, who was a young girl at the time, incidentally, just happens to be one Bernadette Kelly, one of Winston Kelly's ten thousand cousins. She maintains to this day that Glover did attack her, simply punching her in the face for no reason. Winston knew more about this than we did, it seems.'

'It is starting to form a bit of a picture about Glover.' Charlie agreed.

'It's not a picture, Charlie, it's a portrait. Bernadette was persuaded not to make a complaint if he resigned and so he had no criminal conviction. When you go back through his record, he had two other allegations of assault against him, one was for GBH but none were ever proved. The GBH was after he left the job: some youths cornered him, he pulled a blade and cut one of them. He was cornered again, but this time by Mr and Mrs Marriott.'

Ashley spoke to Nobby. 'I can't believe it, can you, Nobby?'

'I'll believe anything on this job, but there is still a lot to prove to convict. It fits but it is all supposition. Have we got anything else, boss?'

'Glover, typical ex-cop, thinks he knows about investigations; thought he could cover his tracks. Fortunately for us, he had not been a copper that long, so he didn't really know what he was doing.'

'Maybe getting off all the other stuff, gave him a bit of confidence?' Steph noted.

'Probably so, Steph. The piece of shit actually waved to me at Paul's funeral, can you believe it?' Stark grimaced.

Nobby's brain was almost visibly churning. 'What about the phone call to Bernie Squires that you picked up?'

Stark was ready with the answer. 'It turns out, Terry Banner had got rid of thirty five video recorders which were nicked from a warehouse the night before, some place out of town. He was just letting Bernie know in his half-cocked way. The two of them and a couple of other idiots have been arrested for a series of warehouse breaks all over the Midlands.'

'We could still use some proof, boss.' Nobby observed.

Stark smiled and drew back a playful punch at Nobby. 'You won't have it will you? Look at this.' He put his hand in his trouser pocket and threw a piece of paper on the desk. 'Have a read of that.'

Nobby picked it up. It was a photocopy of a betting slip. The original safely packaged. He read it aloud. '"Squires Turf Accountants" is the heading and it has a telephone number scribbled in pen across it – 0115 9425675.'

Stark continued. 'Remember in the statement Paul took off Glover, he denied any knowledge of the Marriott family at all. Never heard of them. Guess whose phone number that is.'

'Faye Marriott's' came the chorus.

'It's the same slip that she gave to Charles Lyon. He found it in his jacket the next day and called her.' Steph remembered.

Stark continued. 'It was found in Pete Glover's pocket diary, in his house, stuffed loosely in it with a dozen other similar scraps of paper with phone numbers on.'

'He's a bit shagger, then is he?' Ash commented.

'A bit of a prat. Why didn't he get rid of it?' Nobby grunted.

Stark gave a view. 'I don't suppose it would have crossed his mind, Nobby. You see as always, Faye would have given him her telephone number earlier in the night, before there was a hint of any problem, when everything was cosy. I bet he put it in his diary there and then, with the others, and never gave it another thought. It was several hours after that that he turned murderer, the telephone number long forgotten, no doubt.'

'What about Paul – why him?' Stephanie asked.

'The night that Paul got drunk was the night he was killed, if you remember...'

'How could we ever forget?' Charlie said.

'Yes, sorry. Well, I reckon Glover was either at the pub, where you all were, and then went to Ritzy's or he just went straight to Ritzy's where he knew Paul might be. In fact, I suspect that Glover was using his former friendship with Paul to keep in touch with him to keep a tab on how the investigation was going. Remember we saw him "coincidentally" in the pub next door with that fit bird. Paul was pissed and was probably mouthing off his theories about the smooching man, he was doing it in the pub wasn't he, Charlie?'

'He was, I tried to get him to shut up. I was more worried

about the black brotherhood standing behind us, sending us the voodoo, than anyone else.'

'Careless talk, costs lives, unfortunately it was his own life.' Stark said shaking his head. 'Paul would be mouthing off about his theories in all innocence, we've all done it if we are honest, perhaps showing off a bit to Glover, and whilst these were just theories to Paul, they struck a big chord with Glover, and he started to panic.'

'He thought we were getting close.' Nobby said.

'Well, yes. That's why he waited for Paul, near the club.'

Ashley was curious. 'How do you know all this, sir?'

'The riddle prompted me to double-check everything we had done that involved Glover. Faye's telephone number wasn't the only thing that SOU found. There were other discoveries too. They have found two spots of dried blood on an old sheet, on the garage door, about the size of a ten-pence piece; enough for us to check genetically. My bet is that the blood is Paul's. After the attack on Paul, Glover would have been absolutely soaked in blood. This would have dripped in the garage as he walked through it. He's been fairly clever in that he appears to have disposed of any other bits of clothing, but he has missed the drip factor. I bet he hasn't considered either, that all the fibres and blood that he thinks he has cleaned away in his car, will still have residue evident, once the forensics team tow it away, and get started on it. I will be amazed if they don't find a matching fibre in the house when forensics go in.'

'I thought you said he would have disposed of the clothing, and SOU didn't find anything?' Ashley said.

'I did, Ash, but his other clothing and furnishings at his house will have been in contact with the jumper he wore that night, fibres are like Velcro.'

Ashley nodded. 'Brilliant.'

The group fell quiet. 'Let's get the bastard.' Nobby said.

'Do we know where he is?' Steph asked.

Stark shook his head. 'He's not been home. There has been

a car parked up nearby all night. We know where he works, though don't we?'

'Let's go!' Nobby said again.

'Hold on, Nobby. Let's get organised first, this prat has nothing to lose. SOU haven't found the video, screwdriver or knife, so he could still have the knife on him. He must have been carrying it the night he killed Paul.'

'Good!' said Nobby. 'Cos, I'm going to make him eat the bastard.'

Charlie joined in. 'Yes, let's go and get the little shit.'

'I've just said, Charlie, hang on a minute!' Stark gestured for them to all sit down. 'I want this bastard as much as you do, but we owe it to Paul to get it right. We don't want to lose it on a technicality or lose him because we rush things. Let's not forget that he has already killed one copper. That is one too many. We need to do a bit of planning first. Now, I'm going to be in on the strike when we nick him. Who's coming with me?'

'I will!' The cry was simultaneous and unanimous.

*

Stark was surrounded by computer screens, telephones and radio equipment as he sat in the control room, gathering his thoughts. He regretted the tiff he and Carol had had before he came out the house. He wanted to call her and make things right, but he simply had too much to do. The plan was straight-forward. No need to overcomplicate it. After all options had been considered, it was decided to take Glover within the confines of his own house, if possible. It was quite secluded and would lessen any danger to the public more than if they took him out at work. RCS were to locate and follow Glover, keep control of him from afar. Once they had 'housed' him they would inform Stark and his men, waiting in nearby streets, who would strike and arrest him. There had been a discussion about RCS keeping the decision rights to take him out, if a safe opportunity arose. Stark reluctantly agreed, but it was understood that if possible, Stark and his team would be the ones to arrest him.

Stark walked into the general office. It was empty. He couldn't bear it any longer: he had to phone Carol. He went to the telephone: all the outside lines were engaged. He would wait; he had to speak to her before they left. He didn't like parting on an argument, not today, of all days.

The door opened; it was Nobby. 'We are going to have to get going, boss.' he said.

Stark again glanced at the still illuminated lights on the telephone. He winced as he stood up. 'Come on, then, Nobby. Let's do this for Paul.'

Stark led his loyal troops out of the station. The lights on the phone went out. Paul Fisher's friends drove off in their cars to capture his killer, each of them apprehensive but focussed. None of them was sure how they would react on seeing Glover. He had killed, and he would kill again if trapped – he had nothing to lose.

*

The phone in DI Stark's office rang. There was no reply. She was just about to ring off when it was answered. 'David?' she enquired.

'DI Stark's office, PC Winters speaking.' The young voice was unknown to Carol.

'Oh. I'm sorry. Can I speak to DI Stark, please? It is rather important.'

'I'm afraid he is out at the moment. Who's calling, please?'

'It's his wife, Carol. Do you know when he will be back?'

'I'm afraid I don't, can I take a message?' The PC asked politely.

'No, it's fine . . . actually yes, if you would. Have you got a pen?'

The young PC extracted his black biro from the top pocket of his blue shirt. 'Yes. Fire away.'

Carol felt a little embarrassed, but it had to be done. 'Just put, "Sorry about earlier. Ring me when you can. I love you, Carol."' The PC smiled to himself and added a kiss at the end for good measure, before leaving the note on Stark's desk.

Carol felt unusually uneasy, nervous even, as she paced around her living-room. 'Stop being bloody silly,' she muttered to herself. 'He's probably out in the bloody pub. He'll ring later, when it suits him, I bet.' A shiver shot down her spine. She bit at her lip and stared out of the window at Christopher and Laura, talking on the lawn in the sunshine. The children saw her and waved. Carol smiled and waved back. 'He'll be OK, won't he?

15

'Are you going to come quietly,
or do I have to use earplugs?'

From *The Goon Show*

Pete Glover sat in the small, makeshift kitchen in his insurance company offices. The kitchen consisted of a sink, kettle, and microwave and that was it. He sipped at his cup of tea. He still couldn't believe what had happened. How it had come to this. He reconstructed the events of that fateful night in his disturbed mind. It wasn't really his fault. She'd offered it him on a plate. She had begged him to go in for a coffee; any normal red-blooded male would have gone in. Even when they were in the car, her tongue had played with his, in a passionate kiss, supporting her request. Her hands had explored his erect member as it strained at his trousers and 'coffee' seemed like a great idea. Their passion had continued inside on the soft settee, spilling on to the floor. He could feel her moistness as he rhythmically rubbed at her clitoris. She was loving it. He was just about to enter her, the end of his penis was between her lips, and then she said 'No! You can't!' It was too late he had entered her. She started squirming and pushing at him, and then shouting protests; things were turning nasty. He did what a lot of men do when they begin to lose control of a desperate situation: he used his physical strength. He knew that after all her teasing, he wouldn't be long, so he thought he would carry on and just cover her mouth to shut her up, and then- oh God! Why did she have to be a prick teaser? Why did those idiots have to come home when they did?

It was everybody's fault apart from him. He had panicked; anyone would under those circumstances, surely? He should have just run away . . . and then what? Do life imprisonment? No way.

He got off his chair and began pacing the kitchen. He was getting agitated again. He had to remain calm. He had scarcely slept since . . . since Paul. It had to be done, he thought. It was either him or me. What did he have to go all clever for? Saying that he knew who the killer was. Saying he was going to view the CCTV again at Ritzy's. Was he warning me? He looked so serious, grim, disappointed when he said it, and when he asked, 'is your car diesel, or petrol, then, Pete?' That was the icing on the cake. Surely, he was being sarcastic when he asked if I had seen any good video's lately. He knew all right. I couldn't risk it. He had to be disposed of. Him or me.

Pete threw the plastic cup into the kitchen bin and pondered his next move. If he stayed calm everything would just go away. It was when he panicked that things went wrong. They would never dream it was him, he had helped them. He was a witness for God's sake! He was one of them. In a couple more weeks the enquiry would start to stutter and stall, and then in a couple more, it would start dropping staff off and before you know it, it would be winding down. Some police chief would start looking at their budget and officers would return to their Divisions gradually when the local crime rate rose because of their absence. Or better still another murder or major enquiry, getting priority, as this all fell out of focus. Everything would be just fine, just keep his wits about him. He had covered his tracks well enough. It was a mistake opening that window before chiselling away at it properly. It's hardly surprising, he had just killed three people for fuck's sake! He was bound to make mistakes, same with the bloody diesel. You just aren't thinking straight. If it wasn't for all that, they would still be looking for a burglar, and Paul would still be here. He had to report it as a witness, he understood there is always someone who sees you. If they'd come for him, he would have been a suspect not a witness, he could control things better if he went to them. It was fine. He just had to stay calm and confident and forget that any of it had ever happened.

Pete glanced at his watch: 12.30. He would go home for his lunch. He couldn't stand the thought of dining with the crowd today. As he stepped out of the offices into the street he didn't look twice at the man on the bench, eating his chips. The man was in his thirties, with long straggly hair and a stubble chin. His single ear-ring gave him a gypsy appearance, with tattooed arms and grubby fingers that concentrated eagerly on stuffing in the chips as quickly as possible. His general scruffiness belied his true identity: DC 1219 Sumter of the Regional Crime Squad. He was the 'foot man' to begin with; the 'off' man, and as he disposed of his chips he followed his quarry.

Glover reached his car; parked on a nearby road, and DC Sumter walked past the junction and passed him on to the next surveillance operative. Sumter was picked up by the fourth car as the first three took Glover on his journey, which was to lead to his front door. They had not gone down the country lane but passed on the surveillance to the two crop men. Crop men were experts in camouflage, and they had been at different sides of the field under a hedge since midnight last night, pissing in a bottle and focussing through their telescopes at the house belonging to Glover.

He let himself in. There was an odd feeling to the house. He took off his jacket and prepared to cook his under-the-grill pizza. He opened the cutlery drawer for a knife and fork – he froze. A tingle shot down his spine. He knew the compartmental plastic container, which separated the different pieces of cutlery should be, from left to right, knives, forks and spoons – *not* forks, spoons and knives. If nothing else Glover was a creature of habit. Somebody had been in the house. He looked out of the window and saw two men on the street beyond the hedge, talking. They were not RCS, but Glover did not know that. 'Fucking hell.' His panic rose to fever pitch and a knot formed in his stomach. He ran upstairs and changed into jeans.

White T shirt and bomber jacket. He didn't bother packing; he simply collected his passport from the dressing-table drawer. He had all his credit cards on him. He put the passport in his jacket pocket, vaulted down the stairs, grabbed a large kitchen knife, and ran out of the door to his car. The crop men shouted the alarm on their radios. Glover was back mobile. There was no opportunity to arrest. There was a killer on the loose!

*

Stark and his team had started their engines and were waiting for the call to strike. They were only in the next street, and nerve-ends jangled. RCS had reported that Glover had returned to his house. This was the moment of truth.

Stark's foot revved the engine. 'Come on,' he said to himself more than to anyone else.

Nobby, in the passenger seat, was impatient. 'What the pissing hell is going on? We should be going in now!'

Ashley spoke from the back seat. 'Can't we radio them up, sir, and see what's going on?'

Stark revved the engine again. 'Just bide your time, lads. RCS have got the eyeball, they can see what is happening, and we can't.' The tension in the car had caused the windows to steam up.

Nobby was not convinced. 'We know he's in there. Why can't we just hit it?'

Stark said. 'It's not as simple as that. They have got to make sure that he isn't going to just come straight back out again, as they approach.' He revved the engine again. Being the boss not only included making the decision, it included batting away the myriad suggestions and questions from the team when the tension grew. It wasn't always easy. The silence made the seconds drag out like minutes. 'They have obviously seen him doing something in the house, or there is a complication,'

'RCS to DI Stark.' The radio crackled.

Stark snatched the handset resting on his lap. 'Go ahead.'

'The target has left the house and is moving. We'll continue with the follow.'

'Ten-Four. Keep us posted.'

'Yes, yes. He's changed his clothes, white T shirt, black leather jacket. I hope he hasn't clocked us.'

Stark replied. 'If he has, we'll have to take him wherever we can, in the safest place possible.' His brow furrowed as he put the radio down. 'Shit! Now what's he up to?'

RCS followed Glover's car along the streets of Nottingham and on towards the motorway on the A453, close by. The convoy followed him the short distance to East Midlands Airport, then contacted Stark. The radio contact was not working well, so they had to get the Force Control Room to contact the local control room, to then contact Stark and update him on the local frequency.

Stark replied through the same chain. 'He's obviously sussed that we want him. Contain him at the airport; we're on our way. If he tries to board a plane, arrest him for murder.'

*

Glover was sweating. The carving knife was uncomfortable in the inside pocket of his leather jacket. He was a wanted man. He was nearing the end of his yellow brick road. What was it to be? Death, escape or imprisonment? He had made it to the Airport foyer. He had to appear quite normal, but he felt that everybody was staring at him. He approached the British Midland Airways desk, went through the booking process and clung on to his one-way cancellation ticket to Paris. Once in mainland Europe he could go anywhere from there. It was the furthest he could get away at such short notice. He would have to seek out a non-extradition country, if he could just avoid the Airport Police at Paris. He looked at the clock: 2.22 p.m. Was he being followed? His flight was only an hour before take-off. He would have to ditch the knife at the last minute.

The foyer was thronged with travellers- the information

board indicated that there were no delays and that he should board at Gate 3. He considered hiding in the toilet, but if the police saw him going there, he would be trapped. He didn't think he was being followed, so, if he could just bide his time, he might just pull this off. He decided on the safer option of mingling with the crowd, until the very last second, when he would jump on to his flight and away. He stood at a row of telephone hoods and pretended he was making a call. He didn't want to leave the country, but it was this or a life in prison. He scrutinised every face that came within fifteen yards of him, his mind scrambling with fear and paranoia. He stole a glance at the uniformed policeman standing near the information desk. He felt as if everybody knew who he was, as if there was a big sign above his head with MURDERER displayed on it. There must have been a thousand people milling around, and Glover felt uneasy, jumpy; he felt cornered.

He saw a quick dart of movement to his right. It was the figure of a man appearing in the airport entrance doorway, then deftly stepping aside to hide behind a wall. Glover recognised the face: it was Detective Inspector David Stark. Glover's heart was pounding. He had to do something quickly. He glanced at his watch: 2:42. He had to cause a diversion and he had to do it now. He reached for his knife.

*

Glover's days were numbered, but human nature dictates that you fight for your life, and it was with this in mind that Stark decided to arrest Glover immediately. They had done enough softly-softly policing. The time had come to hit the bastard and to hit him hard.

Stark felt that Glover might have seen him when he arrived in the doorway; but if he had, he hadn't shown any signs of it. Stark was with his detectives near the doorway and the RCS contingent were spread out, but mainly near the bar area and perimeter exits. Their radios were useless in the hubbub of the plane engines, flight announcements, luggage trolleys and a thousand goodbyes.

Stark surreptitiously started to walk across the foyer to inform RCS that they were going to move in and hit Glover now – but he never got there. Initially when he heard the shrill sound, he thought it was an aeroplane reversing. He was wrong: it was the fire alarm. 'Glover!' he said.

What followed was bedlam. Men, women and children panicked en-masse. They were rushing everywhere, in all directions, and mainly towards the area where the detectives stood. Glover had created his barrier and Stark could only watch as he crept through the doors that led to a safe passage to Paris.

Dave Stark fought with all his might against the full force of the tide of people; all thinking that there could be a terrorist attack or fire to escape from. The others were stuck too. Stark alone had a chance of catching the killer. He was closest. The others had no view of Glover. Stark used all his strength to fight against the hordes and get to Glover. Eventually he reached the double-doors behind which Glover had disappeared; the chaos of the alarms and auto-opening fire doors, enabled him to by-pass security while they were distracted. A security guard realising too late that Glover had evaded the search area, stepped in Stark's way: 'I'm sorry, sir, the fire escape is...' He didn't finish his sentence: Stark had knocked him flat on his back as he barged through. 'Police!' he shouted over his shoulder.

Once through the doors, he could see Glover in the queue of people entering the jumbo jet on the tarmac airfield. The two men's eyes met. Glover was about a hundred and fifty yards away from the plane: he knew that he would never make it. He turned and ran, across the tarmac, and under the plane. He pulled out the carving knife from inside his jacket. The blade shone in the sunlight as Glover's arms moved like bees wings to escape the Inspector who was quickly gaining on him, cutting off the corner.

As Stark ran, his mind created fleeting images of his own family; Carol and Chris and Laura, of a family brutally murdered, and a young man cut down in the prime of his life. Stark was angry, the sort of mad-dog angry that can make a man kill. He saw the blade, he thought of Nobby's threat to make Glover eat it: it seemed like a good idea. Stark knew he was going to catch him. He was running towards high fencing. Glover also knew he was going to be caught. He was scared. He stopped and turned around, brandishing the knife. Stark stopped. They had reached the end of the runway, near some shrubbery and thereafter baron land and the fence. They stood fifteen feet apart.

From the area of the boarding gate, in the distance, rows of open-mouthed faces stared down at the two men on the tarmac. Passengers were still streaming out of the terminal with the alarm blaring unabated, all the emergency services had headed *into* the building.

Both men were breathing heavily. Stark stood with his fists clenched at his side, his face menacing and intense. Glover stood with the knife in his right hand, his left outstretched, palm face down.

'Just you and me, then Stark!' he said, puffing and panting.

'*Mr* Stark, to you, kid.' He growled. His anger intensified the grimace on his face, and he bared his teeth. His heavy breathing and his contempt forced grunting noises from his mouth. Stark wasn't there to chat. He was incensed. Enraged. Red mist. Tunnel vision. There were no bargaining chips for a four-time murderer. He wanted to get at him and tear him limb-from-limb. He lunged at Glover. The knife cut into Stark's left upper arm, but he felt no pain, that was for later. Glover was knocked to the ground, with Stark on top of him. The Inspector got hold of his right arm, holding the knife against the tarmac. Stark looked into Glover's eyes and smiled. Glover was afraid, he could feel that Stark was stronger, and it was his turn to deal with someone who was in a position to fight back, for a change.

'Drop it, you bastard!' Stark punched Glover hard in the face, breaking his nose. Glover clung on to the knife, but he was powerless to resist. He was petrified; he had never seen such hate and it scared him senseless. He pleaded for mercy: 'All right, all right. Let me get up.'

Stark punched him in the face again. 'You cunt! Did you give Paul a chance? You killed a decent fucking man!'

An image of young Paul's cut-up face seared into Stark's brain. Glover released his grip on the knife and Stark threw it to one side. He had lost his self-control. He was unhinged. He placed his strong hands around Glover's throat. Glover clawed at Starks hands and writhed around, but to no avail as Stark squeezed hard, forcing a gurgle out of Glover's gullet.

Stark's eyes were wide and maniacal. 'Why don't you kill me, eh, Glover? Why not kill me, you fucking cowardly piece of piss!' Spittle landed on Glover's face, his eyeballs were starting to protrude, and his body started to relax through lack of oxygen. His body was like a rag doll in Stark's hands.

'Sir, no! For Christ sake don't!' Ashley shouted, as he raced towards the two figures, his colleagues close behind. Stark heard the young detective's pleas. His hatred started to subside and again he thought of his young children. This would be murder. This was prison. He released his grip on Glover and threw him down on the floor, the wretched killer's teeth cutting into his bulbous tongue and fetching blood as he choked and gasped, retching, as his body searched for oxygen. He was limp but huge intakes of breath threw out blood and snot as he struggled to survive. It was a close-run thing. Stark stood up over the pathetic sight, riddled with contempt. After a couple of seconds, Glover rolled on to his side, curling into a ball, clutching at his neck and crying and whimpering like a stuck pig. The others finally caught up with Ashley. 'Are you all right, boss?' Nobby asked, ignoring Glover.

'Get him out of my fucking sight!' said Stark.

The men led Glover away, still coughing and spluttering. Stark sat on the tarmac floor and buried his face in his hands.

Nobby looked at Ashley, and then at Stark. 'Go, on Ash, we'll join you in a minute.'

Ashley used his handkerchief to pick the knife up carefully, and then jogged away to catch up with the others. Nobby called after him. 'Tell him he's nicked, if he hasn't worked it out!'

Nobby sat down next to his Detective Inspector in silence. Stark reeled backwards feeling the pain of the cut for the first time. 'Fuck! That hurts!'

The DS put his hand on Stark's shoulder. 'Are you OK, sir?'

'I think so, Nobby.' He blew out a gasp, obviously shaken, and began to press at the wound on his arm to apply direct pressure. 'I should have killed that bastard!'

Nobby laughed. 'I think you almost did.'

Stark laughed with relief. His senses returning. He shook his head. 'If Ashley hadn't come when he did –.' he began.

Nobby interrupted him. 'Ashley did come. It's over with now, Dave. Paul can rest in peace.'

'Yes, I know. You're right. Thanks. Nobby.'

Nobby shrugged and smacked his boss on the back. 'No problem.'

'Ow! Watch me fucking arm!'

'Sorry, boss.' Nobby stifled a laugh. 'Come on, boss, let's get that seen to. It's pissing blood.'

*

Stark lay bare-chested on the gurney in the airport medical centre with his shirt in a heap at his feet. The attractive young nurse with blonde hair smiled at the brave policeman as she bandaged his wounds. 'How many stitches?' he asked her.

'Twenty three, I think.' She said.

'Just a scratch, boss.' Nobby said.

Stark had fulfilled his promise to himself to catch Paul's killer. He had thought he would be elated, but he just felt numb, empty – drained of all emotion. He shook his head.

Why did all this have to happen? It wasn't going to bring Paul back.

The nurse had finished attending to the police's latest hero, and turned to go.

'Excuse me, nurse?' Nobby said

'Yes?'

'I think I may have bruised my groin area, could you rub it better, please?'

'Very funny.'

'Behave, Nobby.' Stark said.

'So it's a no, then?' Nobby asked.

'I hear it every day.' She grinned.

Nobby shrugged. 'It's when you don't hear it, you need to worry.'

'Ha ha. True.' She winked at him as she walked out the room.

Stark swivelled sideways and hung his legs over the side as he sat on the gurney, his arm now in a sling. Nobby helped him drape his bloodied shirt over his shoulders and fastened a couple of buttons.

'I'll get you a gown or something to put over yourself, Dave. That shirt is an exhibit.' Nobby said.

Stark laughed. 'Cheers, Nobby. I guess you're right.'

Stark lowered himself down gingerly until his feet hit the cold floor and he slowly stood up. He still felt a bit shaky. He shuffled to the callbox near the door and rang his wife. It was answered immediately. 'Wow. That was quick. Hello, love it's me...'

He didn't get a chance to finish. 'About time, too. What time do you call this? Where are you? All you do is swan about all day, without a thought about me sitting at home going out of my mind with worry! I bet you've been in the pub all day, while I'm here with the kids hassling me every ten minutes, you're out there having the time of your life. Well, it's not on! Why didn't you ring me back?'

Stark smiled. It was good to be alive. Kind of.

THE END

If you enjoyed the book please take two mins
to leave a review on Amazon, Kindle, Goodreads or the author's web-site:
Keithwrightauthor.co.uk

Follow the author on Twitter: @KeithWWright

Exclusive- witness the opening pages of Keith Wright's up-coming book:

'Trace and Eliminate'

A Novel from the Inspector Stark series – Book 2

1

'But bacon's not the only thing,
That's cured by hanging from a string.'
Hugh Kingsmill

James was smiling as he leaned out of the car window to wave to his wife and child. Sarah stood on the porch, clutching their little girl's hand, and waving back enthusiastically. 'Bye, James. Love you!'

'Love you too.' He began to wind the electric window up, diminishing the sound of Sarah's request: 'Bring some milk back if you can.' He gave a thumbs up sign, indicating he had heard, although it was a pain in the arse.

He wasn't to know this was the last goodbye. That he would never again feel the softness of her cheek against his, or the squeeze of little Katy's all-giving hug. Maybe he should have known. If he had been more aware, and had his wits about him, he might have seen, but he wasn't, so...

He glanced over towards the door as he reversed the car, and saw them troop back inside, into the warmth.

Sarah's good-bye, although distant, had alerted the hidden figure into a state of taut expectation, stomach churning, and mouth dry. There was no going back now.

The route was a familiar one to James, or 'Jim', as he was sometimes called, or if you were his parent's, 'Jack'. His Mum and Dad were the only ones who called him Jack. When Sarah first heard of this anomaly, she used her skewed logic: 'If they wanted to call you Jack, they should have called you John'. That was why he loved her.

James drove the same roads every week-day from home to the office. Despite the bitter chill and depressingly overcast sky of a January morning, the inside of the car was beginning to cosy-up, and his tape of Pavarotti warmed the cockles of his heart. He liked a good old blast of a tenor or two to get the blood pumping. His blood would be pumping soon enough, but he did not know that, because he didn't pay attention.

Although it was eight o'clock, the roads were not as bad as they could be, and James felt he was making good progress. He lowered his foot on the accelerator and let the music flood over him, his deep, slightly off-key voice endeavouring to match the great singer's.

Things were looking up for James. He considered himself to be one of the 'new breed' of solicitors. At Johnson & Brown he was definitely the blue-eyed boy, and at twenty-five the future was looking distinctly rosy. He slowed down as a solitary cyclist pushed his bike across the road. He waved and smiled in acknowledgement. All the efforts he had made and the years of College and University and the law exam, and all that drudgery were paying off. A nice house and a decent car and a beautiful family. Katy was three, the best age, and that innocence and dependency was what he thrived on. What else was there? Maybe two holidays a year instead of the one, but he was working on that.

James slowed down as he approached the rail-track junction, sensing danger, there was something of a commotion. Some guy was farting around in the road, surely, he can't be drunk at this time of the bloody morning. He indicated to turn left, once he had figured out what this idiot was going to do. Was he waving him down? No. All was well. The crazy guy had decided to stagger off back onto the pavement and away down the side street. Maybe it was drugs, or something? His car was almost at a stand-still. James reached to turn the music down a little. His head smashed into the side-window with the force of the blow to his neck. The large carving-knife slid relatively easily through his carotid artery, severing both his trachea and oesophagus and chipping the glass of the window as it exited the other side. The killer held the force of the blow and twisted the knife savagely, grunting with the exertion. Steel could be heard grinding on bone and gristle. The bastard withdrew the knife in preparation for a second blow, but it quickly became apparent that another would not be necessary. James slumped in his seat and instinctively raised his hand to his throat, but it hovered in mid-air, his dying brain not really fathoming what was happening. His body worked hard to pump blood and adrenaline to the source of the trouble, but this was a bad idea as it pumped out of his artery at an alarming rate. With each heartbeat the spray of blood diminished, until it became a mere trickle. The killer opened the rear nearside door and fled, only a second before the car, still rolling, slewed into a telegraph pole. The impact causing little Katy's daddy to flop around like her favourite ragdoll. A whistling sound was emitted from the gaping hole in his neck, which was making his mouth redundant, desperately trying to breathe on its behalf, and failing. The whistling subsided like a boiled kettle, and the trickle of blood halted completely as Pavarotti's final tremulous, diminuendo top C faded. The music stopped.

*

For several minutes the car remained undiscovered, the cassette player, having moved on to the next track, delivering a strident operatic melody.

Outside the vehicle, and a full thirty yards away, a repetitive squeaking could be heard. A young newspaper-boy, cycled towards death. His heavily laden bag tilting him slightly, and his front wheel was weaving. He was still half asleep, as he faced the challenge of delivering the morning newspapers to the neighbourhood to get his two pounds. He cycled past the car, his mind miles away, until it slowly dawned on him. He applied the brake. 'That's weird.' He got off the cycle and looked back towards the vehicle. It was at an angle and appeared to have hit the telegraph pole, it wasn't on fire or anything, so it was probably okay. He could see someone inside, though; the bloke had a funny look on his face, but he couldn't see properly, with the light shearing across the windscreen. Instinctively he felt that something wasn't right. The paper boy was a boy scout and he had sworn an oath to 'do his best' and 'to help others.' In his innocent mind, he felt he should investigate and started to tentatively walk towards the car, wheeling his bicycle. As he reached the driver's side window, his eyes met those of James Deely, grotesquely frozen in death. He stared at the face trying to comprehend what the image was. He took in the glazed eyes, the copious amounts of blood, the displaced swollen tongue, and the gaping hole in the side of his neck. The boy-scout made an assessment. 'Fuck me!'

*

Detective Inspector David Stark sat in the heavy traffic. The frustrating thing was that he could see the side road ahead of him which he knew to be a short-cut to avoid whatever the hell was holding them up miles ahead. 'I bet it's an accident.' He muttered to himself.

David was currently second in command at Nottingham Divisional CID. It was only a temporary role: 'Acting Detective Chief Inspector', whilst Bill Rawson was away on yet another course at Bramshill Police Training College. Bill was only passing through the CID on his route to higher things, Stark was there to stay. He wasn't entirely sure he wanted promotion anyway, as it would take him further away from doing the job he loved.

Still the constant flow of traffic coming the other way continued blocking his opportunity to avoid the queue. He wanted a quiet day today; he had a ton of paperwork to do which he had been putting off for far too long.

'Finally.'

He swung the black Cavalier to the left and travelled along for fifty yards before he turned up the side road towards freedom and Nottingham Police Station.

Nobby Clarke greeted him at the nick. 'Morning, boss.' Nobby had been Stark's Detective Sergeant for several years. He was a tough, unyielding character, if not the brightest star in the sky.

'Morning Nobby, all quiet?'

Nobby followed Stark into his office, trying to contain the cumbersome array of lever-arch files and prevent them falling from his arms. It was Nobby's job to prepare the briefing for Stark each morning. 'Yes, I've got the briefing pads.' They included, the night crime report, missing from homes of note, newly reported crime, that sort of thing. Nobby placed them on the floor in a heap. 'Oh and there's a report of a fatal RTA, car v lamppost, some kid found it on Papplewick Lane, it's only just come in. Traffic are attending apparently.'

'That's nothing to do with us, let Traffic deal with it. That's probably what held me up this morning.'

'I thought you were a bit later than normal.'

'Is that why I can't see a cup of coffee on my desk?'

'Sir, with respect, bollocks!'

*

Police Constable Paul Wood was the traffic officer attending the report of a fatal RTA. He was experienced and qualified to deal with 'fatals'. Not all traffic officers were. He had seen plenty of them in his time, the horror, the gore and the never ending and usually, avoidable deaths of men women and, the worst of all abominations, children.

His eyes were wide and alert as he skilfully raced through the peak-hour traffic, sirens blazing and lights flashing. On hearing the siren some drivers would immediately slam on their brakes instead of easing into the side. 'Get out of the fucking way, you stupid old fart!' Paul cursed as the umpteenth well-intentioned driver stopped in the middle of the road. It was with relief that he hit the country roads leading towards Papplewick and the scene of the reported accident. As he approached the junction he saw an elderly man waving both arms in the air to attract his attention. He was relieved to see that an ambulance was already at the scene, but the relative inactivity of the paramedics had daunting implications. Paul quickly took stock of the situation and parked his car in the most suitable spot to warn oncoming vehicles. Safety first. He had to make do with a 'Police Accident' sign on the other side of the road.

'Morning.' Paul greeted the paramedic.

'Morning, Paul, all right?'

'I'm good, thanks, you?'

I'm good, there's nothing for us on this one, Paul, I'm afraid, he's been dead a while by the looks of it.'

'Okay,'

'We've got another shout, Paul, are we okay to shoot?'

'Erm, okay, sure, send me the report through the post will you?'

'Will do – enjoy.' He slapped the officer on the back.

'Thanks.'

Paul walked up to the blue Volvo and looked through the window of the driver's door. The sight briefly took him aback. Pavarotti singing 'funiculi funicula, funiculi funiculaaa!' was something of a distraction. He noticed the seatbelt holding the body in place as he turned off the engine which was still running and it thankfully silenced the din. Despite Paul's lack of medical qualifications, it was fair to say the driver was dead. He checked to make sure there was no-one else in the vehicle, in the foot-well at the back, and as he could see the rear nearside door was wide open, that no passengers had been thrown out into undergrowth. Nothing. 'Looks like he was on his tod'. He assumed the door was ajar because the Paramedics had done a similar check. Paul opened the front passenger door to clamber on the seat and have a proper close-up look at the body. He had to settle for leaning in as the blood was all over the seat. The vast amount of blood in the car was obvious, but there were no easily recognisable trauma injuries to his head, body or legs that he could see. Paul could see the huge wound to the side of the neck, but what had caused it? He looked at the front of the vehicle and the telegraph pole. Hardly a scratch was evident. He started to get a strange feeling rise in his belly. He returned to look back inside the vehicle. This didn't make sense. The old man tapped Paul on the shoulder.

'I can see you're busy, but do you need me to wait, or can I go home, officer?'

'Did you find them, or did you witness the accident?'

'Neither, I rang in to report it. I reckon the young paper-boy might have seen it. He was the one who told us, like. I only live across the road, and he ran over and knocked on our door. He was worried about finishing his round, so he's buggered off.'

'What is your name please?'

'Jenkins, Derek. We live at twenty-five, it's the one with the red door and azaleas.'

Paul had no idea what azalea's looked like but he could cope with a red door. 'I'll come over later and get a statement from you. What shop does the boy work at; did he say?'

'It's the one at the top of Victoria Street.'

'Excellent. Sorry you had to see all this.'

'Don't worry about that, lad, I worked down the pit for thirty years, I've seen worse.'

Paul smiled. 'Thanks again, I will see you shortly.'

Two other cars had stopped, either out of curiosity or public-spiritedness but none of the occupants had witnessed anything. There had simply been no-one about when it happened. Paul again returned to the car and leaned inside to see what the dead man could have possibly snagged his neck on. Nothing.

There was no way that the 'accident' could have caused the death of the man. So, what had? Could it be some sort of an embolism? Surely not. He wished the paramedic was still there. He shouldn't have let them rush off like that. He pushed his traffic officers peaked cap on to the back of his head and scratched his head. He yet again he peered at the wound. It looked as though he had been stabbed. He wanted to be as certain as he could because he did not want to call the cavalry and end up looking like a chump.

Paul returned to his traffic car and displaced the black radio phone. 'Alpha Quebec Two Five to NH.'

'Go ahead.'

'I am ten-twelve at the scene of the RTA on Papplewick Lane. I can confirm it is a one oblique one, but can you request CID to attend as it looks suspicious.'

There was a pause. 'Confirm request CID to attend?'

'Confirmed.'

'Ten Four, stand-by.'

His little radio message would send shock waves throughout the force.

*

Stark tapped his fingers irritably on the steering wheel. The queue of traffic spanned a good 400 yards in front of him as the road curved to the left, and out of sight. DC Ashley Stevens sat in the front passenger seat, his black hair quaffed back, his solid gold watch and bracelet an indication of the private income he was party to.

Ashley's father had used his redundancy money all those years ago, to invest in a little video shop, hoping that it would give him an interest and sufficient money to live on. Within five years he had twelve similar shops throughout the Midlands and was a millionaire. Today he had over two hundred stores. His only son, however, refused to join his business and remained a detective, albeit a financially secure one. It was an odd quirk that at twenty-eight, Ashley had a better house and car than the Head of CID.

Ash strained to see through the rear window of Stark's car. He could see the red CID vehicle several places back in the queue. He smiled at the ruddy face, seemingly hewn out of granite, of Detective Sergeant John 'Nobby' Clarke who had his head poking out of the driver's side window. Nobby was agitatedly pointing forwards in thrusting motions. He looked annoyed and was shouting something incomprehensible.

Ashley, however got the message.

'I think Nobby wants us to make progress, sir,'

Stark turned and saw Nobby gesticulating wildly. He wound down the window and gave him the thumbs up. Stark's foot became heavy on the accelerator pedal, the rev counter straying into the red. He pulled out onto the wrong side of the road, switched his lights on and pressed his horn. A glimpse in the mirror saw Nobby follow suit. The sudden increase in speed jolted Ashley and he clung to the dashboard. A few seconds later several cars appeared, heading straight for them, but they moved over just in time and motioned their discontent with various movements of their fingers and fists.

'Piss off! We're the Queens' men.' Stark reciprocated.

After a hair-raising drive, the two cars arrived at the scene of the reported 'accident'. By this time there were three traffic patrol vehicles present. The young patrolman had done everything: Scenes of Crime officers had just attended, and a uniformed Inspector was strutting around, barking orders to his underlings. Stark hated this initial stage, with everyone running around like headless chickens. He knew the importance of haste, since any suspects could be in the vicinity, but he was not prepared to sacrifice evidence by poking around too early, before Scenes of Crime had finished. Stark's first job was to extinguish the mania the uniformed Inspector was creating, and he approached him with a smile.

'Morning, Mark. What are we looking at?'

The red-faced Inspector was young in service and scarcely hid the relief he felt on seeing Stark arrive. He used his long black stick with its glistening silver top to point at the car.

'I think the Traffic officer has done the right thing, Dave, by asking you to attend, it looks a funny one. Obviously, you will have a look yourself but it looks to me like the driver has been stabbed in the neck.'

'Okay. What have you done so far?'

The Inspector swallowed. 'Well, erm, we've preserved the scene. As you can see, Scenes of Crime are here, and now you are. I've started a couple of my lads doing some house-to-house enquiries up the road. I've asked for CID support. That's as far as we have got.'

'So basically you have waited until we got here.'

Mark grinned nervously. 'There is nothing else we could do, David, there are no witnesses and hence no descriptions to circulate of possible offenders.'

Nobby had been party to the conversation, hands in pockets, head bowed. He had little time for the new-style 'college inspectors. Nobby as an ex paratrooper hated the 'hairy-fairy' way the Inspector conducted his business. Nobby could be a belligerent detective. He didn't understand, nor did he *want* to understand, the modern management techniques, which he felt were much too cautious and naïve. They were okay in their place, if you like that sort of thing, but he felt the police service was not that place.

'Do you want me to do the biz then, sir?' he asked Stark.

'Please, Nobby. You've heard the set-up, haven't you?'

Nobby turned and returned to his vehicle grabbing the radio hand-set.

'Juliet Quebec two nine to NH.'

The female voice answered promptly. 'Juliet Quebec two nine, go ahead, NH over.'

'Yes, we are at the scene at Papplewick, Juliet Quebec zero two is with me. Still no update on descriptions, no witnesses are evident as yet. Compliments of DCI Stark, request mounted section, Dog Patrol and gain authority for police helicopter to search surrounding fields and woodland, plus a unit of SOU for searching. Also set up a snatch plan immediately. Over.'

'Ten four, NH out.' The young lady had a lot to organise.

Stark joined him at the car. 'Did I hear you ask for a snatch-plan to be put in place?'

'Yes, boss, all the major junctions will have a traffic car on them within minutes.'

'I know what a snatch-plan is, mate, but there is no description or vehicle, what are they looking for?'

'Anything suspicious?' Nobby said with his confidence waning a little.

'I wouldn't have bothered with that just yet, Nobby, but leave it for now, the Control room Inspector might query it, though.' Just as he spoke the radio sounded.

'NH to Juliet Quebec two nine.'

'There you go!' Stark said. 'Just ignore it, let's have a look at the motor.'

Stark peered through the open driver's door. 'I think we can safely say he's dead!' He walked around the vehicle, careful not to collide with SOCO who were putting on their white overalls. He looked through the window, focussing on the severe neck wound, glancing at the minimal damage to the front of the vehicle. Mark, the uniformed Inspector hovered around behind him. Stark spoke to Nobby. 'Any observations, Sergeant?'

'It's a suspicious death all right; somebody's bleeding throated him!'

Trace and Eliminate by Keith Wright.
'He plots and paces well, and the climax is a genuine shock.
A commendable follow-up to his impressive debut.'
Marcel Berlins, The Times.

For the author's blog and news on upcoming books, as well as free short stories visit his web-site: **Keithwrightauthor.co.uk**

Follow the author on Twitter: @KeithWWright

Printed in Great Britain
by Amazon